TO CONTROL THE STARS

In the aftermath of the battle for Sutton and Satterfield, Admiral Josiah Gilbert saw the tide of the war for the Caveness Galaxy turning in favor of the Sondak Confederacy. But there was danger from within: a leak at the heart of military intelligence, and a fanatic poet who had begun a deadly fifth column of terrorism and subversion.

Frye Charltos, Commander of the United Central Systems, faced a harsh truth. Divided by infighting and dissention, reeling from the enemy's bold raids, the United Central Systems were no longer assured of victory. The only strategy that could now prevail was total war, no matter the cost in human lives.

But other factors were destined to radically alter the outcome of the war: the struggle to control a deadly new weapon, a strange alliance between four alien races, and a daring mission by a pair of young lovers.

Acclaim for Warren Norwood's
MIDWAY BETWEEN:

"Fast-paced battle sequences, political maneuvering, and a varied cast of humans and aliens make this a promising beginning to this new series. Fans of space adventure should enjoy this well-crafted novel."
—*Library Journal*

D1397310

FINAL COMMAND

Warren Norwood

BANTAM BOOKS
TORONTO • NEW YORK • LONDON • SYDNEY • AUCKLAND

FINAL COMMAND

A Bantam Spectra Book / February 1986

ISBN 0-553-25554-1

Published simultaneously in the United States and Canada

Bantam Books are published by Bantam Books, Inc. Its trademark, consisting of the words "Bantam Books" and the portrayal of a rooster, is Registered in U.S. Patent and Trademark Office and in other countries. Marca Registrada. Bantam Books, Inc., 666 Fifth Avenue, New York, New York 10103.

PRINTED IN THE UNITED STATES OF AMERICA

H   0 9 8 7 6 5 4 3 2 1

For "The Herd,"
the members of the 173rd Airborne Brigade (Separate),
who served with honor and distinction
in the Republic of Viet Nam
7 May 65 to 25 Aug 71

STYLIZED VIEW OF CAVENESS GALAXY FROM
THE SOUTHERN POLAR PERSPECTIVE

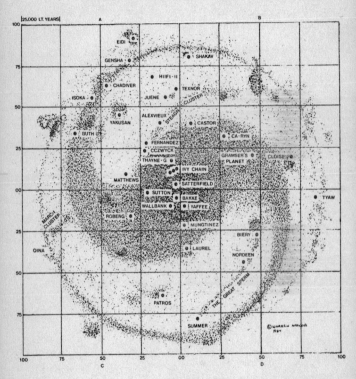

Chronology

Ninety-two years after the signing of the treaty that officially ended the Unification Wars, Earth sent forth the first two generation ships to seek new homes for mankind in the stars.

The *Bohr* and the *Heisenberg* together carried a total of three thousand seven hundred eighty-three pioneers and crew members. Each ship was powered by ten linked Hugh drives that eventually pushed them to a speed of one-point-four times the speed of light relative to Earth. At that speed their Benjamin drives took over, and they crossed Einstein's Curve where relative speed could no longer be measured.

Two hundred forty-one ship years later, the descendants of those first pioneers celebrated the thirtieth anniversary of their landing on the planet they named Biery after the woman who led their forebears from Earth. Much to their mixed surprise and fear, that celebration was interrupted by the landing of an alien ship containing a race called the Oinaise. To everyone's relief—including the Oinaise's—the contact was peaceful.

Nine years later the Kobler calendar was established and set the date of the first landing as New Year 2500. The following chronology gives a brief listing of major events dated according to that calendar.

2530—First contact with the Oinaise.

2575—First pioneers arrive on Nordeen, the most Earth-like of any planet ever discovered in the galaxy.

2599—Approximate date the last generation ship left Earth, carrying fourteen thousand new-human pioneers, genetically altered people known as *homo communis*, whose major difference from *homo sapiens* was a greatly extended longevity.

2648—The anti-intellectualist riots.

2657—Beginning of the early expansionist movement seeking other planets and star systems suitable for human settlement.

2664—Last known message from Earth indicating war, famine, and increasing chaos.

2681—A group of Nordeen's brightest people call themselves *homo electus* and leave aboard the *Mensch* in search of what they hope will be a better home for the intellectually elite.

2723—The Gouldrive tested and proven. Marks the beginning of the Great Expansionist Movement, the settling of many independent systems, and the establishment of true interstellar trade. The phrase, "a planet for every clan," became popular at this time. During the whole movement scientific research and technological progress were extremely limited.

2774—News reaches Nordeen from the so-called *homo electus*'s first contact with the alien Verfen, a reclusive race inhabiting a cluster of star systems near galaxy's center.

2784—First contact with the crab-like, methane-breathing Castorians.

2846—Discovery of Cloise.

2862—Foundation of Sondak, a loose federation of fifty-eight sparsely inhabited planetary systems. *Homo electus* demanded and received recognition as a separate human race as the price of joining the federation.

2893—Foundation of the misnamed United Central Systems, twenty-seven planetary systems inhabited mostly by *homo communis*. The establishment of the U.C.S. marked the end of the Great Expansionist Movement.

3021—The first galactic war between Sondak and the U.C.S.

3024—The U.C.S., unable to match Sondak's capacity for producing the tools of war, sued for peace. After extended negotiations during which the fighting continued, the U.C.S. promised to pay heavy economic reparations to Sondak and the independent systems, and also agreed not to produce new war materials for one hundred years. Neither promise was kept.

3029—Seemingly spontaneous civil disorder broke out on several planets populated mostly by the fair-skinned, racially distinct, politically fractious pikeans. Although called by some the Pikean Civil War, the dissidents had neither the numbers nor the equipment to fight a true war, and consequently were forced to leave their home planets. Many of them chose to go to systems controlled by the U.C.S., where they quickly aligned themselves with the political factions that supported a new war with Sondak.

3033—The Cczwyck Skirmish occurred when U.C.S. Admiral Nance made an officially unauthorized attempt to take control of that independent system just as a Sondak border squadron was making a courtesy visit. There was no serious fighting, but the political repercussions caused the U.C.S. to accelerate its secret rearmament program; caused Sondak to increase its economic pressures on the U.C.S. and also on the independent systems that refused to join the confederation; and caused Cczwyck to become more isolationist.

3034–3042—Sporadic raids on U.C.S.-chartered freighters by unknown agents were blamed on Sondak despite fierce diplomatic denials and a total lack of evidence.

3038—Long-range plans began in the U.C.S. for a new war against Sondak.

3046—The so-called "Double-Spiral War" began with raids on ten isolated Sondak systems and several independent systems. During the year the U.C.S. captured the independent systems of Fernandez, Cczwyck, the water planets of Thayne-G, the three systems in the Ivy Chain, and Ca-Ryn. The aliens of Oina and Cloise found themselves drawn unwillingly toward participation in the war.

Matthews system, strategically located midway between Sondak and the U.C.S., was the target of an attack and invasion planned and directed by U.C.S. Commander Frye Charltos. The attack failed due to the planning of Sondak Admiral Josiah Gilbert, with the help of Admirals Pajandcan and Dawson, and a great deal of luck. The system was saved, but with a great loss of ships and personnel on both sides. Matthews system's principal planet, Reckynop, was rendered a watery ruin by U.C.S. neutronic missiles that exploded over its poles and melted its icecaps. However, the battle for Matthews was considered a victory for Sondak.

3047—The year opens with the launching of new U.C.S. subspace hunter-killers—the hunks. Sondak's forces on Sutton strongly resist the U.C.S. occupation force and with the aid of a newly reformed Polar Fleet defeat the U.C.S. there and in a space battle for the Satterfield system. The prototype for Sondak's Ultimate Weapon is deliberately lost, and the aliens begin bargaining for a neutral alliance.

3048—U.C.S. Admiral Frye Charltos and Bridgeforce declare a victory at Satterfield and commence planning for a final series of strikes against Sondak, while Sondak's Admiral Gilbert and General Schopper begin their plans for a counteroffensive.

Prologue

Chief Warrant Officer Henley Stanmorton, Combat Teller, keyed his thoughts into his computer diary:

> One day this war will be over, and no one knows what the long-range consequences of its outcome will be. But we are again learning the most fundamental lessons that these galactic wars should always make clear to us.
>
> We are again learning that some people fight with great courage under fire and some do not. We are learning that right, truth, and honor are the possessions not of the powers that rule, but of individuals who hold those values in trust and guard them with their lives; and that small units of resolute combatants guarding those values can ofttimes have an effect totally out of proportion to their size.
>
> We are again learning that morale is one of the most important factors in any lengthy war and that nothing increases morale so much as superior weapons and training effectively used to overwhelm the enemy in battle.
>
> We are again learning that exceptional military leadership is usually far more important on the stage of battle than it is in some distant headquarters half a galaxy away; that even the most carefully devised plans can never allow for the chance events and accidents that can alter the course of any battle and thus change the outcome of a whole war.
>
> Finally, we are learning that the heat of war can forge the strongest bonds of love and allegiance between those who fight it side by side but that it will always be a harsh, cruel waste of lives and resources that darkens the life-spirits of everyone it touches.

He paused for a moment, thinking of Mica Gilbert.

Allegiance? Yes. Love? No. Love was the wrong word. Love was a casualty of war—at least that kind of love. It died in battle faster than anything else. Yet allegiance by itself wasn't a strong enough word for the bonding that took place in war—or for what he felt about Mica.

With a dismissive shake of his head he turned away from that thought and leaned back with a sigh. There was more he wanted to write, more he wanted to say about the new alien alliance, about the bravery and heroism he had seen on Sutton, about how this war—regardless of its outcome—would alter Caveness Galaxy forever.

He knew even if the *Flag Report* accepted what he wrote, there was too much evidence that little or none of it would make any difference. These were not new lessons. He hadn't made them up on his own. They had been learned before by other people in previous wars over countless centuries. Yet no one seemed to remember them from one war to the next.

Why? That was what Henley wanted to know. Why?

1

"My father died in a Uke prison. My mother died defending Ca-Ryn," Rasha'kean Ingrivia said. "I ca'not keep sittin' behind a logis-desk somewhere like I been doin' for the past two years and let others fight this war. I hope you ken that, sir."

"I understand it only too well, Colonel." General Schopper gave her a reassuring smile. "And I think, perhaps, that you might be just the officer I'm looking for."

Rasha'kean brushed a loose strand of long blond hair back from her face. "As long as I can be of service in some 'active' capacity, sir, I'm willin' to try almost anythin'." Just get me into the fighting, she thought.

"Unfortunately, the job I need you for won't be active in the way you mean it. In fact, it will require even more desk work than you've been doing."

"But sir, I've been tryin' to tell you that I d'not—"

Schopper held up a heavy hand. "Let me finish, Colonel. I'm working on a plan for the Planetary Force to play a major role in the rest of this war, but I need the best logistics officer I can find to make that work. Your dossier tells me that you could be that officer."

Rasha'kean held her emotions in check. She had to convince Schopper to give her a combat command, and this might be her only chance. "Do you ken what my name means, sir? Rasha'kean means 'she who is born to battle.' I took fooly-pride in that when I was a-growin', but now it's time to live up to the name my parents gave me. I'm a trained combat officer, sir, trained to *fight*, not to be some superclerk routin' supplies around the galaxy. I d'not want to be your logistics officer or anyone else's. I want a combat command. I owe that to my parents—and to Sondak."

"Now listen, Colonel, if we need—"

"No," she said, angered by his tone. "You listen, sir. I have a free commission—purchased with my parents' blood. Since

1

they both died in service, you ca'not hold me in. I can resign my commission any time I damn well please."

She paused and caught her breath, fighting the frustration that boiled inside her—knowing she had not convinced him yet. "Either you find a combat command for me in the Planetary Force or I'll resign this stinkin' colonelcy and enlist as a common spacer on a line ship. At least there I stand a chance of gettin' in the middle of it."

Schopper stared at her for a long moment after she stopped speaking. "Tell you what," he said finally, "I'll offer you a compromise. You join my logistics staff now and help work on the plans for invading the U.C.S., and when we put those plans into action, I'll find a command for you. Is that fair enough?"

"A combat command," she insisted.

"Yes, Colonel Ingrivia, a combat command."

She wanted to believe him, but the Service had made other promises to her that were broken as easily as cheap glass on a hard floor. "You'll warrant that, sir? No tricks, I mean?"

"Dammit, Ingrivia, I said I would do it. What more do you want?" His anger and impatience were clear in his voice.

Rasha'kean instinctively sensed it was time to ease her pressure on him. She tilted her head and blinked quickly as she gave General Schopper the smile her mother had called "the charmer." "I'm sorry, sir. I d'not question your integrity," she said as she watched the lines in his brow soften. "But the Service has broken promises before, and I just want to be sure I get to help fight this war."

"I know you do, Ingrivia, but you can help most by doing it my way and joining my logistics staff first. There will be time enough for you to get into the fighting."

How easy men are to disarm, she thought. The right smile on a pretty face and their resistance is cut in half. Schopper was no more resistant to that cheap tactic than most other men she had known. "All right, sir. I accept."

"Good, Ingrivia. Report here tomorrow morning and I'll introduce you to the rest of my team. And Colonel?"

"Yes, sir?" As she stood up, Rasha'kean tried to read the expression on his face.

"I suggest that you not overuse that disarming smile of yours. Use it too often and it won't be as effective."

For the first time in a long time Rasha'kean blushed. It was only the barest hint of warmth spreading through her cheeks, but she knew it showed. She also knew that she had underestimated General Schopper and would have to be careful not to do that again. "Thank you, sir. I'll remember that." She saluted, a natural smile fighting for control of her face.

"See you in the morning," Schopper said, returning her salute, "about ten hundred hours."

"Yes, sir." As Rasha'kean turned and left his office, her smile settled into a subdued grin. Life had not offered her much humor in the past ten years, so she took it whenever it came her way. That Schopper had seen through her smile made the idea of working with him far more interesting than it otherwise might have been. That he had done it so quickly offered a challenge that took some of the edge off her disappointment.

She threaded her way through the crowded hall with a look of determination replacing her grin. Rasha'kean had come to Nordeen with a single purpose in mind, and General Schopper had diverted her from it—at least temporarily. Furthermore, he had told her that she would have to use more than her natural beauty and a quick smile to make sure he kept his end of the bargain.

Rasha'kean was glad. Sometimes she felt sure that the only reason she had risen so quickly through the ranks was because it was so easy to manipulate those male superiors who reacted positively to her good looks. Sometimes she hated them for making her feel that way and wished she were plain and unattractive. But if she had been unattractive, she might never have wangled this trip to Nordeen out of old General Milligan and thus never have had the chance to present her request to Schopper. If she had been unattractive, she might—

Her thought was broken as someone bumped her against the wall, and she found herself staring directly into the face of an old Chief Warrant Officer who steadied her with a firm grip on her elbow.

"Excuse me, Colonel," he said, releasing her arm with a slight wince. "I'm afraid I wasn't looking where I was going."

"The fault's mine, Chief. I wa'not payin' much attention, either. Did I hurt you?"

"No, not at all. Shoulder's just a little sore." He was

immediately struck by the clarity of her voice and the striking beauty of her pikean features, a beauty that was accented by blond hair worn in a much longer style than was commonly seen around Sondak's Supreme Headquarters.

She looked at his name tag and then at his insignia and immediately guessed who he was. "You're the Teller who wrote all those great stories about Sutton in the *Flag Report*, ar'not you?"

"All compliments accepted," he said with a quick, waving salute. "Chief Henley Stanmorton at your service. And am I safe in assuming, Colonel Ingrivia, that you are related in some way to the late Admiral Ingrivia?"

"Her daughter, Chief. But how did you know . . ."

"I'm sorry," he said quickly. So this was Ingrivia's daughter. The flood of memories that brought to him now was not one he wanted to wade through now, so he dammed it up as efficiently as he could. "I didn't mean to refresh your grief, but the Ingrivia name is rather famous around here. Would I be prying into military secrets to ask what the colonel is doing here on Nordeen?"

Rasha'kean smiled. "Are you always so formal with your questions?"

Henley returned her smile. "No, ma'am. If I ask it again less formally, will you answer it?"

"Only if you'll show me how to get out of this maze—if you have time, that is."

"I'd be delighted, Colonel. I was just leaving myself. Where would you like to go?"

"First I need somethin' to eat. Then you can point me t'wards the Regular Officers Barracks."

"Easy enough," Henley said. Her accent tickled more memories loose in the back of his mind, but he kept them under control. Yet he couldn't resist making her an offer. "There is a fine restaurant between here and the ROB that advertises 'Food from Seven Planets' and actually comes close to living up to that. Since I am fortunate enough to have a skimmer at my disposal, I'd be glad to take you there."

"Lead the way," Rasha'kean said without hesitation. Stanmorton was about to save her from what might otherwise have been a dull evening.

The trip to the restaurant was filled mostly by Henley's trying to answer her questions about the sights along the way. It was only after they had received their drinks and ordered their dinner that he repeated the question he had asked after they bumped into each other.

"Schopper," she answered. "I'm the new addition to his staff."

"May I ask in what capacity?"

"Logistics. But I'm afraid that's all I can tell you for now. What about you? I thought from the tone of your stories that you liked bein' where the action was."

"I do, but for the moment I'm sticking as close to General Schopper as he will let me. I have the feeling that he's going to be in the center of whatever happens next."

"He has a good reputation."

"He's brilliant, Colonel. I was there on Sutton and got to see firsthand how he deployed his troops and coordinated with General Mari's forces and . . ." The thought of Mari brought a quick end to his enthusiasm. Sometimes in his dreams he could still smell Mari dying beside him.

"Wer'not you there—with Mari, I mean—when he died? Di'not I read that in the *Flag Report*?"

"Yes, I was there. And it was such a waste."

"Why? What made it a waste?"

"Are you serious?" He held the rest of his reply until their waiter set two small flower-petal salads in front of them and moved away. "Mari was just showing off for the troops, trying to raise their morale before the area was totally secure. He got me shot and himself killed because of that."

"Your sore shoulder?"

"Yes."

There was a tone in his voice that made her wonder which he was angrier about, his wound or Mari's death. "You think he was stupid, d'not you?"

Henley took a forkful of salad and chewed it thoughtfully before answering. "No, not stupid, just foolish. It didn't have to happen."

"But at least we got victories at Sutton and Satterfield," Rasha'kean said, shifting the subject slightly. She was fascinated by Stanmorton's willingness to talk so freely. Maybe it had something to do with the fact that he was a Teller.

"We can't afford many more victories like the ones at Sutton and Satterfield—and certainly no more like the one at Matthews system." The salad was good, and its slightly bitter flavor matched his mood. "We need to take the war to the Ukes as quickly as we can, not wait for them to come to us."

"And you think Schopper can do that?"

"Isn't it obvious? The Joint Chiefs have decided to back Admiral Gilbert, even after the losses we took at Satterfield. And Gilbert called Schopper back here for intensive planning. Any spacer in the halls could see that—" He quickly cut off the rest of what he meant to say. "I'm sorry, Colonel. I meant no disrespect."

"None taken, Chief." Rasha'kean had not touched her salad, so she began to eat steadily, waiting for him to reopen the conversation. When he did, it was not what she expected.

"You look like your mother," he said.

"You kenned her?"

"Not really," he lied, wondering why he had brought up her mother again. There was nothing to be gained from it. "Did a story on her back in the last war and talked to her a few times after that. She was a very beautiful woman."

"And a damned fine officer," Rasha'kean said, surprised by the vehemence in her voice. Why was beauty the thing he remembered about her mother instead of her achievements?

"And a gorlet addict," Henley added softly as he picked at his salad.

Rasha'kean was startled even more. "You kenned that?"

Suddenly Henley remembered those last few meetings with then Post-Commander Phondu Ingrivia—those personal meetings during which he had tried to counsel her. How could he tell this young colonel what he really knew about her mother? Or the even darker suspicions he had? He couldn't. It would be cruel and pointless to share that with her.

"Yes, I knew that. I tried to find help for her."

There was a long silence between them as their meal arrived and they began eating. Henley concentrated on the food, annoyed with himself for spoiling the evening but uncertain as to how to make amends.

Rasha'kean felt uncomfortable in Stanmorton's presence, but at the same time she wanted to ken more about his connection to her mother. Finally, she had to ask. "You tried to find her help to break her addiction?"

"Yes."

"When?"

Henley looked up into the clear brown eyes and silently cursed his careless tongue for getting this whole thing started. "When you were a young girl. She had given up the gorlet while she was pregnant with you and then years later went back to it. I tried to make her see what it was doing to her, but she wouldn't listen. I wanted to—"

"Why? Why were you so concerned about my mother?" Rasha'kean needed to know what Stanmorton was holding back from her. Her mother had been the most important person in Rasha'kean's life, and she never stopped hungering after new information about her.

Henley couldn't tell Ingrivia the truth, but he was afraid to lie. Somehow he knew she would know if he lied now. "Because she asked for my advice," he said, giving her a half-truth. "She saw me as a neutral, objective party."

Rasha'kean sensed his reluctance. "There's a lot more to it than that, i'not there, Chief?"

"Yes, there is."

"But you'd rather not be talkin' about it?"

He felt grateful and tried to smile. "That's correct."

"Then I w'not be askin' you anythin' else for now. But I might be later."

"Maybe later I can tell you." But I won't, he thought. I can't. I dare not tell her—

"From the frown on your face, Chief, I ken it will be a struggle to get it out of you."

Henley sighed and looked at her half-empty plate. "Well, now that I've ruined your meal, how else can I be of service?"

"I think we ought to get quietly drunk," she said, looking straight into his eyes.

The genes will tell, Henley thought, then immediately caught himself. He had no right to make that judgment.

"It'll take me some alcohol to settle down tonight." And get the rest of this out of you, she added to herself. "Do you ken someplace we can do that without attractin' too much attention? Or shall we buy a liter and take it to my quarters?"

Henley had no intention of drinking in her quarters. "I know a place," he said, "if you have some civy clothes. They're not much fond of the service there."

"Happen to have some in my duffel," she said. "But what about you?"

"We'll check you into the ROB and change, then head for the Millius Tank where you can drink to your nerve's delight."

And where I'll pump you for the rest of truth, she thought. "You're still in the lead, Chief. Let's do it now."

2

U.C.S. Vice-Admiral Frye Charltos massaged his forehead with the tips of his long brown fingers.

Despite what he had told Bridgeforce, despite the victory at Satterfield, and despite the continuing reports of successful skirmishes against Sondak throughout the polar systems, he was no longer sure that the United Central Systems was winning this war it had started under his military leadership almost three long years before. He was not afraid of losing, because he knew in his heart that the U.C.S. could never—would never—be defeated. But true to his early warnings to his staff and line officers Sondak had proved a difficult enemy.

With a long sigh he pulled his hands away from his face and returned to the stream of information still pouring in on his microspooler. There was so much to do—and so little time to do it in—that he couldn't afford any more minutes wasted in worry. So long as he did his job properly, he knew he could lead the U.C.S. to ultimate victory. That was all that mattered, and that was what he had to focus his attention on.

"Begging your pardon, sir," Melliman's voice said over his desk speaker, "but Meister Hadasaki just called to tell you he is on his way down to see you. Didn't say what he wanted to talk about."

"Thank you, AOCO. Bring him in as soon as he arrives."

"Will do, sir. Shall I prepare tea?"

"Good idea, AOCO," Frye replied, and realized again how grateful he was for Melliman's presence, not only in his office but in his whole life.

Moments later Melliman entered the office and went directly to the tiny kitcove to make the tea. Frye watched her openly, admiring the suggestions of her figure that showed through the neat tucks of her uniform, thinking of the joy she had brought into his life.

He blinked and for a brief instant saw not Melliman standing with her back to him, but Vinita—a young, beautiful, healthy Vinita, a Vinita before— With a quick shake of his head and another blink he shook off that image.

Vinita was dead. He had killed her three years ago—killed her to keep her from dying in pain—and it was time to forget, time to scatter those images on the same winds that had scattered her ashes over the slopes of her beloved Irkbie mountains. But he couldn't forget. He would never forget. No matter what happened, Vinita would always be a daily part of his life.

"Are you all right, sir?"

Frye was startled for an instant to see Melliman standing so close to him. "Yes, Clarest. I was just thinking about Vinita," he said, glad that he could tell her that.

"As you always should," she said softly. She reached and straightened the memo-box on the corner of his desk, brushing his hand in the process. "The tea will be ready when Meister Hadasaki arrives, sir. Is there anything else you need?"

He heard the undertone of affection in her voice and was all too aware of her hand brushing his, yet he was pleased beyond measure by the proper military way she conducted herself when they were on duty. "I'm fine, AOCO, for now. Perhaps later, however, we should discuss this."

"As you wish, sir," she said as she left the office. A few minutes later she was back, ushering in Meister Hadasaki.

"Sit, Admiral, sit," Hadasaki said with a wave of his hand as he crossed the office in his long strides. "And you, Captain," he said to Melliman, "serve us some of that tea this office is famous for, then leave us alone."

Frye was shocked and amused by Hadasaki's blunt manner but was willing to wait until after Melliman had served the tea and left before saying anything. "You're in a rude mood today, sir."

"Forgive me, then. But don't waste time worrying about it, Charltos. I have several very important things to discuss with you—not the least of which concerns that renegade daughter of yours."

"Which one?" Frye asked. "I have so many." The look on Hadaski's face made Frye regret his attempted humor. Hadasaki was obviously not in the mood for virility jokes. Especially that one, Frye thought. Yet Hadasaki was the only person who could laugh with him about that. No one else knew.

"You know damn well," Hadasaki said after sipping his tea. "After she deserted on Yakusan, I thought the U.C.S. was done with her. But now Judoff has discovered that your daughter is in league with the Oinaise on some deal concerning a new weapon."

"The Oinaise? A new weapon? Where's Judoff getting all this information? And what does it have to do with us?"

Hadasaki laughed curtly. "Who knows where Marshall Judoff gets anything except the young officers who service her? We know where they come from. But don't ask how I know what Judoff knows. Just tell me what you know."

Frye hadn't heard from Marsha since sending her away to find her Sondak trader, and sadly, he was resigned to the fact that he might never hear from her again. "Nothing you don't, sir. We weren't on the best of terms, you know. She apparently left Yakusan with an Oinaise broker on a lightspeed freighter with neutral Patros registration. After that, who knows?"

"Judoff thinks she knows, so you'd better find out if you can, Charltos, because if her information is correct, she'll use it against you with Bridgeforce, you can bet on that."

Frye nodded, agreeing that Judoff would use anything she could against him but not that he was going to try to find Marsha himself. He had released her from her promise to serve with him and sent her as close to her Captain Teeman as he dared. He had no idea how she had escaped, but he did have one about where she wanted to go—Oina. That was where she had sent the message to Teeman. "You said there was something else you wanted to discuss, sir?"

"Several other things, Charltos, like when will the plans be completed for the next major offensive and when are you going to present them to Bridgeforce? Surely you can see that we're losing time if we don't mount this next attack as quickly as possible—and losing supporters, too."

Frye allowed himself a small smile. "I thought you and

almost everyone else on Bridgeforce wanted the first two bombships finished before then?"

"The bombships be damned! They may never be finished."

"Forgive me, Meister," Frye said with a quick wave of his hand. "I meant no disrespect. The plans should be ready within ten days."

"Good. It's about time. Now the important question is—the one Bridgeforce will demand an answer to—how deeply can we strike without the bombships?"

"It's a three-phase operation, sir, fairly close to the preliminary proposal Bridgeforce approved. If the first two phases are successful, the third phase will be the attack on Nordeen itself."

Hadasaki whistled softly. "Can't get any deeper into Sondak than that, Charltos. But do you really believe we can do it—without the bombships, I mean?"

"Yes, sir, I do." Frye sounded more confident than he felt, but as overall offensive commander of the U.C.S. forces, he had no choice. He had to believe that his plans would lead to the final victory.

* * *

Delightful Childe stroked his long, wrinkled proboscis with a seven-fingered hand and pulled his lips tight over his blunt, yellowed teeth. Humankind was an exasperating species, and individual humans always seemed worse than the norm. Yet despite his feelings of reserve about Marsha, he liked these two humans, and he wanted to be fair to them. By his faith in the Gods, he had to be fair to them.

"The answer to your question, Captain, is that we have agreed to represent the neutral alliance in the festbid for this 'special' weapon my cousin has procured."

"But why?" Lucky asked. "Why in the voids of space would you want anything to do with something like that?" He felt Marsha squeeze his hand slightly and knew she supported his persistence.

"Because, my dear partner, if we gain control of this weapon, then neither the Ukas nor Sondak can use it against one another, nor could they use it against us or—"

"But doesn't that mean the alliance won't be any better—"

"Please, be patient and let me finish. As I was trying to say, if we possess the weapon, we can destroy it. Then it will never be used against anyone."

Lucky shook his head. "I still don't understand."

"Neither do I," Marsha added, "and I saw the damned thing and the scientist who supposedly invented it and—" She cut herself off from adding Inspector Janette to that list. Janette had wanted the weapon enough to steal *Graycloud* to get it. "What makes it so special, anyway?"

"Xindella did not tell you, then?"

"Would I be asking if your arrogant cousin had told me?"

"Easy, Mars," Lucky said softly.

She gave him a half smile, then looked back at Delightful Childe. "I'm sorry. It's just that I can't see why this weapon is so important."

Delightful Childe's proboscis fluttered in a rumbling sigh. "If my cousin is to be believed, this weapon, when completed, would be capable of destroying a star from as far away as eight or ten parsecs."

"Impossible," Lucky said. "It would have to violate the laws of physics to do that."

"Oh?" Delightful Childe cocked a ridge of wrinkled skin over one eye. "Have you become a physicist, now? Do you know how this weapon functions?"

"No, but . . ."

"Neither do I, Captain. However, neither am I willing to take a chance that the Ukas might get their hands on it and find some way to make it work. That is why the alliance is willing to outbid the Ukas and Sondak, regardless of the expense, because that is the only guarantee we obtain for our own safety."

"Tensheiss," Lucky cursed, "there has to be some other way."

Delightful Childe looked carefully at Teeman. "We are open to all suggestions," he said finally, afraid to acknowledge any stirring of hope. He and the council had discussed this through endless meetings with no other realistic alternative being presented by anyone.

"I don't know," Lucky admitted, yet he knew there was something wrong with this approach, something that was biting at the back of his brain. "But I'm sure not ready to give in to this idea just because you Oinaise think—"

"I do," Marsha said. "I mean, I have another idea, another way you might solve your problem." She paused and wondered if they would both think she was crazy—especially Lucky.

"Offer to back the U.C.S. in the bidding—without anyone else knowing, of course," she added. "Then you can talk them into secretly destroying it. Sondak will think the U.C.S. still has it and will have to be wary of—"

"Preposterous," Delightful Childe huffed. "We would certainly get no guarantees from the Ukas—"

"Stop," Lucky said quickly. Suddenly he knew what had been nagging the shadows of his thoughts. "Marsha's idea is no more preposterous than your own. If your precious neutral alliance wins the festbid and possesses this superweapon, why wouldn't Sondak and the Ukes both turn against you? Then what happens to your guarantee of peace? Since when has possession of a powerful weapon ever guaranteed anyone peace?"

"An ugly but persuasive argument, Captain. Yet, I do not believe we have a choice. The festbid will be held regardless of whether we choose to participate or not. It still seems that the least risk to the neutral systems would be to possess and destroy the weapon. Perhaps your argument could be countered if there were observers from both human groups present."

"I doubt it," Marsha said before Lucky could reply. "They won't believe you actually destroyed the real weapon, and as long as there was a mote of doubt in their heads, neither side would take a kindly attitude toward you."

"Then perhaps another way can be considered," Delightful Childe said quietly. "However, it would require your specific involvement, as neither I nor any other Oinaise could take the risk we would ask of you."

"And what's that?" Lucky asked.

"To steal the device from Xindella before the festbid and destroy it yourselves."

Marsha looked at Lucky and saw questions in his eyes, the same doubting questions that were coursing through her own, all surrounding the biggest question of all: Why should they get involved in this?

"We would have to think about that," she said, "and discuss it much more."

"Then by all means, do so," Delightful Childe said. "I excuse you both." As they left, he prayed for relief from their annoying arguments and wondered what they would finally do. He prayed it was something quiet and unobtrusive and assumed that it would be, because they had no reason to risk their lives stealing the weapon from Xindella. No reason at all.

3

The Uke fighters came streaming out of the belly of their launchship as soon as they reached the maximum range. Post-Commander Bacus smiled faintly when they appeared on her screens and sent her own fighters spewing from the *Taxco* against them.

It wasn't her job to wonder why they were probing this uninhabited system or how they had located her ship. It was her job to hold her sector and fight back.

"They've got us outnumbered, Commander," the Tech Mate said from his coordinating computer.

"As usual. Issue the order for standard skirmish procedures, Lieutenant Henry. Then notify POLFLEET Headquarters that we have made contact."

"Aye-aye, ma'am," the young lieutenant replied.

They're getting younger every year, Bacus thought. And I'm getting older—too old for this kind of action. I should be holding down a desk on a headquarters-ship somewhere, telling others how to do the fighting. If there were a way to—

"Unidentified targets, high acceleration, one-eighty full astern!" the Tech Mate shouted.

"Size, type, and range," Bacus demanded.

"Too soon to tell, Commander, but they look like hunks!"

"Full quartering defense!" Nothing scared Bacus like the thought of being pursued by the new Uke hunter-killers. They had blown a ship out from under her at Satterfield, and she dreaded what they could do to her now. She would have to defend *Taxco* against the hunks' long-range missiles as well as hold off any Uke fighters that got through to attack the ship itself.

Commander Bacus had every right to be afraid. Less than ten minutes later the first four hunk missiles were on their way. *Taxco*'s gunners destroyed three of them, but the fourth missile caught *Taxco* with a glancing blow by the stern, temporarily knocking out her maneuvering engines.

After that it became a running fight, with Bacus finally deciding that the only way they would stand a chance was to chase the hunks instead of trying to avoid them. Her change of tactics helped, and it also confused the Uke fighters who broke through *Taxco*'s defense screen.

However, by the time the Ukes withdrew their fighters and their hunks thirty hours later, the *Taxco* had lost ten percent of its fighters, and half the others were crippled. The *Taxco* itself was seriously damaged but still capable of offering some defense for its sector.

The only thing that gave Commander Bacus any satisfaction from the whole encounter was that the Ukes had probably lost as many fighters as she had and at least one hunk. That was too little satisfaction as far as Bacus was concerned.

As much as she hated this duty, she hated not beating the Ukes even more. Someday, she thought, someday, we're going to beat those *homo communis* bastards, and whenever it comes, it won't be soon enough—not nearly soon enough.

*   *   *

The sun settled through an orange haze into the sea, filling the room with an almost-fluorescent light. It had been on an evening very much like this one when Mica Gilbert had come to Rochmon's quarters on the day she joined his Cryptography staff.

Suddenly Rochmon remembered that day with annoying clarity. He had not brought Mica here until later in the evening—after dark—yet his casual memory linked her with the sexual ephemera he had used that afternoon years before. Maybe it was the odor that caused the link—the same heavy odor of sex mixed with the sharp smell of a fading ephemera that laced the room even now to remind him of his major vice.

Rochmon checked his chronometer and climbed swiftly out of bed. He had more than enough time to shower and dress for the promotion ceremony this evening, but he wanted to be clean now—immediately. And he wanted his room cleansed of the smell that had triggered those memories.

Mica was out there with Admirals Dimitri and Pajandcan, out where the fighting was going on, out there in danger. She had ignored his message of concern for her and rejected his request that she return. Instead, she had gone straight to her father for permission to stay with Polar Fleet. She was sending him her own message by doing that, yet he refused to accept it. More and more she haunted his thoughts, and worse—or better, he couldn't decide which—her image appeared with increasing regularity in his erotic dreams.

Hew Rochmon stood in the shower, letting the sharp sprays of water rinse the sweat from his body, and shook his head. It amazed him when he admitted to himself how much he wanted Mica, how much he needed her, and how much she had become a fixation he couldn't shake. But what he didn't know was whether or not he loved her. He wanted to love her. He wanted to allow himself that emotion again. He wanted to let his feelings for her blossom with the wild abandon of unrestrained love. He wanted that and more.

Yet he couldn't get any of it. Something inside held him back. The barriers from failed loves and failed marriages kept him constantly in check. The defenses erected after other emotional failures refused to yield simply because he wanted them to. It would take something greater than lust and desire and a need to love and be loved for him to break through those barriers. It would take something far more passionate than that.

"And the irony is, stupid," he said aloud as he carefully rinsed the cleanser off his body, "the one thing your defenses will never allow is passion. Too dangerous. Too threatening. Hell, too damn frightening. Might as well save the passion for Cryptography and get Mica out of your mind."

In the bedroom his milcom began dinging insistently. Rochmon shut off the water, grabbed a towel, and answered the milcom as quickly as he could. "Rochmon," he said curtly.

"Two things, Hew," Admiral Gilbert's voice said. "First is that I would like to have you share a drink with me before the ceremony this evening. Second is that I think you should be warned that afterward Stonefield may want to talk to you about Bock. Can you come for the drink?"

Bock? A drink? "Uh, certainly, sir," Rochmon finally managed to say. "Will an hour be soon enough?"

"Fine. See you in one hour in the HQ Senior Wardroom."

"Very good, sir." Rochmon shut off the milcom and began drying himself automatically. Why would Stonefield want to talk to him about Bock? He hadn't seen her in over a year, and as much as Cryptography missed her brilliant services, part of him was relieved that he no longer had to endure her acerbic presence. The goldsleeves had never found any evidence to charge her with, and she had quickly found a job with Scientific-Security where at least her talents were being used to some degree. Those two things combined to relieve any lingering guilt he felt for not having defended her more vigorously.

"Guilty until proven innocent," he reminded himself as he began to dress. "Both of us, I guess. So what does Stonefield want to talk about?"

Could they have found some evidence? He doubted it. He had enough contacts in enough places to have gotten at least a whiff of such a discovery. No, it must be something else, but what?

An hour later, as he joined Admiral Gilbert in the Senior Wardroom, Rochmon had pushed that question temporarily out of his mind and tried to put himself in a brighter mood. After all, it wasn't every day that he got promoted to Quarter-Admiral.

"New uniform, Hew?"

"No, sir," Rochmon said, accepting the drink Gilbert handed him. "There's still a materials shortage, so I had the best of my old ones altered. I seem to have lost some weight lately."

"Well, you certainly look fit enough." Gilbert meant what he said. He was as proud of Hew Rochmon as if he had been his son instead of just his protégé. "Shall we drink to victory?"

"To victory, sir." They touched glasses, and Rochmon took a slow sip of the smoke-flavored liquor. "Very nice, sir," he said after the last of the sip dissolved on the back of his tongue. "Very, very nice. What in the galaxy is it?"

"It's called Aquamarie. Mica sent me a liter of it from Sutton, and she told me to expect only trinkets from her for the next few years because it was so expensive."

Mica again. Always Mica. "Maybe I should just soak my tongue in it and absorb it by osmosis," Rochmon said, swirling the Aquamarie in the glass. "Or maybe just take it in by fumes."

Gilbert laughed. "I'm not going to be that stingy with it, Hew. Drink it as you see fit and I'll gladly pour you another."

Rochmon nodded and emptied the glass into his mouth, letting the delicious flavor soak every taste bud as the exotic fumes filled the back of his nose. Then he slowly swallowed the Aquamarie with a pleased sigh and held out his empty glass.

"Second and last drink," Gilbert said as he refilled Rochmon's glass from the quaint blue bottle. "You're feeling too good already for any more than that."

"I'm trying, sir," Rochmon said without thinking as he took the refilled glass.

"Trying? Is there something wrong, Hew?"

"Not exactly, sir. That is, nothing out of the ordinary. The Ukes have started using their Q-3 code for all their major transmissions, and even though we know how they put their Q-codes together, we're having a tough time breaking this one."

Gilbert watched Rochmon's face. "There's something else. What is it? Anything I can help with?"

"Well, sir . . ." Rochmon hesitated, then decided that if Gilbert couldn't help him, no one could. "It's about Mica, sir. You know how I feel about her—how much I care about her, I mean, and I just wish she were back here, that's all. Now don't get me wrong, sir. I'm not suggesting that you call her back or anything like that. It's just that—"

"Wouldn't do any good." Gilbert laughed, but behind the laugh he felt an uneasiness about what Rochmon had said. "She's determined to stay out there come hell or black holes." A soft chime sounded in the Senior Wardroom. "We only have a few minutes left. Shall we finish this drink and go down to get you your gold sleeves?"

Rochmon sighed, then quickly smiled and lifted his glass. "To Mica, sir."

"To Mica," Gilbert responded. As he downed his Aquamarie, his eyes began to water. Strong stuff, he thought, yet he knew that was only part of the reason for the wetness in his eyes.

As soon as they finished their drinks, they walked down the ladders of the Hall of Flags. To Rochmon's surprise, the hall was crowded with senior and junior officers, many of whom signaled thumbs-up as he made his way to the platform.

The ceremony itself was handled quickly and efficiently by Admiral Stonefield's staff. First the new officers were awarded their commissions, then the junior officers were given their promotions, then Admiral Stonefield pinned on the ceremonial gold sleeves and the two space-blackened stars that denoted Rochmon's new rank of Quarter-Admiral.

The reception following took much longer than the ceremonies themselves. Liquor flowed freely from the bars along the side of the hall, but Rochmon was careful to drink very little.

After a respectable period of time that allowed Rochmon to accept a series of congratulations, Admiral Stonefield crossed the hall and said, "Admiral Rochmon, may I have a few minutes alone with you?"

"Of course, sir." Rochmon followed Stonefield through a side door and into a small, richly furnished meeting room.

"Please, Hew, sit down," Stonefield said.

Rochmon settled himself in one of the padded leather chairs beside a small table in the corner, and held his drink in his lap with both hands. Stonefield remained standing.

"I won't beat around the stern tubes, Hew. I've been reading your latest reports very carefully, and it seems to me that you're going to have to break that Q-3 code if we're going to stay ahead of the Ukes."

With a nod of his head Rochmon said, "I agree, sir. It's already becoming their major code." He hadn't been prepared to talk about the code, but he was more than willing to agree.

"Then I think we should recall that Bock person who helped break the Q-Two."

"What, sir? I thought—I mean—I'm not sure I understand, sir. You want to bring Bock back to Cryptography?"

Stonefield stared at him with no emotion showing in his cold, dark eyes. "That's what I want, Rochmon. You'll have to keep tight security on her, but I've checked around. She's the best. And Sondak needs her."

"Does that mean you've cleared her of the spying charges?"

"No, Rochmon, it doesn't. As far as I'm concerned, she's a threat, but if she's as good as everyone claims, then use her."

Rochmon stood up slowly. He didn't know if he liked this or not, but from the angry undertone in Stonefield's voice and the look on his face, Rochmon knew better than to pursue the subject any further. "I'll make good use of her, sir," he said quietly.

"You do that, Admiral. You do that. Now, go enjoy the reception."

Rochmon left the room and rejoined the reception, but after all that had happened that day, there was no way for him to really enjoy it.

4

Leri Gish Geril coiled her body to the proper formal height for receiving visitors and waited for Glights the Castorian to come to her chambers. Ever since the execution of Exeter and the other Castorian criminals, Leri had been very cautious in her dealings with Glights. Despite that caution, she had come to like him, and that made her angry. She had liked Exeter, too, and he had responded by drugging her and taking her aboard his spaceship so that he could eat her.

She shivered at the memory and coiled her body tighter. That memory of Exeter's treachery would serve as a constant reminder never to trust any Castorian, regardless of how friendly and likable one might appear to be.

With a sigh of frustration she spat a fireball across the chamber. Leri was tired, tired of being Proctor of Cloise, tired of having to deal with aliens—especially the humans and the impertinent Oinaise—and tired of Weecs. Oh, Weecs was an excellent lover, with a superior mind and an eager body—and she was not yet tired of that long, sleek body with its red-and-yellow scales still bright with the color of youth and always tinged with the scent of his lust for her. But she was tired of Weecs pressuring her to make personal decisions. She was under enough strain and pressure without his contribution.

A lover was supposed to refresh, not tire. A lover was supposed to provide relief from problems, not new problems to be coped with. Maybe that was why she had refused to totally renounce Ranas. Maybe in some deep way she understood that a long-standing Mate like Ranas offered something more stable and basic that she *needed* even more than she *wanted* Weecs's passion.

Leri sighed again. Hundreds of seasons ago she had been blessed with dreams that developed into a clear vision of the future. She had dreamed of a path through the mists, a way to lead her people away from the Sondak humans who robbed Cloise of its methane. But season after season humans and Castorians and Oinaise had come to Cloise and dragged her and her people deeper and deeper into the galaxy's conflicts. And season after season her vision had become more confusing and muddled. Now when it came to her, it brought little she could understand.

When she had gone to the Confidante, it had asked her a series of questions in its usual way that had only led her back to where she had started. She had no choice but to trust what little of the vision she did understand and to use her instincts to follow it to the best of her ability. But what if the Confidante— Her thoughts were interrupted by the arrival of Ranas and Glights.

"Greetings, Proctor," Ranas said formally as he slithered up beside her.

"Greetings, Mighty Proctor," Glights said through his translator pack while he clacked his claws high over his carapace. "I am honored that you have chosen to receive me."

"Greetings," Leri said curtly. "What do you and our other soulless allies want of me this season?"

"Pardon my contentiousness, Proctor, but I must remind you that we Castorians do have souls, and your references to us as soulless only adds to the friction of—"

"Very well," Leri said, cutting the crab off, "Castorians have souls." Glights did like to prattle on about his soul, and she constantly had to remind herself that if she didn't want to hear about his soul, she shouldn't provoke him. "So tell me what it is you want of me."

"We must speak again about the festbid, Proctor."

"Why? I thought you and the Oinaise had settled on how to handle that abominable problem." Beside her Leri could smell Ranas's disapproval and tried to tell herself to speak more politely to Glights. Courtesy was cheap enough.

"Unfortunately, Proctor, 'that abominable problem' will not be settled until the festbid is completed—and perhaps

not even then. The Oinaise spokesmouth—Delightful Childe
I believe he is called—has suggested some alternatives for
our consideration."

"Alternatives?" Leri spat a fireball over Glights's head,
knowing that its only effect would be to demonstrate her
anger. "Surely your original proposal is sufficient. Outbid the
humans and destroy the blasphemous weapon!"

"Ah, well, yes, Proctor, that would seem the best plan.
However, this Delightful Childe has suggested that if we do,
indeed, obtain the weapon, Sondak and the U.C.S. might not
believe we'd destroyed it and then they'd both turn against
us in order to take it back."

"Then destroy it in front of their fecal faces!"

Glights clacked something his translator pack couldn't find
a Cloisean equivalent for, then said, "Quite impossible. The
broker who is conducting this festbid has made it clear that
he has established double-blind safeguards to ensure that the
party who wins the bid can safely acquire the weapon."

Leri sighed. There was no sense in arguing with him.
Glights had leaned back on his carapace, and she knew he
would just persist until she let him have his way. After dealing
with male Castorians, Oinaise, humans, and, of course, those
of her own race, she had decided this characteristic of relent-
less persistence was one of the few universals they shared.
Males just had to have their say, one way or the other,
regardless of whether anyone wanted to listen to them or not.
"All right. All right. Tell me their new proposals. But do it
quickly."

"As you wish, Proctor. The first is that one of Oina's
representatives attempt to steal the weapon before the festbid.
The second is that the alliance back the U.C.S.'s bid in
exchange for their promise—"

"Madness!" Leri hissed. "Steal the weapon? Back the humans? What is wrong with the Oinaise? What is wrong with
you? I refuse to hear any more of this. Go away. Now."

"But, Proctor Leri, it is necessary for you—"

"Nothing is necessary for me, you soulless crab! Leave me.
Go back to your ship and protect Cloise as you agreed. And
tell the soulless Oinaise that I will have nothing to do with
their insane proposals."

Before Glights could answer, Leri buried her head in the
center of her coil. She heard him leave but refused to ac-

knowledge his departure. Only when Ranas stroked her, smoothing her flared scales, did she finally pull her head back up and let herself relax a little.

"You are rude, my Proctor," he said softly as he continued to stroke her, "but you are right."

"Of course I am right. What is wrong with them, Ranas? What is wrong with us?"

"Questions I cannot answer, Proctor. How can I understand an alien mind? How can we make sense of what they do? We can only cope with them according to our own understanding and—"

"I know. I know. Leave me now, Ranas, and send in the Isthian. I am tired and in great need of exchange."

Moments after Ranas left Leri heard the Isthian scramble unseen into the chamber and felt it climb gently on her back. Without hesitation it began suckling the nipple on her neck, drawing its nourishment from her blood while replacing her vital antibodies. The more it suckled, the more her body relaxed, and Leri let herself slip into the dreamy prelude to sleep. But deep in a hidden grotto of her mind she knew that her escape from the problems she faced was only temporary.

*   *   *

"That is only the preliminary plan, of course," General Schopper said. "The final details are still in the process."

"May I say somethin', sir?" Rasha'kean asked.

"Certainly, Ingrivia. That's why I brought you here."

Rasha'kean ignored that comment. She had brought herself to Nordeen—and not for this. But if she had to buy herself a combat command with work on logistics, then so be it—just as long as she got her command.

"I ken that you've attacked the logistics part of this plan from the wrong direction. If we're goin' to attack our way system by system into the U.C.S., we cannot afford the extended supply routes you got here. Let the Ukes cut even one of those routes, and they could isolate whatever system we were currently engaged in."

"But how else can we—"

"Excuse me, sir, but there are double-other ways. Ar'not there uninhabited systems close to your proposed route of attack where we could stockpile supplies?"

"I'm sure there are, Ingrivia, but that seems like an even more dangerous plan to me."

"I d'not think so, sir. Find me five, six uninhabited systems close to the route and I'll set you up a plan for supply caches that'll eliminate some of your logistic vulnerability."

"Why do you have to have systems? Why not just pick someplace in space?"

Rasha'kean laughed, tossing her blond hair as she did so. The scowl on Schopper's face made her stop. "Sorry, sir, I'm not laughin' at you. I'm laughin' 'cause that's the same question every new logistics officer asks. We have to use systems because they're easy to find. A good ship's navigator can get you to most any star in the galaxy, but only one in a thousand can get you to within a parsec of some random point in space away from any star system."

"I see," Schopper said, his tone implying more humility than his face showed. "All right, then. We get Space Force to locate suitable systems for us. Then what?"

"Then we assign each system to one step in your attack plan and sneak in as many supply ships as we can into those systems ahead of the attacks themselves. Then they only have to make a short hop to keep you supplied and fueled."

"And where are we going to get all these ships?"

She could tell Schopper was not impressed by her idea, but that was his problem, not hers. "We'll get them, sir. We'll get them from the reserve fleet and from the civilian combines and by commandeerin' independents if we have to. But I'm sure you and Admiral Gilbert will find a way."

Schopper stared at her for a long moment before he spoke. "You're uppity-damn sure of yourself, aren't you, Ingrivia?"

"Yes, sir," she said without hesitation. "Have to be if I'm goin' to convince hardheaded old generals that I'm right."

"And you think I'm hardheaded?"

"You said it, sir, not me. I woul'not be sayin' things like that about my superior officer." Rasha'kean gave him a flash of a smile. Over the ten short days she had worked for him, she had learned that smile worked on him, after all—just in a different way than it had worked on others.

"I still think it sounds very dangerous. What if the Ukes catch us at this supply plan of yours? They could stop us dead in space simply by destroying the supplies in any one of those systems."

"I said there were double-other ways to do it, sir. The

supply systems are only part of my idea. The other thing we can do is to use Ca-Ryn sleds."

"What?"

"Ca-Ryn sleds, sir. They're not sleds, actually, and they di'not even come from Ca-Ryn. But that's what they're called. Anyway, they're really just big empty hulls you can fill and tow through space. If we can find enough of them—or build enough—we could fill them with supplies and tow them right along with the attack fleet."

"Does Space Force know how to use these sleds?"

"Of course, sir. At least Border Fleet does. That's where I first saw them used."

Schopper rubbed his chin thoughtfully as he stared up at the ceiling. "So, what you propose is that part of our supplies be cached ahead of us, and part we tow along, and either way we avoid extended supply routes. Is that correct?"

"That's about it. Except for one other thing, of course."

"And what's that?"

Rasha'kean suspected that she should wait to press this point, but she did not want Schopper ever to forget why she was there. "What we talked about before, sir. Once we get this set up and movin', I want to be in command of a combat unit with the first attack force."

"Now look, Ingrivia, we've already been over that. I said I would find you a combat command, but it won't be with the first attack force. Someone's going to have to coordinate this—"

"I resign, sir," Rasha'kean said as she came to her feet. "Take my commission and shove it up your—"

"At ease, Colonel! I'll have no more of this resignation talk from you."

"Then I'll have my combat command." She leaned forward with her hands flat on his desk and stared straight into his eyes. "With the first attack force. That's the deal, sir."

Suddenly Schopper laughed. "You're going to be a damned pain to have around here, Ingrivia. You know that?"

"Only until I get my command."

"In the first attack force," he added.

"You got it, sir," she said as she straightened up.

"Then get your boots out of here and draw up a detailed plan for what you just proposed—and I mean detailed. I want you to put down every contingency, everything that might go wrong, everything and anything that occurs to you that might be important. I want the logistics part of your brain, Ingrivia, and I want it in a report in five days."

"Will do, sir," she said with a quick salute. He ignored her, so she left. Score one for me, she thought as she headed for her office. Score one for me.

5

Marshall Judoff stood with her hands on her hips and an ugly scowl on her face. "And just where in the void did you hear about that, Charltos?"

"Does it matter?" Frye asked. He could tell by the expressions that most of the members of Bridgeforce were as stunned by the news as Judoff was. Only Meister Hadasaki was smiling.

"It's a freespacer's lie," Judoff said, "and I don't have to listen to the likes of that from the likes of you."

"Then you deny any involvement with this so-called Ultimate Weapon? And you deny having the Sak scientist Ayne Wallen in your custody? And you deny that you were aware of this festbid for the weapon? And you deny—"

"I don't have to deny anything." Judoff sat back down and folded her hands neatly in front of her. "Whatever actions I have taken have been on the behalf of the U.C.S.—which is more than we can say for that deserting daughter of yours, Admiral."

Beside her, Commander Kuskuvyet coughed and looked down at the table, making Frye wonder if Judoff's aide were as nervous and clumsy in bed with her as he was in public.

"Come now, Judoff," Hadasaki said, "either these allegations are true, or they are not. Which is it?"

"Believe what you will, Meister."

"Then I accuse you of treason," Hadasaki said softly.

"Treason?"

"Yes, treason. You have betrayed—"

"You're insane! I never in my life committed a treasonous act, nor would I ever—"

"And who lies now?"

Frye slapped his hand on the table. "Both of you are out of order. "We have no indications that Marshall Judoff has done anything that can be considered treasonous, Meister, and none, so far, that she has lied." They were both staring at him, Judoff with a smirk, Hadasaki with anger flushing his face.

"However," Frye continued, "if Marshall Judoff refuses to respond to these allegations, then I believe Bridgeforce will have cause for considerable concern." He looked directly at Judoff and hoped she had gotten the message clearly. The U.C.S. still needed her and the forces she commanded if they hoped to win this war. There would be time enough after they won to expose Judoff for what she really was—a spoiled, ego-powered sex-maniac who in every critical situation thought first of herself.

"Very well," Judoff said slowly, "since you already have half-truths about what has been happening, I suppose it is my duty to give you the facts. I neither informed Bridgeforce of this situation nor involved you because the negotiations have been occurring outside all official channels. I had hoped to be able to obtain this weapon and present it to you without having to involve—"

"More flimsy lies," Hadasaki said.

"Oh, shut up, Hodass, and let her finish," Vice-Admiral Lotonoto said with a quick shake of her head.

Frye was surprised by Lotonoto but held his tongue. Despite his position as chairman of Bridgeforce, he was still the junior ranking member. That required him to allow the other members to express their opinions in ways Admiral Tuuneo never would have stood for.

"Thank you, Lotonoto," Judoff said. "Your respect is appreciated."

"No respect intended," Lotonoto said. "Just want to hear the rest of your lie before I vote to hang you by your dugs to dry in the sun."

"All right. Damn you all," Judoff said flatly. "I'll give you the straight story, then walk out on your apologies. Kuskuvyet here learned through a contact on Patros of a scientist who had defected from Sondak—the Ayne Wallen mentioned before. We managed to arrange for Wallen to be transported to us, but before we could obtain any specific information, Wallen escaped with the broker who had made the original arrangement. We believe this plan was devised as bait to involve us in a festbid for a prototype of the weapon itself."

"And that is all?" Frye asked.

"Not quite. It seems that this same broker managed to obtain the prototype of the weapon constructed by Drautzlab on Summer, so that whoever wins the festbid gets both the weapon and its creator."

"What exactly does this weapon do that makes it so interesting?" Hadasaki asked.

Judoff frowned. "If the limited information we have is correct, this thing that Drautzlab calls the Ultimate Weapon would be capable of exploding stars."

Soft whistles and sighs filled the room.

"Impossible," Lotonoto said. "Such a weapon would have to carry enough mass to make it the size of a small planet."

"Wallen claims it works at a distance. 'Reciprocal action at a distance,' he said."

"Even more impossible. I don't believe for an instant—"

"Pardon me, Admiral," Frye said, "but leaving that aside for a moment, I would like to ask Marshall Judoff if she knows who else is involved in this proposed festbid."

The smile she gave him was one of smug self-assurance. The tides had turned in her favor again. "There are at least two other interested parties: Drautzlab itself, probably with the help of Sondak's Scientific-Security Division, and the new alien alliance including Cloise—which has been supplying the Saks with methane, by the way—Castor, and the Oinaise. A curious group, don't you think?"

Hadasaki sighed and leaned across the table. "So, please tell us again, Marshall Judoff, why, if so many powerful parties are interested in this weapon, you did not see fit to tell us about it voluntarily?"

His question brought chaos to the meeting. Within seconds members were on their feet and yelling at each other in five languages—the kyosei faction, Drew, Garner, and Toso, defending Judoff and her methods, and Hadasaki and Lotonoto leading the attack of those who condemned her. After several attempts to restore order, Frye gathered his things together, declared the meeting adjourned, and left them to their arguments.

As he returned to his office he wondered how they were

ever going to accomplish anything as long as this division between the kyosei and the others kept getting worse. He didn't understand the kyosei now and never had. Their goals seemed self-centered and defeatist to him, and their propaganda seemed deliberately designed to confuse the citizens of the U.C.S.—not to mention confusing him, as well. They claimed to want to win the war, but at the least possible cost, and with a plan of isolationism that would cripple the U.C.S.'s already weak economy.

It just didn't make sense. None of it.

Melliman jumped to her feet the moment Frye entered the office. "We've had some bad reports coming in, sir. I think you'd better take a look at them right away."

"Very well, AOCO," he said, hearing the fatigue in his voice. "Fix me some tea and I'll get started."

Hours later Frye shook his head in quiet dismay. Somehow Sondak had found the ships to reinforce their polar sector. The raids he had designed to cripple the Saks there and rip holes in their defenses were beginning to cost the U.C.S. as much as it was costing the Saks. But why? What had he done wrong? And where had they found enough ships?

He shook his head and wondered if he should call another meeting of Bridgeforce for tomorrow. Then he realized that for all he knew, they could still be up there arguing now. Better just to prepare a summary report for them. How would Tuuneo have handled this? he wondered. Tuuneo had had prestige and respect, and Bridgeforce would have yielded to that. But Tuuneo was long dead, and whether he liked it or not, Frye was responsible for seeing that Bridgeforce was pulled back together.

He leaned back with a sigh and suddenly realized how late it was. "AOCO," he said into his lapel mike, "let's lock the files and go home. I'm tired and hungry."

"Ready when you are, sir," her voice said from the desk speaker.

Frye didn't say much on the trip home, and Melliman respected his silence. Only after they had eaten the meal she had ordered ahead for them and were sitting on the low couch sipping their wine, did he finally open his thoughts to her.

"Bridgeforce went at it again today. That's the third time in six days. You'd think the kyosei were trying to keep us from getting anything done."

"Is that so hard to believe, Frye?"

"What do you mean?"

Melliman set her glass down and put her head back against his arm. "Well, if Drew, Garner, and Toso can stall Bridge-force—even if only for thirty days or so—they could probably use that to force you out and put Judoff in charge."

"Damn," he said, looking first at the overhead, then turning quickly to her. "Clarest, you're brilliant. And you're right, too. But why didn't I see that?"

"Because you're in the middle of it, my love, up to your armpits."

Frye gave her a quick kiss on the nose. "You win the prize for the day," he said with a sudden laugh.

"There's only one prize I want." Her hands slipped gently around his neck, and she pulled his mouth to hers.

For a second Frye resisted. There was so much to do, so much he had to think about, that he wasn't in the mood for lovemaking. But his mouth accepted hers with practiced skill. His arms automatically wrapped themselves around her, and his groin tightened with a desire for her that washed his resistance away. There would be time for thinking later.

Slowly and sensuously they shared long, searching kisses while their hands busied themselves removing each other's uniforms. Then they were finally naked on the floor, Clarest lying on top of him, teasing his need, brushing her breasts lightly across his chest, pressing her hips hard against his, tickling his ear with her tongue.

With gentle pressure he raised his knees so that she slid up his body a little, then pulled her legs up until she was kneeling over him, the heat of her desire pressing against him.

Clarest needed no further encouragement to capture him with a soft plunge of her hips. Then with the ease and grace and exquisite timing that comes from intimate knowledge, she rode his body up the long rise of excitement until they peaked together and plunged over the edge of joyous release.

Frye stroked her hair and her back as they slowly recovered their breath and wondered again at the marvel she was. The best Aide-of-Commander in the whole U.C.S. with a grasp for tactics that continually impressed him; an excellent cook, even if she wasn't as good as he was; a fine companion; and a very talented lover. What more could he want?

Vinita, a voice whispered in his mind.

A quiet smile lingered on Frye's lips. He would never forget Vinita, never be able to love anyone—even Clarest—the way he loved her, but Vinita was gone, and he had mourned enough. The energy he had given over to mourning for her was now channeled toward winning the war. In her honor, he thought, and Tuuneo's. For both of them.

"What are you thinking, my love?" Melliman whispered.

"I'm thinking, my dear Clarest, that if we do not get up from here, I will fall asleep, and I still have too much to do tonight to sleep yet."

She gently rotated her hips. "Are you sure you want to get up right now?"

"Yes, you insatiable delight. If you will help me get some of this work done, and if you're still inclined to use my body later, I think you might find me willing."

"You'd better be," she said as she slowly pulled herself off of him, "because my body is very fond of your body."

Working together, it took them two hours to put together the summary report for the rest of the members of Bridgeforce. Then after sharing another glass of wine Melliman led him by the hand to the bedroom, and Frye made good on his offer.

Afterward, as he lay in the warm love-stupor with Melliman obviously falling asleep beside him, Frye unexpectedly felt himself slipping into a dark mood. It was Judoff and her treachery and her damnable kyosei, and Lotonoto with her arrogant ways, and Hadasaki with his meddling ways, and the whole of Bridgeforce with its arcane politics that depressed him.

Maybe I should just resign and ask for a fleet command, he thought. Wouldn't that foul their brass?

And Judoff would take over. And what would happen to you and the war? And whose brass would be fouled then? Whose, Mister Brilliant-Admiral Frye ed'Laitin Charltos? Whose then?

It took a long time before fatigue won over the questions in his mind and he fell into a heavy sleep.

6

Henley Stanmorton looked up from his almost-empty plate when he heard the commotion and stared across the restaurant at the heavily bearded, garishly made up figure skipping toward him. When he realized who it was, he laughed out loud. "Kinderman? Kryki Kinderman? Is that really you?"

"Krystal R. Kinderman, in the raggedy flesh," the man answered, "every poetic bone metrically intact."

"And then some," Henley said, waving him to a chair. "You're a little more hirsute than the last time I saw you, and a good deal thinner. What are you doing here? Come to harass the powers that be, I suppose."

"Why, Henley, old son, how could you ever think such a thing of me, who has known and loved you so long?" Kinderman's uneven brown teeth filled the orange smile painted on his black beard as he sat down across the table from Henley and carefully arranged his purple-and-red striped longcoat. All around them the other customers in the restaurant slowly turned back to their own concerns. "You know my only purpose in life is to spread the joy and beauty of poetry to the mass of humanity."

"And raise hell with anyone in authority who crosses your path," Henley said, wishing he were more amused by Kinderman's outrageous presence. He could have used the humor.

"Ah, but it usually works in reverse, you snotty old Teller. It is the authorities who raise what you so quaintly call 'hell' with me." Kinderman paused with an exaggerated frown, then brought his hands flat together in front of his face, touched his nose to his forefingers and gave Henley a little bow of the head. "Your humble old friend merely attempts to educate the oppressors of the adorable masses whom they force to dwell under the wretched trials and—"

"Enough! Enough. I've heard you spout all that spacecrap before, remember?" Too many times, Henley thought. He remembered the days when Kinderman had been at the top of his form, traveling around Sondak, issuing poetic manifestos that advocated intergalactic brotherhood. Kinderman had received good coverage from the Tellers as comic relief from the less cheerful news of the day. But that was before the war had started.

Henley hadn't seen or heard much about Kinderman since then except a reference or two in the news journals noting that the once-famous poet had been jailed in cities on several planets for what was euphemistically called creating a public nuisance. "So, Kryki, what do you know—besides some bad poem? Anything that's new and interesting?"

"Everything is new and interesting, Henley—even poetry—to those who open their hearts to hear it."

Before Henley could reply, Kinderman waved his hand dramatically. "Now do not get flushy on me, my plate-headed old friend. However depraved and basically illiterate most members of your profession are, I have always respected you and the truth you fight so hard to reveal in those stories you tell. You really should have been a poet, you know. But anyway, that is why I have come to see you, old son."

"Me? You came to see me? To tell me I should have been a poet? You'll have to give me a better reason than that or I'm going to run and hide."

Kinderman laughed, then looked around the restaurant and leaned over the table. "Would you hide," he whispered with a conspiratorial grin, "if I told you that the puking Ukes have paid me to talk to you?"

Henley was stunned. "They what?"

"Has the war deafened you? I said, the pukin' Ukes have paid me to find you and talk to you. I am a messenger, Henley, shot from the throat of the enemy like the burning light of a stellar laser, come here to share with you truths that other Tellers would kill their offspring for."

"Like what?" Henley asked. Skepticism had quickly replaced his shock, and he wondered what outrageous caper Kinderman had launched upon now.

"Ah, I see you do not believe me, old son. Well, pay for that wretched mess you just consumed and take me somewhere where we can talk privately and drink a bitter liter and I will make of you a believer."

Half an hour later they were sitting in a privacy booth in

one of the many bars within walking distance of Sondak Supreme Headquarters. After they received their drinks, Henley sealed the booth shut. When the green security light over their heads went on and indicated that the booth was soundproof, he said, "All right, Kryki, just what is all this nonsense about the Ukes sending you with some message for me?"

"I lied," Kinderman said with a smile. "It was not the Ukes, exactly, but it has to do with the Ukes and Sondak and the new alien alliance and the whole damnable war."

Henley sighed and took a sip of his drink. "So spread it out for me."

Kinderman looked at the security light as though to reassure himself that the booth truly was sealed, then leaned forward, cupping his glass with both hands. "It is a long story, old son, one that does not bear retelling at this moment."

Henley was relieved to hear that.

"However, what is important is that through the good offices of a friend of a friend, I have received a considerable addition to my cash reserves in return for passing this information on to a reliable Teller."

"Just tell me, Kryki. I don't have the patience to play dance around the virgin's thigh right now."

"Such vulgarity, Henley. I expected better from—all right. All right. Do not become angry with me. I will tell you as simply as I can. According to my source and benefactor, Drautzlab, the military weapons complex on Summer that—"

"I'm familiar with Drautzlab. Go on."

"Very well. As I said, according to my source, last year Drautzlab produced a weapon unlike anything mankind has ever in its most horrible dreams conceived of, and that weapon, along with its creator, is now—"

"What kind of weapon?"

"A cataclysmic weapon, Henley. A star-buster."

"Damn! Are you sure?"

"My source is sure. But if you want all the information, let me finish. That weapon is now in the hands of an Oinaise broker from Patros who will shortly be conducting an auction—festbid, he calls it—in order to sell the weapon and its creator to the highest bidder."

Henley whistled softly; then his natural skepticism stopped

him. "Why?" he asked. "Why wouldn't he just sell it to the Ukes?"

"Apparently he tried that and they cheated him, so he stole the weapon and its inventor back and thus the auction. And now," Kinderman said before taking a deep drink of his liquor, "my source believes the alien alliance will also be bidding on this weapon."

"Who's your source?"

"I cannot tell you that. Suffice it to say that he has contacts in many places—including the U.C.S."

"Then tell me why I'm supposed to believe you and what your mysterious source expects me to do with this information?"

Kinderman smiled ruefully. "As to the first, only your knowledge that I have never lied to you, even when it would have been to my advantage."

"True enough," Henley admitted.

"As for what he expects you to do, why, that should be obvious. You are a Teller. He expects you to tell all of Sondak what I have just told you."

Henley laughed. "Your source must be a very naive person. Even if I could spread this on the newsnets, I wouldn't. But that doesn't matter, because I can't."

"And why not, old son? Why can you not?"

"Because, Kryki, I am back in the Service, and if I were to spread such a story—"

"You are what?" Kinderman stared at Henley in disbelief.

"Back in the Service. You let these civilian clothes fool you, Kryki. When I'm on duty I'm Chief Warrant Officer Henley, even to you, old friend. But on or off duty, I'm still in the Service."

"Of all the stupid, ignorant, obscene, senseless, totally revolting things I ever—"

"Oh, shut up, Kryki. You're already in trouble enough."

"Me? In trouble? How?"

"Because I'm going to have to turn you over to someone who will make sure you don't share this information of yours with anyone else." Henley saw the look of disappointment on Kinderman's face. "I'm sorry, Kryki, but it can't be helped. If what you told me is true, the last thing we need is to have it become general knowledge throughout Sondak."

"But Henley . . . can you not see that the cause of peace—"

"I see only a very clear danger, Kryki—you. Now, will you go with me voluntarily, or do I have to call for assistance?"

"Where?" Kinderman asked after a long pause.

"To see Admiral Gilbert," Henley said quickly. "He's my boss, and he'll have to decide what's to be done with you."

Kinderman sighed, then stared straight at Henley. "You would call for help if I said no?"

Henley nodded. "I'd have to."

"Very well, then. But I will tell you this, Henley Stanmorton—you shall one day regret this."

"I already do, Kryki. But it has to be this way."

* * *

Ayne counted the pieces of gorlet left for the third time. If Xindella did not return in the next few hours and replenish his supply, Ayne knew his withdrawal symptoms were going to become unbearable. He had meant to ration his supply more carefully, but there had been so much gorlet in the box when he started that he was sure he would have enough. Now he was frightened about what would happen to him if Xindella did not return soon—very soon.

His strongest urge was to gobble the seven pieces he had left and live with the consequences. Or die with them, he thought. Reluctantly, he withdrew only one piece, then closed the box and placed it on the shelf over his worktable.

As soon as the sweet dark gorlet was in his mouth, it started to dissolve. Ayne savored its chocolaty flavor until he realized he was sucking on his tongue for the last hints of taste. The gorlet eased the tension in his stomach but little else. Halfheartedly he cursed his addiction as he stared longingly at the box holding his remaining supply. Then, with a sense of determination he knew wouldn't last, he forced his eyes away from the box and turned back to his project.

Most of the engineering on the Drautzlab weapon was fairly easy for him to understand, especially when he recognized what Sjean was attempting to create in her assembly of the components. And it definitely was Sjean's work he was looking at. The whole contraption had her imprint on it, from its compact basic design to its highly efficient wiring scheme. Ayne even thought he understood the functional areas as she had laid them out.

Laid them out. He sighed. That was what he would like to do to her. That's what he always wanted to do to her.

With a quick shake of his head he again forced his attention back to the weapon. There was something beautiful about its asymmetrical design, but something puzzling, as well. Where was the detonator? Surely it couldn't have been attached to the thin strand of cable that had been dangling from the weapon when Xindella picked it up. He rubbed his fingers on his temples as he tried to think, wishing again that he had sufficient gorlet.

No, the cable couldn't be for a detonator. It had to lead to some kind of focusing device that would be far enough away from the body of the weapon to allow for some kind of parallax correction. But if that were so, where was the detonator?

Could it be internal? Ayne had been hesitant to dig into the guts of the weapon, afraid to disturb the inner workings before he understood the outer ones. "But now," he said aloud, "we guess it is time to take chances."

Without thinking, he opened the gorlet box and popped three of them into his mouth. Only when the taste hit him did he realize what he had done.

"Damn. We will suffer sooner than expected if—"

"Why do you talk of suffering, Citizen?" Xindella's voice asked from the overhead speaker.

"Our friend and benefactor," Ayne said in his most supplicating voice, "we despaired of your coming, as our gorlet is almost exhausted."

"Is the weapon ready for inspection?"

"No. It needs much to be understood."

"Ah," Xindella said mockingly, "then how can I give you more gorlet if you have not done your work?"

"Is easy," Ayne said, already starting to shake under the threat. "If our most gracious Xindella does not give us more gorlet, then our work will not get done at all while we go through agony of withdrawal. Will not be then ready for your festbid, and therefore cannot—"

"Shut up. I will bring your gorlet—this time. But you'd damn well better figure out how that weapon works pretty soon, or you will pray for withdrawal as a relief from what I will do to you. Do you understand me, Citizen Wallen?"

"We understand, Xindella," he said softly. "We understand."

7

Rasha'kean sat watching silently as General Schopper read the preliminary summary of her report. His repeated nodding at first was encouraging, but it stopped and was then followed by a slow, almost-rhythmic shaking. Consequently, when he finally looked up at her with a frown on his face, she was prepared for trouble. "Somethin' wrong, sir?"

"Damned right there is, Ingrivia. To begin with, where in the name of Biery are we going to get all the ships for this plan of yours?"

"Wherever we have to, sir."

"That's a space-poor answer," he said as his frown deepened. "I'm afraid this report is totally unsatisfactory."

"But you've only read the summary," Rasha'kean protested, sensing that this was going to be worse than she thought. "How can you judge a report you ha'not read?"

Schopper slowly shook his head again, closed his eyes, and let out a long breath. When he opened his eyes and looked at her, she saw a strange, indefinable sadness there and more than a little anger.

"Please, sir, at least read my complete report before you condemn it."

"I don't have to, Colonel. It's obvious to me that you've rushed through this because of our agreement. Your summary makes it quite clear that this so-called plan of yours is ill conceived and poorly thought out. It won't do at all. Now, what I want you to do is to start over with a different—"

"No," Rasha'kean said firmly as she rose from her chair. She refused to let Schopper bully her into further logistic work. He had asked for a planning report, and she had given it to him. "If you d'not like my report, sir, then you know my standin' resignation offer."

For the first time since she had entered his office, Schopper smiled, but it was a smile without humor. "Sit down, Colonel, and listen carefully to what I'm about to tell you."

Reluctantly, Rasha'kean sat down. She was angry again, but from the tone of his voice she knew Schopper was about to tell her something she did not want to hear.

"Ingrivia, I've put up with as much of this resignation nonsense from you as I'm going to. From this moment on—"

"It i'not nonsense, sir. I meant what I—"

"As you were, Colonel," Schopper said sternly. "Just shut up and listen to me."

"Yes, sir."

"I've talked to Admiral Gilbert and also to the Joint Chiefs about your case since you and I had our last discussion, and I'm going to lay it out for you as clearly as I can. Yes, it is true, you have the right to resign your commission if you should so choose. But under the Extreme Emergency War Powers Act of 3022, the Service has the right to recall you to active duty at your permanent rank, which I believe in your case is Co-Captain. You didn't know that, did you, Ingrivia?"

"No, sir." Rasha'kean's mind rebeled against what he was saying, but she dared not interrupt him again. She also dared not let herself believe him. If what he said was true, then she would be effectively stripped of all the leverage she had against him and the Service.

"I thought not. Furthermore," he continued, "the Service can recall you to a specific duty—under my command, for example, where you would be doing exactly what you're doing now, but with three grades less rank. Is that what you want, Ingrivia?"

"Of course not, sir," she said, hearing the anger edging through her control, "but I'll not be wantin' to believe you, either . . . sir."

"I don't give a spacejack's damn what you want to believe. I'm telling you the way things stand. Now go rework this report. And make sure you do it right this time."

For a brief moment Rasha'kean did not move. She felt numb and cold, and angry, and stunned, wanting desperately to fight back, but not knowing how to do it. Schopper was right, of course. She had rushed through the report. She wanted to get her combat assignment. But all she had succeeded in doing was delaying that and angering Schopper. Slowly and deliberately, she stood up and saluted him.

"Do it right, Ingrivia," Schopper said with a casual return of her salute, "and I'll keep my promise. I'll get you that combat command you want so much. But you have to do your job here, first. Is that understood?"

"Certainly, sir. I ken what you're saying."

"Good. That's all."

As quickly as she could, Rasha'kean left his office and headed for her own. She hardly saw the other people in the halls as she ducked into the stairwell and went down the two flights as fast as she could. When she came out of the stairwell on her floor, she almost bumped into Stanmorton—again.

"Easy, Colonel," he said, stepping aside so she could pass. "What's your rush?"

"Ca'not be talkin' now, Chief," she said, unwilling to meet his eyes as she moved past him.

"We're still scheduled for dinner tomorrow," he said to her back, "aren't we?"

"Yes," she said over her shoulder, realizing that she had totally forgotten about that. "Pick me up at my quarters."

It was only when she got to her office and shut the door that she realized Stanmorton had been in civilian clothes and was accompanied by one of the strangest-looking people she had ever seen—a man in an ugly striped coat with orange paint in his beard. As swiftly as that trivial realization came, she dismissed it and turned on her research terminal.

In less than a minute she had a copy of the Extreme Emergency War Powers Act of 3022 coming off her copier. The document was fairly short, but it took her over an hour to read and understand it—and then to acknowledge to herself that she was wasting time looking for exclusions that were not there. Finally, she tossed the copy onto her desk in anger and disgust.

There were no exceptions for her or anyone else. The government could recall to active duty any previously commissioned officer it chose, regardless of current status, "for the good of the Services and Sondak," the phrase in the act read.

As much as she wanted to lash out at someone, she knew she had no one to blame but herself. If she'd done her background work before, she would have known about the act and could have saved the resignation threat until she was truly prepared to resign. Then she might have gotten away with it. But she had been so busy playing her game with

Schopper that she had failed to gather all the facts necessary to protect herself.

Now she was in a bind she could not get out of. It would be stupid to resign just to go through the process Schopper had threatened her with and end up back in this same office with two-hundred-plus credits less per chit to her account each pay period. That would be stupid, indeed.

But she hated like everything giving up her only weapon against the bureaucracies of government and the Service just because of— She broke her thought with sudden laughter.

What difference did it make? Schopper had promised her a combat command, had he not? All she had to do is what she should have done in the first place, and then she would be on her way.

* * *

"Inspector, you look as tired as I feel," Sjean said as they sat in chairs on opposite sides of Caugust's office. "Maybe you should get some rest."

"I'll be fine, Dr. Birkie, especially after I discuss the balance of this matter with Dr. Drautz."

"But I explained that he won't be back for another five or six hours, Inspector. One of the Lakeside labs is running a series of experimental demonstrations they wanted him to observe, so you might as well get some rest."

"The Thrasher experiments," Janette said.

"I wouldn't know. That's classified information." That Janette knew about those experiments only added to Sjean's tension. She rolled her head around in an attempt to relieve the aching stiffness in her neck.

"Of course it is. But you forget that I have the capacity to monitor such experiments."

Sjean stared at this tiny woman, who seemed to radiate power, and again felt her own sense of helplessness. She was caught up in the system, obliged to work around the clock on the Wallen—or the Ultimate Weapon, whatever they wanted to call it—yet every day she felt a growing resistance to this project and everything connected with it. Did Inspector Janette know about the festbid and Caugust's secret negotiations to get the prototype Wallen back? It didn't matter anymore. Regardless of how important the weapon might eventually be to Sondak, the horrible implications attached to it were becoming far more important to Sjean.

When she realized how her thoughts were drifting, she began to understand just how tired she was. I need rest, she thought, and good riddance from the inspector.

"Are you ill?" Janette asked suddenly as she noticed a little twitch of Dr. Birkie's head.

"No more than you, Inspector." Sjean rose slowly from her chair, forcing her lethargic muscles to hold her upright. "I have to leave you now and get back to work. If you need anything, one of Dr. Drautz's assistants should be able to provide for you."

"I'll manage, Dr. Birkie," Janette said, rising out of politeness, "but I would appreciate it if you would answer a few questions for me before you go. You're still working on the Ultimate Weapon, I assume?"

"What?" Sjean asked, surprised by the sarcasm she heard in her voice. "You mean you don't know? I thought Sci-Sec knew everything that went on around here."

Again Janette noticed the twitch of Dr. Birkie's head. "What is the matter with you, Doctor? Have I said something to offend you, or are you just angry about life in general?"

"Listen, you little bitch," Sjean said, spitting out the last word in a sudden surge of anger. "I don't need you snooping into my life or my health or anything else."

"Please, Dr. Birkie, there is no need for you to get—"

"Damn you! Who in the holy halls do you think you are? Some kind of deity who can meddle in other people's lives?" Sjean heard the rising hysteria in her voice but had no desire to fight it. "Or do you think you're even better than that?"

Janette quickly decided to let Dr. Birkie's outburst run its course. The woman was obviously suffering from extreme fatigue and wasn't thinking right.

"Answer me!" Sjean screamed. "Answer me!" When Janette only stood there, staring at her, Sjean felt a second rush of anger and wanted to knock the smug look off Janette's face. Picking up the ore sample that Caugust kept as an ornament on his desk, she flung it at Janette and felt a great sense of satisfaction when it hit the tiny woman on the shoulder.

The next few moments were a blur as Janette launched herself across the room and buried her shoulder in Sjean's stomach.

Surprise and pain mixed as Sjean hit the floor with Janette

on top of her. As she fought for breath, Janette flipped her over and pinned her arms behind her back.

"What the crazy hell is going on here?" a voice asked from behind them.

Sjean recognized Caugust's voice and felt Inspector Janette turn on top of her.

"Hysteria," Janette said firmly. "She's having some kind of breakdown, I think."

"No!" Sjean screamed. "No! Caugust, help me!"

"Let her up, Inspector."

"As you wish," Janette said, releasing Dr. Birkie's arms and rising quickly to her feet, "but I think you should— Yowl!"

Her statement was cut short as Sjean rolled over, grabbed one of Janette's legs, and sank her teeth as deeply into Janette's calf as she could.

Thirty minutes later, as the sedative began to push her toward sleep, Sjean thought about what had happened as though remembering a dream—a bad dream. Caugust had attacked her! Sided with that terrible Inspector Janette! He shouldn't have. He had no right, no right at all. She hadn't told Janette their secret. She hadn't . . . but she could now . . . She would if she got the chance. Then why had he come back early? Because he deserved it . . . would tell everything she knew . . . damned Caugust . . . not his fault. The weapon, the damned Wallen, that was the problem. Get rid of Wallen . . . have to get rid of the Wallen . . . be all right . . . all right.

8

A deep frown creased Frye's brow. "How did we get this information, AOCO?"

"It arrived in a sealed pouch this morning, sir," Melliman said, "along with all the routine correspondence. I should have noticed it sooner, but with all the—"

"Doesn't matter. What does matter is how reliable this information is and who sent it to me."

"I think the most obvious answer to that is Lieutenant Oska himself. By referring to himself in the third person, he could deny everything contained in that memo if it were intercepted by one of Marshall Judoff's people."

"Or," Frye said with a deepening frown, "that could be exactly what Judoff's people want us to think. Then they could use this method as a source of information we would come to rely upon and later . . ."

"They could feed us false information," Melliman said, finishing the sentence for him.

"Exactly." He shook his head. "So which is it, AOCO? Someone under Judoff's command who wants to set us up for some later deception? Or a patriotic Lieutenant Oska whose true concern is the welfare of the U.C.S.?"

"For the time being, sir, I'd guess the latter."

"Sit down and tell me why."

"Because we have nothing to lose that way," Melliman said, taking the chair beside his desk. "We can evaluate whatever information he gives us as it comes in and get some idea—"

"But either way we're going to get good information to begin with," Frye said.

"True, but I think we'll be able to tell after a while whether or not our source is a loyal Oska just from the information we receive."

"Maybe I'm too tired to follow that." Frye leaned back, closed his eyes, and massaged his temples with his fingertips. "What makes you think we'll be able to tell?"

"Well, in the first place, sir, as one of Judoff's Junior AOCO's, Oska would naturally be limited in the kind of information he had access to. Furthermore, his youth and general inexperience will probably show up in whatever reports he sends along to us. There is a certain innocence in that memo, don't you think?"

"Perhaps, but I'm more interested in your reactions at the moment. What makes it innocent?"

"The fact that he assumes you will be interested in having a spy on Judoff's staff, the fact that he is ready to begin communications immediately because he is sure you will want this information he possesses, and perhaps most importantly, the fact that he dared approach you at all."

Frye quit massaging his temples, resigned himself to putting up with the headache for a while, and opened his eyes. "I suppose you could be right, but I still think the potential is there for a grand deceit engineered by Judoff."

"Of course there is, sir. I wasn't suggesting that we accept this without question, but does that mean that we should totally reject this offer? Might we not learn something from the deceit itself?"

"Very well, Melliman. As long as we are both aware of the danger, I guess it can't harm us to take the first step. How long will it take you to get to the lock-box and back?"

"Less than an hour."

"Then go now. I'd like to know what's in that first packet before this afternoon's Bridgeforce meeting."

While Melliman was gone, Frye drafted replies to most of the day's routine correspondence, which consisted mostly of denying his various space commanders more ships, more equipment, and more personnel. He was sure their requests were legitimate, but he was just as sure that there were no surpluses he could spare for them. Every reserve the U.C.S. had was being prepared for the big push into Sondak. When that came, his sector commanders wouldn't need to worry about their shortages.

He had almost finished the stack of requests when he came to one that stopped him cold. It looked routine. All the proper spaces on the microspooler form were properly filled out. But the narrative explanation set alarm bells off in his head.

It was from *her*. How many years had it been since he had heard from her? Or had it been decades? He didn't care how long it had been. That she had contacted him at all sent an uneasy feeling churning through his stomach. As he deciphered the message coded into the narrative, using the modified Playfair cipher he had taught her, the feeling got worse.

"Father," it said, "if you do not bring this war to a close, I will see that you taste ultimate defeat."

There was no name, but Frye knew exactly who had sent him this message. But how? How had she gotten it into his routine correspondence? How had she known the forms and recognition codes? Where in the voids of space was she?

"Somewhere in the U.C.S.," he said aloud. "Has to be."

But did it have to be? She had surprised him once before by knowing far more than she should have about his actions, chastising him for marrying Vinita, and threatening to claim her birthright as his firstborn. Four messages she had sent him then, and he still remembered every one of them with a dark, hollow feeling under his heart. She hadn't carried out her threat to tell Vinita back then, but only because he had managed to get a response through to her that openly begged for her understanding.

Apparently that appeal had worked, because he hadn't heard from her after that for almost ten years. Then, when he was on the brink of promotion, she had sent him a message demanding that he credit an anonymous account on Patros with five thousand credits. For reasons he wasn't sure of at the time, he had done it. Maybe it had been guilt. He never could decide.

Now, after almost fifteen years, she had contacted him again with a threat that sent chills down his spine, not because he believed for an instant that she could do what she said but because the way the message came made it obvious that she had penetrated countless layers of security.

That on top of the Oska message touched a highly sensitive nerve in his military mind. There was something very wrong with the security around him when messages like this could slip through so easily. What is it? he wondered. What in the galaxy is going—

"I'm back. sir," Melliman's voice said from his speaker, "and you're not going to believe what I found."

"Whatever it is, bring it in," he said with a feeling of resignation. "Looks like this is going to be a day full of surprises."

"It is a 'she,' sir," Melliman said as she opened the door between their offices and ushered in a slightly built woman wearing a dark, formal suit. "Admiral Charltos, I'd like for you to meet Anshuwu Tashawaki, Lieutenant Oska's mother."

* * *

"And I don't care what he told us," Marsha said angrily. "If we fail, if we can't find this Xindella and his stolen weapon before the festbid, the whole galaxy is going to be in a hurt."

"Easy. Take it easy, Mars." Lucky said, running his hand lovingly over her arm. "I'm not arguing with you. I think you're absolutely right. All Delightful Childe said was that if we couldn't steal the thing away from Xindella, there were other alternatives."

"None of which make any sense," she said, shaking off his hand and crossing her arms over her bare breasts. "I can't let him and the snakes back Sondak in the bidding. You know that. It wouldn't be fair."

"But it was Sondak's to begin with. I don't see how—"

"It's not theirs now, though. That's the problem. It's going to the highest bidder. If Delightful Childe and the damn snakes want to be fair, they ought to back the U.C.S. in the bidding. Then each side would have a potential star-buster, and neither would dare use it because they would know the other side could and would retaliate."

"I wish it worked that way," Lucky said as he rolled onto his back and pulled the blanket up over both of them. He hated having discussions like this in bed, yet he knew that Marsha needed to talk about it. "Mars, if the history of war teaches us anything, it teaches that—"

"I don't need a history lecture. I don't care about history," Marsha said. "What I care about is whether or not the U.C.S. gets cheated out of a fair chance to win this war."

"Somebody had better care about history," Lucky said softly, trying to be as patient and understanding as he could. "We'd better hope that the powers that be on both sides care about history, because . . . it teaches that if the opposing sides have equally devastating weapons, the only guarantee is that one side will try to cripple the other to prevent the other from striking first. Why should it be any different just because we're talking about a weapon that can destroy a complete solar system?"

"Whose side are you on?" she asked, avoiding the question.

"Our side," he answered, wishing there were some way he could defuse her anger. "Only our side, Mars. I want us to survive, you and me, and the aliens because they're trying to stay neutral. Beyond that I don't really care."

"You'd better care, because I do."

Lucky pushed himself up on one elbow so he could look her directly in the eyes. "What do you want from me, Mars? You want me to side with the U.C.S.? I won't do it."

"But I thought—"

"No," he said. "Just let me finish. I told you before, and I'll say it now. If I could pick the winner in this war, I'd pick the U.C.S.—but only because I dislike their Trade bureaucracy a little less than I dislike Sondak's. However, I don't like the

way they started this war with sneak attacks, and I don't like
what your father did to us, and I hate all of the restrictions they put on the freespacers, so I don't think I'll ever be
an enthusiastic supporter of the U.C.S. Can't you understand
that?"

As she looked at him, a slight smile tugged at the corners
of her mouth. She shouldn't be taking her frustration out on
Lucky, and she was a little chagrined with herself for having
let the discussion get this far. "Of course I understand that,
Lucky. I know that at heart you are really an anarchist, and I
thought I was, too, until now."

"I still think you are," he said, leaning down and giving her
a quick kiss on the nose. "And a cute one, too."

"Maybe . . . but there's still an awful lot of allegiance to
the U.C.S. in this anarchist's heart."

"Allegiance? Or just sympathy for them? I mean, is it real
allegiance because you really think they're right in this war,
or is it because that's where you were born and it's home no
matter where else you go?"

He wasn't asking her anything new, but then, he didn't
have the same feelings about where he was born as she did.
The only allegiances he had were the ones he gave his word
on—or pledged his love to. Lucky had certainly made his
allegiance to her plain enough. But for Marsha the questions
of allegiance were more complicated, and she had questioned
her motives and true allegiances over and over since the very
beginning of the war.

"Yes," she said finally, "I feel allegiance and sympathy for
those reasons and more. It's allegiance because it's home, but
also because Sondak did such rotten things to us after the last
war, and now we are only getting the revenge we deserve,
and that's why I think the U.C.S. should at least have a fair
chance to get this star-buster."

"And so we come full circle," Lucky said with a sigh. "But
I guess the only real question for you and me is what we do,
not why we do it. Right?"

"Right." She looked up at his wonderful face and wished
there were a way for the two of them to escape all this
together. "So," she said with a teasing smile and a wink, "if
we make love right now, we don't need to know why, do
we?"

"Of course we do. That's one of the few things we do know the reason for."

"Because we're sex-addicts," she said, putting her arms around him and pulling his head down to her breasts.

"Right," he whispered, "because we're sex-addicts."

Marsha let her fingers play along his ribs, enjoying the familiar feel of his flesh as it tightened and prickled under her touch. "Not because we love each other."

"Nothing to do with it," he said as his fingers caressed her thigh. "Nothing at all."

"I didn't think so," she managed to whisper as his tongue started doing erotic things to her nipple.

His only response was to flick his tongue faster, as though his tongue alone could rout the questions that troubled them so.

9

Rochmon saw the smile creeping onto Bock's lips and wished he could signal her somehow to keep a straight face. She wasn't supposed to be amused by Admiral Stonefield's lecture about security and the restrictions that were going to be placed on her, but apparently she was.

As though sensing Rochmon's distress, she gave him a little wink. Then she confirmed his suspicion when she interrupted Stonefield and said, "Tell you what, Stony, you keep the job. I don't need somebody sitting under the pot every time I piss."

"I beg your pardon," Stonefield said, his face flushed with anger and his tone full of indignation.

"Beg all you want," Bock said with a satisfied sneer. "Sci-Sec likes the work I do for them, and I don't have to ask their permission to blow my nose or wipe my ass. I think I'll just stay where I'm respected for the work I do."

Twice Stonefield started to speak, then clamped his jaws tight and turned toward Rochmon and Gilbert. "I expect you to feel free to comment on this, gentlemen," he said through almost-clenched teeth, "as it seems Bock here needs some further persuasion."

Rochmon held his tongue in check. He was angry with Bock and proud of her at the same time. She had been charged without evidence and treated with scorn by the Service. Now the Service wanted her to come back on terms that would be humiliating for anyone, much less someone of her intelligence and talent. He also sensed that something else was going on under the surface of this exchange, but he wasn't about to share any of those thoughts with Stonefield.

"Can't say as I blame her," Admiral Gilbert said, breaking the silence that held the room. He wasn't sure why Stony had required his presence at this meeting; however, that did not mean that he was going to sit quietly by while an apparent injustice was done. "Seems to me, Stony, that you're asking this woman to let herself be degraded and used without giving her anything in return."

"I don't believe this," Stonefield said with a glare. "Are you defending this woman?"

Gilbert didn't want to anger Stony any further, but since the lines of confrontation were already drawn, there was no sense in backing away from them. "Yes, sir, I suppose I am. No one ever produced any evidence of treason against her, and now you want her to accept a job where she'll be treated as though she were guilty. Hardly seems fair to me. I know how I would feel under the same conditions, and it wouldn't be much different than she does right now."

"Your loyalty is hardly at question here, Josiah," Stonefield said.

"And mine shouldn't be," Bock said. There was fire in her eyes now, but her voice was steady and level. "I worked my skinny ass off for Cryptography helping to break the Ukes' Q-Two code, and as a reward you accused me of treason and stripped me of my job. Now you want me to help you break the Q-Three? What will I get if I do that? Life in prison?"

It was all Rochmon could do to keep from cheering, but something besides the look on Stonefield's face helped him repress that urge.

"Don't get sarcastic with me, Bock. I could force you to accept this offer under terms—"

"You can't force me to accept a damn thing, Admiral," Bock said calmly. "You can call me back to active duty and assign me to Cryptography or ship me out to the polar systems or put me in prison—if you're willing to fight Sci-Sec Command for me, of course—but you can't force me to accept anything. You can only move my body around."

She paused as though waiting for him to respond. Gilbert and Rochmon were both fighting to control smiles.

"If the Service wants my help breaking the Q-Three," she continued, "you'll have to give me your personal guarantee that I will be treated exactly as I was before all these stupid accusations began. I'm not asking for anything more than that, but I won't accept anything less."

Rochmon could no longer hold his tongue. "That seems fair enough to me, sir," he said quietly.

"And to me," Gilbert added.

"But not to me," Stonefield said. "I absolutely refuse to put up with—"

"No wonder you're a damned admiral," Bock said with a laugh. "You're so sticky-stuck on yourself you're not fit for anything else. Go seven ways to hell, sir," she added with a mock salute as she rose from her chair, "and have a miserable trip."

She had almost reached the office door when Stonefield said, "Very well. I'll reinstate you with no restrictions."

No one spoke as the three of them stared at his smiling face. "Had to test you," Stonefield said finally, "and I had to know that Gilbert and Rochmon were willing to stand behind you. If you had accepted the restrictions, I would have been convinced of your guilt. As it is, I believe that you—"

"Stick it," Bock said as she opened the door, "where the sun don't shine and the grass don't grow."

"Bock!" Rochmon said in his best command voice as she walked through the doorway. "Get back in here!"

No one was more surprised than Rochmon when she stepped back into the room and closed the door.

She stood with her back against the polished wood, her eyes filled with angry light. When she finally spoke, her voice was cold and clear. "Let me tell you all something, just so there won't be any misunderstanding between us. I'll go back to work at Cryptography with a written exoneration in my files along with a letter of apology from you," she said, pointing a bony finger at Stonefield.

For the first time since this meeting had started, Rochmon

realized that Bock was doing the same thing to Stonefield that she had done to him once years before. She was playing a game, and had been all along. That realization bothered him.

"But," Bock continued, "if I detect the slightest hint of the restrictions you mentioned awhile ago, I'll walk out Cryptography's door without hesitation and never return. Do all of you understand that? Good," she said after they all nodded, "because I won't warn you before it happens. I'll just walk. There's more than one organization in this galaxy willing to pay for the use of my talents."

"The Service does not take kindly to being threatened," Stonefield said coldly.

"No threat, Admiral, just a statement of fact. If I catch your watchbirds looking over my shoulder, then you can find yourself another sucker, 'cause I won't accept it."

Rochmon wanted to say something in support of her, but now that he understood that this was all a game to her, he couldn't bring himself to say anything. He didn't know why she was doing this, or what it meant, but knew he didn't like it at all.

*   *   *

"I am here, Proctor," Ranas said formally as he entered her chamber.

Leri's body was still heavy with the residue of sleep, but she forced herself into a coil of respect. "Thank you for coming," she said quietly.

"As the Proctor commands," he responded automatically.

"No, Ranas, not as the Proctor commands . . . as Leri requests. I asked you to come here as your estranged mate because I feel it is time we had a long talk about us and our future."

"We are not estranged, Leri."

Leri's sensitive nostrils could smell the odor of control around him mixed with a scent of love and respect. "Then what would you call the way we have been living our lives?"

"A temporary separation," Ranas said evenly, "one that I suspect will come to a natural end when the time is right for both of us."

Leri was almost amused by the casual tone of his answer, but whatever he thought, she needed to talk about what had happened to them. "Do you have some timetable for this 'natural end'?"

Ranas hesitated. "There are a variety of possibilities, Leri, and a variety of factors involved. Perhaps after the humans settle their war and you can pass the duties of Proctor on to another, we will know when the time is right."

"That could take hundreds, maybe even thousands, of seasons. Must we wait that long?"

"What is another thousand seasons, Leri? Have I not been patient with you for several thousand seasons already? Have I not endured the presence of Weecs in our burrow for several hundred? What do I care how long it takes? In the end we will be together with the Elett's blessings. That is all that matters to me."

As startled as she was by the rush of his words, Leri did not miss the pain she heard behind them nor the slightly bitter scent of frustration that rose from him. She did not know what to say—how to respond to him—but he had brought up Weecs's name, and she did know that unless they discussed Weecs they would never break down the barriers that had risen between them.

"But what about you, Leri?" he asked. "What matters to you?"

"Many things," she said with a sudden weariness, "but most of all the vision I once had of leading our Cloise to peace and happiness free from all the aliens. That vision has become garbled beyond recognition, and I do not know what to do about it. However," she said, taking a deep breath, "there are also those things that matter to me which have nothing to do with my duties as Proctor—things like our relationship, and mine with Weecs—"

"Of course."

"Do not treat me to your sarcasm," Leri said quickly. "I can smell it on you."

"What you smell is not sarcasm, Leri. It is disdain for Weecs. I see nothing in him beyond his obvious lust for your body that would make him worthwhile in any—"

"That will be quite enough! I will not apologize to you for my affair with Weecs. He came to me when I needed what he had to offer and gave of himself without asking for anything in return. There is nothing wrong or shameful about that."

"Of course not," Ranas said slowly, "except in the way it weakens you in front of our people."

Leri felt the frustration building inside her. This was not at all how she had meant for this conversation to go. But then, little had gone the way she wanted it to since the humans had begun their senseless quarrel. "Then let one of them come forward and replace me," she said, knowing that neither he nor any other of Cloise's people would volunteer for her job.

"I did not mean that you should be replaced."

"Ah, but you did, Ranas, you did, because your vision has us back together after I am no longer Proctor. Is that not true?"

"Perhaps."

"You said it," she continued, "and you cannot withdraw from that. And while you are looking for my replacement, remember that it was Weecs, not you, and not the Council who rescued me from Exeter the Castorian."

"With our aid," Ranas added defensively.

"Yes, with your aid, but he was the only one brave enough—or who loved me enough—to travel into space for me. Perhaps he should be the next Proctor." Leri was as surprised as Ranas was by that suggestion.

"You cannot mean that, Leri!"

"Why not? He is an historian, wise beyond his years, and he certainly has been exposed to the workings of the office under extreme conditions."

"The very suggestion is outrageous. He is too young, too immature, too obviously ruled by his gonads to assume the—"

"Oh, hush! You cannot see Weecs for your jealousy. I will admit to you that this is the first time I have considered this possibility, but the very fact that he lusts after me, not this office, makes him all the more an acceptable candidate."

"Leri, I don't understand how you can—"

"Then listen to me, Ranas. You want me back—us together again? If so, you should be seriously considering every possible candidate to succeed me—if not Weecs, then others. But I suggest you look at Weecs's qualifications very carefully, because if he were to become Proctor, he certainly wouldn't have the time for me as he does now, and without his constant desire for me, I am afraid my interest in him might wane."

"That is a poor reason to choose someone for Proctor."

"But Ranas, I never meant to suggest it as a reason, only as a side-effect that might interest you." Leri could tell from his scent that despite his protests her suggestion had lodged in some positive area of his brain. She would miss Weecs. She was missing him already, but her intuition told her he would make a good Proctor, and she would gladly give up the office to him or anyone else who wanted it.

"Go away now," she said softly. "I am tired and need to rest." And to think, she added to herself.

10

"Sergeant Julianne Denoro, reporting as ordered, ma'am," the trooper said with a perfectly executed salute.

Rasha'kean Ingrivia returned the salute and appraised this lean, well-tanned sergeant in front of her with an eye that told her this woman had been through more than her personnel file indicated. Even in her postduty uniform Sergeant Denoro looked as if she were ready to jump into combat.

"Sit yourself, Sergeant," Rasha'kean said, waving Denoro to the only other chair besides her own in the cramped little office.

"Thank you, ma'am." Denoro sat in the chair at attention, showing the years of discipline that had become ingrained as part of her physical bearing.

"Do you know why you were assigned to me, Sergeant? I mean, did anyone explain your orders to you?"

"No, ma'am, they didn't."

Rasha'kean laughed. "Typical of the Planetary Service, d'not you think—to send you somewhere without botherin' to tell you what it's all about?"

"That's been my experience," Denoro said, allowing herself a well-controlled grin.

"Well, Sergeant, I d'not know if you're goin' to like this assignment, but I can tell you right now that I am needin' you and the benefit of your experience about as much as anybody in this Service. From now until Fate separates us, you will be my executive officer, second in command of any unit—"

"Begging your pardon, ma'am. Sorry to interrupt and all that, but isn't that a bit out of line? I mean, really, how am I gonna order some officer around if I have to?"

Rasha'kean laughed again. "D'not worry about that for now, because there are no officers for you to order. When we get to our unit out on Mungtinez, then we'll worry about it. But you wi'not be the first sergeant to hold the X.O. job, you know."

Denoro shook her head. "I'm afraid I'm a bit confused, Colonel Ingrivia. Maybe I still haven't recovered from that bump on the head I got on Sutton. Let me see if I got this right. We're going to Mungtinez to join a combat unit there, and you're gonna be the unit commander, and I'm gonna be your Executive Officer. Is that right?"

"You got it, Denoro, dead on the bullet."

"But why me, ma'am?"

"For a lot of reasons, Denoro. Let me explain my situation and you feel free to interrupt whenever you need to. And you can drop the 'ma'am' stuff. I'm afraid I still like the oldy form when everyone was called sir. So either call me sir, or colonel, or Ingrivia if that suits you. All right?"

Again Denoro shook her head. "All right, Colonel, but that will take some getting used to."

"Take all the time you need. Anyway, here's my setup. I am currently workin' on a logistics plan for General Schopper's next line of attack against the Ukes. As soon as that is approved, I will be shippin' out to command a Z-company in the first major counterattack against the Ukes. You with me so far?"

"Yes, m—sir."

"Good. Now, I requested that a senior sergeant with combat experience be assigned to me as soon as possible so I could begin my get-readys for command and—" She stopped when she saw the puzzled look on Denoro's deeply tanned face. "A question?"

Denoro hesitated. "Well, Colonel, maybe I shouldn't ask this, but why would a logistics officer want a combat command?"

"Because I'm a combat officer by trainin', Denoro, and I'm only stuck behind this logistics desk because of some experience I've had in this area." Rasha'kean smiled when she saw the look of relief on Denoro's face. "Of course," she said as her smile grew even wider, "you were afraid you were goin' to have to follow a noncombat officer into battle. I'm sorry. I should have told you that up front."

"No problem," Denoro said with a smile of her own. For the first time since she had entered the office, she physically relaxed. "But all that still doesn't explain what you're gonna do with me."

"You're my source, Denoro. I ca'not and wi'not attempt to lead a Z-company into battle with only my trainin' and experience to go on. You're here so I can dig out of you everythin' you can possibly tell me about the actual fightin' you've been through—and that's why you're my X.O. I want combat experience at the top, and there ar'not enough officers around who have it to spare one for a Z-company. Besides, I di'not want a junior officer. I wanted a senior sergeant, and from what I saw of your record, it looks like I got the best."

"Don't know about that, Colonel, but you certainly got a shit-load of experience when you got me. And I gotta tell you something right now, 'cause I don't want you to misunderstand later."

"Go ahead, Denoro. As far as I'm concerned, you should always feel free to tell me anythin' you think I need to know whenever you think I need to know it."

"Good enough. Then this is it: if I'm gonna be your X.O., then I'm gonna do exactly what you just said. This is my second war, and God knows I hope it's my last, but I plan to do everything I can to live through it. Once we get into combat, Colonel, if I say, 'Duck,' you do it first and ask me why later. If I say, 'Jump,' don't ask me how high till you're already in the air, 'cause a lot of what happens in real combat isn't in any of the Corps' training manuals. It comes from more than training and experience. It comes from instinct."

"Looks like your instincts have served you well so far," Rasha'kean said, "and I'm certainly not goin' to buck them. As long as you remember that even when I'm jumpin' I'm still in command, I think we'll get along just fine."

Denoro grinned. "You jump, Colonel, and I'll remember."

"Good. Now, Denoro, what do you know about logistics?"

"Not much, Colonel—at least not the way I think you mean. Most of my experience in that area has been ground combat logistics, and I expect you're talking about something more general than that."

"Well, you're about to learn—probably more than you ever wanted to know. Anythin' you can do to help me with this job means that much more time you and I will have to get on with my education. However, for the time bein', go get yourself somethin' to eat and— Where's your kit?"

"Oh, I've already checked into the Temporary Duty Quarters, Colonel. When do you want me back here?"

"Oh-seven-hundred tomorrow."

Denoro stood and saluted. "I'll be here," she said, then hesitated. "There is one other thing, Colonel."

"What's that?"

"Well, when I got my orders, I asked around, and a couple of people told me that, uh, well, damn—that you were part Uke. Is that true, Colonel?"

Rasha'kean smiled. "No, Denoro, it definitely i'not true. Whoever told you that di'not know anythin' about my family history. Anythin' else?"

"No, sir," Denoro said with a second salute. "See you in the morning."

After Denoro left, Rasha'kean turned back to her logistics plan with a positive glow. Having Denoro in her office had made her feel much closer to realizing her goal. She was going to make damned sure there was nothing in this version of her report for General Schopper to complain about, because she was more eager than ever to get her combat unit and start repaying her Uke cousins for what they had done to her family.

* * *

Captain Mica Gilbert cursed silently. Then, instead of destroying the directive per her instructions, she made a decision that went against all her military training. With very little hesitation she contacted Admiral Pajandcan's office and requested to see her.

Two hours later she was ushered into the planning room where Admirals Pajandcan, Dimitri, and Dawson were huddled around a holomap of the polar sphere.

"—and I still say there has to be some logic to these skirmishes," Dimitri was saying.

"Come in, Captain," Pajandcan said when she saw Gilbert. "Torgy said you needed to see me about something?"

"Yes, I did," Mica said, "but I believe it will have to be in private, Admiral."

"More of your father's secrets?" Dimitri asked in a teasing voice, "or a spy report to send back to him?"

"What are you talking about, Dit?" Admiral Dawson asked.

"Didn't you know she was a spy for her father?"

"Please, sir, I really don't think—"

"That will be enough, Dit. You and Dawson keep working on this. Project all the known skirmishes and see if you can figure it out. I'll be back in a few minutes." Pajandcan welcomed the break from the planning. Standing still for any length of time made her injured back ache, and more than once she had been forced to sleep in traction. The doctors had told her it would probably be like that for the rest of her life, and she didn't relish that thought at all.

Mica followed Pajandcan into a small office off the planning room and was surprised when Pajandcan grabbed an overhead bar, swung her feet up, and proceeded to hang upside down.

"Forgive me, Mica, but this is the only way I can get relief. I hope you won't mind talking to me like this."

"I just hope you don't fall when I tell you why I came here," Mica said with a smile that crept past the seriousness of this meeting. "Admiral, you've seen the reports to my father, but what you haven't seen and didn't know was that I am an honor trustee."

"Doesn't surprise me."

Pajandcan's face looked strange when she spoke upside down as though the wrong part of her mouth were moving. "You mean you knew?" Mica asked.

"I guessed. But I am surprised that you are telling me. Isn't that against regulations?"

Mica sighed and sat down, bringing her face closer to the level of Pajandcan's. "Yes, it is, unless I have determined a need to confide in the overall commander—you—and the directive I received today made me feel like that need had arisen."

"Stonefield laid this on you, didn't he?"

"Yes. And now he wants me to increase my surveillance of you and Admiral Dimitri, and I just can't do it."

"Why? If that's what your orders are, why can't you spy on us more than you have been?"

Mica hesitated. "Please, Admiral, I don't mean to deprive

you of your relief, but it really would be much easier to talk about this if you were rightside up."

"All right," Pajandcan said, pulling herself up to the bar and freeing her feet. "My head was beginning to fill up with blood, anyway." She lowered herself gently to the deck, then sat on the desk, facing Gilbert. "So, go on. Why are you breaking all the honor trustee regs like this?"

"Because, Admiral, I thoroughly despise spying on you for Father, much less for Admiral Stonefield. I hate being an honor trustee. I hate what Stonefield keeps asking me to do. And I hate myself when I do it. There's no way I can go on like this, Admiral. I just can't."

Pajandcan felt sympathy for Mica Gilbert but wasn't sure how she could help her. "So? What do you want me to do?"

"Can't you get me out of it?" That was what Mica really wanted, relief from this onerous duty.

"No. Only Stonefield can do that. The only thing I could do would be to— No! Wait, Mica, there is something, something we can both do if you're willing." Pajandcan only hoped Mica was woman enough to accept her idea.

"I'm ready to try almost anything," Mica said.

"All right, then, listen to me while I talk this out, and remember that I hate this spying business, so I may not be seeing things as clearly as I should. If you force Stonefield to release you as honor trustee, that only means he will find someone else to take your place. However, if you were to keep the assignment, then you could continue sending Stonefield your reports, only Dimitri and I would help you with them."

"You mean falsify reports?" Mica asked.

"No. I wouldn't ask you to do that. We wouldn't tell him anything that wasn't true. The three of us would just agree on what to tell him."

Suddenly Mica grinned. "You know, Admiral, I think I like your idea. Let's do it."

"The three of us will have dinner in my cabin and can do your first report then. You can even tell Stonefield you had dinner with us and were privy to our conversation."

Mica's grin turned into laughter. Oh, if Stonefield ever found out, the garbage would really hit the backblast, but there was no reason he should ever find out.

11

Frye had been surprised to see Lieutenant Oska following Judoff into the Bridgeforce meeting. As the discussion of the attack plans ranged around the table, he had been even more surprised when the lieutenant had caught his eye for a second and given Frye a slight nod.

Perhaps Oska and his mother were to be trusted, but Frye was going to have to ensure that Oska never again allowed himself a public acknowledgment of any connection between them. If Judoff ever suspected that Oska was feeding information to Frye, there was no telling what she would do to the lieutenant. Frye refused to let himself think about that. He had to make sure Oska understood the danger he was in.

Bridgeforce was arguing about the bombships again, not only because the ships still were nowhere near completion, but also because they had become so psychologically linked with the concept of victory that even some of those who had originally opposed their construction now felt reluctant to approve the final attack plan without them.

Frye was bored by all Bridgeforce's repetitious arguments and let his mind drift back to the meeting with Oska's mother just a short six days earlier.

He had risen to meet her when Melliman ushered the tiny woman into his office, too surprised to speak until she gave him the traditional bow from the waist. Only then had he recovered his composure.

"Please, be welcome Anshuwu Tashawaki."

"My honor to be in your presence, distinguished sir."

Melliman had prepared tea for them while he and Madame Tashawaki exchanged pleasantries, and it was only after they had drunk their first cup of tea that Frye dared to ask about the letter concerning her son.

"He is a good son, distinguished sir," she had said, "and he works for the honor of our family and the U.C.S. The shame would be if Marshall Judoff, under whose command he is forced to serve, did not work for the same honor."

"I understand your concern, Madame Tashawaki; however, I must know if your son is aware of what you have done."

"It was he who asked me to do this thing. Were his father, the honorable Sezua Oska—may his soul soar in peaceful winds—still alive, this duty of informing you would fall to him. Since he is not alive, and since by tradition I cannot ask my new husband to assume such duty, I must do as best as a humble woman can to assist my son in keeping his honor."

Frye had marveled at the strict, almost archaic formality of her speech and attitudes, and he had admired her for them at the same time. "You are a noble woman," he had replied.

"You are too kind, Admiral Charltos, yet I must presume upon that kindness on behalf of my son and ask that you accept this honorable commitment he would make to you."

"Most certainly I accept it. You have but to tell us how it may be arranged, and I will attend to the details."

"Sir, since my son dares not communicate directly with you, he asks that you accept my services to forward his communications and return your responses. The difference between his name and mine keeps all but members of our family from knowing our relationship, and none in Marshall Judoff's command are aware of it. Would that arrangement be satisfactory, distinguished sir?"

"Yes, Madame Tashawaki, it is a satisfactory arrangement, but I must caution you that no one discover what it is we do, or your son could be in grave danger."

"He and I both understand that and are prepared to be most cautious and circumspect in our dealings with one another. His communications to me will come through his father's cousin who will believe he carries only personal correspondence. Unless my son tells me of some great urgency, I will wait several days after receiving each letter before bringing it to you."

"Perhaps your arrangement should be with Captain Melliman someplace well away from here," Frye had suggested.

And so it had been arranged, with the unknown cousin as the ignorant go-between for Lieutenant Oska and his mother, and Melliman between her and Frye. He had warned Madame Tashawaki that Oska should not use the channel he used for first contact again unless it was an emergency. She had agreed to everything he suggested, and after a ritual serving of ice water, Melliman had taken her home. All in all it had been a remarkable experience.

Now as Frye listened once again to the arguments around him, he wondered what could come through this channel of secret information from inside Judoff's headquarters.

"And I insist," Meister Hadasaki was saying, "that it is imperative for us to proceed with Admiral Charltos's plan as quickly as possible."

"If we have not lost the initiative already," Vice-Admiral Lotonoto added.

"Well," Frye said, unexpectedly entering the discussion, "one thing is certain. If we continue arguing instead of taking action, eventually either the bombships will be ready or Sondak will have won this war."

"That's a treasonous statement," Marshall Judoff said.

"It is a factual statement," Frye said, letting out the anger and frustration he felt. "I warned Bridgeforce in the beginning of this war that if we wanted total victory, we must never lose the initiative. Then, as now, my warnings seem to go unheeded by the majority of this body."

For a long moment there was silence in the room. Then Meister Hadasaki said, "I move we accept Admiral Charltos's plan and begin executing it at once."

A second was heard, and the motion was approved by a vote of four to three. Lotonoto immediately moved that the vote be made unanimous, and when Judoff seconded the motion, everyone voted affirmatively.

Suddenly Frye felt much better than when he had entered this meeting. "Thank you all," he said. "I will have additional detailed copies in your hands within the hour which we can discuss tomorrow. Until then, this meeting is adjourned."

As everyone was preparing to leave, Marshall Judoff walked to the head of the table and in a barely audible voice said, "I would be careful tomorrow, Charltos." Then she turned her back on him and left, with Kuskuvyet and Lieutenant Oska following close behind her.

Frye smiled at her retreating entourage and thought, I certainly don't need your caution to be careful, Judoff. Your presence is warning enough.

* * *

Henley picked up the com unit on one side of the glass

wall, and Kinderman picked up an identical unit on his side of the wall. "This is not at all what I intended, Kryki," Henley said.

"I know that, old son, but your intentions do little or nothing to make my imprisonment more bearable. Besides, you have already apologized for this injustice. Surely you did not think it was necessary to do so again."

"No, that's not the reason I came. I just wanted to tell you that I'm going to talk to Admiral Gilbert again and try to get him to change his mind."

"He will not do so, I assure you."

"Perhaps not, Kryki, but I must try, and since I think I'll be leaving soon, I have to do it now."

"You are leaving, old son? To where are you bound?"

"I can't tell you that, but I can tell you that I'm going to be much closer to where the real war is taking place."

Kinderman smiled. "Yes," he said slowly, "I should have suspected that. There is a tone of attraction in your stories about the war. Be careful of that, my friend. Those who are attracted to war often die for their attraction."

"I'll be careful. Getting shot once was enough for me." Henley hesitated. "Look, Kryki, if you would promise not to tell anyone what you told me, I think that would go a long way in getting Admiral Gilbert to change his mind."

"Sorry, old son, but I have already explained my position to you on that subject. I am honor bound to do that for which I have already received recompense."

"You could give the credits back. Gilbert could probably even find a way to make up for your loss."

"Good-bye, old son," Kinderman said. Then he turned off the com unit and set it gently in its rack.

"Wait, Kryki! Wait!" Henley waved frantically for Kinderman to pick up the com unit again, but all he got for his efforts was a smile and a wave as Kinderman walked out of his side of the visiting room with a guard behind him.

Damned idealist, Henley thought. He put his com unit in its place and left feeling depressed. Colonel Ingrivia had broken two dinner engagements and then told him she "just di'not have the time to be goin' out socially." Gilbert had put Kryki into protective custody and had indicated he might not let him out until the war was over. And Mica Gilbert had responded to his last message with a cryptic note that did not make him feel she was eager to see him again.

The only thing that had gone the way he had hoped it would in the last ten days was getting Gilbert's approval to join one of the new legions that were being formed for Sondak's next major offensive. Gilbert had hinted that this legion would be leading the counterattack against one of Sondak's systems now controlled by the Ukes. He couldn't tell Henley which system yet, but from some of the rumors Henley had heard floating around, most bets were on one of the systems in the Ivy Chain. Wherever it was, Henley was ready to go.

It isn't that this place is boring, he thought as he walked through the connecting tunnel between the military prison and Sondak Supreme Headquarters. It's just that my stories are beginning to read like headquarters stories. And he didn't like headquarters stories. In spite of the death and pain and dying and fear, combat reporting was still the most attractive thing he had ever done.

Maybe Kryki was right. Maybe he was too attracted to combat. There was certainly something about combat that made a man feel more intensively alive than anything else he knew. Regardless of the dangers, combat was a thrilling experience that was hard to replace in normal life. Kryki was right. He would have to be aware of his attraction just to make sure he wasn't careless when the guns were firing and the adrenaline was flowing.

After being passed by the guards, he caught an elevator and made his way to Admiral Gilbert's office. Much to his surprise, he was told to go in as soon as he arrived.

"Ah, Henley, I have something for you," Gilbert said. "It's a message from Mica."

"For me, sir?"

"Well, through me to you. She said, and I quote: 'Tell that mature Chief Warrant that I understand why he likes it out here so much and give him my love.'"

Henley just stared at Gilbert.

"That's what it says, Chief. Why do you look so surprised?"

"Because," Henley said slowly, "the last message I got from her didn't give any indication that she ever—uh, well, sir, let's just say it was worded far more formally."

Gilbert waved Henley to a chair and sat in his own behind

his desk. He didn't know what had happened between his daughter and Stanmorton out in the polar systems, but he was sure there was a great deal of emotion tied up in it. "Are you in love with my daughter, Henley?"

Henley fought to control the blush that started to rise in his cheeks. "Sir, I don't know how to answer that. Love is a word she and I have skirted around. I'm not sure I can love anyone—at least not the way that Mica talks about love."

"In other words," Josiah Gilbert said, "you are in love with her, but you don't trust your emotions?"

"Look, Admiral, I'm almost as old as you are, and I'm certainly old enough to be her father. What I feel for Mica could be the same thing I'd feel for my own daughter." As soon as he said that, Henley regretted it. Linking his own daughter and Mica uncovered a dark layer of emotions and desires he would just as soon keep buried.

"I see. Well, then, I won't ask you any more, Henley, but I want you to know that the difference in your ages doesn't seem to bother her, and it doesn't bother me—now that I've had time to think about it."

Henley laughed suddenly. "You sound like a father talking to a prospective son-in-law."

Gilbert smiled. "I could be, Henley—someday. But for now we'll just consider the subject closed until you two bring it up again. You're here about Kinderman, I suppose?"

"Correct, sir." Henley was glad for the change of subject.

"The answer is the same. As I told you before, the Service and the civilian government have no comment to make on his information, but we do not want rumors about the Ukes having some terrible new weapon circulating throughout Sondak. That would be very bad for morale. So, until we have Kinderman's assurance that he will not start such a rumor, we have no alternative but—"

"He won't give that assurance, sir. He says it's a matter of honor."

"Then he will stay in protective custody. You understand that, don't you?"

"Yes, sir, I do."

"Good. Now, how soon can you be ready to space out?"

"In a couple of hours at most."

Gilbert handed Henley a packet disk. "Well, you'll have a little more time than that. Here are your orders. The unclassified part will get you aboard the *Taylor* the day after tomorrow. The classified part you can read once you're in space. This is the code sequence," he said, handing another disk. "Good luck to you, and don't forget to keep your head down."

"Aye, sir," Henley said, taking the second disk, "and my ass, too." They both laughed.

12

"How was the General Warfare Center?"

"I didn't get to see much of it, General," Archer replied. "That speed-course you set up for me didn't leave me much time to look at the facilities or soak up the traditions."

"Sorry I couldn't give you more time, but it's finally here," Schopper said. "Admiral Gilbert and the Joint Chiefs have given the go-ahead for the entire planet-hopping invasion plan."

"What about Colonel Ingrivia's logistic plan? Did she finally get that right while I was up there?"

"Yes, and it is a good one, too. The Joint Chiefs approved it last week and started putting it into effect immediately," Schopper said, handing Archer a steaming cup. "It's battle coffee. Hope you like it, because it's gotten so it is the only kind of coffee I really do like anymore."

Archer blew on the cup several times, then took a tiny sip, careful not to burn his tongue. "Whew. Never could get used to this. Guess it's the three hundred milligrams of caffeine per cup that jolts me. I'll bet you're eager to join the invasion force, aren't you, sir?"

"Yes I am, but I have a surprise for you, Archer. I am not going to be commanding the invasion force. You are."

"Me, sir?" Archer almost spilled his coffee, so he set it on the desk. "I'm just a junior brigadier. When you brought me here from Sutton, you led me to believe that I was going to be commanding two legions, not the whole invasion force."

"That was my intention. However, it quickly became obvious to me that you had talents beyond legion command.

General Mari must have spotted those same talents when he promoted you. That's why I sent you up to General Warfare."

"General Mari was a good man and a damned fine soldier, sir, but I don't see why—"

"That he was, Archer. That he was. And it was his reports on you that led me to bring you to Nordeen. Archer, I need a man who is adaptable, someone like yourself, used to unconventional warfare, someone who won't be tied to the book and tradition. So, I picked you. If Mari can promote you, so can I. As of now you hold the temporary rank of Post-General. That will cause some quiet screaming around here, but I think it's justified."

Archer stared at General Schopper for a long moment before he spoke. "That's a helluva lot you're laying on me, sir."

"Such is war, Archer. We all get asked to do a lot more than we want to. However, I am convinced that you are the best man to handle this assignment, and I have persuaded the Joint Chiefs that if they will not allow me to command the force myself, then they have to let me send the officer I have the most confidence in. That's you."

"I appreciate that, sir. I really do, but . . ." Archer paused. "I guess I can assume from all this that the Joint Chiefs have decided on our first invasion target?"

General Schopper gave him a grim smile. "Archer, we have a security leak around here, a serious one, and what I'm about to tell you is known only by a select few—a very select few. Your target has been designated as Vine One. That's Terratane, the system in the Ivy Chain closest to the galactic pole."

Archer shook his head and gave a low whistle. "I don't know, sir. That's a half-inhabited planet with a million or two civilians. Sounds like too big a responsibility for a back-planet soldier like me."

"Quit thinking about yourself, Archer, and pay attention to your duty for a change. The fleet ship *Taylor* is leaving here tonight on a fast run to Mungtinez. That's where we're going to be assembling the invasion force. I'm going to travel with you on the *Taylor*, and by the time you get there, you're going to know everything I know about invasions that I haven't already taught you. Then I'll be heading right back here."

Again Archer shook his head and pursed his lips but did not whistle. "You're going to have to convince me you're right about this, sir, 'cause I've got some serious reservations."

"Like what?"

"Like what kind of response I'm going to get from the senior officers to someone with my experience who has jumped ranks?"

"You let me worry about them," Schopper said with a smile. "What else bothers you?"

"It's all tied to the same thing, sir, like a sled to a beckynoid, and if it's going—"

"A sled to a what?"

Archer smiled. "Oh, sorry, sir, an expression from home. Beckynoids are little draft animals we used to pull sleds across Sutton's deserts. Anyway, if we're—if I'm going to make this thing work, it seems to me that I'm going to need more experience than I have now."

"What are you suggesting, Archer?"

"I'm not sure, sir, but wouldn't it be possible to take on a smaller target before attacking the Ivy Chain?"

Schopper frowned. "It's too late to change targets."

"But sir, you just said you wanted someone flexible, someone who wouldn't be tied to—"

"Don't throw my own words at me, Archer. I said it's too late to change targets. Get used to that idea."

"All right, sir, but I think it's a mistake."

"Dammit, Archer," Schopper said angrily, "two-thirds of your troops and half your officers are going to be veterans of the Sutton invasion. Yet you understand the principles behind an invasion better than most of those officers who have actually participated in one. You are the best officer I have for this job, and you're going to do it with no further complaints. Is that understood?"

"Yes, sir!" Archer said with a quick salute.

"Save your sarcasm and go pick up your new stars and pack your kit. We're leaving tonight. And Archer?"

"Sir?" Archer asked as he rose to leave.

"Try to have a little more faith in yourself."

"Is that an order, sir?" A slight grin and a twinkle in his eyes accompanied the question.

"It is."

"Then I'll do my best, General," he said, the grin turning into a teeth-baring smile.

"That's why I picked you. See you at eighteen hundred."

* * *

As Mica read the incoming message, she felt sorrow and anger at the same time. It couldn't be true. It just couldn't. As soon as the message was completed, she requested a confirmation from the *Phantell*.

When the confirmation arrived, there was no doubt about the truth. Dimitri was gone. With a thick heavy feeling in her throat she called Admiral Pajandcan's quarters.

"Sorry to wake you, Admiral, but I just received a message that I think you need to see immediately."

Pajandcan rubbed at her sleepy eyes and tried to clear her head. "Very well, Captain. You may come to my private office at once."

Mica scrambled up the first ladder toward Pajandcan's deck, as though by hurrying she could get rid of the awful truth she held in her hand. When she started up the second ladder, she realized what she was doing and forced herself to slow down. Nothing would be accomplished by getting there a minute or two earlier—no lives would be saved; no anger and sorrow would be washed away in the rush. There was no way to get rid of the feeling that was churning through her insides. And to think that in her last message to her father she had talked about how glad she was to be out here!

She forced herself to take the next two ladders slowly, giving the extra time to Pajandcan, who, from the sound of her voice, had just dragged herself out of a very sound sleep. It was a small enough courtesy in the face of the message Mica had to give her.

"Tell me the gist of it," Pajandcan said as she escorted Mica into her private office. "I can read the whole thing when you're finished." Sleep was still clinging to her brain like mold to old bread.

"The Ukes got Admiral Dimitri's ship," Mica said as evenly as she could, fighting the quaver in her voice.

"What? The Ukes? Was it a hunk attack?" Pajandcan asked as her brain came fully awake.

"We don't know for sure yet, Admiral." What Mica really wanted to do was to hand Pajandcan the message and run back to her quarters to cry. Dimitri, why Dimitri? "All we do know is that the *Greelee* exploded as it was leaving the system."

"Space-suckers!" Pajandcan cursed. "I told Dimitri it was stupid for him to make this inspection tour himself. But no, he had to do it—showing the flag, he called it." She paused and looked at Mica, surprised that her anger was directed at Dimitri. It was Dimitri's fault that the Ukes had been able to kill him. "Were there any survivors?"

"None," Mica said softly, as if by her very tone she could lessen the loss of so many lives. "By the time the *Phantell* arrived, there wasn't much of anything left. I made them verify before I called you."

"How many?"

"Three hundred fifteen."

Pajandcan felt her stomach turn. Three hundred and fifteen people, gone. Just like that. With no warning. What a waste, a shameful waste. And where was she going to find someone to replace Dimitri? She held out her hand, and Mica placed the message in it almost tenderly. Pajandcan took it to her desk, sat down, and read it word for word, trying to make the connection between this piece of printout, with its series of little symbols, and the robust Dit. No matter how hard she tried, she couldn't do it.

Mica watched her until doing so made her pain that much worse, and she forced herself to stare at the only decoration in the room—a little holo of Reckynop in Matthews system, the way it had looked before the Ukes almost destroyed it.

"All right, Mica," Pajandcan said finally as she stood up and walked slowly from behind her desk with the message clutched in her hand. "Thanks for getting this to me so quickly. Find Admiral Dawson and tell him I want to see him as soon as possible. Oh, and one other thing," she said, laying a hand on Mica's arm as she started to leave.

"Ma'am?"

"Make me a current list of all the senior officers in my command. We're going to have to find a replacement for Dimitri."

"Will do," Mica said. Then on impulse she wrapped her arms around Pajandcan and hugged her firmly, pleased that her hug was returned. Without a word they released each other and shared a look that needed no words until Mica said, "Dawson. And the list."

"Right," Pajandcan sighed.

After leaving the office and closing the door, Mica walked slowly back down the first of the ladders toward the communications center. How could Pajandcan do that? How could she be thinking of a replacement when Dimitri was barely dead? Mica knew the answer to that question, but that didn't make it sit any easier on her mind.

This wasn't the first time that Mica was grateful she didn't have a command out here, because having a command in a combat zone meant losing people you cared about—and having to think about replacements even before their bodies were cold—if there were bodies.

That thought finally brought the tears that had been swelling behind her eyes. She stopped on the deck above the communication center to get herself under control, but she couldn't. The tears kept running silently down her face as fast as she could wipe them away. Two passing spacers stared at her, then carefully averted their gaze. Behind them came a gray-headed old Fleet Gunner. As she started to turn away from him, he put his hand gently on her arm.

"You all right, Captain?"

She looked at him and saw something familiar in his face, something that helped her quell the tears. "Yes, Gunner, I'll be all right."

"It's about the *Greelee*, ain't it, Captain?"

"How did you . . ."

"Word gets around about something like that pretty quick-like on an HQ ship. You sure you're okay?"

"Yes, Gunner, but thank you." Only after he turned and continued down the companionway did Mica realize what it had been about him that had helped her regain control. For some reason he reminded her of Henley, and whatever it was about both of them, it gave her the reassurance she needed.

With a wondering shake of her head, she descended the last ladder to the communication center, knowing more about herself than when she started the climb and now faced with more questions she would have to answer about her relationship with Henley.

13

"Well, what do you think, Sergeant? From your professional point of view, I mean. Am I anywheres near ready to lead a Z-company into battle?"

"Honest truth, Colonel?"

Ingrivia felt a quiet flash of resentment against Denoro's less than total acceptance of her, but she let it pass because she knew that acceptance would only come with time and experience. "Of course I want the truth. Hav'not you learned yet that I never want to be lied to?"

Denoro stared at the pale gray-green ceiling of Colonel Ingrivia's cabin, then slowly tilted her head back down until her eyes rested on the colonel's. "I'd say . . . that you . . . as a colonel, that is . . . when all your handicaps are taken into—"

"Gush it up, Denoro. Yes or no?"

"Almost," Denoro said simply with a wide grin on her face.

Despite Denoro's grin, Rasha'kean was not sure how she should take that. "What do you mean, *almost?*"

"I mean you're about as ready as anything short of actual battle experience can make you. And that I can't give you. You'll have to get it from the Ukes."

"Would you follow me into battle?"

"Yes, Colonel, I would," Denoro said without hesitation.

"You woul'not be foolin' your commandin' officer, would you, Denoro? I woul'not take kindly to that."

"You told me not to lie, Colonel, so what you get from me is the bare-butt truth. If we had to jump into combat tomorrow, I'd follow right behind you without thinking about it twicet. You got good sense, Colonel, and that puts you about ten strides in front of half the officers I ever served under. Most of them were—well, maybe I shouldn't be talking like this."

"No, I mean, yes, go on," Rasha'kean said. "I need to ken what I do that makes you think I'm a good officer. If I ken what the bad ones did wrong in your estimation, then maybe I can keep from makin' the same mistakes." She meant what she said and realized that having Denoro's respect was very important to her.

Denoro hesitated; when she spoke, she did so very deliberately. "You have to understand that I don't mean to be bad-mouthing officers in general. But like I said, there were some officers that was just damned hard to fight under." Again she hesitated.

"You see, Colonel, I've been in this woman's Service a long time, going on twenty-seven life-years, it's been, and if I've learned anything about officers during that time, it's that none of them can be trusted till they prove themselves."

Rasha'kean cocked an eyebrow. What Denoro said made sense, but Rasha'kean had never considered the necessity of an officer proving herself to her troops. "How? How do they have to prove themselves?"

Denoro smiled. "It's easy in wartime. You just put their butts on the firing line and see what they do. If they choke up and go stiff on you, you get rid of them as fast as you can ship them out. If they scrabble up the hill no matter how scared they are, then you keep 'em."

"I ken I'm gettin' an education here," Rasha'kean said. "But go back to gettin' rid of them. How does a sergeant get rid of an officer?"

"Lots of ways, Colonel, but the easiest is to turn them in to officers who've scrabbled up the hill themselves. They'll find a way to get you a replacement, 'cause they don't want nobody like that on their flank if they can't depend on them."

"Sounds like common sense to me. But how do they prove themselves in peacetime?" Rasha'kean asked. This was turning into an amazing conversation.

"That's a bit harder, 'cause you see, Colonel, somehow an officer—say an officer like you—has got to prove herself to the troops so they know she's gonna get them through the tough spots if war ever does come. So what usually happens in peacetime is that the senior sergeants put their heads together and figure a way to test that officer."

"You mean an individual test for each officer?"

"Sure. No other way to do it. Like you say your whole unit was sent to one of the Service's Mountain Schools, and suppose in the middle of a real-time cliff-scaling exercise, on a course up a cliff that this officer chose for them, some of the troops got tangled in their lines halfway up the face."

Rasha'kean had a strange feeling about what was coming next as she remembered a similar incident back when she was a very young Post-Lieutenant, but the look on Denoro's face told Rasha'kean nothing, so she held her tongue and let Denoro continue.

"Now, an officer's got a handful of simple choices in a case like that. She can order some of her troops down to get them unsnarled, or she can order a sergeant down to do the job, or she can go herself with or without help."

"I'd go myself—with help," Rasha'kean said.

Denoro smiled. "That's exactly what you did, Colonel."

"You mean—but how did you ken?" Rasha'kean asked. "That was fifteen, sixteen years ago."

Denoro's smile got wider, splitting her narrow face. "Seems there was this young trooper in your squad that day who until a few days ago was a Tech Sergeant working in S.S.HQ. It took me a little time to find him, but when I did, he told me the story."

Rasha'kean chuckled and shook her head. "I d'not believe this. You mean, Sergeant Denoro, that you were checkin' up on me? How did you do it?"

"It's not too hard, Colonel. You see, whenever she can, a sergeant wants to now what her C.O. is going to be like, so I pulled a few strings, using what you'd already told me about when you were a troop leader. A buddy of mine ran all that through HQ's magical mystery computer, looking for matches with anyone on Nordeen who's ever served under you. Was just lucky that I found Millyus, 'cause he was the only one, and he had orders to ship out to Roberg. Caught him right before he left."

Rasha'kean shook her head. "Millyus? Ah, I remember him. Rowlf Vilhelm Millyus. I'm surprised he stuck with the service."

"You remember him, Colonel?"

"You bet I do. He was the slowest lump of spacemud in my platoon—and he was one of those tangled in their lines!"

"Right you are, Colonel. You got a good memory. He said that if you hadn't gone bad, I should give you his best wishes."

"So," Rasha'kean said slowly, "that whole snafu on the cliffs was just a test? I still ca'not believe it. Denoro, do you ken that I got called up before my legion commander and thoroughly brain-busted for that little *test?*"

"Did you blame it on your troops?"

"Of course not. What do you think I am, some kind of— You already ken that, didn't you?"

"Colonel," Denoro said, "Millyus didn't tell me that, but he did say he respected you, and his respect told me more than a day full of details."

"This is a strange feelin', to ken that you could dig up so much of my past. Do all senior sergeants have that kind of power?"

"Haven't you heard, Colonel? The senior sergeants run the Service. Without us the whole damn show would stop."

"Well, if I di'not believe that before, I do now," Rasha'kean said. "Maybe we should find us some whiskey and toast the senior sergeants."

* * *

"You want me to what?" Sjean asked. What in the path of free electrons was Janette up to?

"I want you to help find the alien, Xindella, and Ayne Wallen. Why is that so hard to comprehend?"

"You're fluxing right it is. After everything that's happened and what you did to me? That's the craziest thing I ever heard."

Janette felt a touch of pity for this woman but quickly pushed it aside. "Because," she said slowly, "you don't want the Ukes to have this weapon any more than Sci-Sec does. In fact, I'd say you don't want anyone at all to have this weapon."

Sjean held her gaze steady on Inspector Janette. How did she know that? Or was she just guessing? Guessing, Sjean decided. No one but her parents and Caugust knew how much she hated the Wallen. "If that were true—and I'm not saying it is—why would I want to help you find it?"

"Can't you answer that for yourself? Do you want *them* to have your Ultimate Weapon?"

"It's not mine," Sjean said quickly. "It is a Drautzlab—"

"You designed it." Janette let her anger bite through her words. "You supervised its construction. You're the one who determined how to put Wallen's equations into a practical piece of engineering. It is yours, whether you like it or not, and because it's yours, I think you have a certain obligation to see that it doesn't fall into the wrong hands again—no, more than an obligation, a duty, a moral duty."

Sjean laughed bitterly. As far as she could tell, there wasn't much morality left in her world.

"You think what I said was humorous?"

"Very humorous, Inspector. I used that same moral argument on Caugust once, but—"

"But what?"

"Well, Inspector," Sjean said with a slow shake of her head, "you can't have me building a new Wallen here and be out with you looking for the old one and its father at the same time. Which is more important to Sci-Sec?"

"Neither. I had no intention of taking you anywhere—not yet—but I did hope you would be willing to spend some time giving us everything you know about Ayne Wallen, anything that might give us clues that would help us find him."

"I've told you everything I know. What more do you want?" For a moment Sjean wished she were back in the hospital where the medics had shielded her from Janette.

"Yes, you've told me everything you thought you knew, everything that your conscious mind remembered, but I'm hoping that your subconscious knows more—something that will help us find and capture Ayne Wallen—with the prototype."

"My subconscious mi— Oh, no," Sjean said when she realized what Janette meant. "You're not going to use any of those brain-searching techniques on me. I've read about them and how they have driven people insane. You're crazy if you think for a minute that I would let you—"

"Doctor," Janette said firmly, "calm yourself. I don't need your permission to brain-search you, but I want it. The people who suffered mental difficulties afterward were people who had resisted the techniques. That's why I'm asking you to—"

"What do you mean, you don't need my permission?" Sjean felt a growing sense of panic that made her want to run from her office and hide somewhere. Could Janette really—

"The law says you can be forced to submit to the process for the good of Sondak, but I don't want to force you, Doctor Birkie. I want you to volunteer your help. If you do, I might get the information I'm looking for, and you will be none the worse for the experience. Can't you see that this is the best way?"

Before she answered, Sjean looked up and saw Caugust standing in the doorway. "Is it true? Can they really do that to me?" she asked in a quavering voice.

"I am afraid it is," Caugust said. "They've already set up their equipment."

Janette wanted to slap his mouth for telling Birkie that.

Sjean was terribly frightened. For a second everything went black. Her mind blinked, once, twice, turning itself on and off, detaching her from what was happening, making her numb. A distracted kind of panic tightened her chest. Then her mind blinked a third time, and she relaxed with a long sigh.

Nothing to be afraid of. This had happened before. Many times. Many times. The last, when? She couldn't remember. The first? A bright picture flashed through her mind.

The party, Uncle Rusty's party, a special, secret party. Sjean took her clothes off to go swimming. So did he. She squeezed her eyes shut when he took off his pants. It frightened her when Uncle Rusty made her look at him.

The picture darkened. Suddenly they were lying down. She bit her tongue when his body pressed down on her, and then—

Her mind blinked rapidly, and she relaxed again. It was all right. Everything would be all right. Uncle Rusty had promised. Every time. Everything would be all right.

"All right," a hollow voice whispered. It sounded as if the words were coming from somewhere else, but Sjean knew it was her other voice speaking.

"Do it as soon as you can," her other voice said, more loudly this time. "I don't want to think about it. I can't."

Maybe this is best, Sjean thought as Janette took her arm and led her out of the office like a lost child. If I don't make it, then I don't have to work on the Wallen anymore. I'll be free of it, and Janette and Caugust and, and . . . everything.

The hallway seemed strange to her, as though she had never seen it before, yet the empty office they took her to looked vaguely familiar. It was; it was Ayne's old office. But they had done something to it. There was something different—a bed where his desk had been, a bed with a stainless-steel box over one end of it.

Sjean was frightened. Her mind blinked again.

Someone helped her up on the bed and spoke soothingly to

her. Janette? No. Yes, but with a new voice. Janette with a new voice. How funny, she thought, as she felt a burning prick in her left shoulder.

Then another voice spoke to her. It asked her questions she didn't understand. Her other voice answered those questions, but she couldn't make out the words. They were both so far away, so very far away, on the far side of a wall. Then both voices faded into dark silence.

"She's under," Janette said to the technician. "You ask the questions. She seems more responsive to your voice."

For over an hour the technician asked questions and Dr. Birkie answered them. When Janette finally told him to stop, she had learned very little about Ayne Wallen that she didn't already know. The only thing of any promise was that several times Wallen had mentioned to Dr. Birkie that he had a powerful friend on Nordeen, a woman he referred to as Barra.

What Thel Janette had learned about Sjean Birkie, however, was enough to make her cry. But she couldn't allow herself that freedom. Xindella's auction was fast approaching, and if she didn't find him soon, the whole galaxy could be at risk.

14

"Still no signs of any other ships in this system. Are you sure this is the one Delightful Childe told us to check?" Marsha asked for the second time.

She and Lucky still had not decided exactly what they were going to do if they found Delightful Childe's cousin and his star-buster. Lucky wanted to drop it into the nearest star or blast it into space junk. Marsha didn't like either of those options, so they had decided to put off their decision until they actually had control of the thing. If they didn't find it and the festbid went on as scheduled, they had also agreed to do their best to see that no one else got the weapon if the U.C.S. didn't win the bid.

"This is the only system within two hundred parsecs that matched to within half a light year on the Oinaise curve-charts and our nav-holos. Since we couldn't feed their data into *Graycloud*'s nav-computer, we had to assume that this was what he called Jamiliskey's Star."

"Sounds pretty iffy to me," Marsha said. "So how long do we stay here based on those shaky assumptions?"

Lucky checked *Graycloud*'s bank of coordinated chronometers. "No more than three hundred ship's hours. If Xindella is here, he'll have to leave by then to make it to the festbid by the specified time—and so will we."

"And what if we don't find him? What if we're out here on a stray asteroid hunt? What then?"

Lucky knew something was bothering her, but he was almost too tired to ask what. He also knew that until she talked about it, he wasn't going to get much rest.

"All right, Mars. What's shorting your circuits now?"

"Nothing," she said, concentrating on the little nav-screens. She could feel him looking at her, but she covered her lie by refusing to meet his gaze.

"Then why am I receiving all these tension signals from you? The three of us are partners in this, remember? Something's bothering you, and you might as well get it out of your system."

"Lucky, nothing is bothering— Uh-oh."

"See something?"

"Yes, and I don't like it."

"You want to be more specific?"

"Look," she said, pointing to her center screen. "Nav-signals. Sondak-type. Eleven, fourteen, maybe fifteen of them entering the system behind us."

Lucky moved quickly to her side. "What the tensheiss are that many Sondak ships doing out here in the March Cluster? And why here? There's nothing in this system worth fighting for."

"Do you think they could know about Xindella?"

"Impossible. Delightful Childe only knows because he and Xindella sometimes used Jamiliskey as a transfer point for illicit cargo. How would Sondak know about that?"

"Don't ask me," she said with a worried frown. "Ask them. They're braking, but they're still closing on us awfully fast, and we're smack between them and the sun."

Lucky shifted his gaze to the larger nav-screens, and suddenly he understood. "Ukes! They're looking for Ukes. That's the only thing that makes any sense. Time to go," he said, throwing himself into the nav-chair. "Get us out of here, Mars. We'll head for Oina."

"And Xindella?" she asked as she opened the throttle on the meth-engines and increased the pressure in the Gouldrive.

Lucky was calling up course coordinates for Oina on the nav-computer. "Damn Xindella. If he's here, he's going to have to get out, too. Either way I sure don't want to get caught by some damn fleety asking a bunch of snoopy questions—especially if they're expecting Ukes and looking for a fight."

Seven sets of coordinates rolled onto his screen and stopped. "Numbers up," he said, throwing the input switch.

"Drive temp fifty-percent," Marsha responded.

"Incoming message on a standard Sak channel. Think we should answer it?"

"We'll be ready to accelerate in three minutes and they're still five or six hours out. Sure, answer it. Tell the damn Saks to go take a walk in space."

"Maybe I'd better find out what they want first. No reason to get them excited about us. What do you think?"

"No harm, I guess," Marsha said reluctantly, "but unless there's a good reason not to, *Graycloud's* going to be leaving here in short order."

Lucky flipped the channel open.

"—is imperative that you identify yourself immediately to forestall hostile action on our part. . . . Fleet Ship *Rualt*, calling unknown lightspeed freighter. Identify yourself. Repeat. Identify yourself. It is imperative that you identify yourself immediately to forestall—"

"A loop," Lucky said, closing the channel. "I'm going to send them the Oinaise registry information but nothing more."

"Two-fifteen to acceleration," Marsha said. She didn't care what Lucky sent them.

"Easy, Mars. We're all right. Besides, you said they were five hours away."

"Doesn't matter. We're leaving."

"Right," Lucky said with a shake of his head. Whatever was bothering her hadn't gone away just because the fleeties had shown up. He switched the registry signal to the Sondak channel and pushed the transmit button. As he looked up at the nav-screens, he realized they had waited too long. "Missiles, Mars," he said as calmly as he could, "two of them on a true course for us."

For the first time in hours Marsha grinned. "Stupid Saks, shooting at an Oinaise trading ship at this range. Don't those idiots know we'll be hours gone before those missiles get here?"

Lucky laughed suddenly.

"It's not that funny."

"Yes it is. This whole thing is funny. As much as I may have argued with them in the past, I learned that you don't mess with a Fleet Gunner."

"Lucky, what are you talking about?"

"Don't you see, Mars?" he said with a delighted grin. "They're just trying to scare us. There's probably not a Gunner in the fleet who couldn't tell you within twenty meters of where his missiles were going to hit and within fifteen seconds of when. They have no intention of hitting us."

"I doubt that. They just launched two more. If they didn't want to hit us, why would they do that? And why would those missiles be accelerating like that?"

"Spaced if I know," Lucky said. His grin was gone as he leaned forward in the nav-chair. "They're sure coming faster than anything I've ever seen. Like I said before, Mars, it's time to get out of here. I'm ready when you are."

"Meth's on full power. Thirty seconds till Gouldrive."

"Inertial dampers on. Course set. Take us away, Mars."

There was a prolonged silence in the cabin as they watched the Gouldrive build to maximum thrust pressure. When Marsha said, "Go!" and started *Graycloud* acceleration, they both sighed in relief. Regardless of how far away the missiles were, neither of them liked being shot at.

Ten minutes after they entered subspace, Marsha turned to Lucky with tears in her eyes. "You want to know what's bothering me? Well, I'll tell you. I'm bothering me. Lucky, I"—the tears overflowed and rolled freely down her face—"I'm bothering me. I don't know who I am anymore."

*   *   *

According to Lieutenant Oska's letter, Judoff had arranged for one hundred fifty thousand freetrading credits to take to this weapon auction she was so determined to attend. Frye shook his head. He would have bet the soles of his feet that most of that amount was government money, not hers.

But worse than that, the date Oska gave for the auction was only one U.C. Standard day before the attack fleets departed for the first full-scale attacks against Sondak since the battle for Satterfield.

This time Frye was determined to keep Judoff from robbing him of vital ships. If she thought this auction was important enough for her to miss the departure, so much the better. He didn't need her. But he did need her fleet.

"AOCO," he said, calling Melliman on his lapelcom, "we've got work to do."

"Bad news from our friend?" Melliman asked as she entered his office.

"Depends on how you look at it. Judoff's auction is the day before fleet departure. What you and I have to do is find a way to make sure she can't take her ships with her."

"What about Vice-Admiral Lotonoto and Meister Hadasaki? Couldn't they help with this?"

"Excellent idea, AOCO," he said. "See if you can locate them, and try to set up a meeting within the next fifteen hours."

"Can do, sir," she answered quickly.

As she left his office, Frye thought again of how grateful he was that she had returned to serve at his side. If only Marsha had— He quickly cut off that thought, but he couldn't get rid of Marsha so easily. His whole relationship with her from the days of her childhood had been a history of *if onlys*. She was a daughter without the strength and courage of her mother, and he was a father who had failed his daughters in more ways than he cared to think about.

Daughters. Plural. Two daughters, one happily off with her lightspeed trader, the other threatening him from somewhere beyond his knowledge and control, and both of them as much of a disappointment to him as he was to them. He might one day live up to Tuuneo's estimation of him by becoming the best military commander in U.C.S. history, but he would never be able to live up to the expectations of his daughters.

For the first time in his life he wondered which was more important—not to him, personally, he knew the answer to that—in the final summing up of his life. Which would count for more in the hereafter, what he did for the U.C.S.

or what he did for his daughters? He knew the answer to that question, as well, and it sent a cold chill to the center of his bones.

With grim determination he pushed all of that out of his mind and concentrated on the work at hand. Every detail of the upcoming invasion of Sondak seemed to be crossing his desk, and at this moment he was very grateful for the distraction from his dark thoughts that the invasion provided. But five hours later, when Hadasaki and Lotonoto arrived for the meeting Melliman had arranged, the chill still had not left his bones.

"Meister. Admiral," Frye said as they entered his office, "I am pleased that you both could find time for me on such short notice. Please make yourselves comfortable," he continued, indicating the informal group of chairs at one end of his office.

"This is about Marshall Judoff, I understand," Vice-Admiral Lotonoto said, taking the only chair with its back against the wall.

"Yes," Frye said, surprised that she so abruptly brought up the subject when normal courtesy called upon her to wait. "And the auction for this mystery weapon she is trying to procure," he added. He and Hadasaki sat facing Lotonoto, and Melliman began serving tea.

"I need your assistance," Frye said after they had all finished their first servings of tea and Melliman had refilled their cups. "I see no way or reason to dissuade Marshall Judoff from attending this 'festbid' of hers, but we need the ships of her fleet to succeed in the first phase of our invasion."

Hadasaki smiled grimly. "She controls one hundred seventy-two ships, doesn't she?"

"Two hundred eleven if you count her supply ships," Lotonoto said. "Of all those, I believe we have planned to use all but six of the fighting ships and all but one of the supply ships."

"That is correct," Frye said.

"What, then, is the problem?" Hadasaki asked.

"We have to ensure that those ships launch as scheduled with the other fleets, don't we, Admiral Charltos?"

Frye was pleased that she had such a firm grasp of the problem. For an officer with kyosei sympathies, Lotonoto was remarkably independent in her thinking. "Correct again," he said with a slight bow of his head.

Hadasaki nodded. "I see now. You're afraid she'll pull them out until she returns with this weapon of hers?"

"Or try to take them with her," Frye said.

"And your proposal?" Lotonoto asked.

"To realign the fleets so her ships are divided among all the fleets and under the fleet commanders whose first loyalties are to Bridgeforce rather than to Judoff."

"That will take a big fight," Hadasaki said.

Frye smiled slightly. "Only if Marshall Judoff is present."

Lotonoto's frown wrinkled her forehead up past her hair-line. "I suppose it could be done, but I do not like it."

"Nor do I," Frye said quickly. "However, I firmly believe it is necessary if we wish to succeed in our plans."

"Your plan," Hadasaki corrected him.

"His plan as accepted by Bridgeforce," Lotonoto said.

Looking down at the floor, Frye said, "I would rather think of it as our plan, for every member of Bridgeforce made significant contributions to it."

"Very well," Hadasaki said gruffly. "Our plan. But even if we do meet without Marshall Judoff and suspend the rules in order to divide her fleet, can any of us guarantee that she will abide by our decision?"

"Yes!"

The sharpness in Vice-Admiral Lotonoto's tone startled Frye, and he was eager to hear what she was going to say.

Lotonoto gave them both a wicked smile. "I can ensure that she will be away from Yakusan until after her fleet is physically dispersed. Once that happens, it will be too late for her to call them back and attend her auction at the same time. From all that has happened, I suspect she will choose the auction with an eye to reforming her fleet later."

"Yes, but how would you do it?" Hadasaki asked.

"I won't," she answered. "The kyosei will."

Frye let out a long sigh. "Admiral," he said slowly, "the U.C.S. will be greatly in your debt if you accomplish that."

"No, Admiral Charltos," she said softly. "It is I who am forever indebted to the U.C.S."

There was a moment of silence, then Hadasaki asked, "How quickly can you arrange this?"

"Two days, no more," Lotonoto said as she rose from her

chair. "We can call the special Bridgeforce meeting as soon as she is gone."

Frye and Hadasaki stood at the same time. "Yes, as soon as she is gone," Frye said, wishing there were some way Judoff would be gone for good. "I thank you both."

15

Hew Rochmon sometimes wished he had never gotten involved with the Service and Cryptography, and especially with Bock. For all her intelligence and skills, it took enduring patience for him to abide her presence. There was no doubt that Cryptography had been less effective without her than it had been when he and his staff had her mind to draw on. But there was also no doubt that none of the strange personality types who seemed drawn to Cryptography were half the trouble that Bock was.

In the seventy days since she had returned to work, she had managed to anger or frighten everyone on staff who hadn't known her before and half of those who had. Her attitudes concerning cooperation were totally self-serving. Bock openly lusted after every male under thirty-five and every female under forty-five whom she came into contact with. Department heads had demanded that he not allow her in their departments. Senior officers had Military Guards physically ban her from their floors and then complained over his head. Now Admiral Gilbert was thinking about sending her back to Sci-Sec.

That would have been fine with Rochmon except for one thing. In the seventy days since she had returned, she had made more progress in breaking the Uke's Q-3 code than the rest of his cryptographers had in three hundred days. For all the valid reasons that he would be glad not to have to put up with her, Rochmon needed her. Sondak needed her.

He glanced at his clock. Admiral Gilbert would be here in less than an hour, so he might as well start getting Bock ready for this meeting now. He punched her number on the intercom.

"What?" her voice asked curtly.

"I want you to come to my office as soon as you can."

"Can't. Busy. Get someone else to play with."

Before he could reply, the intercom's light went off, and he knew she had broken the connection. With patience born of experience he punched up her number again. "Bock," he said as soon as the light went on, "you will come to my office now, if not sooner. This can't wait."

"Everything can wait. You want the Q-Three or not?"

"Don't ask stupid questions. Just get over here."

"Damn! You love to slow me down. Why can't you—"

"Now, Bock," he said, using the command voice he had learned on the drill field as a fuzz-faced cadet. "You will report to my office immediately."

Her answer was to disconnect again, but three minutes later she charged into his office without knocking and slammed the door without breaking her stride as she moved straight to his desk. "What's your problem this time, you motherless whelp?" she asked as she slammed her hands on the edge of the desk and leaned forward with raw anger in her eyes. "Did you lose your manhood and need me to find it for you?"

If Rochmon hadn't seen all this before, he would have been furious. Instead, he just laughed. "Sit down, Bock, and save the act for someone else. Or better yet, why don't you just—"

Bock cleared her throat, then spat in his face. "Save that, poker," she said with a cruel smile.

Without thinking, Rochmon slapped her as hard as he could, then backhanded her as she fought to retain her balance. Her body twisted across his desk, then fell to the floor with a loud moan as a stack of reports slid after her.

As quickly as he could, Rochmon moved around the desk, wiping his face on his sleeve. The only thing he felt at that moment was anger—anger at her for what she had done and anger at himself for misjudging her mood. He felt no regrets about slapping her.

She looked up at him with both hands holding her face. "You're faster than I would have figured," she said slowly. "Not bad . . . for a man." She held up one hand to him.

"Think you can act like a civilized human being for now?" he asked as he helped her to her feet.

"If that's what happens to the uncivilized, I guess I'd better," she said, one hand still holding her jaw. "I had that coming, I suppose."

"You did. And you've got a lot more coming if you don't pay attention to what I'm about to tell you."

She sat in the overstuffed chair beside the door. "I'd just as soon you didn't hit me again."

Rochmon sat on the front of his desk, ignoring the mess on the floor for the moment. "I'm not about to hit you again, but Gilbert might—not with his fists, but he might use the power of his office to slam you hard. Hang it all, Bock, why can't I get you to understand that you can't run rampant through this headquarters insulting people and sexually assaulting people without having to pay for it sooner or later?"

"So that's what the problem is," she said with a smile that quickly turned into a grimace. "You really hurt me."

"You hurt yourself or cause other people to hurt you. Did you know that in the largest country on Laurel if you spit on someone they can legally demand that your tongue be cut out?"

"So, who's on Laurel that we care about? And why should I have to nambyfoot around this headquarters? We're all big boys and girls and neuters here, and it's a tough world."

Rochmon sighed, then crouched down and started picking up the reports and putting them back on his desk. "Gilbert will be here in a few minutes. He'll want me to defend you and explain why you shouldn't be sent back to Sci-Sec, or worse. And he'll want you to defend yourself." He paused as he picked up the last of the reports. "I think I'll just let you defend yourself. No one person, however intelligent and valuable she is, can be worth the disruption you cause in my headquarters."

"Now wait a minute, Hew. If you think I'm going to—"

"I don't care what you think, Bock." He stood up and moved back behind his desk. "It's harder to defend you than it is to remember your full name—which, I gratefully believe, I have totally forgotten."

"Jectiverdifiaad Barrabockerman Montivillieo Questen Pasqualini," she said in the musical accents of her homeland. "Did I ever tell you what my name means, Hew?"

"No, but don't bother."

"It means the child of whore Pasqualini born in the gutters of Montivillieo. Nice name for a child to grow up with, eh?"

"If you want my sympathy, Bock, it's way too late for that. The travails of your childhood do not make up for your actions as an adult." The sad expression on her face stopped him from saying anything else. He'd never seen her look like that, and despite what he had said, he felt sorry for her.

"You think Sci-Sec will take me back?"

Rochmon sighed. "Look, Bock, go back to your office and bury your head in the Q-Three. I'll take care of Gilbert for you one more time. But this is the last time. Either you act in a civil manner in this headquarters from now on, or you face whatever Gilbert wants to throw at you. You don't get another chance."

"I'll try," Bock said as she stood. "Thanks, Hew." When he didn't respond, she turned and quietly left his office.

As he watched her go, Rochmon had a strange and sudden thought. Why had she told him the meaning of her name? In all the years she'd known him and all the times she had teased him about being the only person who could remember her complete name, she had never given him the slightest hint that it had such a meaning. Why now?

He made a note to check her personal file again and to request that another in-depth background check be run on her parents. Rochmon didn't know why he thought that was important, but the decision made him feel better, and that helped him prepare for Admiral Gilbert.

"The Admiral's here," Rochmon's aide announced a few minutes later.

"Show him in, Farrandy."

"I don't have much time, Hew," Josiah Gilbert said as he strode confidently into Rochmon's office, "so I'm going to give it to you by the book and get out of your way."

"By all means, sir, go ahead." Rochmon could tell that the old man was in no mood for bartering.

"You will do two things, Hew. You will tell Bock that if I receive one more complaint about her conduct, she will be called back to active duty and then be court-martialed if she so much as blinks in the wrong way. Then you will tell her that as of today she is being placed under restrained movement and will be accompanied all her waking hours when she is not in her office by one or more MGs."

"Isn't that pretty harsh, sir?" Rochmon asked.

"Yes it is, Hew. But it was either that or have Stony lock her in the prison over there for 'disrupting military during wartime.' Any further questions?"

"No, sir, I'll tell her."

"Good. Oh, and Hew. Tell her I'm sorry about the MGs."

* * *

"Not again," Sjean said. "Please? Not again."

"I'm sorry, Dr. Birkie, but there are some things I believe are buried in your subconscious that I have to know, and we just don't have time to dig it out any other way. Besides, you came through the last brain-search with no trouble. Why are you so afraid of doing it again?"

"No trouble? You call not being able to sleep more than two or three hours at a time no trouble? You call this constant headache I have no trouble? What's the matter with *you*, Inspector? Did they make you surrender your compassion when you signed up for Sci-Sec?" This discussion was making Sjean's low-grade headache turn into a real temple-pounder.

"I didn't know about your headaches," Janette lied, "but I doubt if they were caused by the brain-search."

"You know damn well they were. I never had these kinds of headaches before that."

"I am sorry, Doctor," Janette said again, "but it has to be done. Please?" She held out her hand. "Don't make me force you. I told you that an unwilling subject was the most likely to suffer side-effects."

Sjean stared at Janette until tears blurred her vision. Reluctantly, she took the Inspector's hand and followed her down the same hall to the same office where she had gone through it all before.

When they entered the office, Sjean felt suddenly calm, as though a distant voice inside her was telling her everything was going to be all right. She didn't understand it, but she gave in to it, glad to accept any reassurance.

Again she lay on the table with the box over her head. Again she felt the burning prick in her arm and heard Janette speak soothingly to her. Again the questions started, and the other voice inside her answered them until both of them blurred into quiet nothingness.

Thel Janette truly felt sorry for Sjean Birkie and wished there had been some other fast way to get the information she needed. Since there was no other way as quick and accurate as this, she had no choice. But that didn't mean she had to like what she was doing.

"Dr. Birkie, do you know why the prototype weapon you tested did not function properly?"

"Did function properly," Dr. Birkie answered in a slow, thick voice.

"I don't understand. The test was a failure. Why do you say the prototype functioned properly?"

"Wasn't supposed to work."

That startled Janette. She had never suspected that the test was a deception. "Why wasn't it supposed to work?"

"Funny. Caugust called it dud, D-U-D, dud."

"What does that mean, D-U-D?"

"He said it. Dud. Daringly Undestructive Device."

"You mean it wasn't a real weapon? Just some piece of junk you put together?" Janette was finding this hard to believe, but if it were true—no. It couldn't be true. Why would Drautzlab be willing to enter the auction for a piece of junk?

"Oh, yes . . . it was a real . . . It could have worked."

"Why didn't it work?" Janette pressed. "Why?"

"Don't understand. Couldn't work. Incomplete."

"What was missing?"

Dr. Sjean Birkie giggled. "The detonator. Didn't have a real detonator. See? Isn't it funny?"

Janette bit her tongue to keep herself from giving an answer to that question. It was anything but funny. But she didn't have time to worry about that. There were two more questions she had to have answers to. "Did you build a real detonator?"

"Of course."

"Where is it?"

"Secret. Can't tell. Caugust said hush-hush."

"Tell me where it is," Janette said slowly. "I can keep a secret."

"Mmm. All right. Here. It's here. In the main test lab behind the blast doors."

"Just relax and sleep now, Sjean," Janette said. "Sleep peacefully, and when you wake up, you will feel fine, and your headaches will be all gone. When you wake up tomorrow morning, you will feel healthy and happy, and you will not have any headaches. Do you understand me?"

"Yes. Sleep. No headaches."

Janette patted her arm. "Good. It's time to sleep now."

"Slee-e-e-ep. Goo-o-o-od."

As quickly as she could, Janette turned off the equipment and took the head unit off the bed. After covering Dr. Birkie with a light blanket, she dimmed the lights in the office and left in search of Caugust Drautz. She found him in the first place she looked, his office.

"Have you finished questioning her?" he asked when Janette knocked on his doorframe.

"Yes. Now I have some questions for you, Dr. Drautz."

"Like what?"

Janette knew from the tone of his voice that he was totally on the defensive. "Like why did you use fake equipment when you tested the Ultimate Weapon?"

His already-ruddy face got redder. "We did no such thing."

"Don't lie to me, Doctor. The weapon prototype you sent around GA-72-6694 was real enough. If it weren't, you wouldn't be so interested in getting it back. But the detonator was a fake. Dr. Birkie told me all about your DUD."

Caugust laughed unexpectedly. "Equipment failure, Inspector—yours, not ours. The detonator and the weapon were both real. Doctor Birkie lied to you."

Suddenly Janette had doubts, but only small ones. "Then why didn't it work? Why didn't it explode two stars?"

"Ask the Inspector Admiral's Office. They have all the data. They can tell you."

"I've seen that data, and it would take months, maybe years, to analyze it, even if they knew what they were doing, which they don't. Either you give me the truth now, or I'll question you the same way I did Dr. Birkie."

"Oh, no. Not me, Inspector. You're not getting me in your torture rack. No chance."

"Then tell me the truth. Why didn't it work?"

Caugust sighed heavily. "It was programmed to fail."

"Thank you. Now, I want the detonator you have stored away in the main test lab."

"You what? Inspector, I don't know what you are—"

"Either you turn it over to me," she said menacingly, "or

I'll have you locked up and take this complex apart piece by piece until I find it."

"You win, Inspector. You win," he said with a look of defeat. "But why do you want it?"

"So that when I get the other part in this auction, Sondak will have a complete Ultimate Weapon to use against the Ukes, of course. Why else would I want it?"

16

Henley walked slowly down the hill, wishing he had done a better job of distributing the weight in his combat pack, because no matter how he tried to adjust it, he felt as if he were leaning slightly to the left. He paused for a moment to wipe the perspiration from his face and looked away from the bright orange heat of Mungtinez's sun. He was sweating freely now in the warm, humid air and wanted nothing more than to find his unit and get out from under the sun and his pack.

Putting his cap back on, he continued down the hill. The orderly rows of hundreds of stretchlon tents in the shallow valley below him reminded Henley of the beehives he had seen one time on Wallbank—or was it Yaffee? He couldn't remember.

Here and there among the rows of troop tents, larger domed tents indicated unit headquarters or officers quarters. According to the clerk back at legion headquarters, Delta Company's tent was in the seventh row of Z-companies from the north.

The clerk had been wrong.

After asking directions several times and getting completely turned around once, Henley finally found the tent he was looking for on the ninth row. An orderly who was leaving the tent as he approached it told him he could go in.

"What are you doin' here, Chief?" Rasha'kean asked, rising from her chair as Henley came through the flap.

"Following your career, Colonel." He took off his pack and smiled with relief. It was noticeably cooler in the tent.

"Get truthful," Rasha'kean said, returning his smile.

"Colonel!" he said with mock dismay. "You caught me. I'm actually here to make you keep a dinner date."

Rasha'kean snorted.

"All right," Henley said, "the truth. I requested an attachment to a combat unit, and General Archer asked me if I had any preferences." He paused to wipe his face.

Rasha'kean's smile had turned into a slight frown. "And you chose my unit?" She did not think she liked that idea.

"Not exactly." He had noted the quick shift of her expression and wondered what she was thinking. "The general said he would assign me to a Z-company, which was fine with me. I didn't know until I received my orders that you were the commanding officer. You don't look too happy about that."

"I'm not sure I am, Chief. But I'm not sure I'm unhappy about it, either. Maybe I just d'not ken what to do with you. Please, sit down," she said, sitting back in her chair.

Henley was grateful for the chance to sit, even in a collapsible field-chair. His hike had tired him far more than he thought it should have. Got to get in shape, he thought, or I'll never make it. "You don't have to *do* anything with me, except put up with me—and tell me when I'm in your way or out of line," he added.

"I see," she said slowly, then asked the question uppermost in her mind. "What is it that you're goin' to do in this unit?"

"What I do is pretty simple," he said, "too simple, some people would say. Basically I will stay with your company from now through the invasion. I'll watch, listen, try to get to know your troops, and write my stories for the Service Archives."

"And the *Flag Report*," she added.

"Yes. For the *Flag Report*, but also the *Courier-Times*, and *Intraworld News*."

"Uh . . . ar'not those civilian controlled?"

"More like civilian-government controlled. Actually, it's rather complicated. I submit some of my stories through the *Flag Report* Editorial Office to the Tri-Cameral's Information Release Committee. They decide which stories to release to Efcorps, and Efcorps controls both the *Courier-Times* and *Intraworld*."

"But that's censorship!"

"Of course, Colonel. You seem surprised."

"I am shocked," Rasha'kean said.

"But why?" Henley asked. "You don't think the Service would release just anything I wrote, do you?"

Rasha'kean hesitated. "Perhaps not, Chief, but on Ca-Ryn such censorship is very much against the law."

Henley laughed. "It may be against the law, Colonel, but I'd bet you a year's pay that it happens all the time. No government can afford uncensored reporting. How do you think the Efcorps started?" It was a rhetorical question, but he paused, anyway, and gave her a chance to answer.

When she didn't, he continued. "Efcorps was the censorship arm of the original government on Biery, but it wasn't called Efcorps then. That strange name is a rather recent addition. However, no matter how many times the name changes, the results are the same. News is censored for the good of Sondak and its citizens."

"Not on Ca-Ryn," Rasha'kean said stubbornly.

"Yes, on Ca-Ryn. Believe me, Colonel."

"I d'not, Chief, nor will I until I have some better proof of it than a Teller's word for it. You'll not be takin' offense to that, I hope?"

"Not at all," he lied. He resented her refusal to believe him—or her naive approach to the government, he wasn't sure which. "However," he said, "if I were you, I wouldn't bet any credits I wasn't willing to lose on that."

Rasha'kean did not want to pursue this discussion any further and decided it was time to change the subject. "Have you met my Executive Officer?" she asked.

"No. Your orderly said the X.O. was supervising some training this morning."

"Well, Sergeant Denoro should be returnin' soon, and I'll let her find a place for you. If you want stories, I think you'll find her an interestin' trooper."

"*Sergeant* Denoro?" Henley asked, barely waiting until Ingrivia had finished speaking.

"Yes," Rasha'kean said. "Does that surprise you?"

"I suppose it does. Not too many officers around anymore who would make a senior sergeant their X.O."

"Well, I'm one who d'not think all the oldy ways are bad, Chief, and experience is more important in my X.O. than rank."

"I didn't mean to sound critical, Colonel. I was just flat-foot startled. Takes good sense to choose experience over rank."

"And you di'not think I had good sense?" Rasha'kean teased.

Henley shook his head. "You know better than that. How about dinner? I'll even cook it myself if you can get us some F-rations. Brought my own kingjun hot sauce."

"When we get into combat, maybe." She saw the flash of disappointment in his eyes and added, "For the F-rations, I mean. Tonight we can eat in the Officers Tank."

"If that's what you want, Colonel," he said with a tone of resignation, "but I guarantee that what I do with F-rats and hot sauce beats the normal fare at any Officers Tank."

"It's easier to take risks in combat, Chief. Tonight I'll take the safe menu."

"There you go again, Colonel, selling me—" He stopped as a thin, dark sergeant entered the tent.

"Denoro," Rasha'kean said, "I've got a new charge for you. Chief, this is my X.O."

"Pleased to meet you, Sergeant," Henley said, giving her a casual salute.

Denoro looked him up and down for a few seconds. "Combat Teller, old one, too. Been around, haven't you, Chief?"

Henley was puzzled. "A few times, Denoro. Why?"

" 'Cause you ought to know better than to salute me," she said sternly. Then her face broke into a grin. "I'll be grounded before I'll be mistaken for an officer." She gave Rasha'kean a quick wink.

"Aw," Henley said, "take it while you can get it. Won't be any saluting once we hit the dirt."

"Truth enough," Denoro said, holding out her hand.

Henley shook it.

"You here to do a story on our colonel?" she asked.

"I'm tryin' to get him to do one on you," Rasha'kean said.

"On both of you, and the whole company. There is something I need from both of you, I guess, before I do stories on anyone. Today's hike convinced me that I'm out of shape, so I want to join the physical training program you're putting the troops through."

They both smiled, and Denoro said, "Never had a chance to kill a Teller before. What do you think, Colonel?"

"Permission granted." Rasha'kean looked critically at Henley. "I want all that fat off him before we launch."

He shook his head slightly. "Why do I have the feeling I'm going to be very sorry I asked for this?"

"You'll love it, Chief," Denoro said. "You really will."

* * *

"Ranas, I do not understand what you mean," Leri said, shifting her coil back and forth to scratch an annoying itch close to her tail. "Are we or are we not receiving messages from the mysterious Verfen?"

"We are, that is, we think we are, but the messages are so weak and garbled that we cannot be sure."

First the new recurring dream-visions of entering huge alien jaws, then the methane raiders, and now messages from the Verfen. There was nothing she could do about the vision. The raiders were being coped with by the Castorian and human patrols on the fringes of Cloise's atmosphere. But everything she knew about the Verfen disturbed Leri even more than the vision. And now they were sending messages. No one she knew had ever communicated with one, but at least there was a definite precedent for such communication.

"When was the last message received?" she asked finally.

"Three seasons ago," Ranas answered.

"And you are just now telling me this? Why?"

Ranas shifted his own coil before returning her gaze. "Because, Proctor, we have, or more accurately, our specialists have, been attempting a translation."

"And why is that taking so long?"

"Leri, what is the matter with you? You know very well why it is taking so long. No one now alive has ever done one before. And those who were trained to do this are working with garbled fragments. The Verfen seem to be concerned with protection, but whose protection and why, we do not yet know. I only told you now so you would be aware of their efforts and might consider other possibilities."

She stopped scratching and stared at him. "What other possibilities?"

"Our experts agree that we need to take our transceiver equipment outside the atmosphere."

"What about the raiders?"

"We will arrange for protection. Glights the Castorian has already been notified of the possibility."

"I see. And you have found volunteers for this?"

"More than we need."

That surprised her. "Very well, Ranas, you may send the volunteers and the transceiver into space."

"I will lead them, not send them," Ranas said simply. "I was the first volunteer."

She smelled a rush of emotions—fear, dismay, resentment, love, and anger—that filled the chamber with a confusion of scents. Ranas? To space? But why? "But why?" she repeated aloud. "Why are you going?"

"Because I am needed."

Leri knew he was frightened, but now the strongest thing she smelled from him was the sharp scent of determination. That was the thing she did not understand. "There are others who can fill that need," she said slowly.

"Yes, but they did not volunteer quickly enough. I have chosen, Leri. Do not try to dissuade me."

"Then explain to me why you feel this sudden gulping-rush to do something so dangerous? You, who are afraid of space? Why? I want the real reason."

Ranas tightened his coil and looked past her. "It is as I said, Leri. I was needed, and I was the first volunteer."

"Can't you see that is a contradiction," she said angrily. "Either you were needed and had no choice, or you were a volunteer. I want to know the real reason."

"I smell your anger, Leri," he said very slowly, "but it will not force me to give you my personal reason for making this decision. I will go with the specialists and serve them as I can. When they return, I will remain in space with our guard—"

"No! No, Ranas. Don't say such a thing. I need you here. You hate space, remember?" Her heart was suddenly beating like a night-thumper.

"I hate myself, more," Ranas said, starting to uncoil. "I bid you good-bye now, Proctor, Leri, mate of my nest."

For the briefest moment his words froze her in place. Then, without thinking, she struck out and threw her long body toward the entrance, blocking his way. She was angry and very much afraid at the same time. "I have to know," she said softly. "Are you doing this because of what I said about Weecs?"

"No, mate of my nest, I do it because I must do it for myself. Please let me go now. There is much preparation to be made, and we do not know how long the Verfen will continue sending their message."

Reluctantly, she pulled herself back from the entrance. "I smell deceit in you," she said, trying to keep the emotions out of her voice.

He swung his head to hers and rubbed his topscales against her throat. "Good-bye, mate of my nest," he said lovingly. Then, with a quick turn, he slithered out the entrance and was gone.

His gesture had been so familiar, so intimate, and it had been so long since she had let him rub her, that she was caught in a swell of affection and guilt. And it was the guilt she felt that made her let him go.

Good-bye, he had said, but he had meant good-bye forever. She knew him too well, his scent, his tones. He felt sure he wasn't coming back. And he was doing it because of the stupid thing she had said about him not loving her enough to try to rescue her from Exeter.

Stupid. Stupid. They were both stupid, she for having said that and he for letting it goad him into space.

Leri's inclination was to curl up in a corner and slip into the stupor of grief that was already slipping over her, but she knew that was as stupid as trying to stop him. No, there was only one place she could go for comfort, and that was to her Confidante.

As quickly as she could, she slithered from her chamber through the dark tunnels to the cliff, then carefully down the cliff until she came to her chosen grotto. Without pausing, she slithered into the darkness. As her tail cleared the entrance, a pale light began to fill the grotto and revealed the looming gray bulk of the Confidante.

"Have you need of exchange?" the Confidante asked.

"No."

"Would you like it, anyway?"

"Yes, I would," Leri answered. "But first I must ask you a question. Why has my vision gone so wrong?"

"Has it gone wrong, Leri Gish Geril? Or do you wish it to be something it is not?"

Leri shuddered. "I dreamed that I led my people into the jaws of gigantic aliens, but . . . I felt no shame in doing it. What is happening, Confidante? I don't understand?"

"Do you believe in your vision?" the Confidante asked.

"Yes . . . I did. I guess I still do."

"Will you let the Isthian mount you now?"

"Yes." Almost before she said the word, she heard the Isthian scrambling along the floor. Moments later it was up her neck and suckling.

"Can you learn to trust yourself?" the Confidante asked.

"Yes," Leri answered, enjoying the Isthian's enthusiasm despite her mood.

"Will you rest now?"

"Yes," she said. Her body was already beginning to relax. "But the questions. What about the questions?"

"Can you not wait for answers?"

"I can . . . I can." Then Leri, with the Isthian suckling contentedly on her neck, slept.

17

For a full day Frye had wondered what to think about this new message from his daughter. Either she was crazy, or a traitor, or a patriot, or this new message was some kind of Sondak trick and wasn't from her at all. Or perhaps it was from her and she was in on the trick.

He didn't know how to sort out the truth from those options yet, but there were two things he was sure about. Whoever had sent the message had made the connection between himself and his daughter, because the message was signed *Barra*. Furthermore, that person had found a wormhole in the security around his communications network. The message had come straight to his microspooler.

No matter how he looked at it, the problem compounded itself. If he believed her claim that Sondak was going to invade the Ivy Chain in an attempt to regain control of those systems, he might move his forces in such a way as to fall right into their trap. If he ignored the claim, he could proceed as planned with his own invasion of Sondak. He decided to do nothing about the message. For the time being, that was the only thing that made sense to him.

By the time he got to his office the day after receiving that message, he was tired and irritable. Melliman had tried to put him in a better mood with tenderness and affection, but her efforts only seemed to make things worse. As usual, his microspooler was loaded with information, but he wasn't ready to turn it on. All he could do was stare at it and wonder if *she* had broken into it again and left another surprise for him.

She. Barra. Was that what she was calling herself these days? Or was she using that name in the message to mock him? With an angry swipe he flipped on the microspooler, then chided himself for his actions. If he wanted to do something useful, he should have called the Comnet Security people as soon as he got the first message and told them to change all access codes as quickly as possible. Then she might never have gotten to him a second time.

He smiled ruefully, thinking that he probably had not called in Comnet just so she *could* reach him. Might as well do it now and stop this harassment, he thought.

As he reached to turn off the microspooler, his smile faded. It was too late. She had reached him a third time.

> Admiral, however much I might once have hated you, I am still a daughter of the U.C.S., and as such, I understand where my duty lies. If you did not believe my last message, I understand, but if you check with your spies on Mungtinez, you will discover a large buildup of Planetary Forces there destined for the invasion of the Ivy Chain. I cannot send much more than this in one message. Please trust me—Barra.

"Melliman," Frye said loudly into his lapelcom, "get the head of Comnet Security up here immediately." He paused for a long second. "No. Never mind. You get in here."

"What is it?" Melliman asked moments later as she stood in front of his desk.

Frye pointed silently to the message on his screen. "Come around here and look at this. It is the second one that has come in like that. Do you know what that means?"

Melliman moved around the desk and bent over slightly so she could see his screen. "I have no idea what it means," she said after reading the message. "Who is Barra?"

"That's a long story, Clarest, one I'll tell you as soon as we have time. For now, let's just say that Barra is someone I used to know who is apparently living in Sondak—where I don't know. But she appears to have access to some of Sondak's important military information."

"A spy, sir?"

"No. At least not an official spy. Perhaps she's a distant relative with good intentions."

"So why are you so upset?" Melliman asked, letting her hand brush against his arm as she straightened up.

"Ah . . . I was hoping it didn't show. Part of the reason I'm upset, Melliman, is that this Barra has found a nice little crack in our communications security network through which she is sending these messages."

"And you want Comnet Security to close the crack? But something, or someone, is giving you serious second thoughts. Am I right?"

Frye smiled up at her with a great deal of affection. "You are, Clarest. That's one of the reasons I value your assistance so much. You have a talent for getting directly to the center of things. The problem for us is twofold—first, determining if this information is valid, and second, finding the crack through which it comes."

"How well do you know this person, sir?"

"Not very well, why?"

Melliman knitted her brows as she answered. "Because, sir," she said slowly, "if you don't know her very well, why should you have any reason to trust her at all?"

Frye paused before he answered but decided it wasn't time yet to tell Melliman the truth. "A valid question, AOCO, to which there is but one answer—she is a relative who might well be worth trusting."

"Hardly a valid answer, sir. I think you should call Comnet Security and let them handle this. And if you don't—" she hesitated, then quickly went on, "well, by the rules and regs, if you don't report it, I must. You know that, don't you, sir?"

"Yes. Of course," Frye said slowly. There was no way of avoiding the truth now. "She's my daughter, Melliman."

"Captain Yednoshpfa, sir? How would she—"

"My other daughter," Frye said softly.

"Pardon, sir?"

"My other daughter," he repeated, "the daughter only three other people in the galaxy ever knew about. And two of those people are dead. You see, Clarest, this Barra claims to be my illegitimate daughter, and I believe she is. Now do you understand the problem?"

Melliman gently put her hand on his shoulder. "Yes, I do. But if I am going to help you, I have to ask you something."

"Go ahead."

She took a deep breath and let it out slowly before she resumed. "I am assuming that Vinita is not Barra's mother but that Vinita was one of those who knew, and Barra's mother knew, and both of them are dead."

"You are correct."

"Then the question is: Who is the other living person who knows about her?"

Frye almost smiled when he looked at her. "Meister Hadasaki," he said, watching her reaction, "and I don't believe for a minute that he is involved in this."

"Nor do I, at least not yet, anyway. She paused and rubbed the end of her nose with the knuckle of her thumb. "There is another alternative, of course, that someone completely unknown to you discovered that she was your daughter and is—"

"That would have to be pretty complicated," Frye said pensively. "Wouldn't it? That person would not only have to know about Barra and how to penetrate our communications but would also have to know about our spies on Mungtinez and about a troop buildup there that could be verified."

"Then it has to be Hadasaki," Melliman said quickly. "He is the only one with access to all that information. He doesn't have to penetrate security. He has access to the information from the spies, and he knows about your daughter."

"I thought about Hadasaki last night and rejected him immediately for one simple but important reason. He never knew my daughter's name. Even if he had found that out, he wouldn't know to use the ekename, Barra, that I gave her mother. Only Barra's daughter would know that."

Melliman sat on the edge of the desk. "All right, sir. If we assume that these messages are from your daughter, what do we do about them?"

"Nothing. Not yet, anyway. For the time being we must proceed without taking the messages into account. Even if the Saks are increasing troop strength on Mungtinez, we have no confirmation that they are planning to invade the Ivy Chain."

*   *   *

"There are times, Admiral," Mica said, "when the service's demand for secrecy seems to get out of hand."

"You think your father should have told us more?" Pajandcan asked. "You think that just because you're his daughter you should be treated differently than—"

"Go easy on her." Dawson smiled. "I don't think that's what she meant at all."

"He's right. I didn't mean that, Admiral," she said quickly. The last thing she wanted now was for Pajandcan to be angry with her. "What I was, and still am concerned about, is how do Admiral Dawson and I prepare for our new assignments when we don't know what they will be."

"You'll find out soon enough." Pajandcan felt some of the same frustration, but she knew better than to share it with her subordinates. "I'm sure that when you two join BORFLEET, all your questions will be answered."

"Sounds like you quoted that from the book," Dawson said.

"No, sir," Mica said to Dawson, "she is right about all that." For some reason Mica thought about how much she was going to miss POLFLEET's officers and crew. No, that wasn't it. She hadn't really made any close friends in POLFLEET. It was Pajandcan she was going to miss. Now she understood what had been bothering her since she had gotten her orders.

Pajandcan saw the strange look on Mica's face and wondered what it was all about. "Something else, Captain?"

"Uh, not exactly, Admiral, but, well, I would like a few minutes of your time before Admiral Dawson and I leave."

"Certainly. In fact, you can have it right now if Dawson doesn't have any further questions."

Dawson shook his head. "No questions, Admiral, not from me. Remember, I'm just a civilian you tricked into this position. Since I can't get out of the system until the war is over, there's no sense in arguing with it."

"You like it, Dawson. Admit it," Pajandcan said. "If you didn't have a war to fight, you wouldn't know what to do with yourself."

"Not true," Dawson said, holding up his hands. "I was once a happy tree farmer on Granser's Planet before Sondak forced us to fight for our rights. You still don't see it, do you, Admiral? Sondak—namely, the Joint Chiefs and their militaristic government—is the cause of all this."

Pajandcan had heard this speech from him before. "That doesn't change what I said. You like what you're doing because you're so good at it."

"Eat dirt," Dawson said as he stood up.

Mica was surprised by the anger in Dawson's voice. She had never seen him this way before.

"Go pack," Pajandcan said quietly. "Captain Gilbert and I still have some business to attend to. Oh, and Dawson," she added as he was halfway through the doorway, "just for the record, I do understand."

Dawson mumbled something unintelligible and was gone.

"He's a good man," Pajandcan said absently, "but a very bitter one." With a quick shake of her head she let go of Dawson and turned toward Mica. "Now, Captain, what is it you wanted to talk to me about?"

"Well, uh, I—" Mica shut her mouth. *Just say it*, she told herself. "It seems to me, Admiral, that, well, that there is some unfinished business between us, and I didn't want to leave without trying to clear it up."

"Like what?" Pajandcan suspected that Mica was talking about their personal relationship, but it wouldn't hurt to let her introduce the subject.

"Well, for one thing, I wanted you to know that I never said anything derogatory about you in my reports to Father."

"I never thought you did."

"You're not going to make this any easier for me, are you?"

Pajandcan hesitated. "Until you make it clear to me what it is you want to talk about, I don't know how I can do anything but listen, Captain."

Something about Pajandcan's attitude made Mica feel awkward and uncomfortable. "Look, Admiral, I know you haven't exactly appreciated my presence in your command, but I think we just started off on different frequencies. I have a great deal of respect for you now that I didn't have before, and . . . and . . ."

"And what? If you've got something else in your exhaust, so blow it out." The subtle hostility in her voice made her wonder just how much Dawson had gotten to her.

It was as though Mica's mind were blank, as though she

had never really had anything to say at all—but she did. She knew she did. "I never really knew my mother," Mica said suddenly, surprised by the words coming out of her mouth. "Oh, I mean, she was around, but she was never quite *there*, if you know what I mean. She had a problem coping with everyday life, so we tried to protect—"

"What does this have to do with us?" Pajandcan asked tensely. The last thing she wanted to hear about was Mica's mother.

"Please, Admiral." Mica didn't know exactly why she had brought up her mother, but she knew intuitively that by talking about her mother, she might be able to make Pajandcan understand what she was feeling. "This is very difficult for me," she continued. "I have to tell you in my own way."

"No." Pajandcan was angered. How dare Mica presume that she had a right to discuss her mother? Pajandcan knew no reason why she should have to listen to this. "Either tell me what all this has to do with me—and us—or keep it to yourself."

Mica felt a tremor under her ribs and did her best to steady herself. "All right. I'll try to say it as simply as I can. My father is going to Bakke, and you are going to meet him there, right?" When Pajandcan nodded, Mica rushed on, desperate to get it out. "When you see my father, if anything happens—between the two of you, I mean—tell him I love him and I think you'd be good for each other."

For a long moment Pajandcan didn't know what to say. Her anger was gone, and she was touched and a little amused. Mica was giving her permission to resume her affair with Josiah! If Mica hadn't been struggling so hard and so seriously to get it out, Pajandcan would have laughed. This child, his child . . . and suddenly it made sense. Pajandcan's heart tingled with an emotion she couldn't identify.

Mica watched Pajandcan's expression go from amusement to something else that ended in a slight reddening of her face. "Do you understand what I mean?" she asked, needing to have some assurance that Pajandcan hadn't misunderstood.

"I'm not sure," Pajandcan said finally, "if you are giving your father and me permission to have an affair, or if . . ."

"Not just that," Mica said. She leaned forward and touched Pajandcan's hand for a second, then sat straight in her chair and pulled her hands into her lap. "More than that."

With a quiet laugh Pajandcan said, "Mica Gilbert, I believe you're playing matchmaker."

It was Mica's turn to blush, but the laugh had broken the awkwardness she felt. "A woman could pick a lot worse for a second-mother."

"Thank you, Mica." She felt the moistness in her eyes and hoped she could hold her tears in check. "That's probably the highest compliment I could ever expect to receive."

"I'd better go pack," Mica said, standing up quickly. "Good-bye, Admiral."

"Good-bye . . . Mica. Be good to yourself."

"I will. You, too." As she left the office, Mica thought she would always remember the smile on Pajandcan's face.

18

Somewhere deep in her dreams Marsha had been aware that the ship was braking, but it was only when that awareness stopped that she awoke. She pulled on her jumpsuit, zipping it closed as she headed for the cockpit, where she found Lucky still at the controls. "Where are we?" she asked sleepily as she moved up close beside him.

"Unless we've made a severe navigational error," he said, putting his arm around her waist and giving her a little hug, "we are sunside of the ninth planet from the star designated—"

"Are we here?"

"If we're not here, Mars, we're nowhere!" Lucky cried as he checked the nav-readout in mock panic.

"Don't tease me. I'm not awake yet. Is this where Xindella told us to meet him?"

"It is indeed, my sleepyheaded partner," he said with a grin, "and it looks like we're the first ones here. Now, go wake yourself up and then come back and take over so I can get some sleep." He slid his hand down and began rubbing the back of her thigh in the way he knew she liked.

"Did you try calling him?" Marsha's brain was slowly registering the facts as her body responded to Lucky's caressing massage of her leg.

"I did, all the way into the system. No answer. That's why I assume we are the first to arrive."

"All right," she said, yawning. "You go get some rest. I'll watch the ship."

"Are you awake enough?"

"I'm awake enough," she said, pulling him up and giving him a quick kiss on the nose. "Go. Sleep. You'll need it. I'll put out a call every hour or so on the frequencies he gave Delightful Childe. Now, go. Go."

Lucky kissed her, thought momentarily of doing more than that, then headed for bed, suddenly very aware of how tired he was. He had meant to eat something first, but now the only thing that really interested him was sleep.

Five long, boring hours later Xindella finally responded to Marsha's call.

"Welcome, Captain Yednoshpfa," Xindella's voice said over a steady crackle of static from the speaker. "Am I correct in assuming that you and Captain Teeman are here as representatives of my cousin and the neutral alliance?"

"Correct," Marsha answered, wondering exactly where Xindella had hidden his ship, "but I'm no longer a captain, remember? If you'll broadcast a beacon, we're ready to join you."

"Please, then, Citizen Yednoshpfa, how foolish do you think I am? I have no intention of conducting this festbid, uh—how do you humans like to say it?—face-to-face? Yes. This will not be conducted face-to-face."

"Then what are we supposed to do? Just sit here?"

"Another of your quaint phrases, but an accurate one. Yes, Captain Yednoshpfa, keep your ship where it is right now, and as soon as all interested parties have assembled, I will give you all the rules and the festbid will begin."

* * *

Inspector Thel Janette had been sitting in her small Sci-Sec Lightspeed-Packet-Runner monitoring Teeman's ship since it had entered the system, waiting for Xindella to reply so she could move against him before the Ukes arrived.

Now as she listened to Xindella's conversation with the woman Yednoshpfa, she cursed aloud and tried to get a fix on Xindella's transmission. What she discovered gave her cause to smile. Xindella was smart. His ship was somewhere directly between the ninth planet and the sun. It would be impossible to get a fix on him because of all the radiation interference from the sun itself.

She had not accounted for this possibility in her hasty planning. Foolishly she had assumed—as Yednoshpfa and Teeman had apparently assumed—that Xindella would conduct the festbid face-to-face, as he said. His way was much safer for him because no one need see him at all, and no one was going to be able to track him down until he moved.

"But wait," she said aloud, "there is something else I could do. If I could take readings from five or six different locations, I might be able to get a close approximation of where his ship is—assuming it isn't moving and that I have time to shift at least three times to locations enough apart without being detected getting there."

She paused and considered the problem. "Big assumptions, old girl," she said softly. "Very big assumptions. But I won't know unless I try, will I?"

This habit of talking to herself was a new one, and she vowed to break it—after she got the weapon back to Sondak space. If her glass-lidded supervisors had listened to her instead of Caugust Drautz, they'd have sent a whole team in a heavily armed ship. "But no, he convinced them the Wallen was only a harmless prototype, not worth the effort," she said sarcastically. "And they believed him. Idiots."

After a long sigh she sat up straight. "Can't worry about them now, can I? Just be glad they gave me a ship big enough to bring the damned thing back in—and maybe enough credits to win it." As quickly as she could, Janette picked a theoretical spot, set the controls, and began accelerating. She had barely turned the LPR over for decceleration when she heard the Ukes calling Xindella.

* * *

"Make them identify selves," Ayne insisted, popping a piece of gorlet into his mouth.

"You consume that far too quickly, Citizen Wallen," Xindella said. "Our gorlet supply is not unlimited, even with faith."

"Your problem," Ayne said, eating another one. "You do not give us the gorlet, we cannot work. Is simple, you see. You provide gorlet. We work."

"Is not simple," Xindella said, mimicking Ayne's gentongue

dialect as best he could. "You eat all the gorlet before we can get more and you be very sick scientist."

Ayne felt only a momentary flash of fear, followed by an unnerving anxiety. He quickly squelched that with yet another piece of gorlet, savoring its gentle sweetness as he pressed it against the roof of his mouth and let it melt under the pressure of his tongue so that the flavor slid in a delicious trickle down his throat. If it was necessary, Xindella would provide.

Xindella watched his human companion for a moment, then reached out with one of his seven-fingered hands and closed the gorlet drawer, pushing the hidden lock at the same time.

"No!" Ayne was dismayed.

"You must wait," Xindella said. "If necessary, I will ration your supply. It would make me sad to see you sick."

"No, no, no," Ayne repeated as he tried to unlock the drawer. "Two more. Please, Xindella, just two more. Just two, that's all. Just two more. Then you can ration us."

"Wait," Xindella said sternly, "and stop begging, or I will put you back in the—"

"Will not work," Ayne said, crossing his arms petulantly over his chest. "No gorlet, no work."

"No work, no food. No work, no sleep. No work, no gorlet, Citizen Stupid Scientist," Xindella said shrilly. He punctuated his statement with a long snorting sound through his proboscis that caused Ayne to clamp his hands over his ears.

"Stop! Stop! Will work," Ayne said as Xindella made the sound a second time. It was a sound he had come to hate as much as he loved the gorlet, for it was a sound that roared straight to the center of his brain in a grinding whirlwind filled with pain. "Stop, please, stop," he said again.

Xindella stopped and bared his blunt yellow teeth in the Oinaise approximation of a human smile. Then he opened the gorlet drawer and took out two pieces. When Wallen grabbed them, Xindella quickly shut and locked the drawer again. "Go work," he said simply.

Ayne gobbled the first piece, wanting it, needing it, afraid Xindella might take it back. The second he held tightly in his hand, afraid not to have any gorlet left, afraid he would need it worse later than he did now.

"Work," Xindella repeated. As Ayne edged out of his seat, Xindella turned back to the transceiver. "U.C.S. ship registry seventy-seven-two-oh-nine, identify your commander."

Ayne was almost out of the control room when he heard the Ukes answer.

"We are commanded by Marshall Judoff, who sends the trader Xindella her special greetings and admiration."

Without thinking, Ayne ate his remaining piece of gorlet and immediately hated himself for doing it, Xindella for not letting him have more, and Sjean Birkie for having driven him to this point in his life—but most of all, he hated himself.

* * *

"The alien demanded that it speak directly to you, sha," Group Leader Kuskuvyet said with an odd leer, "but I told him you were resting and would talk to him when and only when you—"

"You dirt-brained fool," Judoff said as she rolled out of bed and reached for her clothes. "You weren't suppoed to aggravate him. How will that help us any?"

"But, sha, I only meant to make sure he understood who was worthy of the most respect."

"Double-fool! You insult him and then expect us to be able to obtain the weapon? He is already angry because you cheated him out of ten thousand credits. If you hadn't done that, we wouldn't be facing this problem now."

As she fastened her trousers to her blouse, she stared at him, standing there, head hanging, feeling sorry for himself. "If you hadn't been such a sexual magician," she said slowly, "I would have done more than demote you from Vice-Commander to Group Leader, Tana. And I suspect that someday in the not too distant future I'm going to pay a higher price for your body than I ever intended . . . just because you are so stupid."

"I am sorry, sha," he said, raising his eyes to meet hers, "very sorry, but . . ." His voice trailed off under her glare.

"Come, Tana. It's not that bad." She put her hand on his arm. "Let's go talk to Xindella."

They went directly to the bridge and had the communications officer call Xindella. It quickly became obvious that he was not about to speak to them when no one answered their call.

"Keep trying," Judoff said, giving Kuskuvyet a withering glare. "If we have to, we'll go bump his ship."

"We have not yet located it, sha," a handsome young Third Actual said. "We have the other two ships, but not the alien."

"And why not?"

"Many pardons, sha, but the alien is somewhere between us and this sun. Our equipment could not screen out enough of the interference while he was transmitting. We might be able to locate him with a few changes in the equipment, but now, since he is neither moving nor transmitting, we are like blind men searching for light in a cave."

"That is all very poetic, Actual," she said, obviously measuring him with her eyes, "and I would certainly be interested in hearing about any changes you think might improve our equipment—some off-duty watch when you have the time. But have you no suggestions for what we can do right now?"

The Actual shook his head, a slight blush coloring his cheeks. "Nothing, sha, until he transmits or moves."

"Very well. We'll do what we can to get him transmitting again. Group Leader," she said, turning to Kuskuvyet, "I want you personally to keep calling until Xindella answers. Also, prepare three homing missiles and lock one each on the two targets we know and the third on the alien when we find him. I will be in my cabin."

Kuskuvyet was almost hoarse by the time Xindella deigned to answer the call. In less than a minute after the answer came, Judoff was sitting at the ship-to-ship transceiver.

"How good to talk to you again, Xindella," she said, "especially after the unfortunate misunderstanding that ended our last transaction."

"Lies. Human lies. It was no not-understanding thing, Judoff. You cheated me. Now you will pay through your Uka nose until it hurts you," his voice said through heavy static.

"Let that be in the past," she said, "and let us talk about the present. When can we examine the weapon?"

The static rumbled. "When you own it," Xindella answered. "Only the festbid winner can examine our prizes."

"But we must examine it. Otherwise we would be bidding blind, accepting only your word that it is in satisfactory condition and useful to—"

"It is in satisfactory condition. How you use it is your affair, not mine. In a short while I will explain the rules and the bidding will begin."

"Absolutley unacceptable," Judoff said, leaning closer to the transceiver. "We cannot, will not, bid until after we have inspected the weapon and assured ourselves that—"

"Then leave, Judoff," Xindella said, once again interrupting her. "That would mean less competition, but there is absolutely, to use your word, no way anyone except the winner will be allowed to inspect, examine, or even know the whereabouts of the weapon."

Judoff raised an eyebrow. "Do you mean that you don't have it? That it's not here?"

"In a short while I will announce the rules and the bidding will begin," Xindella repeated.

"There has to be some way we can compromise on this," Judoff said. "Surely you understand that we cannot bid until we are sure the weapon is intact and all that you claim it is."

"The winner will do that before paying."

*   *   *

"Lucky," Marsha called for the third time, "wake up."

A groggy answer came back over the intercom. "Why? What? What's happening?"

"Xindella just announced that he is about to give the rules. Grab a couple of cafpicks and get yourself up here."

Minutes later Lucky stumbled in and handed her a cafpick. "Okay, when's he going to do it?"

"Soon," she said, "but I have a feeling that this may take longer than any of us expected."

Lucky rubbed his eyes. "Why?"

"Because Marshall Judoff is the U.C.S. representative."

"Judoff? Didn't you tell me something about her?"

"Only that she's mean and dirty and doesn't like to play by the rules but will, if she can, bend them her way."

"Sure. I remember," Lucky said, rolling his neck around. "She's the one who pulled her ships out."

"One and the same. Anyway, she's arguing that she isn't going to bid for anything she can't see and is demanding inspection rights."

"And our host objects? I don't understand. You mean he—"

"Attention, all bidders," Xindella's static backed voice said from the ship-to-ship speaker, "I am pleased to announce that all interested parties have arrived, and I can give you the rules. You are listening, little Sondak ship, aren't you?"

A long interval of uninterrupted static came from the speaker before Xindella spoke again. "It is very simple, little Sondak ship. I saw you enter the system. I know where you are right now, and I assume you are trying to locate me. In a moment I will give the rules and open the bidding. If you are no longer interested in participating, we would all appreciate it if you would withdraw from the system. Otherwise Marshall Judoff and her battle cruiser might mistake you for a hostile force. That would indeed be a shame if it were to—"

"Tell the dirty Sak we already consider it hostile," Judoff's voice cut in.

"Sondak ship registry Laurel-twelve-twelve-four-four," a clear female voice announced."

"That's Janette!" Lucky said angrily. "I should have known she would be here, but I damn sure—"

"Inspector Janette?" Xindella's scratchy voice asked.

"Yes," she answered.

"How undelighted I am to hear your voice again, Inspector, and I must warn you that there are some here even less delighted than I. However, now that I have everyone's attention, and since I have personally met at least one member of each bidding delegation, I trust you will take me at my word for manner in which this festbid is about to work. Now if you—" A long burst of static cut him off.

Marsha looked at Lucky. "Wonder what's going on?"

"Who knows, Mars. Sunburst, maybe?"

"Pardon the interruption," Xindella said a few moments later. "A member of my crew seems suddenly to have become ill. If you would, please, indicate your readiness to proceed, starting with the representative of the Neutral Alliance."

"Ready," Marsha said quickly.

"Sondak?"

"Ready," Janette's voice said in a distracted tone.

"United Central Systems?"

"I still must insist that we be allowed inspection of—"

"Judoff! Either you are ready, or I will terminate this festbid and give the weapon to someone worthy of it."

"The U.C.S. is ready—under protest," Judoff said slowly.

There was another burst of static before Xindella spoke

again. "The rules are simple. The bidding will begin at fifty thousand credits, an amount offered to me prior to this meeting, and will proceed until none of you are willing to raise the bid. Once that occurs, the other two parties will leave the system, and I will make arrangements with the winner . . .

"Oh, and one more thing. Should any of you harbor foolish ideas about doing violence either to me or the winner, I must tell you that I have provided for that possibility with an armed escort that would be only too happy to earn the bonus I promised them for blowing you to dust if you break the rules."

"Fifty thousand," Janette said.

Lucky nodded. "Sixty," Marsha said.

"Sixty-two," Janette responded.

"Sixty-five," Judoff said, entering for the first time.

Marsha put her hand over the microphone. "No bidding while she has the top, right?"

Lucky sighed. "That's what we agreed on."

"Sixty-seven," Janette said.

Marsha waited, expecting Judoff to raise the bid.

"One hundred thousand credits," Judoff said confidently, as though she expected no opposition beyond that.

"Thank you, Marshall Judoff," Xindella said. "Your bid allows me to inform you that we have a silent bidder who instructed me to open her offer only after the bidding had reached one hundred thousand."

"Unfair!" Judoff cried. "How do we know that you are not the silent bidder?"

"You have no way of knowing that, Judoff. However, I have only one offer from this party, which I am neither authorized to raise nor to lower. If none of you are willing to top that offer, then the weapon and its creator go to the silent bidder. If you are willing to exceed that bid, you will hear no more about her."

"Tell us, you scoundrel."

"Why Inspector Janette, what harsh words you use sometimes. The silent bidder offers one hundred fifty thousand credits."

Marsha and Lucky listened intently to see if either Judoff or Janette was willing to go over that.

"What do you think, Mars?" Lucky whispered. "We sure didn't expect this."

"No. I don't know what to do. Delightful Childe said we could go up to two hundred," she whispered back, "but who else would be bidding?"

"I don't know, but I think we'd better offer more."

"One hundred fifty-five," Janette said.

"One sixty," Lucky responded.

"Who was that?" Xindella asked.

"One hundred sixty thousand credits from the Neutral Alliance," Marsha answered.

The next pause lasted several minutes, until Xindella said, "In a traditional festbid the festmaster says, 'For the bidder to have. For the bidder to hold. For the bidder to keep.' If there are no interruptions before the festmaster says to keep, the bidding is concluded. So I begin. For the Neutral Alliance to have. For the Neutral Alli—"

"One hundred seventy thousand."

Marsha looked at Lucky with a sigh of relief. That was Judoff's voice.

"One hundred eighty," Janette said almost immediately.

"Go to two," Lucky whispered to Marsha.

"But what if Janette—"

"She won't. I think she's in over her head already. Besides, I think both sides are willing to let us have it. That's why Judoff waited so long."

"That doesn't make any sense."

"Just do it, Mars."

"Two hundred thousand credits," Marsha said reluctantly.

Again there was a long silent pause before Xindella said, "For the Neutral Alliance to have . . . For the Neutral Alliance to hold . . . For the Neutral Alliance to Keep!"

"He sounds pleased enough," Marsha said.

"I thank you all," Xindella said. "And now I must ask the other parties to withdraw from this system."

* * *

"Good-bye," Judoff said, "and good luck." She switched off the transceiver and turned to her Attack Coordinator. "You're sure the third missile will pick up the alien once he starts to move?"

"Yes, sha. Positive."

"Then launch your missiles. Kuskuvyet, as soon as the missiles are launched, head us out of the system, slowly."

"Yes, sha."

Judoff turned to the image of this almost deserted system on the holomap and stared at it, seemingly lost in thought.

"Missiles away. Beginning departure procedures," Kuskuvyet said from close beside her.

"This has to work, Tana, and it has to work quickly," she said. "I'll be busy enough reorganizing our fleet once we return. I don't want to waste any more time here because of stupid mistakes."

"I understand, sha. We will get the weapon."

Judoff's only response was a worried shake of her head.

* * *

"Why have you not begun departing, Inspector Janette?" Xindella's raspy voice asked.

"Just a minor problem," Janette lied as she fired the tiny homing device toward *Graycloud*. "But I have it fixed now. Good-bye, you soundrel."

"Good-bye, Inspector. May we never meet again."

"Can't tell about those things," she said as she fired the LPR's maneuvering rockets. "Keep your nose clean." In spite of herself she laughed when she thought of Xindella's half-meter-long nose.

* * *

"When those two have cleared this system, I will contact you with further instructions," Xindella said. "I guarantee this on my honor as Delightful Childe's cousin. Our friends are departing rather slowly, probably trying to listen to what I tell you, so I suggest you rest for a while, as you will not have much time to do that later. Is that agreeable?"

"It is agreeable," Marsha said; then she turned to Lucky and whispered, "What do you think?"

"I think," Lucky whispered back, "that Judoff and Janette haven't given up yet. We'd better be extra careful, Mars."

She could only shake her head and wonder where all this was going to lead.

19

If his insides had known how to do it, Henley would have swallowed his heart. Instead, his heart threatened to escape up his throat, and it took all his control to hold it down.

He tried to distract himself by thinking about the last fifty days since his arrival on Mungtinez. In that time Sergeant Denoro had managed to whip him painfully into top physical condition along with the rest of Ingrivia's Z-company, and he had managed to form some interesting friendships among her troops. Most of the company couldn't understand why someone as old as he was would volunteer for their heavy training schedule, but later many expressed their respect for him because of his efforts, and that made him feel good.

Now Ingrivia's Delta Company and two other Z-companies from the Three Hundred Seventy-First Legion were packed in a landing craft that was plunging through the dense atmosphere of a planet code-named Fruitbasket, in a system code-named Vine One. As the landing craft vibrated and shuddered it reminded Henley far too much of the ride down to Sutton that he had taken with Caffey almost a year earlier. The worse the shuddering got, the more he strained to hold back that same kind of nausea.

Rasha'kean looked across the narrow aisle in the crowded troop bay and sympathized with the pale expression on Stanmorton's face. No matter how much they had practiced mock landings back on Mungtinez, nothing could have prepared them for the real thing, because the real thing was frightening. Crammed onto the decel-benches were more troops and equipment than the landing craft was ever meant to carry. The air was heavy with the smell of sweat, and nausea, and fear.

But Rasha'kean felt more exhilaration than fear. She was proud to be here, proud that her unit had been chosen to be part of the first assault, and more proud that she was finally going to get the revenge on the Ukes for her mother, for her father, and, in some symbolic way, against the treacherous Uke cousins her mother had told her about.

All of that made up for the queasiness she felt under her exhilaration and on impulse she gave Stanmorton a thumbs-up sign. Just as she did so, the landing craft lurched heavily, then seemed to float for a second before slamming to a bone-jarring stop. They were down.

Immediately the deboard horn filled the craft with its staccato series of blasts. Seconds later the big, square loading hatch opened, and Denoro was already standing in the narrow aisle between benches, shouting for them to unbuckle and move out, cursing the ones who were too slow, and physically jerking some of the troops onto their feet.

Henley stood with a sense of relief and followed the troops in his company. His nose was almost touching the pack in front of him, and the trooper behind pressed against his back. They moved slowly down the narrow aisle until they reached the hatch where the pressure from behind them spewed them out onto Fruitbasket's spongy soil.

Several craft had landed before them, but everything looked chaotic. Commanders shouted orders. Troops ran in every direction. Two, then three, more landing craft burned their way out of the sky close to them. In the distance the firing of heavy weapons rolled toward them with dark certainty.

Someone screamed. Henley turned in that direction in time to see a landing craft crash and crumple atop a low, rocky ridge eight hundred meters away.

"Let's go, Chief!" Denoro shouted.

Henley shook his head, saw her waving, and ran to join the company as it formed a double-staggered-V and began moving toward the sound of the heavy weapons.

"You keep to my right flank," Rasha'kean told him when he caught up with her and Denoro. "I want to know where you are at all times."

"Will do," he replied. "Where's Archer?"

"He's supposed to come with the second wave." She paused and sighted through her polar compass. "We'll guide on that split rock to the left of the gap in the ridge, Denoro."

"Guide to the left of the gap!" Denoro shouted to the platoon leaders, "On the double! And keep your military eyes open!"

Her order was relayed by the platoon leaders. The point

troops turned, and the company shifted behind them. They jogged slowly across the spongy field, then ran at a well-disciplined pace when the ground got harder as they approached the ridge.

Henley wished they would run faster. He hated the open field and the danger it represented. The heavy weapons fire sounded as if it were just on the other side of the ridge. If they could get to the rocks, at least they would have some cover.

A piercing whistle filled the air. Henley was diving for the ground even as someone yelled, "Incoming!"

Two rounds exploded behind them. Then three more. A light shower of mud and rocks spattered their backs.

"Move out!" Rasha'kean shouted. "They d'not have the range. Move out! Move out!"

The troops were on their feet quickly with Henley close behind, their V-formation ragged but still intact as they ran from the explosions. They scrambled up the rocky ridge, weapons ready, fear riding behind them as the explosions got closer.

The point troops had almost reached the top of the ridge when the air rattled with automatic weapons fire. Three troops fell. Another screamed and clutched her gut as she tumbled backward down the slope.

Henley ran a few more steps and dodged behind a low, flat-sided boulder, his heart pounding insanely.

Twanging bullets splintered the rock just above his helmet. Fear burned in his gut. He pressed himself closer to the rock and tried to see if there was anyone else close to him.

Upslope he could see people firing back at the unseen enemy. Downslope another company was pinned down by the light artillery fire that chewed up the ground between them.

Then he saw Ingrivia worming her way between the rocks, belly hugging the earth, with Denoro hard on her heels and the Commo Tech close behind Denoro. Another burst of fire splintered his rock, and he ducked as low and as flat as he could go.

With her rifle cradled in the crooks of her elbows, Rasha'kean crawled past a wounded trooper. "Check her, Denoro," she said without pausing. Her first priority was to control this ridge and secure the landing zone for General Archer.

Ahead she could see two bodies, lifeless and bent, and another wounded trooper already being bandaged by a fourth. Slightly beyond them in a narrow defile between slab-shaped rocks, five of her troops were pouring fire back at the enemy. As quickly as she could, she crawled up the defile until she reached the first of them.

"How many are there?" she asked.

"Don't know, Colonel," the trooper said, his pale face dripping with sweat. "Can't see them."

"Cease fire," she ordered. Four more startled faces turned to look at her. "Count your ammunition and sound off."

None of them had more than one hundred rounds left.

The enemy had paused, too, as though waiting to see what she was going to do. Denoro crept up the defile beside her.

"Menikos will live, Colonel. We have two dead and three more wounded. I called for fire support. We should have it any time."

"Good. Get some more ammunition up here and Lieutenant Haultcour with the rest of his platoon. As soon as the mortars cut in on our reception committee, Haultcour can take his platoon to the head of this defile and flank them. Or lead us out of here if the mortars are doin' their job."

Henley waited twenty or thirty seconds after the firing subsided before trying to see what was happening. As he did so, he heard a roar. Looking up, Henley saw a larger landing craft with a fireball clinging to its tail wobbling out of control down toward the field behind them. He barely had time to bury his head in his arms before it crashed in a tremendous explosion.

A fierce wind filled with debris tore at his clothes. The heat scorched his exposed neck. He fought for breath in the stifling air. Only the shelter of the rock kept him from being wrenched free and swept away. He felt an odd pain in the back of his head, and everything went black.

Before the wind had subsided, Rasha'kean had her platoon leaders checking their troops. Meanwhile, her point troops had gained the top of the ridge without taking further fire. Apparently the enemy had withdrawn. Haultcour's platoon secured the top of the ridge, and after she had satisfied herself that everything was in order, Rasha'kean joined Denoro and the Commo Tech in the shallow depression between rocks where the medics were treating the wounded.

"That was General Archer's ship," Denoro said when Rasha'kean sat beside her. "And the chief caught a rock in the head."

Rasha'kean's stomach turned several times. "You sure about Archer?" she asked, praying it was not true.

Denoro nodded slowly. "We're sure."

"How's the chief?"

"He'll be all right except for a minor concussion and a fierce headache. He's just a little groggy right now."

"We'll leave him here with the rest of the wounded and get the rest of the company to the top. Haultcour's spread pretty thin up there."

"Will do," Denoro said, rising to her feet. "Then what?"

"I d'not ken," Rasha'kean answered. "We'll hold what we got until we find out who's in command and what they want done."

*   *   *

Frye released a long sigh and looked straight into Hadasaki's eyes. "I have reason to believe that my eldest daughter is privy to Sondak military secrets," he said slowly. "She warned me that the Saks were going to hit the Ivy Chain, but I didn't believe her."

"You mean you knew this was coming?" Hadasaki asked angrily.

"I meant what I said, Meister. I received a warning that I could not verify. Consequently, I put the occupation commander out there on alert, and at least they were not caught totally unprepared by the Saks."

"Why wasn't Bridgeforce informed of this?"

"Because, Meister, until you and Bridgeforce relieve me of my command, decisions like that are mine to make. As soon as I received the first verification that Sondak ships were entering the Ivy Chain, I notified you."

"I am disappointed in you, Charltos. Very disappointed."

"Then relieve me," Frye said quickly, his own anger overflowing. "Either I am in command or I am not. Decide. Call a Bridgeforce meeting and decide. It's Bridgeforce that has endangered us in this—"

"Be careful. Be careful, Charltos. Do not let your frustrations cause you to do something rash."

"Dammit! I'm up to my chin in your conservatism. Bridgeforce chose this war. It chose to attack Sondak. But ever since then it has been retreating from the kind of commitment necessary to win the war. You take it. You command. I quit." Even as he said that, Frye felt relieved.

"You cannot quit," Hadasaki said patiently. "We will not let you quit."

Frye wanted to turn his back on Hadasaki in the ultimate gesture of disdain, but he forced himself to remain calm. "Order as you will, Meister Hadasaki," he said in carefully controlled words, "but do not allow yourself to be surprised if your orders—Bridgeforce's orders—are slow in being carried out."

"I believe that is called treason, Admiral."

"No, Meister. That's disgust. No one wants to win this war more than I do. But no one is more hampered in his attempts to win it. I have to put up with the kyosei and Judoff. I have to put up with the damn bombship project. And I have to live with Bridgeforce constantly second-guessing everything I do and compromising every plan for victory I present."

Hadasaki smiled. "You're getting better, Charltos. I must admit that I have had my reservations about you—too reserved, too polite, too stuck in the conventions, too timid for the job you were given. But now, now I think you might be stronger than I believed."

"How long have you known me?" Frye asked.

"Since you were an officer applicant," Hadasaki said, "Why?"

"Because you should have known before now whether or not I was strong enough. If you didn't, you were stupid."

Hadasaki laughed. "I believe you're right, Frye. So how are we going to adjust to this new Sak move?"

"We'll have to divert part of our invasion fleet to harass them in the Ivy Chain and prevent them from advancing any further. Then we'll need to—wait." Frye suddenly realized what he was doing. "I thought you were disappointed and ready to get rid of me?"

"You're the one who brought up that foolishness about leaving. And I was disappointed. But this enjoyable display of aggression from you has helped me overcome that. Now, back to what you were saying. What elements of the invasion fleet do you want to use for this harassing defense?"

If was Frye's turn to smile. "The flank reserve fleet under Commander Fugisho."

"Why? Half of that fleet belongs to Judoff, and she'll be screaming for it when she gets back from her auction."

"True," Frye said, "but even she wouldn't pull them out of a defensive position. In fact, I think she would find certain advantages there."

"You will have to enlighten me."

"Judoff's long-range goals seem to be ones of coming out of this war with more power than anyone else. If she is in the defensive position, she is closer to Gensha, closer to the seat of power, and closer—at least in her estimation—to achieving her goal."

Hadasaki shook his head. "If you are right, then what you suggest is dangerous."

"I understand the dangers, sir. But I believe it makes the most sense from a military perspective. The flank reserve fleets are made up of mostly older, slower ships. Why shouldn't they be the ones used in a defensive effort while we use our newer, faster ships to strike at Sondak? Besides, I think Commander Fugisho functions better heading an independent force."

"Like when he attacked Oina?" Hadasaki asked sarcastically.

"Exactly. He was only acting creatively on the basis of Judoff's orders. Not bad having someone with a little imagination in charge of defense."

"I suppose not, Admiral. Shall we confer with the rest of Bridgeforce on this?"

"Give me a day, sir. Then I can present a unified plan for consideration," Frye said, rising from the chair.

"Very well, Charltos." Hadasaki gestured for him to sit down. "There is something else we have to discuss—your newly emerged daughter. Where is she?"

"I don't know," Frye said. He didn't sit down because he did not want to be trapped into a long, pointless discussion about Barra. "All I know is that she seems to know what the Saks are planning and has found a way to relay that information."

"I see. Well, then, I suppose I should let you get to work.

But you will notify us immediately of any further information you receive from her."

"Of course, sir. I'll let you know personally as soon as I hear from her again. If I hear from her, that is," he added, wondering if she would contact him again.

20

"Why did Ranas not accompany you?" Leri asked. She knew the answer, but she still had hope that he would change his mind.

"He declined, Proctor." The translator on the back of his carapace squawked seconds behind his clacking whistles, and Glights twisted a claw around to adjust it as he spoke again. "Ranas did not give a reason, and I did not press him for one. However, he did say he would contact you as soon as he had anything further to report on the messages from the Verfen."

"Do you have any opinion about this, Glights?"

"No, Proctor. I only wish we could communicate with home to see if the Verfen have tried to contact Castor, also."

"How soon before you will know?"

"Ten of our seasons. Maybe twelve. There is a fairly strong radiation storm somewhere between Cloise and Castor, but my technicians assure me that it should dissipate fairly soon."

"And in the meantime you fight the pirates."

"We try, Proctor. The human ships are heavily armed, and they are using collecting techniques we have never encountered before. Their main ship seems quite capable of collecting methane while moving, so they collect, and we chase them, and periodically they pause for reasons we do not understand, and then we fight. It has not been an easy thing."

"I do not want your excuses, Glights. I want you and your human mercenaries to fulfill your agreement and rid Cloise of the pirates. Can you do that or not?"

"We are trying, Proctor, but the humans are dangerous and cunning, and now they have two of the new collecting ships, each with ten ships guarding it. It is no easy thing."

Leri spat a fireball over his head in frustration. "Leave me, then, and go do this difficult job of yours. And tell Ranas I want a full report."

"As you wish, Proctor," Glights said, backing from the chamber and clacking his claws over his head.

Every time a Castorian did that, Leri felt a small chill curl down her spine. It was a gesture she would always equate with the treacherous Exeter, who had tried to eat her and whom she had executed in the fires of revenge.

As quickly as she could, she dismissed those thoughts and turned on the music of Shetotem, her favorite composer. She called for the Isthian who had been waiting to exchange with her since before Glights's appearance and then began her meditations. As usual, the Isthian slipped into the chamber unseen and climbed quickly up her back to the nipple on her neck. She felt its reassuring presence and said, "Welcome, tender one."

"May the Elett bless you," he replied.

"And may you share the blessing."

"The mighty Verfen are coming to Cloise, Proctor. Does that interest you?"

"The Verfen? Coming here? How do you know that, tender one?" If he had told her she would bear a Castorian's guplings, she could not have been more surprised. A message from the Verfen was troubling enough, but to have them come to Cloise?

"My Confidante told me. Shall I tell you more?"

"Of course! Yes, please, tender one."

"Let us make the exchange first. I sense you are in need."

Leri did not want to wait, but she would never have insulted an Isthian by demanding anything. Already he was sucking on her nipple, replacing her antibodies while taking his nourishment from her blood, and despite her anxiety about the Verfen, she felt herself relaxing. As Shetotem's music swelled around her, the Isthian settled into a steady, gentle rhythm, rocking against her, pulling back, stretching her nipple with firm strokes in time with the music. Slowly Leri gave herself over to it, letting her mind drift as her body warmed to the exchange.

She never felt the Isthian stop and was slightly surprised when he spoke softly, his breath cool on her wet nipple.

"My Confidante said the Verfen were coming for an exchange."

"Are they like us, then?"

"I do not think so, Proctor Leri. I do not believe they seek this exchange, yet I cannot say what it is."

"How does your Confidante know these things?"

"That, too, is a mystery. Perhaps it learned these things from one of my brothers in the sky. My Confidante does not tell much, and the questions are hard."

Leri smiled to herself. "What else do you know, tender one?"

"Very little." The Isthian paused. "My Confidante said it had been a long, long time since the Verfen had been here, since before anyone can remember, but their coming—"

"They've been here before? I don't understand. There is no record of the Verfen actually coming to Cloise."

"That is true, Proctor, but my Confidante seemed quite sure about that and said that their coming would be a time of peace and turmoil, and questions and answers."

Leri shivered. "This frightens me, tender one."

The Isthian gently stroked her nipple. "Do not fear, Proctor. I caught no sign of concern from my Confidante. Now, forgive me, but I must leave."

"May your blessings double, tender one."

"By the grace of the Elett," he said before scuttling off her back and disappearing behind her.

Leri was confused and upset, and that made her angry. Exchanges were usually times of rest and meditation, a release from tension, and a surcease of worry that left her feeling stronger and more content than before the exchange. They should not be times for disturbing questions.

What could the coming of the Verfen mean? Who knew anything about the reclusive aliens from the center of the galaxy? Why would they want to come to Cloise? And how did the Confidante know they were coming?

Should I question a Confidante? she wondered. Would it do any good? Or would I only get questions in return? Only once in all her experiences with Confidantes had one actually made a positive statement. Every other time they only asked questions, good questions, to be sure, questions that helped her find solutions to her problems, but not statements.

Yes. She would seek her favorite Confidante.

Weecs entered her chamber just as she started to leave. "Ranas wishes to speak to you," he said.

"Good. Yes, of course," she said quickly. Perhaps he had some of the answers she needed. She slithered past Weecs and rushed to the communicator in the adjoining chamber. "I'm here, Ranas," she said anxiously.

"Greetings, mate of my nest," his voice crackled from the ancient communicator crystal. "I have disturbing news for you and for all of Cloise."

"The Verfen are coming," she said.

"How did you know?"

"An Isthian told me. He said that he had learned it from a Confidante. Is it true, Ranas? What does their message say?"

"I believe it is true. I will read our translation of their message, but you must keep in mind that we cannot be sure of our accuracy."

"I understand. Please read it." Her heart pounded as she waited for him to read.

"Very well. It begins, 'To Leri the Proctor of Cloise, and all (something untranslatable) of Cloise's burrows and (we believe the next word means *deep* or *depths*), the (untranslatable) of the Verfen and all (the same word as before) from our *depths* assure you that your protection will begin upon our arrival, being ready to (something) and accept our trust.'" He paused.

"Is that the whole message?" she asked.

"No. The rest of it was easy to translate because it was mostly binary numbers, several dates, and two sets of coordinates. The problem is that they don't mean anything to us. We have no equivalency chart to tell us what their dates mean relative to ours. We don't know what the coordinates are for or why they are included in the message."

"And nothing else, Ranas? This doesn't make any sense."

"We think the last part is a request for confirmation."

"The more I learn, the more this frightens me, Ranas. I want you to return to help me determine what can be done. While you are doing that, I am going to a Confidante to seek—"

"No. I'm sorry, Leri. I cannot return."

"But Ranas. I need you here."

"And I must stay where I am. It is my decision, Leri. Do not anger yourself over it."

She trembled. "By the grace of the Elett, I will try to accept your decision," Leri said slowly, "but by the same grace I pray that you will reconsider."

There was a long silence before his voice spoke again. "You question a Confidante. I will stay here and encourage your translators. Together we may come more quickly to a solution. I will talk to you again at the end of the next season."

"By the grace," she said, "be careful."

"By the grace, mate of my nest, I will."

As she left to go see her favorite Confidante, Leri felt as if a hard, thin tail were wrapping itself around her heart.

*　　*　　*

"Archer's dead, sir," General Schopper said as soon as the aide let him into Admiral Stonefield's office. All the Joint Chiefs were waiting for him. "We just received the news. The Ukes shot his lander right out of the sky. Brigadier Newby, Colonel Langford, and most of Archer's staff died with him."

"Damn," Stonefield cursed.

"Who's in overall command?" Josiah Gilbert asked as he thought about Mica being with the invasion fleet.

"Dirtside, it's Colonel Elgin. He's our most experienced officer out there right now. For the fleet, it's Admiral Ticjicsic with Dawson as his second."

"What were their initial losses?" Avitor Hilldill asked. "How bad was it?"

"Heavier than we expected. The first-day summaries from Elgin and the legion commanders indicate that the Ukes were waiting for us."

"A security leak?" Stonefield asked. "Or efficient Uke preparation?"

"Whatever it was, they were defending three of the four landing zones we picked and had closed on the fourth one within two hours of the landing," Schopper said. "I request the Joint Chiefs' permission to go forward immediately and take overall command of this operation."

"That's how we lost Mari," Erresser said sharply.

"I'm hardly the ranking general in the Planetary Force" Schopper said. "McLaughlin, Novak, King, and Danielites, all have either seniority or rank over me."

"No," Stonefield said. "We cannot afford the risk of—"

"Then who are you going to send if you don't send me? There aren't enough generals around with combat experience who aren't pretty creaky in the joints right now."

"I think he's right," Gilbert said. "We can bring General

McLaughlin in here immediately. She's already somewhat familiar with the planning and goals of our operations."

"But she's in the hospital," Admiral Lindshaw protested.

"She got out yesterday."

"But is she fit for duty?"

"The doctors said she was," Stonefield said, "and of all the senior generals, she probably had more combat experience in the last war than the others."

Gilbert was pleased that Stony was making Schopper's case for him and hoped the others saw the logic in the decision. "I think McLaughlin's the logical choice. With her experience and familiarity with the planning, plus her availability, do we have any better choice?"

"I suppose not, Josiah," Stonefield said. "But sometimes I think we're crazy to send our most talented people forward."

"That's where the war is," Hilldill said. "Don't tell me you haven't wanted to chuck this administrative job and get out there yourself, Stony?"

Stonefield ignored the question and turned to Schopper. "It looks like we've decided that you can go, Thedd. How long will it take you to turn over your office to McLaughlin?"

Schopper smiled grimly. "If she's ready, two days at most to get her current and enhance the background she already has."

"Unless anyone has something to add," Stonefield said, looking at the rest of the members of the Joint Chiefs, "I think you'd better get started immediately. I'll get someone down in transport to find you a route that involves the least hassle, and Josiah, you can contact General McLaughlin. Anything else?"

"Maybe there is something else," Schopper said suddenly. "You asked me if I thought Uke intelligence had sniffed out our plan or if they were smart enough to pick the right places. I think I'd like to know which it was."

"So would I. I'll put Fleet I.D. on it."

Gilbert snorted. "Fleet Investigations couldn't find its face with a mirror. My clerks are better investigators."

"Then what do you suggest?"

"Put Hilldill's people on it. Flight Corp has better intelligence networks than anybody else." Gilbert knew that Stonefield wouldn't like that suggestion because he didn't like Hilldill, but Gilbert hoped he would accept the facts and put his personal likes and dislikes aside. With Stony he was never sure.

"Can you take care of that?" Stonefield asked.

"Yes, sir," Hilldill said with a smile creeping onto his lips. And I thank Admiral Gilbert for his vote of confidence."

Schopper saluted. "I'll be going now."

"Check with me before you go, and make damn sure you take care of yourself out there," Stonefield said. "And tell McLaughlin—well, never mind. I'll tell her myself. You'll have enough to do."

"Good luck," Gilbert said as Schopper started to leave, "and God's speed."

"Thank you, sir. Thank all of you."

As he left, Gilbert watched him with a sense of trepidation, which was interrupted by Admiral Stonefield.

"When are you leaving for Bakke, Josiah?"

"Ten days at the outside."

"Then we'd better finalize these modifications to the plan. Are you sure that your fleet is going to be strong enough?"

"I am. Don't forget that we're going to add those ships that are waiting now in the March Cluster."

"I haven't forgotten that, Josiah. I just don't want to leave anything to chance."

Nothing to chance, Gilbert thought as he turned his attention back to the plans. His brain would try to leave nothing to chance, but the element that his heart wished most was more certain was totally outside his control, and that element was Pajandcan. He wished Mica hadn't spoken to both of them, but now that she had, Gilbert was surprised to find himself emotionally eager to see Pajandcan again, and that pleased and annoyed him at the same time. But even as he worked over the modifications with Stonefield, he sensed that part of his mind was still thinking about his meeting with Charlene Pajandcan.

21

The first thing Sjean Birkie remembered after Janette questioned her the second time was waking up in a darkened hospital room to the sound of someone screaming. Only after a nurse had come in, turned on the lights, and given her an injection did Sjean realize that she was strapped to the bed because she was the one who had been screaming.

After that, things got worse.

When she slept, she had nightmares about giant insects crawling around inside her skull and eating her brain, or of ice-cold talons that shredded her flesh, or of falling down an endless well while fluorescent demons laughed at her.

Again and again she would wake up screaming. Again and again someone would come into her room and give her a sedative. And every time she would try to fight the sedative, slapping herself to stay awake, haunted even in her stupor by the horror on the other side of consciousness. Yet no matter how hard she tried, she always lost the fight and the insane cycle would repeat itself again and again and again.

Sjean had no idea how many cycles she went through. All she knew was that one day she woke up with light shining through her window and she wasn't screaming. Her head ached with a dull, pounding pain, but she wasn't screaming. Something inside told her that she had exhausted the nightmares, and she clung to that hope-filled thought.

It wasn't true.

The nightmares returned. But after that day of sunlight, they did not come every time she slept. The headaches were still there, pounding away in the top of her head, yet gradually, very gradually, she knew she was escaping the terror.

Her doctors were impressed. They encouraged her, taught her mental-relaxation routines to go through just before she went to sleep, and carefully monitored her progress. Finally, after fifteen days with no nightmares and only minor headaches, they released her from the hospital.

The morning after her release, Sjean went to her lab, discovered that the Wallen detonator was missing, and immediately left to find Caugust. When she stormed into his office, he looked surprised to see her. "What did she do," Sjean demanded, "steal it? Or did she sweet-talk you into letting her have it?"

"Slow down, Sjean. Slow down. The doctors said you should avoid excitement, so calm yourself," Caugust said, "and tell me what you are talking about."

"You mean you didn't know the detonator was gone?" Sjean was sure that couldn't be true, but she was willing—no, wanted to give him the benefit of whatever small doubt she had.

"That project has been on hold since you went into the hospital," he said, avoiding her question. "It will take a while to put together a new team for you. That will give you—"

"What happened to the detonator, Caugust?"

"The project was put on hold," he repeated. "As I was saying, while we are putting a new team together—"

"Dammit," she said putting her hands flat on his desk and leaning straight into his ruddy face, "answer my question. What happened to the detonator?"

Caugust tilted his chair back and looked at the ceiling, slowly shaking his head. "Janette took it," he said in a heavy tone of resignation.

"Just like that? She just walked into my lab and hauled it away?" Her head was pounding, and as she straightened up, a wave of dizziness swept through her.

"Sit down, Sjean. You look terrible."

"Yes," she said, leaning heavily against the arm of the chair as she sat down. "All of a sudden I feel awful." She paused and tried to read his face, which had a pained look of its own. "But that doesn't change the fact that the detonator is missing and you haven't told me why."

"Sjean, do you know how much of our business depends on the good will of Sci-Sec?"

"No. And I don't care. We're talking about something much bigger than—"

"We're talking about seventy-five percent of Drautzlab's business under government contract," he said sternly. "Janette would have gotten the detonator from us whether I gave it to her willingly or not. She was quite prepared to use the brain-search on me to find it and have it taken out of here."

"So, you let her brain-search me, but when it came your turn, you noviced out and gave the detonator to her." The sarcasm only made Sjean's head hurt all the more, but by now she had a great deal of experience in living with the pain.

"Yes, if that's the way you want to look at it."

"And do you know what she plans to do with it? Like attach it to something, some innocuous little device we'll all come to know and love?"

"I couldn't help it, Sjean. She'd have had it one way or the other. What difference does it make?"

"It makes a big difference. You could have tried to stop her or made her take the answers from you. At least then you'd have something left, some integrity . . . *something!*"

"All right. You've made your point. I'm a spineless scientist, afraid to stand up to the little inspector. There. Does that make you happy? Or would you rather I broadcast it throughout Drautzlab so everyone will know how worthless I am?"

Sjean felt suddenly embarrassed for him. "I'm sorry, Caugust. That's not what I meant to, I mean—"

"Of course it's what you meant, because it's the truth. Do you think I have no conscience at all? I've been over and over what happened, but there's no way I could let myself off the responsibility circuit."

"I believe you," she said softly, "but that doesn't change what you did. Or what you're asking me to do," she added.

"What am I asking you to do that's so wrong?"

He looked genuinely puzzled, and that distressed Sjean as much as anything. "You just said we would assemble a new team to go back to work on the Wallen. I can't do that, Caugust. Not now. Not after what's happened—and what may happen if Janette manages to get the other half and make the damn thing work."

With a sigh he said, "It has to be done."

"No it doesn't. That's the point, Caugust. It doesn't have to be done."

"Do you know who was here while you were in the hospital?" he asked suddenly. "An oversight investigation panel from the Tri-Cameral and the Combined Committees. Seems that Sci-Sec reported the weapon's existence to them and they came to assure themselves that we were making sufficient progress and had everything we needed to get it into production. Do you understand that, Sjean? They want us to produce fifty or sixty of the damn things."

"What did you tell them?" For the first time she fully realized how deeply troubled he was by all this and was sorry she had been so harsh in her judgment.

He shook his head sadly. "Luckily I was warned that they were coming, so I faked it—put your full team in the lab and told them to look damned busy when the panel snooped around. Then I told the panel that we were trying to work through some major difficulties."

"And that's it?"

"No. They were—how shall I put it?—most eager to have us run a successful test and begin production, and they made it very clear that our failure to do so would be reflected in the amount of government funding we would continue to receive."

"So you want me to go back to work on it?"

"That's up to you, Sjean. I don't have a choice. I need you on this, but after what happened, you might not be able to carry the necessary workload. However, with you or without you we have to resume the project. We can't afford not to."

Sjean hesitated, but she knew what she had to say. "I can't do it, Caugust. I can't be a part of that project any longer. And you shouldn't, either. You shouldn't let them run up your—"

"I have no choice." There was a weary darkness in his voice. "Drautzlab is my life. If I fight them, I could lose everything."

"Maybe you already have," she said sadly. "Maybe you already have."

* * *

"Charltos has gone too far," Kuskuvyet said as he entered her cabin. "We must cease the pursuit of the alien and return to Gensha at once."

"What are you talking about?" Judoff asked.

"This message from Brig Meister Owens. She says Charltos has splintered our fleet in this new offensive he has planned."

Judoff started and rose to take the message from him. "He what? How dare he? No one splits my fleet. No one!"

"Shall I give the order to make way for Gensha, Marshall?" he asked as she read the message.

"No."

"But Marshall, how can we continue chasing—"

"Shut up, you idiot, and let me think." Judoff looked up from the message and stared at the bulkhead for a long moment. "You are right, Tana. I must return to Gensha. But that does not mean that we should stop following Xindella. He has the weapon that can win this war for us with one sure stroke. That is too important an opportunity to abandon."

When she looked at him, there was a strangely cold affection in her eyes. "The *Kasavara*," he said suddenly. "We brought the *Kasavara*. And we have the crew to spare to . . ."

"To get me back to Gensha while you continue the chase," she finished for him. "It is a big responsibility I place in your hands, Tana, a very big responsibility." She watched his eyes drop. "But I am sure you are quite capable of dealing with the alien and bringing back the weapon. You have my confidence."

"Thank you," he said quietly as he raised his eyes again and straightened his posture. "I guarantee that either we will possess the weapon or no one will."

"That is good, Kuskuvyet, except for one thing," she said with a slight impatience in her tone. "Guarantee only that we will possess the weapon. It is far too valuable to be destroyed. Just get it for me. When you have done that, return to Gensha at once unless I tell you otherwise."

"Yes, sha, I will get it." He turned to the bridgecaller. "Prepare the *Kasavara* for launch immediately," he ordered, "minimum crew, and notify Marshall Judoff when all is ready."

He paused after receiving the acceptance of his order as though studying the distracted expression on her face. "What will you do once you get to Gensha?" he asked finally.

"I do not yet know," Judoff admitted. She sat down and rested her chin on a clenched fist. "I must pull our fleet back together and crush Charltos once and finally, and I have to do both things at the same time with the greatest amount of surprise and effectiveness. Have you any suggestions, Tana?"

"No, sha—I mean, I've hardly had time to think about it in the way you laid the problem." He hesitated. "However, given Charltos's almost-foolish reverence for tradition, would that provide some route of attack?"

"Yes, Tana, it just might. But I will have to be very careful. Bridgeforce has approved this division of our fleet, and Bridgeforce will be part of whatever method I use to pull it back together. Hmm . . ." She stopped speaking and again stared at the bulkhead.

Kuskuvyet broke the silence after only a few seconds. "I think there are loyalties at question that we previously took for granted. Lieutenant Oska should have sent this warning."

"Very good, Tana," she said, looking at him with a little smile. "You are learning. Take no loyalty for granted. Assume nothing. Prepare for the worst. If I had paid closer attention to that advice myself, this would not have happened."

"Uh, there's another thing. Didn't I read once that there used to be a confederacy agreement that auxiliary forces could not be divided without the commander's permission?"

"Yes, you did, but that rule was set aside during the last war, and I don't think— Wait, Tana. You're right. The rule wasn't rescinded. It was only set aside!" She smiled.

"And unless they have set it aside again, it has stayed in effect since the end of the last war?" Kuskuvyet asked.

"Exactly. Charltos and Bridgeforce have broken a rule of the confederacy."

Kuskuvyet frowned. "But couldn't they just set the rule aside again?"

"Perhaps," she said, the smile still lingering on her lips, "but they might be forced to put our fleet back together again before they could muster the vote to set the rule aside." She stood up, moved to her locker, and began putting her personal possessions in a small hyleather flight bag.

"Tana, I think we might just use that old rule to knock Charltos out and get the fleet, too."

22

"Another message from Barra, sir," Melliman said. "If this one is as accurate as her one about the Ivy Chain, we're going to have to adjust again."

"How in Heller's Fleet am I supposed to conduct a war based on intermittent messages from a long-lost daughter, Melliman? Read it to me."

Melliman cleared her throat. " 'Father,' it says, 'General Schopper and Admiral Gilbert plan a three-pronged attack on the U.C.S., beginning with coordinated attacks against Buth, Shakav, and either Fernandez or Cczwyck. Further plans are to blockade and bypass weaker systems like Thayne-G and strike toward Gensha and Yakusan. More to follow.' It's not even signed this time. I think she filled the burst she sent it in."

"And dared not send another? Dammit, Melliman, where is she and how do we know this still isn't a trap? It will take every ship and soldier in the U.C.S to defend all those systems at once. If we believe her, we'll be forced to abandon any offensive whatsoever."

"I know that, sir, but if we don't believe and act on it, the Saks could get behind us and be attacking Gensha in a matter of months."

"No," he said with a quick shake of his head. "This one we cannot believe. There is no way that Sondak could have enough warships to make a three-pronged attack, much less the ground forces it would take. And what about logistics? A set of attacks like that would require massive logistic support, and they don't have that kind of reserve. It's been all they can do to control our skirmishes in their polar systems."

"You're right, sir. I guess the first impact of her message made me feel very defensive."

"As it was meant to," Frye said with a frown. He had been struggling with how he must regard Barra ever since her warning about the Ivy Chain had proven true. Now he felt certain that her very first message had revealed her true sentiments. She had threatened him with defeat, and if he reacted to this warning of hers, he would most certainly be defeated.

"Something else?" Melliman asked.

Just looking at her could sometimes take a frown off his face. "Yes, Clarest. I've decided that until we can get some solid confirmation of this, all we need to do is raise the alert level in all our border systems. Otherwise we will proceed with the offensive approved by Bridgeforce."

"And if we get the confirmation? Shouldn't we have an alternate plan that will allow us a fast recovery and counter-strike?"

He saw the knitting of her brow and that strange look she got when she was concentrating on a problem. It had taken him a long time to acknowledge it, but Melliman had demonstrated over and over that she was smarter than Vinita had ever been. Once he admitted that to himself, then he had been forced to deal with what effect that had on his memory of Vinita. In the end he had decided it didn't have any effect. Vinita was Vinita, and Melliman was Melliman, and the better he came to know Melliman, the more he realized that he loved her for increasingly different reasons than he had loved Vinita.

"You have something in mind?" he asked when she didn't expand on her statement.

"I might if you can spare me for the rest of the day."

"Get Lieutenant Nellnix or Raybourn to handle the front office, and the rest of the day is yours," he said with a smile, "on the provision, of course, that I get you back this evening and you explain to me in detail what you're thinking on this."

"Can do, sir."

"Then why are you standing around in my office, AOCO?"

"I'm gone, sir." She started to leave, then turned back. "I'll be home by nineteen hundred. I have to meet Anshuwu Tashawaki at eighteen."

"I'll look for you then."

* * *

Leri heard her people hissing in the tunnels before Weecs, followed by several members of the Council, made his appearance. She knew at once that something was terribly wrong.

"Forgive us," Weecs cried.

"Forgive us, mother of hundreds," the Council responded.

Ranas! No! It couldn't be! Not Ranas. Oh, please, not Ranas. Her mind was a rush of confused prayers and grief.

"All hearts are in anguish."

"The many mourn his passing."

"The Elett are gracious," Leri said automatically. It was the litany of passing, and there was no way to avoid the truth. With each verse and refrain the surety of it sank into her heart. Ranas was dead. Ranas was dead, and it was her fault.

"By the grace of the Elett we were blessed with his coming."

"By the grace of the Elett he passes beyond us."

"By the grace of the Elett, our Ranas is gone."

Suddenly the litany was over, and everyone withdrew from her chamber, even Weecs—or especially Weecs, she thought, for he had already felt his share of the guilt about Ranas going to space and now must feel it even deeper. But not as deep as she.

Leri immediately regretted her selfishness. This was not the time to think about guilt. It was time to send her personal prayers to the Elett for the sake of Ranas's soul.

Instead of the music she favored for meditation and prayers, she put on the Deavor's Melodies, deliberately choosing those upbeat songs Ranas loved most, and tried to fit her chanting to their spirited beat. For some reason it worked almost without effort, and the syncopated rhythm whisked her through her private litany much faster than normal.

But when she was finished, Leri was disquieted by a sense of incompleteness. She almost felt as though Ranas could still slither into her chamber, saying, "Greetings, mate of my nest," and present her with some new problem or request. Of a sudden she knew what was incomplete. She was incomplete. There were so many things they hadn't settled between them, so many things she needed and wanted to say to him now that she could no longer say anything.

Leri felt angry that he had left her this way to deal with the dangling cords of their relationship by herself. If he hadn't been so stubborn, so determined to prove something to her, this wouldn't have happened. Why had he . . . Most of the answers were all too simple. She had caused the great rift between them. She had stupidly, falsely, accused him of not loving her enough, and in proving how much he did love her, he had died. Now she would have to cope . . . but not by herself, not now. There were too many other things pressing on her now.

As she had so many times in the past, Leri fled the confines of her chamber for the sanctuary of her favorite Confidante. When she slithered into the cave, it was already lit, and Leri sensed that she had been expected.

"Are you troubled, Leri Gish Geril?" the Confidante asked as Leri coiled her body loosely in front of the Confidante's great, gray, wrinkled form.

"Yes, I am troubled by many things," she answered.

"Are grief and guilt what trouble you most?"

"Yes," she said, letting her head relax on her coil.

"Have you chosen your successor?"

The question so startled Leri that she didn't know what to say. "Not exactly," she answered finally.

"Is Weecs not suitable?"

"Yes. He is very suitable, mostly because for all that he is fit for the duty, he does not want it."

"How soon can he take your place?"

"I don't understand, Confidante. Are you suggesting I should resign? Now, when there is still so much to be done?"

"Can Weecs not properly serve?"

For the first time since . . . since when? Since she had struggled with her ascension to Proctor. For the first time since then, Leri heard exasperation in a Confidante's voice. "Weecs is fit for the duty and can perform it," she said, using the ritual words of nomination.

"Are you ready to accept your grief?" the Confidante asked, changing the subject again.

"I am ready," Leri answered, and even as she prepared to do so, she felt a great burden lifting from her heart. Weecs would be the new Proctor. He would have to deal with the Castorians and the humans and the coming of the Verfen. Leri Gish Geril would be free of those troubles and might finally know peace.

"My grief has no bounds," she said, beginning the litany she had repeated so many times over her lost guplings, but for the first time, understanding it—really understanding it. "My grief has no attachments. It falls like the cold rain and flows through my heart. The way of grief is pure grief. It has no beginning. It has no end. The way of grief is old. . . ."

* * *

"Have you found a way for us to attack and defend at the same time?" Frye asked as Melliman sat across from him in one of the soft chairs.

"I think we'd better read Lieutenant Oska's message first," she said, taking it out of her small belt pouch and leaning forward to hand it to him. "Madame Tashawaki seemed greatly agitated when she gave it to me."

Frye tore open the double envelopes, took out the single sheet note, and read, " 'Brig Meister Owens has informed Marshall Judoff of your disposition of her fleet, and I have just received notice that Marshall Judoff is secretly returning to Gensha.' That's the sum total of it, Clarest," he said, handing the note back to her.

"This could mean serious trouble," she said.

"We're prepared. Hadasaki, Lotonoto, and I have already discussed this possibility. Did Madame Tashawaki indicate why she was upset?"

"She fears for her son, I think.".

"As she should. But we have been careful, and I don't think he's in any real danger." Frye stood and held out his hand, hoping that Lieutenant Oska had also been careful. "Now, Clarest, I put some food in the warmer, and you can tell me about this plan of yours while we eat."

"It isn't anywhere near a plan yet," she said, taking his hand and rising. "It's still a rather weak idea. Maybe my telling you about it will help me put the pieces in a more coherent order."

Only after Frye had served the food and they were seated at the table did she continue. "Among the many things I tried to get done today was accumulate a list of all, and I mean *all*, available civilian and commercial ships that we might be able to utilize. I don't think I realized until today how many different bureaus we have in this government of ours who have something or other to do with spacecraft." She paused and took a big bite of her meat.

"Too many, I'm sure," Frye said as she chewed. A briefly amusing thought occurred to him. They had talked so often over meals that they had developed a pattern. He talked while she chewed, and she talked while he chewed, and thus both fully participated, and neither had to eat their hot food cold or their cold food warm. Now it was his turn to chew.

"About forty-two major bureaus," she said, "some of which obviously duplicate the work of others but all of which are extremely protective of their interests and domains. In fact, there are ten bureaus, each of which regulates only commercial ships within a specific range of cargo capacity."

"The Bureaus of Class and Standards," he said before taking a sip of his wine. "I always thought that was a wasteful arrangement."

"So did I until I realized they had exactly what I wanted. I now have ten registration rosters sorted by size and last known location. Frye, if we only armed twenty-five percent of them, we would be doubling the size of our armed fleet."

"You mean with something more than the light lasers they're allowed to carry? That would be a dangerous precedent. Seems to me there were good reasons in the Confederacy Papers for keeping them from carrying heavy armament."

"Well, now we have a good reason to change that. Don't you see? If we put one military ship in command of every ten armed commercial vessels, we only deplete our offensive military capacity by ten percent and create a huge defensive force we never had before."

"The peace-traps would scream about that, and no telling what the Amarcouncil will do, unless . . . Clarest, suppose we proposed an idea like this so that the commercial ships were guarding their home systems? That would probably take a lot of the resistance away, don't you think?"

"I think you're right. I'll get the rosters."

"Finish your meal first. No sense in trying to do this on a half-empty stomach."

23

Pajandcan stood in the Admirals Receiving Lounge at the Garner Starport on Bakke and waited impatiently for the arrival of Admiral Gilbert's ship. It had been a long, long time since she'd been this eager to see him, and she wondered momentarily what that meant. Nothing, she assured herself. Absolutely nothing. But of course it did mean something, and the meaning was all connected to her last conversation with Mica Gilbert.

How strange it had been to have Josiah's daughter almost invite her to become part of the family. Even now it brought a nervous grin to her face. For all she knew Josiah might already have someone . . . or might not want anyone else in his life. And what did she want?

Pajandcan wasn't sure. The old differences she had felt so strongly about between her *homo electus* pride and his *homo sapien* egalitarianism now seemed childish and far in the past. She had learned a great deal since their young years together, not the least of which was that the *homo electus* were different only because they said they were. When it all came down to rivets and plates, there were no differences that mattered.

The most unexpected result of Mica's emotional revelation to her had come days later when Pajandcan suddenly realized that underneath all her years of shallow bitterness and petty complaints against him, Josiah Gilbert was one of the most decent, wonderful, lovable men she had ever known. That didn't mean that she still loved him. It only meant that she would now be seeing him with unprejudiced eyes for the first time in many, many years. At least that's what she told herself it meant.

For the tenth time in as many minutes she looked up at the arrival board again. Then she checked her chronometer. Josiah's ship should have been dirtside already. With a sigh she turned away from the board and sat in one of the heavily padded chairs.

There were seven or eight junior officers in the lounge, but they had given her wide berth after she had given them all cold stares. Now she was sorry she had done that, because talking with someone would help the time pass.

Just as she stood up and decided to take a fresh approach with them, the overhead speaker cut on with a sharp crackle of static. "Attention. The *Holden* is now landing at the senior gate. Repeat. Now landing at the sen—"

The *Holden*'s landing roar drowned out his repetition of the announcement, and Pajandcan relaxed for a second, knowing that the waiting was over, then tensed up almost immediately, thinking of how she would soon be seeing Josiah.

"Ah, Charlene. It's good to see you again."

It had been so long since anyone had used her first name aloud that it surprised her. "And you, too, Admiral," she said with a sharply executed salute.

Three of the junior officers stood slightly off to the side, obviously waiting to present themselves. "They yours or mine?" Gilbert asked.

"Must be yours, sir." Pajandcan smiled at them. "This is Admiral Gilbert. Are you going to stand at attention all day?"

A graying Fleet Captain named Tappan introduced the other two in quick order, then said he had transportation ready for Admiral Gilbert.

"That won't be necessary, Tappan," Pajandcan said. "Just see that Admiral Gilbert's baggage is taken to his quarters. He'll leave any further orders for you at the TOQ later this evening." As she returned Tappan's salute, Pajandcan saw the look of amusement on Josiah's face. "That is all right, isn't it, sir?"

"Most all right, Admiral. I just had a feeling that we'd done all this before."

"We did this more than once a few years ago," she said with a short laugh that took the tension out of her. "Old habits die hard."

"Especially good habits," he said, touching her arm. They turned away from the gate together. "So where were you planning to take me that those nice young officers couldn't follow?"

"Captain Tappan didn't look all that young. But to answer your question and get that amused look off your face, I was going to offer to feed you, seeing as how you probably haven't eaten in a few hours, and then I was going to grill you on why I'm here."

"We can do both at the same time," Gilbert said.

"I was going to let you eat in peace, but if you can put up with my questions, we'll do it your way. Here's your skimmer."

The guard held the door as Gilbert climbed into the passenger compartment. "The Senior Officers Club," Pajandcan said to the driver before following Gilbert and sitting opposite him facing the rear.

Once the doors were closed, the passenger compartment was soundproof, cut off from the driver and guard by a triple sheet of glastic above the seats. As the skimmer lifted and started to move, Gilbert leaned forward. "It really is good to see you again, Charlene, but I have a strange question for you."

Pajandcan noted the return of his expression of amusement and wondered what he was thinking about. "Ask away."

"Just what in the name of holy spacers have you and Mica been talking about? I received the strangest message from her before I left Nordeen . . ." The blush on Pajandcan's face made him pause. "Is there something wrong?" he asked innocently.

"Not exactly," Pajandcan said, "but since you brought this up, I'm going to give it to you as straight as I can. Your daughter, your bright, talented, sensitive daughter, has taken an inclination to play matchmaker." To her surprise, Gilbert showed no surprise.

"So that it is," he chuckled. "That's how I interpreted her message, but it was so out of character for her that I could only believe I had misunderstood." After a moment's hesitation, he decided to ask the question he'd been thinking about all the way from Nordeen. "What do you think of all this, Charlene?"

It was her turn to laugh. "Runs in the family, doesn't it? All this jumping to conclusions, I mean? Look, Josiah, we have a lot of things to talk about, military and personal. Let's see what we learn from that." For some reason Pajandcan felt panic creeping into her, as though a whirlwind were about to sweep her away. "I will say this, though. I haven't been this pleased to see you in years."

Hours later, as they lingered over wine, Gilbert said, "So, you understand the layout of the invasion plan and how we're going to coordinate your fleet's invasion of Buth with my invasion of Shakav, but we haven't touched Mica's subject."

"Is that what we're going to call it? Mica's subject?"

"You have a better name for it?"

"I'm not sure there is an *it*, Josiah. And I doubt if we'll find out in the short time we're going to have here."

"Are you saying that—"

"I'm saying that I don't know, and I won't know anything except that I'm glad we've finally gotten our friendship out in the open. Beyond that we need some time to make sure that friendship is deck solid, and then some more time to truly get to know each other again. We've been separated these many years, Josiah, and managed to keep some kind of affection for each other. Whatever it is we have won't go away before the war's over."

Josiah Gilbert wanted more than that and sooner than that, but he remembered from their years before that she did not like to be rushed. "That's quite a speech," he said. "Maybe you should write it down for me so I won't forget and start to make untoward advances." He smiled to hide a blush, unable to remember the last time he had been so openly flirtatious.

She laughed. "You, Admiral Josiah Gilbert, sir, have my personal permission to make all the untoward advances you wish. However, you must promise on your honor as an admiral of the fleet not to laden my responses with any meaning not immediately obvious." Pajandcan knew that the alcohol had loosened her tongue, but it only let her put into words some of the signals her heart was sending.

"Then I suggest that we retire to my quarters where we can relax and discuss this further in private."

"An excellent idea," she said, feeling twenty years younger and happier than she had been in a long time.

As they were leaving the Officers Club feeling good about themselves and each other, Captain Tappan walked in the door.

"Priority message for you, sir," he said handing the envelope to Gilbert, "from Nordeen."

Gilbert tore it open and read it, then silently handed it to Pajandcan. Her eyes filled with tears as she stared at the words. Admiral Dawson had been killed in a mass hunk attack off the Ivy Chain.

* * *

"I fear, Captain Teeman, that we are being followed by both parties," Xindella's voice said from the speaker. "That is going to make the consummation of our arrangement much more difficult than I had hoped it would be."

"You mean you didn't plan on this? I can't believe you thought either the Ukes or Sondak would simply let us take the weapon and go," Lucky said. "From what I've heard, you're supposed to be much shrewder than that."

"Flattery, Captain, is quite meaningless in this particular situation. I did expect one or the other to follow, since I expected one or the other would win the festbid. I never assumed that you—the Neutral Alliance, that is—had a real chance. My contigency plan, unfortunately, did not allow for dual pursuit."

"Your equipment must be better than ours. How far behind are they?"

"One thousand exatrens."

"Can you convert that into tachymeters? I never did quite understand exatrens."

"I cannot, but it does not matter, Captain. Suffice it to say that they are close enough to follow us out of subspace as easily as they followed us in."

Marsha leaned over Lucky's shoulder. "I have an idea. Couldn't we close with you, make the transfer, then head in opposite directions?"

"An excellent idea, citizen, except for one thing. What is to keep them from closing with us while we are closing with one another? Your prize isn't something I can hand you, you know. It fills almost half of *Profit*'s main bay."

"Then what are we going to do?"

A deep fluttering sound came over the speaker, followed by a long moment of silence. "Captain, stay close. We are about to exit subspace close to—never mind. Just coordinate your exit with mine."

"Understood," Lucky said. Two minutes later they exited subspace, and Lucky began to brake *Graycloud*.

"Where did he go?" Marsha asked from the nav-chair. "We've lost him, Lucky. No, wait. We passed him. But if you don't put on full dampers, we will lose him."

"Hold on!" Lucky cringed and put the inertial dampers on full. *Graycloud* began shuddering as the dampers absorbed too heavy a load all at once. "Xindella! What the tensheiss are you doing?" Lucky screamed into the transceiver.

"Zzzaug-dit-dit Gouldrive failurrrssss," his voice came back. "At-t-t-try starrrrr—"

"Fix on the closest star, Mars," Lucky said as he eased off slightly on the dampers. The shuddering was reduced to a low vibration.

"I've got it. Deflect forty-five toward the fix. That's as close as we'll get until we recover maneuvering."

"Wonder what happened to our escort?"

"One of them just overshot us by about sixty thousand kilometers. I don't see any sign of the other."

"So what do we do now, Mars?"

"Ride out the curve and then see if we can find Xindella," she said. "What else can we do?"

"We could just get the tensheiss out of here and leave Xindella to Judoff and Janette. They all deserve each other."

"We can't, Lucky. You know that. We have to complete our part of the agreement. Then if you want to take off for somewhere else, you'll get no fight from me."

"Why? Really, Mars, what difference would it make?"

"All the difference in the galaxy." Marsha understood his frustration, but she also had confidence that deep down inside he didn't mean what he had said.

"I suppose," he said finally, "but sometimes I wish we could just fly away from it all and find someplace quiet where we could do whatever we please without having to cope with galactic government and war and greed and plain lightspeed stupidity."

She reached over and put her hand on his arm. "I don't know where there is such a place, but once we turn the weapon over to Delightful Childe, I'd be more than happy to go look for it with you. Will that do?"

"Mars, I love you. Yes, that will do."

"Good. Now go fix us something to eat while I keep an eye and ear out here. It will be at least three hours before we can start searching for him."

Lucky got out of his chair, leaned over, and gave her a kiss. "Three hours, huh? Lotsa things can happen in three hours."

"But who would watch . . . or does it matter?" she asked after he kissed her again. "Probably not. I don't think we've ever made love in hard decel before."

He pulled her to her feet and wrapped his arms around her. "First time for everyone," he said.

*　　*　　*

Henley stood with Sergeant Denoro across the road from Ingrivia's company. They had finished their meal, and Denoro had suggested they take a casual walk. Despite all the walking he had done in the past ten days, Henley agreed, and they set off down the road at a pace that would have been considered casual only by Denoro. They hadn't walked far, but Henley was glad when they returned to the company area and stopped. He was tired.

"Tell me, Denoro, do you understand what happened? Why didn't the Ukes put up more of a fight?"

"Looks to me like once we broke through their initial resistance, they didn't have much fight left in them or enough troops to fight with. They were sittin' thin all 'round, as my old training sergeant used to say. Anyway, what does it matter? The occupation corps will be down soon, and we'll be up and heading for rest and retrainin'."

"You're beginning to sound like the Colonel," Henley said. "Pretty soon you'll be using her odd contractions."

"Already caught myself at it once or twicet. Got to admit, though, her way of talkin' i'not as hard on the ear as some I've been hearin'."

Henley laughed. "If she catches you making fun of her like that, you're liable to hear something else that's hard on your ears."

"I'm careful. Besides, Chief, the Colonel's all right. Even if she heard me, I don't think she'd mind."

"I woul'not mind what?" Ingrivia asked from behind them.

Henley and Denoro looked at each other, then fought to smother their laughter.

"How many private jokes do you two have at my expense?" Rasha'kean would have loved to have been in on their secret, but in a way she was glad she was not. That gave her something to tease them about. "Never mind the answer," she said. "Denoro, get the company to scour their equipment and pack it tight for travel."

"Orders?" Henely asked.

"Orders," she replied, "but d'not even begin to ask for where. General Schopper wa'not tellin' us, and I ca'not be tellin' you what I d'not ken."

"I'll get 'em started, Colonel," Denoro said with a quick salute. She immediately headed across the road where Delta Company was lounging out under the shade of an orchard whose blossoms made the air heavy with their scent. Many of the troopers were obviously sleeping off their midday meal.

"Schopper didn't tell you anything?" Henley asked, hoping for something he could grab onto for a story. The Ukes on this planet had fallen so quickly, that after the landing assault Ingrivia's company had not been involved in anything that would count as a real battle.

"Only that we were going to hit another planet as quickly as we could reassemble and ship out."

"Is that his plan? To hop from one planet to another, system to system, straight into the U.C.S.?"

It was at times like these that Rasha'kean wished Stanmorton were somewhere else. She would probably never understand why he constantly asked questions she could not answer. "Ask him yourself, Chief. He's hot on his way here from Nordeen to get us ready for the next hop, as you put it."

Henley smiled. "That's it Colonel. This was all his plan to begin with. We're all going to be part of General Schopper's Planet Hoppers."

Rasha'kean was amused in spite of herself. "I d'not believe the general would like such a name."

"General Schopper the Planet Hopper. General Schopper's Planet Hoppers." Henley repeated the two variations several more times. "Has a sound to it, doesn't it?"

"A childish sound, Chief. Bairn-rhymes, my mother would have called them. And not to be changin' roles, but might I ask a question? Is your equipment squared away? If I'm rememberin' correctly, you're still attached to my unit, are you not?"

Henley could see what was coming and tried to dodge it. "I am, Colonel, but I need to get this story—"

"You need to get your equipment ready, Chief Stanmorton. Your story will wait, but I wi'not. I suspect your 'Planet Hopper' would be displeased if I di'not take proper care of you, so get to work."

Henley saw the twinkle in her eyes and decided to see how far she was willing to play this game. "But Colonel, if I do that, I'm going to miss my—"

"That's an order, Chief. By the regs I can only give you orders as regard your health and safety, and this is one of those times. Now move."

As he started to cross the road, she cursed.

"Colonel?"

"There was something' I was meanin' to ask you, Chief. Have you heard the rumor that we lost an admiral up there?"

"Yes, but as far an I know, it's nothing more than a rumor. The Ukes could have started it for all we know."

She motioned for him to come closer. "Chief, I d'not want this gettin' down to the troops, but I suspect it's more than a rumor. We're short one ship—Admiral Dawson's. Part of our briefing after General Schopper signed off was how we were going to adjust for the lost space."

Henley never liked to give credence to rumors, but what she said made a certain amount of sense to him. "You're probably right, Colonel. Rumor says the system was full of Uke hunks after we landed. But you're also right in not wanting the troops to know. They'll hear it officially soon enough. No sense in knocking their morale down with it now."

"Thank you, Chief. I appreciate your opinion on this."

"Colonel, you can have my opinion any time you want it. You may not always appreciate it, but you're certainly welcome to it."

"Better get your equipment ready," she said.

This time he didn't argue with her.

As she watched Stanmorton cross the road and enter the orchard, Rasha'kean was annoyed by all the ambivalent feelings that were tangling her thoughts. Part of her was glad she had Stanmorton around, and part of her wished he was gone. Part of her was sure it would be a mistake to mention Dawson's death to her troops, and part of her thought she should be honest with them. No matter what she decided about those things, she ken she would second-guess herself.

With a shrug of her shoulders she followed Stanmorton, grateful that she did not have that kind of trouble when they were fighting the Ukes.

24

As Quarter-Admiral Rochmon scanned the preliminary investigation report, he had an odd feeling that something was missing. This report covered the same basic information that the last security investigation on Bock had covered. Date and place of birth, parents, grandparents, acquaintances, schooling, previous employment—it was all here, as neat and concise as the analysis reports Bock herself wrote for Cryptography. Even the innuendos and hearsay comments fit neatly into a pattern.

Maybe that was it. Maybe it was too neat, too concise. There should have been some evidence in here of Bock's bizarre sexual appetites, not just rumors, and some indication of her unruly temper—but there wasn't. Why? he wondered. Fleet Investigations should have been able to find something more than rumors about those things. It didn't make any sense, and Hew Rochmon needed for it to make sense.

Ever since the spitting incident, Bock had been acting in an unnaturally polite way. He could have accepted her new-found civility as evidence that she had taken his warning to heart, but he knew better. Bock was playing some game with him. Too many times before she had misled him, dragging him so far into her private game that by the time he realized what was going on, it was almost always too late.

The first time had been the worst, because she had used him sexually and then invited him to a party with some of her more unusual friends. Only when the lights went out and the projector went on did he learn that the purpose of the party was to view a video recording she had made of their lovemaking. It still embarrassed him just to remember it. That incident taught him to be on guard against her, but she still tricked him in little ways after that.

The problem, the damnable problem, was that she was a better cryptographer than anyone he had ever known. Even now, in the midst of this new game, she was making huge dents in the Ukes's Q-3 code and with any luck would break it in the very near future. For that reason alone he would put up with more from her than he would from any ten other people.

He sat up straight, took a deep breath, and as he let it out, flipped back to the first page of the report, ready to go through it one more time. He began reading slowly, looking again for some solid clue to what was bothering him.

"Bock to see you, Admiral," his aide said over the intercom.

"Send her in," Rochmon ordered, closing her folder.

She was through the door and making straight for his desk almost before he finished speaking. It was obvious that she was very, very angry.

"What it it, Bock?"

"Hew Rochmon, you motherless son of a Castorian turd, I ought to walk out of here right now and let you break this stinking code yourself."

"Sit down, Bock," he said steadily, "and tell me what you're so all worked up about."

"You, you sneaking vermin," she said, waving her arms. "You put the scabbing FID on me! I can't go anyplace. I've got the damned MGs with me every hour of the day that I'm not right here in this section. Isn't that enough? Did you have to put the FID on me?"

"Not me, Bock. You put them on yourself."

"Like crap I did!" She glared hard at him. "You get them off me or I quit. You understand that?"

"You sit down and listen to me," he said calmly. "Now." He waited until she finally seated herself before he continued. "You can't quit. Remember? Stonefield said he'd pull you back into the service and then court-martial you. When will you learn, Bock? I'm not the one who's been stirring up the goldsleeves. You are. You kick a beast, you expect to get bitten. What I—"

"But I've been so nice," she complained.

"Yes, you have. But this current FID investigation started before your new nice game."

"What do you mean, game? I'm just doing what you told me to do—treating people with courtesy."

"Bock, if I believed that, I'd be the stupidest man in the Service. I've watched you in action too many times to believe what I see on the surface. Something's working in your head, something I'm sure I'm not going to like."

Arms folded, she leaned back in her chair. "I want them off of me, Hew. I want them off of my past and out of my life."

"Talk to Stonefield. He's the only one who can stop them now," Rochmon lied. "Or learn to live with the fact that someone in FID is going to know everything there is to know about you." To his surprise, he thought he saw a flash of concern cross her face. "Does that worry you?"

"No. I have nothing to hide. It's the intrusion I hate." She paused as she stood up. "Do you have to make the appointment for me to see Stonefield, or can I make it myself?"

"Either way. But I don't know why you're bothering. You know he isn't going to stop it."

"Maybe yes, maybe no, but . . . Hew, just what is it they're looking for, anyway? I don't understand."

"Sins, Bock. All your sins. You have committed a few sins,

haven't you?" Again he saw a flash of concern alter her face for a second.

"It's my parents, isn't it?" she asked slowly. "They're looking for some mistake my parents made, something with the right hint of scandal that they can use against me. Admit it."

"Not as far as I know," Rochmon said. "It's your mistakes they'll space you for, not your parents'."

"My parents didn't do anything like that. My father had the bad luck to die when I was very young. My mother worked hard, kept me fed, and educated me as best she could to prepare me for school. Then she married my second-father and got another chance at happiness. She hated the investigation that got me my clearance, and she hated last year's even more. Now the FID snoopers are asking all her friends questions again, all because of me."

"Can't be helped. You've angered Stonefield. You've angered Gilbert, who used to defend you. And you've angered almost every senior commander attached or assigned to Cryptography. You can't anger that many powerful people and not expect to catch some flak for it, Bock." He shook his head. "Why can't you understand that?"

"And you don't think Stonefield will call it off?"

"I know he won't. Just ignore it. Tell your parents that it's all routine and let it go. FID'll stop sooner or later."

"They damn well better, or I'm going to give the goldsleeves something to really get angry about." She turned on her heels and left his office.

Another act, Rochmon thought to himself, but frayed around the edges this time. Sooner or later she was going to say or do something that would give her game away, and he only hoped he was there to see her fall.

*   *   *

"Marshall Judoff's back," Melliman said, "and she's raging through the building like the Terminator of Texnor."

Frye smiled. "Amazing. One thing about her, she never ceases to amaze me. What possible good does she think a temper-tantrum is going to do her? And why in public? Why not save it for the Bridgeforce meeting?" Looking at Melliman standing there in her sharply pressed uniform made him feel good. "Are you ready?"

"Yes, sir. I'm ready for anything, including the Mad Marshall."

He put his hand on her arm and pulled her to him. Giving her a quick kiss, he released her with a wink. "Were you ready for that?"

"No. I thought you said—"

"Just wanted to make your day more interesting."

"You did it. Too bad we don't have more time to—"

"Not while we're on duty, Clarest."

"That's what you said about kissing."

Frye winked again. "Pardon my momentary lapse in military decorum, AOCO. I assure you it will not happen again."

She gave him an exaggerated pout as she picked up her briefcase. "Now I'm really disappointed, sir. I request that you reconsider."

"Let's go face Judoff," he said. "We'll discuss this later . . . in a more appropriate setting."

Her face brightened. "Yes, sir."

As they left the office, Frye didn't know why he was feeling so playful, especially when he had a set of serious problems, including Judoff, to look forward to. But for some reason he wasn't in the mood to get serious yet today.

When they entered the Bridgeforce meeting room, his playful mood evaporated. Judoff was already there, giving Meister Hadasaki a rapid-fire lecture about the impropriety of splitting her fleet. Hadasaki was listening stoically, refusing to respond to her anger.

"And you!" she said when she spotted Charltos. "You're the one behind all this, and you're the one who's going to pay the highest price for what you've done. AOCO," she snapped at Lieutenant Oska, "give me the Confederacy Papers."

"Greetings, Meister," Frye said to Hadasaki, "and good day to you, sha. It's nice to see that you've returned safely from the auction you were so excited about." He walked past her and took his place at the head of the table. "Did you get that little weapon you went after?"

"Yes." She took the bound papers from Lieutenant Oska and shook them in Charltos's direction. "I'm going to burn you with these, Charltos."

"Why don't you save your histrionics until the remainder of Bridgeforce arrives? I'm sure they'll be as interested in your little performance as I am. How is the March Cluster this time of year?"

"How did you know I went to the March Cluster?" she asked as she shot a sideways glance at Oska.

Frye knew he shouldn't have said that, but he recovered quickly. "Bridgeforce has a vital interest in your welfare. Do you think we would let you wander off without keeping a watchful eye on you?" As he spoke, the remaining six members of Bridgeforce filed into the meeting room with their aides and translators.

"I demand an official roll call," Judoff said, "so that future historians will have no doubt about who was present at this meeting."

"Very well," Frye said. "By rank and seniority, according to the rules. Meister Hadasaki?" Ally, Frye added in silent evaluation of the most important part of this roll call.

"Present and ready to fight," Hadasaki said with a grin.

"Vice-Admiral Lotonoto?" Sympathetic, swing vote.

"Present."

"Meister Baird?" A liberal ally with kyosei sympathies.

"Present and concerned," her translator said.

Frye did not hesitate. "Marshall Judoff?" Bitch.

"Present, of course," Judoff said with a sneer.

"Marshall Langford?" Isolationist with debts to kyosei.

"Unh," Langford grunted. "Why is time wasted on this ritual? Are we at loss for better things to do?"

"It was Marshall Judoff's request, sir, and by the rules we must respect it. Vice-Admiral Drew?" The most conservative of the kyosei, Frye thought, but also the fairest of them.

"Present," his translator said.

"Vice-Admiral Charltos, present," Frye said with a smile. "Force Meister Toso?" The only kyosei liberal.

"Present."

"And Commander Garner?" Even more party-line kyosei than Judoff.

"Present."

"Noted and recorded that all members are present, I believe that our first order of business should be some new business that Marshall Judoff wishes to present us with. Marshall?"

Judoff gave him a nasty smile, then rose to her feet. "According to the Confederacy Papers," she said, holding the copy up for all to see, "this body has committed a grave error by reassigning portions of my fleet to various other commanders. I read Section A, Rule Seven-Seventy-One. 'In the normal pursuit of balance and alignment of forces, all auxiliary fleets must be treated as singular units unless a division of forces is agreed to by the fleet commander and the governing military—' "

"We rescinded that rule," Hadasaki said, "and for an unusual change the Ararcouncil publicly endorsed our—"

"You what? You had no right to do any—"

"The vote, I believe," Frye said gently, "was seven in favor and one opposed." It was a joy to see her defeated this way.

Judoff stared at them for a long second, then slowly turned to look at Oska. "Why was I not informed of this, AOCO?" she asked, her face bright with anger and humiliation, her fists clenched at her sides. "And who told them I went to the March Cluster? You, Oska!" she screamed.

Before anyone realized what was happening, she was charging him with her short ceremonial dagger in hand. "Traitor!"

Oska tried to ward off the blow, but she struck home, shoving the dagger up under his ribs. As Judoff pulled back for a second strike, Melliman threw herself between them.

Frye scrambled to get to Judoff, but Marshall Langford grabbed her first and pinned her arms to her side. Lotonoto wrenched the knife away from her.

"Two-faced bastard! I'll kill you!" Judoff screamed. "Let me go," she said through clenched teeth. "Let me go."

Langford and Lotonoto dragged Judoff from the room. Hadasaki called for the medics, while Baird, Toso, and Garner huddled with Melliman and Frye over Oska's bleeding form.

Hours later Melliman came back to the office from the hospital still wearing her bloodstained uniform. "He's in stable, but critical condition," she said. "Judoff punctured his lung and cut an artery, and he had a lot of internal bleeding."

"What do they think?" Frye asked. "Will he make it?"

"They're not sure . . . How could she have done that, Frye? How? And why?" Melliman asked, with tears suddenly running down her face. "Madame Tashawaki asked me how Marshall Judoff could act so uncivilized, and I couldn't give her an answer."

Frye took Melliman into his arms. "Because Judoff's crazy, Clarest," he said as he held her tightly. "The woman lives in an insane reality occupied only by herself and a few of her most devoted followers—like Kuskuvyet. Insanity is the only way you can explain something as irrational as public murder."

* * *

"You will no longer be dealing with me, Glights," Leri said, "and that does not displease me. Within this season Historian Weecs will become the new Proctor, and I shall retreat from the affairs of Cloise. You may stay and witness his investiture if you wish."

"I do not understand, Procter Leri. How can you do this?"

"With joy and pleasure."

"Then you are about to die?"

Leri wasn't sure his translator had correctly phrased the question. "No," she said, "I am nowhere near death. Why do you ask that?"

"Because, Proctor, as I understand it, only death or fore-knowledge of death can end a leader's rule."

"On Castor, perhaps. Here we are more sensible."

"I see no sense in disposing of a perfectly capable leader in the midst of a crisis and installing a new, untested one."

"What you see does not matter, Glights. Ah, here is Weecs now." As Weecs slithered into her chamber—soon to be his chamber—she thought he already showed signs of the burden of office. His red-and-yellow stripes seemed somehow duller, the black stripes separating the red and yellow somehow shad-ing toward brown. "I have explained to Ambassador Glights that you will soon be Proctor, but he is not impressed with your worthiness to serve."

"Proctor, I never meant—"

"No reason he should be," Weecs said. "I'm certainly not impressed or even convinced that this is anything but madness."

"Both excellent qualities in a proctor," Leri said, "modesty and a self-assessment of limited abilities. You will make an excellent Proctor, Weecs, if you can keep those things."

"This is not funny, Leri," Weecs protested. "I neither want nor am prepared to accept this responsibility."

"The Council has chosen. The ceremony will shortly begin. Will you deny Cloise your services?"

"Of course not, but perhaps this should be delayed so that I might spend time observing you more closely in order—"

"I had no such luxury," Leri snapped. "I was made Proctor with no experience in the midst of a crisis. You, at least, know a great deal about the workings of this office. Do not beg special consideration from me, Weecs. Complain to a Confidante—or to the Verfen when they arrive, if they arrive with their so-called protection." Leri was shocked by how deep her anger at him was. "Complain to Glights the Castorian or to our human mercenaries who allowed Ranas to be killed. But *do not* complain to me."

"He certainly has rationale to complain," Glights said.

"Shut up, Castorian. Or leave if you cannot control your clacking," Weecs said before turning back to Leri. "I am sorry, Leri. I had no intention of angering you."

"Then accept your responsibilities and do what you must."

"Yes, of course. My shortcomings are my own problem."

Loud hissing whistles filled the chamber.

"It is time," Leri said. "Good-bye, Glights. Good-bye, Weecs. Trust your judgment, and do not neglect the Confidantes when you are in need." She slithered off the dais and quickly moved to the back wall where she coiled in wait of the Council.

"Is Historian Weecs present?" a voice asked from the main entrance.

"Is the new Proctor here?" asked another.

"I am here," Weecs answered.

"Take your place," Leri hissed.

Reluctantly, Weecs slithered up on the dais and coiled himself into the position of formal greeting.

"The old Proctor is gone," Leri said as the first of the Council members entered the chamber. "The new Proctor is waiting." Their chant of "Weecs, Weecs, Weecs," echoed behind her as she slithered out a side tunnel and left that chamber for good. Instead of the relief she had anticipated, she felt only a strange numbness. But that didn't stop her from going to her new home with her favorite Confidante.

Leri had never heard of anyone living with a Confidante, but when her favorite had asked, "Can you not live here?" she had quickly assented. There was no place else she would rather be.

When she arrived, the Confidante asked, "Is it done?"

"Yes," she answered. "Weecs is Proctor, and I am free."

"Can you listen to me before you rest?"

Leri thought the question a strange one. "Yes, Confidante, I can listen."

"Is your faith in the Elett strong?"

"My faith is strong."

"Can you hear the truth?"

"You know me, Confidante," Leri said, staring up at its wrinkled bulk in the dim light. "Why do you ask these things?"

"Can you hear the truth?" The Confidante repeated.

"I can hear the truth," she answered impatiently.

"Your decision was correct. Weecs will deal properly with the Verfen, and Cloise will be safe for all time."

Leri was so shocked to hear her Confidante make not one statement but *three* that when she opened her mouth, nothing came out. It must be a great truth for a Confidante to phrase it in a statement rather than a question. Such was the lesson she had learned so long before from the only human document she had ever found of value: the only true statements were absolute presuppositions, the bedrocks of one belief. All other statements were actually questions in disguise.

For the first time since she had assumed the duties of Proctor thousands of seasons ago, Leri felt truly at peace with herself and her world.

25

Despite the unanticipated exit from subspace, following Teeman's ship into this system had been easy. Now Janette was faced with the problem of locating Xindella—and what to do when she found him.

She had only caught a fragment of his last transmission to Teeman and Yednoshpfa, but it was enough to tell her that Xindella's ship had some major problem with his Gouldrive. He had put down somewhere on the surface of a small planet, and from the cratering she saw, Janette guessed that the planet had little, if any, atmosphere. That pleased her, because a lack of atmosphere would complicate any external repairs Xindella and Wallen might have to make and thus give her more time to decide what she should do next.

The Ukes had apparently overshot the system, and Janette hoped they were so far past that they'd never find their way back. For the moment, anyway, they were at the bottom of her list of problems.

"In order," she said aloud. "First I find the *Profit*, then land close enough to get to it on foot with sufficient air in my suitpack to return to the LPR. Then I have to gain access to the *Profit*, subdue Xindella and Wallen, hike back to the LPR, move it as close as possible to *Profit*, and transfer the weapon to the LPR. Nothing to it, girl," she said with mocking chuckle. "Won't require anything more than several minor miracles to pull this off.

"Find the *Profit* first, and maybe by then something else will occur to you. . . . Damn! Bad enough to be talking to myself, but to address me in the third person is sick."

With a little growl she reached inside her jumpsuit and adjusted her booster strap. Her breasts just weren't comfortable in gravity without a booster, and her shoulders weren't comfortable with one. If her stomach hadn't disliked weightlessness so much, she would have done away with the artificial gravity and taken her booster off.

On Patros she had almost purchased a booster with little countergravs—micro versions of the ones used in skimmers—under the cups, but the gadgetry had made it too expensive, and she had told herself it was a luxury, not a necessity. Instead she had treated herself to a fancy, but considerably less expensive spider-lace booster, and of course it had straps that cut into her shoulders, and now she wished she had bought the expensive one.

"Quit it," she said. "You're getting a little weird in your old age, Thel. Instead of worrying about your booster, you should be figuring out the shortest series of orbits around that rock that will let you cover it all and find Xindella." She switched on the Orbit and Landing Program and began feeding in the information it would need to calculate her search pattern.

Once the last datum was in and the OALP began processing the information, she leaned back, unconsciously reached inside her jumpsuit, and adjusted her booster strap.

* * *

Whatever eagerness he might have had to see General Schopper had been rattled out of him by the shuttle ride from his troop transport to the *Walker*. The first thing he wanted to do now was relax and rinse his mouth with something more potent than water. But as he stepped through the lock, the boarding officer waved him aside.

"Chief Stanmorton?"

"That's me, Lieutenant."

"General Schopper sends his compliments and asks you to join him for dinner in the senior wardroom at twenty-hundred hours."

"Ship time?" Henley asked. "What time is it now?"

"Nineteen-fifteen, sir."

"Well, point me toward my cabin, young lady, so I can at least change uniforms."

"Watch Mate," the lieutenant said to a round young woman across the companionway, "take the Chief and his kit to number seventeen on the brass deck."

"You must have a shortage of goldsleeves aboard," Henley said. "Never bunked on the brass deck before."

"Follow me, sir," the Watch Mate said, taking his main kit bag and starting up a ladder. Up four ladders, then down a long companionway she opened a cabin door.

"Thanks, Mate," Henley said as he entered the cabin. Whatever luxury he had expected on the brass deck wasn't evident in this cabin. The only thing it had was a little more space than his previous cabins on lower decks and its own toilet-cleanser-sink combination.

"There you go, sir," the Mate said, putting his kit bag in a locker beside the bunk.

"Which way to the senior wardroom?"

She looked pensive for a second. "Don't get up there much, sir, but it should be left down the companionway to the butt, then right and up the next ladder you see."

As soon as she left, Henley started to undress. Then he saw the message on the tiny fold-down desk. He opened it quickly and sighed when he read it. Kryki Kinderman had blown his way out of prison, and Fleet Military Guard wanted Henley to tell them anything he could about Kinderman as soon as possible.

Henley wearily finished getting undressed, stepped into the cleanser, turned on its hot jets of water, and allowed himself the privilege of just standing there for a few minutes before scrubbing down. It was the first time in fifty days he had felt truly clean. He wondered what Kryki was doing now and where he could be hiding. One more thing to worry about, he thought as he reluctantly put an end to his long rinse. Only then did he realize he hadn't gotten a towel out of his kit. To his surprise a big disposable towel popped out of the wall beside the cleanser as soon as he had turned the water off. Twenty minutes later and barely on time, he presented himself at the senior wardroom.

"Chief on the deck," the spacer at the door announced.

There were only seven or eight people in the wardroom, and Henley didn't see General Schopper, but to his great surprise he did see Mica Gilbert.

Mica smiled and motioned for Henley to join her. As he crossed the room, she wasn't at all surprised by how pleased she was to see him.

"How's my former aide?" he asked Mica.

"Glad she's not your aide any longer," Mica said. "I understand you were dirtside on Terratane."

Henley laughed. "That I was, but after the skirmish when we landed, it wasn't bad at all." His laughter died quickly. "It was a pretty bloody skirmish, though."

"That's what we heard," Mica said. "General Schopper should be here shortly. Did you stay with Colonel Ingrivia's unit the whole time you were down there?"

"That I did. She's a hard-core commander, Mica, and her X.O. is even tougher. But in that situation no one complained."

"Hard-core? That's a word I'm not familiar with."

"Old word I picked up from a dictionary somewhere. Means determined and unshakable, I believe. The modern term is—"

"Windtall?" Mica offered.

"Yeh, I think so. Now, may I ask you a question? What are your duties now?"

"I'm Schopper's new fleet liaison officer. What are you doing here?" That wasn't what she really wanted to ask him, but the other questions that were boiling up inside her would have to wait until they had some private time together.

"You know me. I'm just an old Teller looking for a story." He decided there was no point in mentioning Kryki's breakout to her. What did she care about a mad poet?

"General on the deck," the spacer at the door announced.

"Good to see you, sir," Henley said as he and Mica both saluted Schopper.

"And you, Chief. I hope you're both hungry."

"For news and food."

"As we eat," Schopper said, motioning them to a table, "I'll give you some news for the record. Then, if you're interested, I'll give you a lot more off the record."

"Interested?" Mica said. "He'd rather get that than eat."

"Both, Mica. I was smart and didn't eat before I got on the shuttle, and now I'm famished." He saw the puzzled looks on both their faces. "Another old word. Means ready to eat everything in sight," he said with a laugh.

Mica enjoyed seeing him laugh. His good humor made her feel even better for some reason. Whatever it was, she was glad to be with him and was determined to make sure they had the time and opportunity for a long talk.

The food was served quickly and without much flair by two young spacers, but the hot food was steaming, and the cold food looked as if it had come straight from the icer. "Eat," Schopper said. "That's pepper-grilled thighback with broiled onions and star-bird gravy."

"Is that on the record, or off?" Henley asked as he cut a piece of the thighback. When he put it in his mouth, he winked at Mica, then quickly cautioned himself not to let what he felt about her become too obvious. But there was no denying that her presence had triggered a sense of peace and contentment in him.

"For you," Schopper said with a smile, "on the record."

"It is delicious," Mica said.

"The secret's in the gravy and the peppering."

"It certainly is delicious," Henley said as he finished chewing the tender meat, "but if that's secret information, how can it be on the record?"

"Henley! What is the matter with you?" Mica asked.

Schopper grinned at her and then at Henley. "He's just battle-addled. Occupational hazard for noncombatants."

"Shuttle-addled is more like it, sir. Shuttles and weightlessness are my least favorite parts of any trip."

"Amen."

"You, too, General?" Henley asked. "That surprises me."

"I'm strickly a dirtside general, or waterside, given where we're going next."

"Thayne-G?"

"Tell him, Captain."

"You guessed right, Henley. The water planets of Thayne-G

are our next targets, and they will be much more difficult than Terratane if only because the troops will have to contend with Ukes spread out on islands."

"So they'll have to hop from island to island," Henley said. "Well, sir, that just adds to your new nickname. The troops are already calling you General Schopper the Planet Hopper."

Schopper smiled. "Thayne-G is for the record. The rest of what I'm about to tell you is off the record, and even with that restriction I can't give you many details, so don't even ask."

Henley nodded as he chewed another piece of thighback.

"We're the center zone of attack," Schopper said. "As we hit Thayne-G, at least two other strike forces will be attacking the Ukes or Uke-controlled systems."

"Sounds pretty ambitious, sir," Henley said after swallowing quickly. "I didn't think we had the ships for that kind of offensive."

"No one thinks we do," Mica said, "including the Ukes."

"And that's why it will work. The only other thing I can tell you," Schopper continued, "is that if you stick with the Three-Seventy-First Legion, you won't miss much of the action in this zone—and that's all I can tell you at the moment."

"Can I ask you about something else?"

"Certainly, but I may not be able to answer."

"I understand that, sir." Henley took a drink of his tea and set the cup down carefully. "I picked up a rumor from the shuttle pilot before we left. He said the Castorians have been secretly working for us and that they're about to openly—"

"Don't know anything about the aliens," Schopper said quickly, "and if I did, I couldn't tell you."

"Is that a nonaffirmation affirmation?" Henley asked.

"It is exactly what General Schopper said. Now let's finish eating before our food gets cold."

Following Mica's suggestion, they finished the meal with only general conversation about the success on Terratane and the minimal Uke resistance there and in the rest of the Ivy Chain. As their sweet liquor was served, Schopper waved his off.

"Sorry, but I have to get back to work. You two enjoy yourselves. Check with me after sixth watch, Mica."

"Will do, sir."

"Don't get up," Schopper said as he stood. Then he left.

Henley suddenly realized that he and Mica were the only two officers remaining in the wardroom. He raised his glass to her. "To Schopper," he said.

She touched her glass to hers. "To Schopper," she repeated.

As soon as they both set their empty glasses down, Henley said, "I could stand some exercise after that meal. You?"

"Yes. How about a walk around the exercise deck?"

"I think we've been there before." He smiled. "But you'll have to lead the way from here."

Mica had a strange feeling as they walked down two ladders to the exercise deck and was pleased that the deck appeared to be deserted. For a minute or so they walked in silence.

"How's your shoulder?" Mica asked.

"Gets stiff in the mornings, but otherwise it seems to be completely healed. Hard to believe that the last time we saw each other was right here and I had my arm in a sling."

"Not hard to believe at all, Henley. That's why I suggested it." She hesitated. "I want to pick up where we left off."

"We left off with you going away," Henley said. "I hope—"

"Where we left our conversation. You remember, don't you?"

"Distinctly, Mica." Henley glanced intently at her as she walked beside him. "But I'm not sure what you mean."

Again Mica hesitated. "I want to talk about us, Henley, you and me. I've learned a lot about myself since then, and I've clarified how I feel about you."

"Which you told your father, but not me," Henley said teasingly.

She stopped and put her hand on his arm, making him look directly at her. She knew if she was going to tell him what she felt, this was the time. "Yes, Henley, I told my father. I told him that I love you."

"Mica, I . . ." Henley didn't know— "Mica, words are my livelihood, and I don't know what to say to you. I care a great deal about you, but I don't know if I can love anyone . . . at least not the way I think you mean it."

His words settled heavily around her heart, but she knew instinctively that words didn't matter. "I understand, Henley. I'm not asking for what you think. I'm offering you my love and my self. All I want . . . is for you to accept me, just like this, with the love I have for you. That's all."

Henley took her hands in his, looked into her eyes, and saw a warmth there he had dared not even dream about. "Mica, it's been a long, long time since anyone made me feel this good, but I don't think it's love, not yet, and I can't promise you that what I feel will turn into love." He saw the tears filling her eyes and knew he was hurting her.

"I'm not asking for promises," she said as the tears rolled down her cheeks. "I just want you to accept what I want to give you—what I need to give you. Please. Can't you at least do that?"

"It's hard," feeling the moistness in his own eyes. "I've never had a relationship where someone loved me more than I loved them. It's always been the other way around."

"Take a chance," she said, smiling through her tears.

"I can't," he said, pulling her against him and wrapping his arms around her, "not yet. Later maybe. When the war's over."

"That's what I said the last time," she whispered.

"I know. I know. But I think we have to wait."

For several minutes they held each other and wept quiet tears, neither of them fully understanding why.

*　　*　　*

Delightful Childe smiled with pleasure, gratification, and relief as the Tender severed the umbilical cord that attached him to his son. It had taken much longer than the normal year to reach this moment. Nindoah blamed his involvement with the complicated duties he had to perform, but he felt she had made it all the more complicated by her demands.

Now it was finally over, and he would no longer have to listen to Nindoah's constant complaints, her interruptions when he was conducting business, and her intrusion on his meditations. In the name of all that was holy she had tried his patience and his body, and he was grateful that his obligation was at an end.

The Tender severed Nindoah's umbilical, then quickly took the two cords, knotted them close to the child's belly, and cut off the long ends. She presented Nindoah's to Delightful Childe and his to Nindoah, then asked the ritual question. "What is this yearling's name?"

"Patience," Delightful Childe said.

"True Patience," Nindoah added.

The Tender looked from one to the other, then at the

yearling. "True Patience, I accept you into my care and into the citizenship of Oina."

"It is done," Nindoah said, completing her part of the ritual. She turned her back on them and walked away.

"Yes, thank the gods, it is done. Take the yearling, Tender, and treat him well."

"His needs will be served."

"Thank you." Delightful Childe turned away from her and walked away holding Nindoah's umbilical cord. He would have it processed, of course, and hung with the other seventeen in his private meditation room where he knew that duty would require him to hang many more before he died.

It was a problem, one to which there were no answers. The population of Oina was dwindling, and there were more females available for parenting than males. By all good moral judgment he should sell his business enterprises to some nonbearing female and devote his attention to the preservation of his species. But the thought of spending the next five or six decades attached to one offspring after another and the females that necessarily went with them sent shivers through Delightful Childe.

No. He wouldn't do it. Not yet. Right now all he wanted to do was to take a ship into space and experience the joys of detachment and freedom. His thoughts were interrupted by a checkdroid.

"Realtime communications for Delightful Childe."

"From whom?"

"Oinaise registered freighter number four-four-seven-ay-two-two-nine-three, name *Graycloud*."

Delightful Childe rushed past the checkdroid toward his communications cell where he found another checkdroid waiting.

"Most unusual," the checkdroid said, its gestures poor imitations of Delightful Childe's own. "This appears to be a human freighter with Oinaise registration."

"Out of the way, droid," Delightful Childe said as he seated himself in front of the screen. "Captain Teeman?"

A quiet buzz of static preceded a weak response. "Xindella down and in trouble. Saks and probably the Ukes are both closing on our zzz-zzzt . . . instructions, and need for assistance."

"Understood, Captain. I have your coordinates. Assistance and instructions on the way immediately."

Without waiting for Teeman's response, Delightful Childe left the cell and went straight to his office. There he learned that four of his ships were available, three of which were too large and slow. He chose the *Housa*, ordered it made ready, and went to gather personal things he would need. It was quite evident that Xindella's festbid had not proceeded as planned and that Teeman was unable to cope with this new situation.

That was the problem with humans. They had such narrow horizons they couldn't see solutions standing right beside them—and Teeman was one of the most competent humans he had ever known. That gave Delightful Childe hope. If Teeman was having trouble with choosing a course of action, the Ukes and the Saks couldn't be much better off.

Nine days later the *Housa* climbed through Oina's atmosphere, heading for space with a checkdroid crew and a happy Delightful Childe piloting. The checkdroids had driven him to distraction with their insistence on the delay. But it wasn't the delay that dampened his joy about being free and in space again. It was the prayer that he wouldn't be too late.

26

"Somehow, Denoro, I was thinkin' we'd have more time than this. A trick of the mind, I guess." Rasha'kean smiled. "Think we're ready for a new assault?"

"Does seem like an awful fast seventy days," Denoro said, "but I'm sure the company's ready—and I know you are, Colonel."

"Thanks. I'll have to admit I wa'not sure I would live up to your expectations until after that first day under fire. Somehow after that I quit thinkin' or worryin' about it."

"You're a damned fine officer, Colonel, but don't get too sure of yourself. Every hill's a new hill, and you got to bust them one at a time."

"Secure all stations! Assault descent begins in three minutes. Secure all stations!" the overhead repeated.

"I'll check 'em, Colonel," Denoro said, standing in the aisle of the landing craft. "Check yourselves! Then check your buddy!" Denoro shouted. "Sound off by platoons!"

"First and Second Platoons, all sticks secure!"

"Third and Fourth Platoons, all sticks secure!"

"Fifth and Sixth Platoons, all sticks secure!"

"Recon, all sticks secure!"

"Company's secure, Colonel," Denoro said, cramming herself back onto the bench beside Ingrivia and strapping herself in.

"Delta Company, all platoons secure," Rasha'kean said into her new hand-held communicator. She had barely tucked it back into her shoulder pocket when the landing craft shuddered in the first wave of turbulence.

"What ever happened to the Chief?" Denoro asked.

"He's still aboard the *Walker*. Something about that fanatic, Kinderman. Broke out of prison back on Nordeen," Rasha'kean shouted over the noise. "Ca'not worry about the Chief now."

But she did worry about him a little. He was an intriguing man, full of interesting contradictions. Stanmorton was unabashedly frightened under fire, yet he forced himself to stay where the action was when he could just as easily have retreated up to some safer echelon of command. He claimed to hate war, yet he was openly fascinated by it from top to trooper. Perhaps the contradiction that fascinated her most was that while he denied any religious inclinations, Stanmorton radiated a quiet, reassuring kind of spirituality.

Rash'kean forced her thoughts back to the task ahead. This was no time to be thinking about anything but the coming assault. If all went as planned, her company would be landing on the largest island on Thayne-G Two. The Fleet had been reluctant to soften the Ukes up with missiles for fear of harming the civilian populations, so the legions were told to expect strong resistance. She could only hope that it was no worse than that first day on Terratane.

The landing light flashed. The craft lurched sideways. Its hull rang like a smattering of bells. Rasha'kean braced herself as they came to a bouncing, twisting halt, her stomach clenched with fear.

The troops were on their feet before the deboard horn blasted, pressing against the landing hatch as it opened. They had done this before.

Rasha'kean and Denoro were out the hatch with the first twenty troopers. Automatic weapons fire tore up the earth all around them. Rasha'kean dove forward between two of her troops.

"Down! Down!" Denoro shouted as the rest of the company flooded out of the hatch.

"In that tree line," Rasha'kean said to the co-squader beside her, pointing to a dark green row of low trees and thick underbrush two hundred meters to their left front.

The co-squader nodded and shouted over his shoulder, "Grenadiers, front and center!"

Almost immediately two grenadiers crawled up to join them. Rasha'kean noted that Denoro was already spreading the company out on its belly, ready to move forward. They were firing into the trees, but the enemy fire did not slacken.

Screams of pain filled the air as a second automatic weapon opened fire on their exposed flank.

"They're under that tallest tree on the left," Rasha'kean said. "Blast them out."

Both grenadiers took aim with their stubby launchers and fired together. Moments later the ground in front of the trees exploded.

Rasha'kean heard the hollow sound of grenade launchers to her right and knew that someone was taking care of their flank.

Again her grenadiers fired and this time were rewarded by two explosions in the trees. The Uke fire stopped. Then the company stopped firing, and for a long moment an eerie stillness hung over them, spoiled by the ringing in their ears and the moans and cries of the wounded.

"Delta, move out!" Rasha'kean shouted. Her order was repeated down the line, and her Z-company came cautiously to its feet and began forming an assault-V as they moved toward the trees. She assured herself that the wounded were being cared for and that the company was moving out in good order, then took the communicator from her shoulder pocket.

"Leo One, Leo One, this is Delta One. We have suppressed fire and are movin' to secure the perimeter," she reported.

"Affirmative, Delta One. Report when perimeter is secure."

"Will do. Delta One, out." Only as she tucked the communicator back in its pocket did Rasha'kean realize how excited she was. Her system was so charged with energy she wanted to run to the tree line. Only common sense and good training stopped her.

"Company's on line," Denoro shouted from her right.

Rasha'kean grinned and signaled her acknowledgment. This was promising to be a good day.

Then the tree line erupted with fire, and her company hit the ground again.

*   *   *

"That's right, sir," the MG said. "Bock is still here."

"In her office?"

"No, sir. She's working with the archive translator."

"Thank you. That will be all for now," Rochmon said, dismissing the MG. What was Bock doing with the archive translator? It didn't make any sense, and he was fed up to his ears with things that didn't make any sense. As he left his office and headed for the archive translator, he decided to confront her with the new information FID had finally uncovered.

Her natural father hadn't died. He'd been a Uke soldier who had deserted her mother. Rochmon wanted to know why Bock had lied about that. Was she afraid that being half-Uke would harm her career? Or was it something more than that?

The door to the archive translator was locked. That was a normal security procedure, but when Rochmon punched the numerical sequence on the lock that should have opened the door, nothing happened. That was not normal.

He took his security override card from his pocket and stuck it in the top of the lock. This time the door did open. At first he didn't see Bock. Then he realized she was sitting at the burst transmission composer in one corner, so intent on what she was doing that she didn't hear him enter.

Closing the door as quietly as he could, he walked slowly across the computer-crowded room, his mind filled with sudden suspicions and fears. The soles of his hyleather boots made a scuffing sound on the antistatic mat, and Bock spun around to face him.

"What the—" She turned back quickly and furiously began entering the delete code.

Without thinking, Rochman threw himself at her, flailing his arms against hers and knocking her out of the chair. He landed on top of her with a grunt as the air was forced from his lungs.

Bock growled and twisted and clawed. She fought her way out from under him and tried to get to her knees. Rochmon realized that she was reaching for the composer and hammered the base of her spine with his fist.

As she fell, she threw out her hands and scrambled out of his grasp. He barely caught the top of her left boot and yanked as hard as he could, pulling her back and himself forward as he struggled to get on top of her again.

"Aaa!" she grunted. "Let go of me!"

Rochmon got his arms around her waist and was surprised that she still managed to stand up. He let his arms slip down and threw his shoulder into the back of her knees.

Arms flailing, she fell forward. Her head hit the corner of the composer with a soft crunch. Then her body went limp as it slumped to the floor.

Panting to catch his breath, Rochmon forced himself to his knees. He crawled up beside her still form and rolled her onto her back. His stomach turned over as he closed his eyes to the sight of bloody pulp in the center of her forehead.

Finally, he forced himself to look at her again and placed his hand on the side of her neck. She had no pulse.

He turned away again and forced himself to his feet. Weak knees and nausea threatened to overcome him. With grim determination he made his way to the door, opened it, and shouted. "Security! Security! On the double!"

The first MG to arrive called for a second. The second called for a security officer and the medics. As he waited, Rochmon calmed himself, anxious to read the message Bock had given her life for but knowing the formal procedures had to be followed. After all, he had killed her.

Thirty minutes later, the medics had removed Bock's body; a senior security officer stood beside Rochmon and two MGs stood behind him as he retrieved Bock's message from the burst transmission composer.

At first what he saw was meaningless. Then, when he realized what it was, he couldn't believe it. "I'll need some help on this, Commander McSpadden," he said to the security officer. "There's a staff list posted on the duty board. I want everyone on the A-One section of that list back in this office as soon as possible."

Even with help it took Rochmon and his staff the better part of ninety hours to break through Bock's security screen and decode her message. Rochmon's initial suspicion had been correct. The message was written in the Q-3 code.

That was revelation enough to absolve him of any guilt he felt about Bock's death. She had broken the code without telling anyone. That was treason, or something close to it.

The message itself was a warning to the Ukes that the attacks now taking place against Shakav, Buth, and Thayne-G would be followed by assaults on Gensha and Yakusan. But now the message wasn't as startling as the greeting to its addressee, Admiral Frye Charltos of the U.C.S.

It began, *"Dear Father . . ."*

* * *

Delightful Childe felt an irresistible urge to exit subspace even though he was nowhere close to Teeman and Xindella. He tried to shake it off, but the more he fought the urge, the stronger and more compulsive it became. Only after he set the controls to exit did he feel any relief, and then it was only momentary.

As soon as the exit was complete, he applied *Housa*'s full inertial dampers to slow his ship down. But why? the rational quadrant of his brain kept asking. He had no answer.

The ship-to-ship communicator suddenly started pinging, but his scopes indicated no ships within their scanning range. With a depressing sense of confusion he turned the communicator on.

"Greetings, Delightful Childe, offspring of Dawn Air and Naffow, tendered by Xidie. We welcome you in peace."

Delightful Childe checked his scopes again in disbelief. "Who in the name of all that is holy are you? And where are you?" he asked.

"We are nearby," the strangely musical voice replied. "As to who we are, that is simple. We are those you call Verfen."

Only then did Delightful Childe realize that the voice was speaking perfect Vardequerqueglot. He stroked his proboscis with both hands. If this was true, it was a most interesting and unexpected development, but given the voice, he doubted the truth of its statements.

"I do not believe you," he said simply. "How would a Verfen know who I was, and those who birthed me, and she who tendered me? Is this some kind of illogical attempt a humor? I see no humor at all."

"Are you not the trader Delightful Childe?" the voice asked, "Oina's emissary to the Neutral Alliance and partne with the humans Benjamin Holybear Teeman and Marsha Lisa Cay Yednoshpfa? Have we called the wrong ship to us?"

"What do you mean, 'called' the wrong ship? No one called me."

"Then why did you come here?"

Delightful Childe had no answer for that question. He had no answer for any of this. "I do not understand. How did you call me here? What, why . . . I just do not understand."

"We did not mean to upset and confuse you," the voice said. "We seek your counsel on a matter of great importance to us all."

With a deep fluttering sigh Delightful Childe felt himself relax. Then immediately he stiffened. They were doing this to him. They were manipulating his emotions.

"Again we apologize," the musical voice said. "We had no idea that our actions would upset you. We have avoided contact with the six other sentient phyla for so long that we have forgotten the necessary customs and conventions to be observed."

"Are you reading my mind?" Delightful Childe asked.

"No. We only receive emanations—as we transmit them. When you reacted so strongly to our calming transmission, we felt your aversion."

"Why doesn't your ship show up on my scope?"

"We have no idea why this should be. Perhaps its materials are incompatible with your detection device."

"Why do you speak Vardequerqueglot? Why not gentongue?"

"We speak all sixty-three of the "major intergalactic languages," the voice said in gentongue. "Do you not also?"

Delightful Childe shook his head. "I did not even know there were that many major languages." Suddenly he realized he had missed something. "Did you say six other sentient phyla?"

"Yes. Are there more than that?"

"I am at a loss again. I only know of five phyla."

"That is understandable. Neither the Marcadelitins nor the

Quadiecommastoleons have much contact outside their systems."

"This is all very fascinating," Delightful Childe said, "but I need to proceed to my destination." His curiosity begged to know more about the reclusive Verfen, but his head was worried about Captain Teeman and Xindella—and more than that. He was afraid. "You said you wanted my advice about something?"

"We do, Delightful Childe, but please accept those better than we to explain." There was a brief silence before a new voice spoke. "Greetings, Trader Captain," it said in a tone even more musical than the first voice.

"Greetings, Verfen. How may I be of service?"

"We wish to know how this struggle between the two human factions can be halted."

"Is that all?" Delightful Childe asked.

"Yes."

"You are serious? How would I know how to stop their war? They attacked us, and we are neutral. They steal from the neutral Cloiseans. We have no idea how to stop them."

"That is highly regrettable," the Verfen voice said. "We had great hope that you would be able to assist us. However, since you cannot, we offer to Oina, through your good offices, our eternal protection."

The offer was so absurd that Delightful Childe had no response.

"Do you belittle our offer?"

"I find it incomprehensible."

"Our apologies, Delightful Childe."

"You have no need to apologize." He waited, but there was no response. "Verfen? Are you still there?" he asked. Again there was no response. After several more attempts he gave up. They were obviously no longer in a communicating mood.

With a wrinkle of his shoulders he began reprogramming his navigation computer. It was only when *Housa* reentered subspace that he appreciated the full frightening impact of his meeting with the Verfen. Whatever they were, they had fearful powers he couldn't begin to comprehend, and he could only hope they had the wisdom to use those powers peacefully.

27

Ayne Wallen stared with morose disdain at the worthless weapon. Ultimate Weapon! There was no such thing. This was a terrible hoax perpetrated on him by Sjean Birkie and Caugust Drautz.

And Xindella—the one and only same Xindella who had handed him ten pieces of gorlet an hour before and told him there was no more gorlet aboard the ship. Ayne had four pieces left.

He hadn't believed Xindella at first, but now he did, and he knew that no matter what happened, he was going to have to suffer through the agonies of withdrawal. For what? he asked himself. To remain a slave to Xindella? To fix the Gouldrive so Xindella could turn him over to the Yednoshpfa woman and her partner? What would they do? Make him work on the weapon?

And when he finished that, what then? They would dispose of him because he would no longer have any value to them. Why live for that? Why suffer through withdrawal to end up useless with no place to go in the whole galaxy?

He wouldn't do it. He would kill himself first.

As soon as that thought hit him, Ayne knew it was the only answer. Death alone could free him from the slavery, from the agonies of withdrawal, and from a hopeless future. Death was a doorway out, a way to show them all that he was a free man. "Death is the final answer to the questions of life," his *grandmere* had been fond of saying.

Before Ayne killed himself, he wanted to make one final mark against those who had been so cruel to him. But what? As he stared at the weapon, an idea came to him that was so simple it almost made him laugh. With a few spare parts from the Gouldrive he would turn Sjean Birkie's weapon into his own, a weapon that would destroy anyone who tampered with it.

He prayed that Xindella would be the one, but he could

not be choosy. Anyone who wanted the weapon badly enough to move it off this planet would receive his final salutation to the living.

Putting one piece of gorlet into his mouth, he sat and savored its sweetness until only a hint of its flavor remained in his mouth. Then he put the other three pieces of gorlet on the shelf beside him and went to get the parts from the Gouldrive. That is where Xindella found him.

"What progress are you making on the Gouldrive?" Xindella asked.

"Good progress. With true fortune we should have it ready before withdrawal begins," Ayne said, trying to force a smile onto his face. "You can help us." He knew Xindella's hatred of any physical labor and hoped for the same response he had received before when he suggested that Xindella assist him.

"I would only be in your way," Xindella said. "I am sorry about the gorlet, Citizen Wallen, but you must remember that I tried to warn you."

"We remember that. If you will not help, then please leave us alone so we may finish quickly." To Ayne's great relief Xindella left, and Ayne prayed that was the last he would ever see of the Oinaise scoundrel.

For the first time since they had landed on this airless planet, Ayne was grateful for something. Its light gravity enabled him to carry all the parts he wanted in one trip. He gathered them together and walked back to the cargo bay.

There he ate another piece of gorlet and, as he sucked on its sweetness, began assembling the parts. While eating the third piece, he coupled his new mechanism to the weapon and connected its wires carefully so that they looked like all the other wires. Only Sjean Birkie could have recognized that something was wrong.

Finally, he looked around the cargo bay and decided that the overhead winch would have to serve his purpose. His hands began to shake as he wired a small timer into the winch's controls, but he only had one piece of gorlet left to stop the shaking, and he was saving that for the end.

When everything was ready, he picked up the last piece of gorlet, slipped a loop of the winch's steel cable around his neck, started the timer, and popped the last piece of gorlet into his mouth.

Fifteen seconds later, as the taste of the gorlet was disappearing down his throat, the winch began winding in its cable. Suddenly, Ayne didn't want to die—not like this. There had to be a better way.

He tried to reach the winch's controls, but it was too late. The cable was already tightening, biting into his flesh. He tried to stop it, to hold the noose open with his fingers.

Call for help, he thought. Call for help. Only a gurgling sound came from his mouth. Then his kicking feet left the deck.

When Xindella came back to check on Wallen an hour later, he found a bug-eyed corpse with a face blackened by blood hanging from the overhead winch.

*   *   *

"More hunks, Admiral!" the Watch Leader exclaimed.

"Steady," Gilbert said. "That's why our fighters are out there. They'll take care of them." He made a mental note to have that Watch Leader replaced if she didn't calm down. No commander needed anyone that excitable in the Battle Center. "What's our range to Shakav?"

"Two hundred eighty thousand kilometers, and closing at point one per hour, sir."

Gilbert turned to the young Quarter-Admiral beside him. "Dixie, what's our current disposition?"

"All attack flights have launched, sir. Fighter defense is at range. Reserves are ready. *Madison* is underway with a skeleton crew, the rest having transferred to the *Curtis*."

"I think you should hold your reserves, Dixie. Don't you agree, Pilot Dougglas?"

"I do for now, sir."

"For now is all we're worried about. Pull the fighters in a little closer if you have to, but don't launch the reserves before the refueling changeover unless you both agree that it is absolutely necessary."

"Understood, sir."

"Excellent. I'll be in the senior wardroom getting something to eat if you need me. If not, as soon as I've eaten, I'll relieve you so you can do the same." He accepted her salute and left the *New McQuay*'s Battle Center.

The senior wardroom was less than a hundred steps away, so he didn't feel as if he was really leaving. His stomach had been complaining for an hour, and now that the engagement with the Ukes was settling into a pattern, there was no necessity for him to be in the Battle Center every minute. After twenty hours there he felt as if he deserved thirty minutes for a quiet meal.

Uke resistance was proving to be stronger than he had hoped it would be but less than he had prepared for. Whatever else anyone wanted to say about the Ukes, their space forces had proved to be excellently trained, and steadily determined when they went into combat.

When the wardroom steward brought his food, Gilbert forced himself to eat slowly. He wondered how Mica was doing with General Schopper and if she had found the opportunity to tell Henley Stanmorton how she felt about him. That reminded Gilbert of his brief days with Charlene Pajandcan, and a flood of feelings and questions followed that thought, the most important of which was how she was faring in her battle against Buth.

Suddenly, he realized his plate was empty, and he was still hungry. He stood up and stretched his tired muscles. He could have asked for more food, and it would have been brought to him immediately, but he believed that a little hunger was good for a commander in combat. Hunger gave him an edge. A full stomach usually tended to make him drowsy. "It's age," he muttered.

He made a quick trip to the head to relieve the pressure on his bladder, then went back to the Battle Center to relieve Admiral Dixie. The first thing he noticed was that a veteran Tech Mate had relieved the excitable Watch Leader. The second thing he noticed was a great deal of activity on the perimeter screens.

Dixie followed his gaze, then said, "We've counted twenty-two hunks so far, including five of the Wu class. We've destroyed or disabled four of the old hunks, but none of the Wu class."

"They worry you, Dixie?"

"They do, sir."

"Me, too." Gilbert watched the screens for a few seconds, then said, "Dougglas, how long before the refueling changeover?"

"Forty minutes, sir," the Flight Corps commander said.

"Suppose we send part of the reserves out early to chase hunks? Would that help?"

Pilot Dougglas grinned. "It would, sir."

"Then do it. Dixie, go get something to eat—and then try to get some sleep. I'll call you if we need you."

"Aye, sir."

Gilbert watched as Dougglas's orders were acknowledged and executed. A new swarm of fighters formed on the screen and split into little attack groups to chase the hunks. So far only the *Madison* had sustained serious damage, and Gilbert wondered how long their luck could last. Even with the fighters absorbing the brunt of the Ukes' counterattack, he expected more of them to break through to the line ships.

Maybe his tactic of getting as close to Shakav as possible was having the effect he had hoped for. That's what he wanted to believe, but it was far too soon to try to make that kind of judgment.

As if in response to his thought, the Tech Mate said, "Perimeter breakdown, Admiral, seventh sector."

Gilbert saw it as soon as he looked at the screens. Three, possibly four Uke cruisers had broken through the fighters and were coming at the body of his fleet from fore-underside of the imaginary sphere in which the planet Shakav was the locus and his line of flight determined the arbitrary equatorial plane.

"Launching all reserves," Pilot Dougglas said.

Again new swarms of fighters appeared on the *New McQuay's* screens and in attack formations of four or eight went straight for the Uke cruisers. It quickly became an unfair fight, and everyone except the Ukes seemed to know it. They weren't prepared to ward off that many fighters at once.

Three hours later Admiral Dixie returned to the Battle Center in time to see Dougglas's fighters knock the last cruisers out of action. The remaining Uke hunks had retreated to fight battles they were better designed for.

"I think we're winning," Dixie said.

"Never count your victories, Admiral," Gilbert replied, "until the war's over and won."

*   *   *

"It's all bad news," Frye said as Melliman entered his office. "The Saks now have total control in the Ivy Chain. Our defensive fleet is retreating from Thayne-G. Shakav is taking a beating. Only Buth is putting up solid resistance, but the reports from there indicate shortages of everything except courage." He shook his head sadly.

"What I don't understand, sir," she said as she sat beside his desk, "is where are they getting all the ships to do this? And how are they supplying them?"

"They must have had one incredible crash building program going on since the war started—and even then I never would have guessed they could amass enough trained crews and ground troops to launch a three-pronged attack."

"I hate to say this, sir, but it looks like Barra's warning was correct again."

"And that's another thing, Clarest. What's happened to Barra? Her last message was only a fragment, and nothing has followed it. I'm afraid for her." How strange, Frye thought, to be afraid for a daughter he never really knew while rarely ever thinking about Marsha anymore.

"I've been afraid for her from the beginning." Melliman hesitated. "I'm also afraid I have to add to all the bad news. I just received a call from Anshuwu Tashawaki. Lieutenant Oska died this morning."

Frye cursed softly. "Does anyone know where Judoff is?"

"She was here yesterday, but I don't know if—"

"In Decie's name, Clarest. Find out. I want to know where she is from now on."

Melliman stood up. "Let me send Lieutenant Nellnix down to Watchguard with a request in your name to keep constant track of her, and I'll send Raybourn to see if she can find out where Judoff is right now."

"Yes, good—I'm sorry, Clarest. I didn't mean to sound—"

"I understand," she said as she headed for the door. "Don't worry about it."

During the thirty minutes she was gone, Frye tried to set aside his anger and frustration by composing a note of condolence to Madam Tashawaki, forcing himself to use the most strictly traditional language and form for that courtesy. It was as though the discipline required to compose the note reinforced the discipline necessary to control his emotions. When he finished, he felt better for having done both.

"Brig Leader Lawrence was most receptive to your request," Melliman said as she reentered the office. "Nellnix wasn't available, so I went myself. Seems Lawrence was fully prepared to have Watchguard begin monitoring Judoff as soon as someone asked him to. But Lawrence asked me a question I couldn't answer. Will Bridgeforce formally deny Judoff now?"

"I don't know, Clarest. As far as I know, there's no precedent for this. Lotonoto has already submitted a written motion for Denial and Indictment. Hadasaki wrote the second, but we have no third."

"Can't you do it?" she asked as she sat down.

He shook his head. "I wish I could, but the rules say no. Normally I can vote to break a tie, but I can't second or third a motion. In this case with seven of the nine members eligible to vote, there will be no tie."

"Won't Langford or Baird third the motion?"

"Baird might, especially now that Oska has died. But Drew, Toso, and Garner are almost guaranteed to vote against the motion regardless of what they think of Judoff, which leaves Langford as the probable determining factor."

"And he's in debt to the kyosei," Melliman said.

"Exactly. And this is one of those times they'll demand his allegiance. He's gone against them too often on little things, and I'm sure they've already reminded him of his debt."

Melliman leaned back, closed her eyes, and sighed. "Maybe we could give him a way out. Suppose Baird was to third the motion and Langford were to abstain from voting?"

"The kyosei would scream."

"They might, but from what I've seen, Langford seems to enjoy upsetting them. Besides, before they had influence over the majority of Bridgeforce, they used abstentions all the time."

Frye smiled at her. "All right, someone talks Langford into abstaining. What then?"

"Then you could vote to break the tie."

"But first Baird has to third the motion. If Hadasaki can convince her to do that, then I think he would have a much better chance of convincing Langford to abstain."

"Shall I contact Meister Hadasaki?"

"No. I'll do it." Frye picked up his lightpen and started writing on the small padscreen built into his desk. In his clear, concise hand he outlined the possibilities, signed the note, and punched in Hadasaki's private memo code.

"There," he said, pushing the transmit button. "That will go straight to Hadasaki, and he can deal with it as he thinks best. Now, Clarest, let's review this civilian auxillary plan of yours one more time before we present it to Bridgeforce."

28

"Nothing yet," Marsha said as Lucky walked into the cabin and slumped into the pilot chair. They were both tired and irritable after four hundred fruitless hours of trying to find Xindella's ship on the airless rock they were circling. "You'd think he'd be sending some kind of signal we could pick up."

"Unless they crashed," Lucky said grimly, "in which case all of this is for nothing."

"It's for nothing, anyway," she said bitterly.

Her tone jolted Lucky. "What do you mean, Mars? I thought you were the one who insisted that we follow through on this?"

"That was before. This is now. If Xindella and Wallen die on that oversized asteroid, who are we to care?"

He reached over and put a hand on her arm. "Is that it? I'm sorry, Mars. I thought—I hoped we had worked through your identity problem."

His assumption irritated her. "I love you, Lucky, but sometimes you're so damn sympathetic that it drives me to the edge. I told you, it's not an identity problem. It's that I just don't know where I fit in anymore. You're the only solid thing in my life, but I can't expect you to support me all the time. I have to stand by myself."

"You want to talk about it some more?"

"No. Not now. Later maybe, okay?"

"Mars, you know that I would be glad to—"

"*Housa* calling *Graycloud*. *Housa* calling *Graycloud*. Are you receiving me, Captain Teeman?"

"Well, look who finally showed up," Marsha said.

"Yes, Delightful Childe," Lucky said with a sigh of relief. "We are receiving you very clearly. What took you so long, partner? Can you follow our signal in?"

"I can," Delightful Childe's voice said. "Have you located my worthless cousin?"

"No. But we have a fairly accurate idea of where he isn't."

"What an odd way you have of phrasing things, partner. Now that I have your direction firmly established, I suggest that you continue your search."

"What the tensheiss do you think we've been doing while we waited for you, partner?" Lucky asked sarcastically. "Trading with the natives?"

"My apologies for the delay in reaching you. Remind me later to tell you of the most phenomenal occurrence I took part in on the way here."

"We're just damned glad you're here."

"Certainly you are. I understand that this has been a most difficult task for you."

"And a stupid one," Lucky said. "Once you reach us, I don't think we're going to hang around very long."

"Hang around? Ah, yes, I see. Well, I would remind you that we have an agreement and would ask at least that you ensure that I have possession of the device before you leave. And where will you go, partner?"

"I don't know. Marsha and I haven't decided that yet." He reached for her hand and smiled. "Someplace peaceful. Someplace that isn't involved in the war."

"Oina, perhaps?"

"Hunh. Oina's involved. Remember I told you once that it was your war? I didn't realize how true that was going to be. You're in the war, too, Delightful Childe—you and Oina and the snakes from Cloise and the creepy Castorians. All of you are in the war up to your—up to whatever it is that you have in common. But we're done with it. Marsha and I want out."

"A noble desire, partner, one with which I fully sympathize. Help me get this weapon from Xindella—or destroy it—and we will withdraw from the war together."

Lucky covered the microphone. "You hear that, Mars? Do you believe it?"

"Do you?" She squeezed his hand affectionately, then released it. "Has he ever lied to us before?"

"Childe, if you're serious, we have something to talk about. But what about the Neutral Alliance?"

"The Alliance stays neutral. That was our original agreement, and that is what we shall do. Perhaps you had forgotten?"

"I hadn't forgotten. I'm just not sure I ever really believed that you all were going to—"

"Lucky! I found him."

"Wait a minute. Marsha thinks she's located Xindella's ship."

"I'm sure I have," she said. "Look. It's a weak signal, but it's his. Right in the middle of that flat crater."

"Partner, how long will it take for you to get to us?" Lucky asked. "We've got Xindella pegged."

"Six of your hours at the most."

"Then get in here, because if we've picked up Xindella's signal, Janette can, too. The Ukes overshot us, but if they've found their way back to the system, you can bet they'll be hard after us all."

* * *

"What will you be working on?" Caugust asked.

"Dr. Rizinger wants me to form a team to do some research for his ultra-high-voltage switching lab," Sjean said, trying to sound enthused by the project. "Basic physics, really."

"At least you're not leaving Drautzlab altogether."

"No. I told him I would move down to his end of the lake as soon as I finish all these summary reports on the weapon."

"Then maybe we'll get a chance to see each other."

He looked like a sad, overgrown child at that moment, and Sjean had to suppress an urge to get up and give him a long hug. "I expect that we will, Caugust. Maybe we could have dinner together sometime."

For a few moments he stared over her head, seemingly lost in his own thoughts. Finally, he lowered his gaze to his hands, resting on the neat stack of blue folders containing the first half of her reports. "Sjean, did you know that in less than a year C.J. will have his doctorate and be ready to come home? It doesn't seem possible, does it?"

"No, it doesn't. Seems like only a year ago that he left for graduate school on Biery." She didn't know why Caugust was talking about his son, but if it would help cheer him up, she could talk about Caugust Junior all day long.

"How long did he work in your lab? A year and a half? Two years? The dates all seem to run together now."

"Two years. He was one of the sharpest interns I ever had in the lab. Takes after his father."

"More like Helen—his mother—I think. She was the analyst in the family. I was always the administrator. You never knew her, did you?"

Sjean shook her head, wondering why he was suddenly opening up to her about his personal life after all these years. He had never talked about his wife with her before. "You told me she died the year before I came."

"Cancer," he said, "the one disease that man never beats. She was strong, Helen was, but not strong enough. By the time she died, it had invaded every part of her body." He paused, breathing deeply two or three times.

"She would cry because the pain was so bad. Nothing our doctors had could overcome it. I read everything I could find about the pharmacology of pain. I found out that on Nordeen they grew opium-poppers, a kind of flower that they made a drug called harwin out of. There was some stupid law there that made the export of harwin illegal, but I got some. It cost me almost four thousand credits for a kilogram, but I got it, and our doctors gave it to her . . . and . . . at least she didn't die in pain."

Sjean felt embarrassed for him as the tears rolled openly over his ruddy cheeks. "I'm sorry," she said softly. "I had no idea it was that difficult. No one ever told me."

"Only the doctors knew. And C.J. and me. But you know why I'm telling you this, Sjean? Because you're good—deep down inside you're a good person, and I was a good person, once."

"You still are, Caugust. No one ever said you weren't."

"They didn't have to. I knew. I knew when I bought the harwin that I was doing something wrong, but I balanced it out by thinking about the good it was going to do Helen. But you know what? Once you've bent a rule or broken a law to suit some idea you have about right and wrong—once you've done that, it's like you've crossed over some invisible line, and you can never get back. You're stuck on the wrong side forever."

"I don't believe that. And I don't believe that you're bad or evil or anything like that just because you broke a stupid law in order to save your wife from suffering."

Caugust wiped the tears from his eyes as though he had become aware of them for the first time and was surprised to find them there. "Well, anyway, that's not why I came to see you. I just wanted you to know that I appreciate your tying up all the loose ends for us on this project. I know how hard that must be for you."

"It is my responsibility," she said, "as a scientist as well as an employee of Drautzlab."

"Thank you," he said, standing and holding out his big hand across her desk, "for everything, Sjean. I'm proud to have known you and worked with you."

"Don't make it sound so final, Caugust," she said, shaking his hand. "I'm going to insist that we have dinner."

"Yes, of course. It's just my way. Good-bye, Sjean." He picked up the reports and walked quickly out of her office.

"Dinner. Next week," Sjean called after him as she watched him go, his tall frame bent by some unseen burden. She blinked and suddenly realized that there were tears in her eyes. He had touched her not only with what he said but in the plaintive way he said it, as though part of him was crying for help that no one could give. For a moment she was afraid for him.

Taking a small handkerchief from her pocket, she wiped away the tears and told herself it was ridiculous to worry about Caugust. He had everything he needed to be a continuing success—a thriving business, a brother and sister who supported him, and a brilliant son who would soon be home to join them. Most of all he was one of those people with the will to succeed.

The war was doing strange things to everyone, and Caugust was only going through a bad time because of the pressure he was under. Soon after coming to work for him, Sjean had learned that Caugust was stronger than most people. His actions had only reinforced that knowledge over the years, and she was sure that in a week or even less he would be back to acting like his old robust self again.

*   *   *

Knowing that she had little time, Janette decided to gamble and landed her LPR as close to Xindella's ship as she dared. Then, after quickly suiting up, she grabbed the countergrav sled, went outside, and walked cautiously over to the *Profit*. Much to her surprise the *Profit*'s external hatch was open. Then she found her second surprise. Three meters from the hatch lay the freeze-dried corpse of Ayne Wallen. From the looks of him, he had been dead a while before Xindella had thrown his body out.

Stepping carefully around him, she put the countergrav sled on the ground, entered the hatch, and cycled it to admit her to the ship. Her third surprise was that Xindella was waiting for her.

"So, Inspector, we again meet face to face. I had hoped we could have avoided this, but fortune has not been too kind to me lately. Tell me, Inspector, is that a weapon you are pointing at me? And if so, why?"

"It is," Janette said, "and the why is simple. I can hardly trust you, Xindella."

"How sad, Inspector. I had so hoped you might feel otherwise. However, now that you are here and confronting me, can I safely assume that you have some new and persuasive proposition to offer me?"

"Yes, Xindella, a very simple proposition," Janette said. "You help me transfer the weapon to my ship, and in return I haul you off this rock and save your life. What better deal could you ask for?"

"Two hundred thousand credits from the Neutral Alliance," he said without taking his eyes off the stubby pistol in her hand.

"The Neutral Alliance has deserted you. The Ukes have deserted you. If you don't help me, I'll take the weapon by myself and I'll desert you. Doesn't seem like you have much choice if you want to live." She desperately hoped he would accept her bluff, because she had little faith that she could transfer the weapon by herself.

"Not true, Inspector. My transmitter is not functioning properly, but my receiver still works. Even now my cousin joins with his partners to claim their weapon as is their right."

Janette raised the pistol. "Suit up, Xindella, or pray for your soul, if you have one, because with or without your help I'm taking the weapon now."

"I always did think you had a predisposition toward violence, Inspector."

She watched him open a large locker and take out an orange suit that looked more like a deflated balloon. He put it on much faster than she expected him to. "What frequency is your radio?" she asked.

"One hundred Sondak Standard."

As soon as he put on his helmet, she tested the radios. "Can you hear me?"

"Of course I can, Inspector."

"Then listen carefully. I have a countergrav sled outside. We'll move from here to your cargo bay, open its doors, and you will bring in the countergrav sled. And don't try to do something stupid. I'm not as careless as Ayne Wallen."

Xindella began opening the hatch to the cargo bay. "Citizen Wallen killed himself because there was no more gorlet, a truly unfortunate occurrence, Inspector, but not one for which I share any responsibility."

"I'll bet."

It only took a few minutes to get the sled, pick up the weapon with the winch in the bay, and put the weapon on the sled. When she was sure it was secure, she said, "It will take both of us to maneuver this to my ship, Xindella. I want your guarantee that you won't try anything that would make me shoot you."

His head shook inside the bubble helmet. "Inspector, I have no wish to die."

Even with both of them straining against the overloaded sled, they were barely able to get it across the ground and into the LPR. But they did. Janette locked Xindella in the LPR's tiny sleeping cabin, then prepared to take off. As the engine warmed, she flipped on the communicator and heard.

"—a Sondak ship beside his, Captain, and I believe it is preparing to—yes. It is lifting now. Wait. It looks like the *Profit*'s cargo hatch is open."

"Inspector Janette," Teeman's voice said, "you are stealing property that belongs to the Neutral Alliance. I demand that you transfer that property to the *Housa* which is now landing—"

"Fly it in space," Janette said. "I have only recovered what has always belonged to Sondak." She opened full throttle on the meth engines, and the LPR lifted with gathering momentum off the rocky little planet.

"Inspector, we'll take it by force if we have to," Teeman warned.

"Don't even think about it."

"No, don't," a new voice said. "Inspector, this is Group Leader Kuskuvyet. You will home on my beacon and surrender the weapon to us, or we will blow you to space junk."

29

Pajandcan was deeply tired and frustrated. The Ukes around Buth were putting up a much stronger fight than anyone had anticipated. More and more she was sure her fleet was going to be late for its rendezvous with Schopper's for their attack on Yakusan. If Buth was hard to crack, Yakusan was going to be next to impossible. The best she could hope for was that this temporary stalemate was forcing the Ukes to use ships they would need more over Yakusan—ships they would ultimately miss in their defense of Gensha.

"Status report," she snapped as her senior communications aide entered the Battle Center.

"No change, Admiral," Torgeson answered. "We still haven't been able to contact either the *Hise* or the *Tweener*."

"But we still have visual contact?"

"Yes. The *Connally*'s captain reports that he should reach *Hise* in two hours or less, and the *Tweener* is just beyond—"

"Dammit, Torgy, what can that space merchant do? That's what I need to know. Is the *Connally* equipped to make any kind of rescue attempt?"

"He claims he is. Thinks he can lock on if he has to and evacuate *Hise*'s complete crew and salvage some of its equipment." Torgeson smiled. "Don't like working with these civilians, do you, Admiral?"

Pajandcan thought for a second, then said, "It's not working with them that I mind. Saints know I worked with them enough in Matthews. It's not knowing what their capabilities and equipment are that grinds my nerves sometimes." She shook her head. Thoughts of Matthews inevitably led to thoughts about Dawson and Dimitri and the millions who had died on Reckynop. "But enough of that. At least something's being done for the cripples and the Ukes can't get to them."

"Doesn't look like that's what they're planning, anyway, but they're up to something. Look at this, Admiral."

Pajandcan stared at the bank of screens in front of Torgeson and immediately saw what concerned him. It looked as though the Ukes were beginning to mass their ships in three separate locations. "Counterattacks, Torgy? Why would they do that? It's been all they can do to defend the planet. They counterattack and they'll be open to a breakthrough."

"You'd think that, wouldn't you, Admiral? But suppose it's not counterattack they're thinking of? Suppose they were planning to distract us with one of those groups while the other two escaped?"

"A retreat?"

"They'd probably call it a defensive withdrawal. They know our fleet isn't big enough to attempt an invasion, so maybe they think we wouldn't do anything more than blockade Buth. Maybe they think they can live with that."

"Well, I can't. Every Uke ship that escapes from here is one more we'll have to fight later. And if they think we won't use neutronics against their planet, they've forgotten what their Admiral Charltos did to Reckynop. But I'll tell you what, I damn sure haven't forgotten."

The harsh bitterness of the Matthews system disaster seemed always to be hovering on the edge of her mind. This was Pajandcan's first real chance for massive revenge, and she wanted the Ukes to suffer under her vengeance. Millions had died on Reckynop, and millions of Ukes could pay for that on Buth.

"You want the neutronics readied?"

Pajandcan heard a hint of censorship in Torgeson's voice, but she ignored it. "Yes. Prepare the orders for a polar attack, six R-grade missiles from the *Mervell* against the north pole and six from the *Rath* against the south pole."

"Six each?" Torgeson asked in disbelief.

"Affirmative," she answered sternly. "But first I want all ships except the *Mervell* and the *Rath* to prepare for attack and pursuit as soon as the Ukes make their move."

Nine watches later two Uke groups moved into their old-fashioned cone-shaped attack formations, and Pajandcan ordered half the ships in her command to make ready for them while the other half prepared to attack the third and largest of the Uke groups.

Those preparations were not yet complete when the Ukes attacked. Their methods were exactly what Pajandcan had expected, but the ferocity of their attack surprised her. However, neither of those factors was important. The Ukes had left Buth weakly defended, and Pajandcan gave the final order for the neutronics.

Mervell and *Rath* maneuvered quickly but carefully toward their respective positions. Eleven hours later they launched their neutronic missiles. As the battle raged in space around it, Buth spouted fireballs that shattered its ice caps at both poles.

Pajandcan released a grim smile when the fireballs burst like tiny flowers on Torgy's screens. The Ukes here were much closer to defeat than they realized, and Pajandcan's heart quietly rejoiced in the knowledge that within a few days millions of Buth's citizens would join those who had died on Reckynop.

*   *   *

"You know exactly what I mean," Janette said.

"How many times must I tell you? I understand little or nothing about—about that," Xindella said with a contemptuous flip of his proboscis in the direction of the weapon.

"I don't believe you. You? Xindella? The nastiest, shrewdest broker Patros has ever seen? You want me to believe that you never even inspected the weapon?"

Xindella snorted as he leaned against the custody straps that held him to the bulkhead. "I looked at it, of course, Inspector, but Citizen Wallen was the one who inspected it for me. I have no technical knowledge. I hire humans for such things. Now will you release me from these bindings?"

"Of course not. Do you think me stupid, Xindella?"

"Totally," Xindella said with a baring of his blunt yellow teeth. "In a few hours the Ukes will take your prize away from you, and you will have nothing left but me—assuming they let you live, of course."

"And you," Janette said. "Now shut up and let me think." Xindella was right. She knew that. But that knowledge and what she should do to change it were totally different matters. For a long moment she stood with one hand holding the opposite elbow and the thumb of the other hand hooked under her chin while the forefinger rubbed her nose.

Maybe she couldn't keep Marshall Judoff from taking the weapon. But if she could dismantle it—or better yet, disarm it in some subtle way—then she could agree to jettison it in exchange for her life. And Xindella's life, she thought rudely.

But what if Judoff demanded Wallen? If she told him Wallen was dead, what would keep Judoff from blasting them to spacedust anyway? Nothing. Absolutely nothing.

One thing alone was perfectly obvious to Thel Janette. So long as she had the weapon, her chances for survival were much stronger—especially if Judoff did not know that Wallen was dead. Even so, she thought, it wouldn't hurt to take a piece or two out of the weapon—just for insurance.

"Xindella, you're about to become a mechanic," she said. "I want you to show me exactly what part of this Wallen was working on before he died."

"But Inspector, I told you I know nothing about—"

"And I told you I need your help—help that could very well save your worthless life. The Ukes don't have any use for you. Why would they let either of us live after gaining possession of the weapon? They're not too happy about your role in—"

"All right, Inspector, all right. Your point is well made. However, I cannot be of much assistance bound as I am."

"Then I will free you," Janette said as she stepped closer to him, "but you must swear by whatever gods you honor that you will not attempt to overpower me and take control of this ship."

"I am at your mercy, Inspector. I have no choice but to agree to your terms."

Janette reached to release his straps. "Oh," she said as she hesitated and smiled at him, "there is one more thing you should know. The ship is set to self-destruct if anyone but me tries to pilot it—not that you would do anything like that, of course, but I thought it only fair to warn you."

"Thank you, Inspector," Xindella said with a fluttering sigh when she finally released the straps. "In return for your unnatural kindness I offer you here and now everything I know about the weapon. See that darker panel in the center? Wallen believed that the coupler for the detonator lay behind that panel, and that was the only part of the weapon I ever saw him work a tool upon."

"Open it," Janette commanded.

Xindella shook his great head. "I don't know how."

"Put your hands on it and find—"

"Two hours, Inspector Janette," boomed a voice from the

overhead speaker, "until we reclaim our equipment. We hope you have reconsidered our offer to—"

Janette cut him off with a flip of the bulkhead switch. "We have to get a piece out of this thing, Xindella, so that if they do take it from us, they won't know what's missing and won't be able to make it work. Open the panel."

Again Xindella shook his head. "If you insist, Inspector, but do not blame me if it cannot be done."

One hour later the large brown panel slid aside to reveal one square meter of neatly tangled colored wires running to hundreds of tiny switches and microchips.

In the center of the tangle was a sealed glass tube partially filled with green liquid. And the liquid was bubbling.

A chilling wave of apprehension rippled up Janette's spine as she stared at the liquid and wondered what in the galaxy it was.

*   *   *

"How far away are we, Mars?"

"Farther than the Ukes."

"Delightful Childe? Did you hear that?"

"I did, Captain Teeman. How long do you estimate it will take you to reach the Sondak ship?"

Lucky cocked an eyebrow at Marsha and she said, "About one hundred minutes for us. The Ukes look like they'll beat us by approximately twenty minutes."

"Will that give them time to link up?"

Marsha nodded. "It should if they have a good Close-Maneuvering Pilot aboard." For a moment she wondered who to care about in all this. Why not just let Marshall Judoff and Inspector Janette fight for the weapon? Why didn't she want that to happen? Her mind had hardly formed the question when she knew the answer. She wasn't doing this for the U.C.S or for Delightful Childe and the Neutral Alliance. She was doing it for herself, and for Lucky, and for whatever hope the future held for the two of them. There was no other reason that mattered to her.

"I suggest that you close with them at the fastest safe speed," Delightful Childe's voice said from the speaker. "Perhaps your approach will slow them down enough to prevent their linking with the Sondak ship."

"And what if they blow us from space, partner?" Lucky

asked. "Seems to me like we ought to brake harder and stop well away from them."

"This is no time for caution, Captain. Since I cannot reach their position for another five or six of your standard hours, you must do everything in your power to prevent—"

"The only thing we have to do is survive," Marsha cut in. "And your idea sounds foolhardy and stupid to me."

Lucky saw the determined look on her face and felt a sudden rush of love for her. Regardless of what happened here, he knew he never wanted to be separated from Marsha again. "She's right, partner," he said softly, then repeated, "She's right."

"But you have the laser cannon!"

"Against a Uke cruiser?" With a slight shake of his head Lucky turned to Marsha and whispered, "What now, Mars?"

"Suppose we tell Marshall Judoff that we won't interfere, but as representatives of the Neutral Alliance we demand the right to observe?"

"Captain? Citizen Yednoshpfa? Is there something wrong?"

"No," Marsha said too loudly. "Switch to standard frequency seventy-seven. We're going to try to talk to the U.C.S ship."

"But why?"

"Switch and find out," Lucky said before resetting *Graycloud*'s ship-to-ship transceiver. "Go, Mars."

"Neutral ship *Graycloud* calling U.C.S. ship *Enaha*. *Graycloud* calling *Enaha*—"

"This is *Enaha*. What do you want?"

"Request permission to speak to Marshall Judoff."

"Understood. Wait one."

During the long pause that followed Marsha thought once again about the strangeness of her situation and the confusion of her loyalties. She reached over and stroked Lucky's hand.

"This is Group Leader Kuskuvyet."

"Group Leader, we need to speak to Marshall Judoff."

"I am in command here, traitor. What do you want?"

As Marsha clenched her teeth, Lucky answered. "Group Leader Kuskuvyet, we understand that you are going to take the weapon from the Sondak ship. We also understand that we cannot stop you. But as the representatives of the Neutral Alliance we demand the right to observe the—"

"You have no right to demand anything."

"Very well, then. We request your permission to observe the transfer of the weapon."

"For what purpose?"

"Uh . . ." Lucky knew he had been caught.

"For the purpose of seeing that no violence is done," Marsha said. Even as she spoke she realized how foolish she sounded.

"And if we refuse? What will you do then, traitor?"

"Align the neutrals with Sondak." Delightful Childe's voice signal was clear and strong.

"Who said that?" Kuskuvyet demanded.

"Just another member of the Neutral Alliance, Group Leader."

Kuskuvyet's answer came surprisingly fast. "Very well. *Graycloud* may maneuver to within two kilometers and observe the transfer. Any attempt to interfere will result in your prompt destruction. That is all."

The transceiver buzzed with the static of emptiness.

"That's better than nothing," Marsha said as Lucky turned their transceiver off, "but I'm not sure why we're even bothering with this."

"Because it fulfills our agreement with Delightful Childe. Once Kuskuvyet has the weapon, we can knock the spacedust off our engines and get out of here, Mars."

As *Graycloud* braked to a slow halt ninety minutes later, Marsha and Lucky could see the coupling device leading from the *Enaha* like a long tentacle to Janette's ship. Just as Marsha adjusted the focus on the viewscreens, a flash of fire consumed the center of Janette's ship. A quick series of explosions followed, spreading up the coupler to the *Enaha*.

Then a second series of explosions ripped the *Enaha* apart.

Marsha and Lucky stared in horror as thousands of fragments from both ships flared out into space.

"Sheiss and tensheiss, get us out of here, Mars!" Lucky finally shouted. But it was too late. Already the smallest of the fragments were pinging off *Graycloud*'s hull, and there was no way they could accelerate away from the waves of debris.

Instinctively, Marsha flipped the switch that sealed all the inside hatches. "Strap in!" She buckled her own straps, grabbed

Lucky's hand, and prayed as *Graycloud* shuddered under the impact of a larger fragment.

"Hold on, Mars," Lucky whispered with a forced smile on his face. "This is going to be a nasty ride."

30

Automatic weapons fire chattered over her head as Rasha-'kean crawled slowly up the narrow slimy trail that twisted through the underbrush toward the head of her company.

The wound on her neck throbbed. Her muscles ached. Her wet uniform had plastered itself to her body and chafed every joint. Her feet itched and burned with a fungus that left them red, raw, and oozing despite the medic's treatment and her constant attempts to keep them dry and clean.

Dry and clean. That would be nice, she thought with a damp shiver. About three days of sleeping warm and dry and clean somewhere off this nasty wet planet. That was all she wanted. But she kenned she was a long way from enjoying anything like that.

The weary look she saw on Denoro's mud-speckled face as Rasha'kean crawled up beside her almost made Rasha'kean smile. Was it possible that her X.O. was finally feeling the fatigue that had weighed down the rest of Delta company for the last ten days of heavy fighting in this jungle? "Have you spotted them?" she asked in a low voice.

Again a rattle of bullets chewed up leaves and branches over their heads. They both hugged the ground as the shower of water and debris spattered their bodies.

"No," Denoro said, looking up after the shooting stopped, "but they've sure as stars spotted us."

"How's the hand?"

"Still good enough to hold my rifle," Denoro said, flexing her fingers around the wad of bandages. "Takes more than a giant thorn to put this grunt out of action."

"I'm glad to hear that, Denoro, because we ca'not let these

Ukes hold us up. If those new damned communicators ha'not died in this humidity, we'd ken if the rest of the legion is behind us like they're supposed to be. Now we just have to assume they are and break out of here."

"Agreed, Colonel. The only question is, how?"

"We cut our own trail."

"Through this tangle?" Denoro asked with a skeptical look on her face. "The Ukes will hear us for sure."

"But they'll have to cut their own trail to get to us, and then we'll hear them."

Denoro smiled grimly. "Just might work—'specially if we hack it out twicet fast as they do."

"Right. Now to begin with, I think we should split the company. Recon's exhausted, so they ca'not take the lead. I'll take Third and Fourth platoons as the lead elements, and we'll cut a two-abreast trail. Once we have it started you follow with the rest of the platoons at spaced intervals. Keep the wounded with First for a while, and Haultcour can bring up the rear with Sixth and Recon."

"Why don't you let me take the lead, Colonel?"

"Because it's my turn, Denoro," Rasha'kean said as she turned herself around. "We'll stay as close as we can to a heading of three-five-zero from that big tree we passed halfway down the hill. Once you hear us go to cuttin', have these platoons begin driftin' back down the hill." When Denoro nodded, Rasha'kean started slithering back down the trail.

Slithering. Crawling. Fighting, then crawling some more. That seemed to be the pattern the Ukes defense had forced the legion to follow in the daytime. At night the Ukes withdrew to new positions, and the legion edged forward to regain contact. Rasha'kean had grown to hate every minute of it. Only her pride in her company kept her from complaining.

Fully a third of the company had been evacuated or killed, and there was hardly anyone left without a wound of some kind, either from the Ukes or from the jungle. Yet every day and most nights they forced their tired bodies to do what had to be done, eating on the march, sleeping when they could, but never with anything more serious than casual griping. Only the distant stares she saw in their eyes told her how truly exhausted her troops were.

Now, as she made her way down the hill, she gave each

trooper she passed a quiet word of encouragement or a pat on the shoulder, because she wanted each and every one of them to ken how proud she was to lead them. She prayed that headquarters was right when they told Colonel Elgin this would be the legion's last major confrontation with the Ukes. Delta company desperately needed some rest and recuperation time.

With a shake of her head she pushed that thought away when she saw Sergeant Bradley who had taken over Fourth platoon. It was time to think about their mission, not about rest. Distraction now could get them killed.

An hour later Third and Fourth platoons had only progressed a sweaty two hundred meters up the hill on their new heading. Every five minutes the two cutters would pass their hackchets to the next troops behind them and take their places at the end of their platoons. Rasha'kean was disappointed by their progress but pleased that so far the company had taken no new casualties. The Ukes had not responded to this new tactic with anything more than sporadic firing over their heads.

The underbrush thinned as the cutters neared the crest of the hill, and they made faster progress. Staying as close behind their swinging hackchets as she safely could, Rasha'kean tried to see through brush ahead, looking for any sign of the enemy. Every time the cutters paused, she strained past the chronic ringing in her ears to hear any sound of the Ukes cutting.

Then as two fresher troops took up the hackchets and began their turn at the exhausting work, she stopped them. "Down," she whispered loudly as she dropped to one knee and signaled the troops behind her to get down. There was something wrong up ahead, but what? What?

She forced herself to scan the area instead of trying to focus on one thing, and finally she saw it—a pattern. The underbrush grew lower in three irregular lanes that led to the crest of the hill. Rasha'kean kenned immediately that they had to be firing lanes. She had led Delta into a trap.

As though sensing her discovery, the Ukes opened fire. The air was suddenly alive with the sounds of screaming bullets and chattering guns.

Rasha'kean pressed herself flat into the wet jungle floor.

The pungent odor of decay filled her nose like the smell of rotting fish. She wanted to burrow into it, to get below ground and below those awful fragments of death. But she did not. She pointed her rifle up the hill and fired on instinct.

From downslope she heard troops growling in pain. Delta was taking another battering. But her Third and Fourth were returning fire, blindly sending their bullets up the hill in a desperate attempt to stop the Ukes.

Firing. Reloading. Firing again. She wanted to tell them to stop, to quit wasting ammunition, but she could not even stop herself. To cease firing would be like surrendering.

For seemingly endless minutes the Uke firing chewed up the jungle above them, and their own firing chewed back. Trees shook. Branches split and fell. The air cracked with the rattling sounds of death.

On it went, and on, like some cacophonous machine with an endless supply of ammunition. The sound rose and fell in deafening waves colored by the cries of the wounded

A dull whump stilled the wave. Then another and another as the crest of the hill erupted under the mortar barrage. Somehow Denoro had managed to get Delta's two remaining mortars in action and zeroed in on the hill.

Suddenly the Uke firing stopped. Rasha'kean could ken by the change in sound. Slowly her troops stopped firing, and the mortars were quiet. A ringing stillness held the air for a long moment before a noisy breeze lurched out of the jungle and twisted through the cordite haze over the battle zone.

Cautiously Rasha'kean rolled to her side, pushed up on one elbow, and peered up the hill. The area in front of her looked as though some giant scythe had mowed the brush down to a ragged half meter. Here and there the remains of a tree, draped in splintered limbs, stood a forlorn watch over the devastation. But the pattern she had seen before was covered by a dense strewment of branches and vines.

Were the Ukes gone? Or were they waiting for her to make a move? Probably waiting. Have to assume they were waiting, she thought, but have to take the initiative. She looked back down the slope and signaled for Sergeant Bradley to join her. Much to her surprise, crawling right behind Bradley was Denoro.

"How many casualties?" she asked as soon as they reached her side.

"Eleven new wounds. Two dead," Denoro said, "Lillian and Carl. Lieutenant Stewart is on the edge."

Rasha'kean shook her head. "Good timin' with that mortar help. We really needed—"

"Wasn't us."

"Ca'not worry about that now. Bradley, circle Fourth up the left to the crest. I'll take Third to the right. Stay low and be careful. Denoro, you pull the rest of the company up and hold what we've got."

"Maybe I should take the Third, Colonel."

"No. It's still my turn. I'm over the cliff, Denoro." Rasha'kean felt a hard knot in her stomach, but she was not about to fall back and let Denoro take the risks. "Let's get moving."

With hand signals and whispered orders the platoons formed and split around the edges of the unnatural clearing. Crawling through the underbrush was slow, noisy business, but as they topped the crest of the hill, Rasha'kean kenned she had made the right decision.

It was more a ridge than a hill, and the other side was a rocky slope sprinkled with a few bushes and trees and the backs of a hundred or more Ukes retreating into a broad valley filled with Ukes climbing aboard troop shuttles. There was no time to waste on an elaborate plan. In a very few minutes the closest Ukes would be out of range.

Once again Rasha'kean cursed the worthless communicators. How was she going to let Elgin ken what they'd found? And where was the air support Schopper had promised?

A long glance to her left revealed that Bradley's platoon had also topped the crest. She quickly spread her troops along the edge of the ridge, and Bradley followed her example. Even before they were all in position, Rasha'kean gave the signal to fire, and forty-nine rifles sent misery down the slope.

Ukes fell. Others turned and dropped, firing wildly as they did so. Most fled downslope, kenning in some instinctive way that they could quickly get out of range. The ones who had returned fire soon attempted to join their comrades.

"On line!" Rasha'kean shouted. She looked over her shoulder and saw Denoro bringing the rest of Delta as fast as she could through the tangled underbrush. "Together . . . Forward!"

Third and Fourth platoons began a disciplined advance down the hill. Rasha'kean wanted to run, to chase the Ukes to the brink of damnation. However, neither the loose rocks nor her military training would allow that.

A dull roar echoed across the valley as one of the Uke shuttles began its slow climb into the sky. Rasha'kean raised her rifle and fired a shot at it in frustration, then grinned when the troops who saw her gave her quizzical looks.

Suddenly a strange crackling explosion made them all stop and look up. Rasha'kean could not believe it! The shuttle was breaking apart!

A cheer went up from her troops, and a familiar voice said, "Nice shot, Colonel, but I think the rocketmen will get credit for the kill."

She spun around to find herself facing a grinning Henley Stanmorton. "Where the blazes did you come from?" Her words were almost drowned out by the roar of fightercraft over their heads, racing toward the Ukes with cannons blazing.

"Legion HQ," he shouted. "Been humping with Elgin all day to catch up with you. Sorry I missed the action."

"No you ar'not." She turned away from him. "Bradley, call a rest. Let the pipe jockeys take care of the Ukes." Suddenly she felt weak and tired and gently lowered herself to the rocky ground. The sky above the valley was now swarming with fightercraft, all wreaking destruction on the hapless Ukes.

"You look like hell," Henley said as he sat down beside her, "but I sure am glad to see you alive."

"You d'not look so good yourself." She gave him a weary smile, and unexpectedly wondered how her mother had seen him. "You glad enough to see me to tell me about my mother? I ha'not forgotten, you ken."

"Now?" he asked, totally surprised by her question. "This doesn't seem to be the ideal time and place to—"

"No time is ideal, Chief." She looked back up the slope and waved to Denoro. "No place is ideal, either. But if you're goin' to keep hangin' around my company, you're gonna tell me what you ken about her. I'not that right?"

Henley drew in a breath and let it out with a deep sigh. "All right, Colonel. You pick the time and place, and I'll tell you everything I can."

"Good," she said as she forced herself to her feet. "Come

see what help you can give weary troops and wounded, and
then I'll be findin' some time to pick your brain."

"Like I said, I'll tell you everything I can." He stood and
followed her up the slope—the battle still raging in the valley
was of little consequence to either of them now. But he
wouldn't tell her everything, of course. There was no reason
to tell Ingrivia everything about her mother. He would tell
her the good things, and the sad things, but not the things
that could cause her shame.

What good would it do for her to know that her father
was probably the pikean drug dealer, Kizera, and not the man
whose memory she revered? What good for her to know that
the man who had died in the Uke prison mines was a drunken
pikean adventurer whose arrogant stupidity led to his imprisonment? Or that only her pikean features assured Henley
that *he* wasn't her father?

There was no good in any of that—especially now. She had
earned more of his respect than her mother ever had, and he
would never tell her anything that would hurt her unneces-
sarily.

Rasha'kean was already planning how to evacuate her serious casualties and get her troops some rest and medical attention. Yet in the back of her mind was the question of what the
Chief really kenned about her mother and why he was so
reluctant to tell her anything.

31

"We have to shrink our defensive sphere," Frye said as he
began the grim litany of failures. "Fugisho's defense fleet has
been defeated and dispersed. Thayne-G has been abandoned.
We now have confirmation that Sondak used neutronics against
Buth"—Bridgeforce gave a collective gasp, but Frye barely
paused—"and we have reason to believe that two of Sondak's
fleets are already advancing toward Yakusan. Shakav surren-
dered its space less than thirty hours ago. I have ordered our

commanders to evacuate Fernandez and Cczwyck and will direct—"

"Outrageous!" Force Meister Toso exclaimed. "This is all totally outrageous."

Frye agreed with Toso but for very different reasons. The outrage was Bridgeforce's inability to act quickly and effectively. "Military prudence, Meister," he said in a controlled voice. "If we can save those forces, we can better defend Gensha and Yakusan. If we do not, then Yakusan will surely fall into the hands of—"

"But you told us that with the civilian ships we—"

"Shut up, you despicable old fool," Meister Baird said without using her translator. Her accent was thick, but everyone understood her and now had confirmation of their suspicions that she didn't really need a translator.

Commander Garner was on his feet. "As the newly appointed representative of the kyosei party, I—"

"In Decie's name!" Frye shouted as he pounded his gavel on the table. "I will have order." Even he was surprised by the depth of his anger as he glared at the members of Bridgeforce. "I told you what our forces might be able to do—that was if *and only if* we moved swiftly to garnish the necessary civilian ships. But first this body—you and you and you and you," he said, jabbing a finger at them, "you all hesitated. Then Amarcouncil hesitated. Now most of the ships we needed have scattered away from the Sak invasion."

He paused to draw in a long, intentional breath and realized how very, very tired he was. For over five years his life had been consumed first with the planning, then with the conduct of this war. But directly under his fatigue lay a bedrock of determination to keep on fighting for victory. The U.C.S., Vinita, Tuuneo, and his grandfather all deserved no less than that. There were still ways to win, and he would find them.

"I have *warned* Bridgeforce repeatedly that this could happen if we waited too long, and I was obviously right."

"You destroyed half my fleet," Judoff said as she walked through the doorway, "and you claim your decision was right? I move that Admiral Charltos be removed—"

"Sit quiet. And save your tongue," Hadasaki said as he rose to greet her. "It's you and your stupid kyosei partisans that created this problem with—"

"How dare you accuse me of—"

Hadasaki grabbed her arm and flung her into an empty chair. "I told you to sit quiet, murderer," he said menacingly.

Admiral Drew was giving his translator rapid instructions. "The Admiral wishes to hear the rest of Marshall Judoff's motion for the removal of Admiral Charltos," the translator said, "but the Admiral wishes to make it perfectly clear that his request is only for the purpose of measuring the depth of his disgust with Marshall Judoff. Furthermore, Admiral Drew expresses regret and shame for his previous affiliation with the kyosei."

For a long moment Frye and Bridgeforce sat in stunned silence. The kyosei ranks had broken. The implications could be staggering, but Frye wondered ruefully if it was all happening too late. He glanced over at Melliman, but her attention was totally focused on Judoff and Hadasaki.

"Admiral," Hadasaki said, "I believe we charged you with a message for Marshall Judoff."

Nothing was proceeding the way Frye had hoped it would, but he accepted his responsibility and cleared his throat. "Marshall Judoff, it is my duty to inform you that by a secret ballot of four votes to three, this body Denies you all privileges from your office and Indicts you for the murder of Space Corps Lieutenant Sezuason Oska in the presence of these witnesses."

"Ahgheee!" As she sprang to her feet, the sound that came from Judoff's throat was half growl, half wail.

The side of her left hand slammed against Hadasaki's throat as she pushed off of him and her chair. A dagger flashed in her hand. She slashed Hadasaki's aide and fought to reach Frye at the head of the table.

He bent slightly at the knees, ready for her, almost eager to settle this dispute the only way it could be settled. His hand clenched the small gavel. It wasn't much, but he had nothing else. "Judoff . . . don't do something stupid."

She growled again and slashed at his gut. He stepped back. When she slashed again, he tried to hit her hand with the gavel. The tip of her dagger ripped open his sleeve.

Something loud popped. Judoff hesitated, her eyes growing wide in disbelief, her hands rising to her breasts. Blood seeped from the front of her uniform. She dropped her dagger and slumped to the floor with a strange gurgling sound.

Frye let out a long, shuddering sigh and looked quickly around the room. Hadasaki was slowly getting to his feet as Melliman put a small dart pistol back into her shoulder bag. The smile he tried to give her trembled at the corners of his mouth.

Suddenly everyone in Bridgeforce was talking at once. Commander Drew knelt by Judoff and felt for a pulse. "She's dead," he announced.

"Get her body out of here," Hadasaki ordered. Then he turned to Frye. "Where do you propose establishing this new defensive sphere?"

The question caught Frye off guard, and he answered automatically. "With Gensha as its center and Chadiver, Eidi, and Hiifi-II roughly on its perimeter."

"And Yakusan?"

Frye slowly shook his head. "If we are to save the U.C.S., I believe that Yakusan must stand or fall on its own."

*   *   *

Sjean Birkie was worried. No one had seen Caugust for three days. When her messages to his home went unanswered, she decided to call Security.

"Captain Logfer speaking."

"Captain Logfer, this is Dr. Birkie. No one in any of the labs has seen Dr. Drautz in three days. His admin assistant doesn't know where he is, and there is no answer at his home. Can you tell me where I might find him?"

"No, Dr. Birkie, I can't. And it isn't like him to go anywhere without telling us—even when he's totally wrapped up in an experiment. In fact, my supervisor and I were just discussing the possibility of going to his home."

"May I accompany you?"

"Certainly. We'll wait for you."

It took Sjean fifteen minutes to walk to the security station, but she used the time to review the last conversation she had had with Caugust. He had turned down her invitation to dinner for the third week in a row, and despite his claim that his workload was too heavy, she knew that was only an excuse. She knew from the monotonal sound of his voice that he was on the brink of exhaustion, and still fighting depression, as well.

Then near the end of their conversation his voice had brightened almost as though he'd felt a sudden lift in spirits, and he had agreed to have dinner with her this very evening. She had first called him two days before to confirm their arrangement. By this time she was harboring the darkest pictures of what might have happened to him.

But that was stupid. He probably was wrapped up in some project, something so fascinating that he had lost all track of time. She and Security would go barging into his house only to find him in his basement lab tinkering with his electronic equipment in an attempt to make it do what someone had told him couldn't be done.

Thirty minutes later when they did barge into his house, Sjean went immediately to the lab with one of the officers. She turned on the lights, and at first she didn't see him. When she did, she rushed to the cot where he lay. The officer went to tell the others.

"Caugust? Caugust?" His eyes stared blindly at the ceiling. When he didn't answer, she was almost afraid to touch him. Was he dead? His eyes were open, but that didn't mean anything.

She knelt down and forced herself to pick up his hand. It was cool but not cold. Quickly she felt for a pulse as Captain Logfer came in and knelt beside her. "He has a pulse," she said, "but very weak. Get a doctor."

Logfer stood. "Milligan, call the crash team," he said. Then he bent over again and picked up an envelope from the bed beside Caugust's leg. "It's addressed to you, Dr. Birkie," he said, handing it to her.

Only after the doctor and a team of medical technicians arrived did she move from Caugust's side and consider opening the envelope. As she read, tears filled her eyes.

Dear Sjean,

I am sorry to do this to you, but part of what I have come to understand about myself is how few people in this galaxy I actually care about and trust. You are one of them.

I have deposited sufficient funds in your account to sustain you in research for the next ten years. All

I ask is that you make a trip to Biery to see C.J. and
give him a copy of my Vid-Legal will.
    Again, I am sorry.

Caugust

Why? Why? Why had he done it? No matter how she
twisted it around in her head, Sjean could find no reason in
his life worth trying to kill himself over.

"Will he be all right?" she asked as the medical team
maneuvered him through the lab on the countergrav stretcher.

"Look for anything he might have ingested," the doctor
said, "anything at all. We'll pump him and test his blood, but
if we don't find out what's in his system very soon, I don't
hold much hope for him."

The doctor followed the stretcher out the door, and Sjean,
Logfer, and two of the security officers began a systematic
search of the lab.

"This could take days," Logfer said, opening a cabinet
filled with small containers.

"We don't have days," Sjean snapped. "Maybe minutes or
hours. Just take out anything that looks suspicious or out of
line."

Twenty minutes later they were told they didn't even have
hours. "Dr. Drautz died on the way to the med center,"
Logfer said after responding to a call.

Sjean burst into tears. She was filled with grief but also
with anger. How could he have done this to her? And to
C.J.? How could he claim to care about them and then do
this? It wasn't right. It wasn't fair.

It took her days to calm down enough to realize that there
was no way to change what Caugust had done and no way to
change how she felt about that. The only things she could be
responsible for were her own actions. That was all and enough.

She would go to Biery and give C.J. the Vid-Legal Will.
Then maybe she would go home for a while to see her family.
But she knew that in the end she would return to Drautzlab.
It was where she belonged. Caugust's death had swept away
her foolish notions about giving up research. Research and
development were the two things she liked best and did best
in this life.

And life was too short not to do what gave her the greatest
satisfaction.

* * *

"Do you have visitors?" the Confidante asked.

Leri was startled by the interruptions to her meditation, but she quickly uncoiled and slithered to the mouth of the grotto. There to her surprise she found Proctor Weecs and the Council.

"We come bearing sad information and strange requests," Weecs said.

"Speak and be gone," Leri said without trying to hide the irritation she felt.

"The Castorians have left to join the Sondak humans, and the Verfen have arrived."

She did not care about the Castorians, but the Verfen? "When? When did the Verfen arrive?"

"Just a few seasons ago, Proctor."

"Do not call me that! You are Proctor now, not I. Have you spoken with the Verfen? What are they like? Why have they come?"

Weecs hesitated. "We have not seen them, but they have spoken to us and promised to ensure our safety and neutrality. But it is not that simple."

"It never is. Learning that is part of being Proctor, and the learning never stops." She felt a warm glow of satisfaction that whatever advice she gave, ultimately the problem was Weecs's to cope with, not hers. "What do they want in exchange for this promise of theirs? Methane?"

Again Weecs hesitated. "No, Leri, they have no interest in Cloise's methane. They want you."

"What?"

"They want you—as guarantor of the peace to provide—"

"What by the grace of the Elett do you mean, they want me?" A sudden image of Exeter the Castorian planning to eat her sent a shiver down her spine that curled her tail and increased her anger. "Am I to be some fine meal ordered up for their burrow's feast? Is that what is rippling your tongue, Weecs?"

"No, Leri, no. Nothing like that." Weecs drew back into a subservient posture. "When Ranas communicated with them, he told them you were the ultimate power on Cloise. They refuse to deal with anyone but you and seem to have no concept for succession of authority that does not involve death. When I told them you were not dead, they demanded that you be brought up to their ships immediately."

"Ships? As in more than one? How many—"

"Who knows? They do not appear on any of our devices."

"This is stupid and ridiculous," Leri said. She smelled Weecs's sincerity, but she refused to respond to it. "Be gone and take the Council with you. I must meditate now."

"Please, Leri, hear me out. The Verfen said that before you refused you should seek the advice of your Confidante."

She was speechless. How could the Verfen know about Confidantes? Did they use them also? Is that why they had visited long ago? To seek Confidantes? That made no sense. None of it made any sense. "Very well," she said finally, "I will seek the truth with my Confidante."

"We will remain and await your response."

"You will go! Proctor or no Proctor, you will go. Tell the Verfen they will have my response when I am ready to give it." Without waiting to see or hear the reactions of Weecs and the Council, she turned and hurried back into the grotto.

"Do you have questions?" the Confidante asked even before Leri had settled back into her coil.

"Yes, I have many questions."

"Do I have the answers you seek?"

"I don't know. Do you?"

For a long, long moment the grotto was silent. Then the Confidante said, "Yes, I have answers."

32

"We've tried almost everything we can think of, but we're still trapped in the cockpit," Marsha said into the transceiver. "Given what the remotes show us, it's a wonder *Graycloud*'s life support system is functioning at all."

"Yes, I can see numerous holes in your hull and fragments of the other two ships," Delightful Childe said. "Where is Captain Teeman now?"

"In the access tunnel, trying to reach the suit locker. I cleared the wiring from the first twenty meters, and he's trying to clear the rest of it."

"He is safe?"

"He damn well better be. If he dies, I'll kill him."

"Such strange things you say at times. You are safe?"

"So far we're both safe." It had finally sunk in to her when she was in the access tunnel just how seriously *Graycloud* was damaged. Now she really wasn't sure they were safe at all, but until the situation got worse, she continued to assume that she and Lucky would find a way to handle this problem.

"We have a good supply of air, and the Gouldrive is still supplying power. We're maintaining decent pressure in the cockpit despite the leaks but there's no telling how long that's going to last. Can't you send someone over to help us?"

"No. *Housa* is crewed by checkdroids, and without someone to lead them, there is no accounting for what they would do if and when they reached you."

"And you cannot lead them?"

"Then who would pilot *Housa*? I am the only True Person aboard."

"So you're going to just sit there and watch us die?" The word popped out of her mouth and unintentionally revealed how thin her hope for survival had become. She was down to operating on blind faith. For a brief instant she thought of her father, then she pushed him from her mind. For all he cared she could be dead. She refused to waste energy worrying about him.

"No, Partner Yednoshpfa, I cannot just sit and watch you die. I will attempt to bring *Housa* into direct contact with *Graycloud*. If we can clamp onto you, then I can direct the droids in opening the emergency hatch or cutting through your hull."

"What's he saying?" Lucky asked as he drifted feet first out of the access tunnel.

Marsha smiled with relief. "He's going to try to latch onto us and have his checkdroids perform the rescue."

Lucky wiped his face as he floated over to her. "Tell him not to bother We can reach the survival capsule through here. The air's getting bad, but once we get in the capsule, we'll be all right. It will be a lot easier for him to pick up the capsule than to latch onto *Graycloud*."

"I heard most of what you said, Partner. Where on *Gray-cloud* is the survival capsule?"

"Amidship fore of the dorsal hump," Marsha said.

"We'd better start, Mars. I don't know how much longer we'll have usable air in the tunnel."

"Keep your fingers crossed—all fourteen of them."

"I pray for your success," Delightful Childe said.

Marsha unbuckled her harness and turned to Lucky as she floated off her chair. "You first, my love. You're the smallest."

"What does that have to do with anything?"

"Just go." She pushed him gently toward the access tunnel.

Lucky couldn't understand why she wanted him to go first, but there was no time to argue. Taking a deep breath, he guided his body into the opening, caught the first handhold, and pulled himself in.

Marsha followed as close behind him as she could without getting kicked in the face. As soon as her body was completely in the tunnel, she realized how stale the air was in there and was glad she had made Lucky go first. It had gotten much worse since her first trip, but at least Lucky had a good chance of making it to the survival capsule.

Hand over hand they pulled themselves through the dimly lit tunnel. Lucky paused and coughed, and Marsha's head hit his feet. "Keep going," she said in a high, squeaky voice.

"Helium backup," Lucky said in the same octave. "We're almost there. Another ten meters."

But almost there and being in the survival capsule were two different things. The turnbolt stuck. Then the hatch.

"Sheiss and tensheiss," he cursed as he put as much pressure on the handle as he could. The hinges squealed. He pulled harder. They were both gasping for air.

The hatch sprang open with a loud clang. A burst of dusty air highly charged with oxygen blew out in Lucky's face. He took a heaving breath before pulling his head and shoulders through the hatch.

Marsha smelled the air but couldn't get enough of it into her lungs. Desperately she grabbed his foot and let him drag her into the capsule.

As he fought for breath, Lucky managed to turn himself around and close the capsule's hatch. For a minute or two they both floated in the tiny sphere, heaving in oxygen.

"Grab something," Marsha said. When she was sure he had a handhold, she grabbed one of her own, flipped the cover off the ejection button, and slammed it home with her palm.

Graycloud's outer doors popped open, releasing the cocked spring under the capsule, which thrust it into space.

"There's the *Housa*," Marsha said as she stared through the capsule's only port. "We're headed straight for it. Stay still. We don't want to alter the trajectory."

Using *Housa*'s double grappling arms, Delightful Childe made several inaccurate attempts before he eventually caught the capsule and drew it into the main loading bay.

It took thirty minutes to fully pressurize the bay, but finally Marsha, then Lucky, climbed out of the capsule and were greeted by a Delightful Childe with his wrinkled arms outstretched and all his yellow teeth bared.

"Thank the gods," he said.

"Amen to that," Marsha answered, sending up her own silent prayer of thanks.

Lucky put his arm around her waist and gave her a squeeze as he looked at Delightful Childe. "You don't mind two passengers back to Oina, do you, Partner?"

Delightful Childe fluttered his proboscis in an approximation of human laughter. "Not for the rest of my life. What is mine is yours, Partners."

Lucky and Marsha looked at each other and smiled. "Then let's head for Oina," Marsha said. She kissed Lucky, and they both knew that for them the war was over. They were going home.

* * *

"The LRRS report more Uke hunks headed our way, Admiral, estimated to reach effective firing range in two-point-two hours."

Josiah Gilbert glanced at the external viewscreens and wondered how the Ukes could afford to send so many of their ships against him. Had Schopper and Pajandcan been beaten? It had been over four hundred hours since Nordeen had relayed any word about either of their fleets, and he was growing more and more concerned. Could the Ukes have defeated both fleets and sent all their ships to intercept him?

Or was this a to-the-last-ship effort to keep his fleet from striking against Gensha? For the moment the answers didn't matter. As long as the Ukes were harassing his fleet, there was no way it could make an organized subspace jump to Gensha.

"Dougglas, what is our fighter deployment strength?"

"Forty percent, sir."

"Increase to sixty, and let's get these Ukes out of our way. Dixie, give me the latest on the fleet's status."

"Of our thirty-four ready ships, two cruisers and the launchship *Tems* are still questionable for subspace. The *Stern* is taking as many of the *Tems*'s fighters as it can carry. The *New McQuay* will take on the rest."

"Which gives us how many fighters, Dougglas?"

"Approximately nine hundred seventy-five operational, sir."

Gilbert allowed himself a small smile. "Admiral Dixie, hold that fighter transfer order. Dougglas, I want all the *Tems*'s fighters operating from her bays in one hour. For each of those you put up against the Ukes, pull one back for us or the *Stern*. When that is complete, pull all our fighters back."

"Aye, sir," Dougglas said slowly, "but that will put a tremendous load on the *Tems*. And won't it also slow down our attack departure?"

"Yes, and yes. Dixie, I want a double squadron assembled around the *New McQuay* and the *Stern*. That will leave seven ships to support the *Tems*. Prepare the squadrons for a mass subspace flight to the Hiifi-II attack coordinates." He saw the immediate look of doubt on her face. "You have a question, Admiral?"

"Uh, sir, it's just that—well, sir, isn't a double squadron of twenty-six ships rather weak to be attacking Hiifi-II? I thought that was Schopper's target?"

"It was, but we're going there first. If he needs help, we'll give it. If not, we'll join forces for the attack on Gensha. If the Ukes have sent most of their ships to fight us here, the other systems are bound to be more vulnerable. Now execute that order."

"Aye, sir."

"Tech Mate, I want to send a message to Nordeen, informing them of my intentions."

"It will take four relays from here, sir."

"I don't care how many it takes. Just set it up."

Fifty-three hours later Gilbert's double squadron broke through the Ukes off Shakav and entered subspace with twenty-five ships. Uke hunks caught three more ships in subspace before he exited eighty tachymeters off the Hiifi-II system with a fleet of twenty-two.

Much to Gilbert's relief and surprise, the initial Uke resistance was light as he closed on Hiifi-II. With a little more luck his fleet might be able to capture and control Hiifi's space before the Ukes knew what was happening. Then all he had to do was hold what he captured until Schopper arrived to support him.

* * *

"For some reason your father has changed the plan. According to Nordeen his fleet should already have reached Hiifi-II," Schopper said. "We should have direct contact with him in a few hours. In the meantime, I want to present you with something. Along with the messages from Nordeen came these orders for your promotion to Post Commander. Congratulations."

"Thank you, sir," Mica said, accepting the sealed packet he handed her, "but I don't understand why they promoted me. Am I to be reassigned?"

"Not that I know of. There are also several personal messages for you in that packet. I'll notify you when we make contact with your father."

"Thank you again, sir," Mica said with a quick salute. She left his cramped office and headed for her own, eager to see what the packet contained but more eager to hear from her father. When she reached her tiny combination office-cabin, she shut the door and quickly tore open the packet.

The dispatches were routine information and intelligence updates. She glanced over their title pages and told herself there was no reason to read them right away.

There were three personal messages, one from Rochmon, one from her father, and one from Henley. She read his first and smiled. He wanted her to pick a place for them to meet when the war was over. Apparently his emotions were not as guarded as he wanted her to believe.

The message from her father was his usual query about her health and cryptic references to their mutual activities. The message from Rochmon stopped her cold. It was clearer than anything he had ever said or sent to her—a proposal of marriage.

But why? What had she ever done to encourage his feelings in that direction? Nothing, she decided as she reread the message. He wasn't proposing to her. He was proposing to some ideal of what he wanted her to be. She quickly convinced herself that Hew Rochmon had never really tried to know her as anything but the young girl who had flirted with him—some sweet, innocent child that had captured his warped devotion.

It was enough to make her cry. She liked Hew, but after she entered the Service, she had never truly felt anything stronger than the affection of friendship for him. Maybe she had done some things that he misunderstood, but nothing to lead him to this.

"Captain, uh, Commander Gilbert, we've made contact with your father's fleet," Schopper's voice said through her speaker-phone. "Meet me in communications."

"On my way." Mica put the personal messages aside and quickly stuffed the dispatches back into the packet. Tucking that under her arm, she had a feeling that she was missing something, but she was in too much of a hurry to worry about it.

When she arrived at the communications center, it was crowded with the normal complement of technicians, plus all of General Schopper's staff, the Space Commander, Admiral Flowers, and as many of his staff as could squeeze into the room. They made room for her, but she had to suck in her breath and work her way in on tiptoe.

"We're all assembled, Admiral," Schopper said.

"Thank you," Admiral Gilbert's voice said over the static. "First I want to compliment all of you on the fine job you've done thus far. All indications are that the Ukes are disorganized and on the fly. We have—" A loud cheer covered his next words.

"—reform our attack plan. Resistance here has been minimal, but Admiral Pajandcan's fleet had serious problems at Buth, and her LRRS report a heavy buildup of Uke shipping in the area of Yakusan. Consequently, Admiral Flowers, I want you to split your war fleet as evenly as possible into two task forces numbered Ten and Twenty.

"General Schopper, send me your five reserve legions with Admiral Flowers and Task Force Ten, then take Task Force Twenty, including the rest of your legions, as quickly as possible to Yakusan to support Pajandcan. Is that all clear?"

"Clear, sir," Admiral Flowers said.

"Yes, sir," Schopper said more slowly, "but if I send my five reserve legions to you, by headcount I only have enough troops left to form six tired and battered legions to support Admiral Pajandcan, plus her inexperienced six."

"I understand that, General, but most of the battle for Yakusan should take place in space before you ever have to land those troops, so yours will have some time to rest. I want your reserves because I plan a simultaneous ground invasion and space attack on Gensha."

Mica was startled by her father's decision, but even through the static she could hear the pride and determination in his voice.

"If there are no further questions," Admiral Gilbert said, "I will confirm these orders by message and expect to see Task Force Ten within eighty hours. Gilbert out."

As he signed off, everyone in the communications center seemed to be talking at once. Only Schopper's booming voice stilled the noise. "All staff officers to the strategy room on the double," he announced. "Fleet coordination officers will pass the readiness orders to the legion."

Mica followed the crowd out of the center toward the strategy room. A sudden feeling that she had missed something grabbed hold on her mind, and as soon as she got to the room, she parked herself in a corner and reopened the packet. She found what was nagging her in the third dispatch.

The Castorians had joined the war on Sondak's side. Furthermore, it was rumored that the mysterious Verfen had sent emissaries to the other neutrals. She was pleased about the Castorians and knew her father would be pleased also, but she didn't know what to think about the Verfen. Surely if the rumors had been important, Cryptography would have made a point of saying so.

She dismissed the Verfen and made quick note to tell Schopper and Flowers about the Castorians. As busy as everyone was going to be, she wanted to be sure she didn't forget.

33

"Send them this message, AOCO. Tell them I want a full strategic retreat, with as many of their ships as they can break away to rendezvous at Alexvieux. And tell Marshall Zonazuza that if he wants to remain Senior Commander, he will give us no more excuses."

"Why Alexvieux, sir?" Melliman asked.

"Because that is the last place the Saks will think to look for a fleet. From there we can take the northern polar route to Nordeen and smash Sondak's nerve center."

"Uh, sir, it seems to me . . ."

His face wrinkled into a frown at the negative tone in her voice. "Spit it out, Clarest."

She looked down for a brief second before turning her face up and meeting his gaze. "It seems to me this is a terribly big risk for us—maybe our final shot. We lost so many ships at Shakav and the polar systems that—"

"Dammit, Clarest!" he said as he stood up behind his desk and glared at her in annoyance. "Don't second-guess me. If we don't form a new fleet and strike immediately, Sondak will isolate and cripple the rest of our systems one by one. We should have done this a long time ago. But between the conservatives and the kyosei, my hands have been tied like a ginga hung for slaughter." To emphasize his point, he slapped his wrists together as though they were bound.

"You know that," he continued. "You've been here. You've seen what they've done. Can't you understand that—" Abruptly he stopped himself. The expression on her face finally made him hear what he was saying.

Slowly he lowered his hands to his side. "I'm sorry, Clarest. I didn't mean to fly off at you like that." He reached out, and she placed her hand in his. "It's my frustration talking—the three years of frustration that brought us to this dilemma. Sometimes it all just overwhelms me."

220

"I understand," she said softly. "I only want to make sure that you've considered all the options."

"Of course. I know that. And no one understands the options better than you do." He released her hand and sat back down. "Let's start over again. Give me all your ideas and *all* your reservations."

She sat across the desk from him and leaned back, rotating her head to loosen her neck muscles. "Your plan might work, sir. It certainly would be the last maneuver Sondak might expect from us. But then again, it might not work. And if it doesn't, you haven't left yourself any way out. In effect what you're saying is this: if the attack on Nordeen doesn't succeed, the war will be conceded to the Saks. That's what bothers me."

"But we would continue to fight," he said vehemently.

"A losing battle. Even if we totally destroyed Nordeen, the Saks wouldn't quit fighting. They would only be at a severe disadvantage. The same for us, but how long could we hold out against them? Years? Decades? Decades of what? Irregular warfare?" She paused and took a long breath as she shook her head.

"Then what?" she continued. "Would we fight a guerrilla war until we couldn't beg, borrow, steal, or capture any more fuel, food, and ammunition—not to mention spacecraft? I think we would better serve the U.C.S. by throwing up our defenses here at Gensha than taking a chance on losing everything."

He understood her logic, but he couldn't agree with her. His mind was made up. "No. The best defensive strategy is to mount a strong offensive. We can't give up now. We have to bend like a triggerpault spring, then crush them from behind. Let them win at Yakusan and Hiifi-II—but while they're doing that, strike at their heart and they'll be hurt and confused, and *their* conservatives will slow *them* down—maybe even stop them."

Again she shook her head. "Sounds like you're asking for a terrible sacrifice with little promise of reward at the end," Melliman said with a sigh. "How can we possibly let Yakusan and Hiifi-II and maybe even Gensha fall to the Saks?"

Only his determination not to kept Frye from cursing. Melliman was beginning to sound like Marsha had after the

battle of Matthews system. But he knew that unlike Marsha
Melliman would support him once the decision had bee
made. "Are those all your reservations?" he asked finally.

Her response was slow in coming. "Yes, sir, I believe the
are. There's nothing more I can add to what I've said."

Frye heard something else in her voice, the barest hint of
whine that sounded like pain and weakness. He quickly chos
to ignore it—for the time being. "Very well, AOCO, we wil
begin ordering the withdrawal of ships to Alexvieux an
preparing a battle plan for an attack on Nordeen."

*   *   *

Henley picked up the handful of messages that had accu
mulated for him over the past few days and filed his lates
story for the *Flag Report* in the *Menard*'s communication
center. He hoped they would publish it before the war wa
over, because it told about the bravery and courage of th
troops in the Three-Seventy-First Legion.

The first message angered him. It was a demand from
Headquarters, Fleet Military Guard, ordering him to repor
to the ranking M.G. officer aboard and provide that office
with all the possible locations he knew about where to fine
one Krystal R. Kinderman. He'd already told Lieutenan
Conlaura everything he knew about Kryki. What more di
they want from him?

Reluctantly, he went straight down to the lower decks an
knocked on the door of Conlaura's tiny cabin-office.

"What took you so long?" Conlaura asked with a friendly
smile as they exchanged salutes.

"Just picked up my messages, Lieutenant. But I'm afraic
I'm not going to be much help to you or your headquarters. I
told you everything we knew the last time we did this."

"I'm sure you did, Chief," Conlaura said, waving him to
the bunk that served as a seat across from her desk. "How
ever, I'd like to go over it with you one more time—just fo
the sake of the formalities, you understand. Who knows, i
might jar something loose that you didn't remember last
time."

Henley smiled at her. "I doubt it, but it can't hurt to try.
As I told you before, if Kryki got off Nordeen, there are
hundreds of places he could have gone where he would have
been safe. He's a hero on Biery and a celebrity on Patros
and—"

"He hasn't left Nordeen," Conlaura said. "H.Q. told me to tell you that. They have evidence that he is still on Nordeen, being hidden by one of the antiwar groups, possibly the Last Signalcrew Society."

" *'And you don't need a signalcrew to hear the screaming voices of the people as they're killed by the ones who made the choices.'* "

"Pardon?" Conlaura asked.

"That's where the society got its name—from one of Kryki's most famous antiwar poems." Henley smiled. "You mean you've never heard it?"

"Can't say that I have, Chief."

"Doesn't matter. So, your people think he's still on Nordeen, and you think I might have missed something when we last talked about all this?"

"Correct. Let's begin by reviewing what you said . . ."

Henley listened as Conlaura read the transcript of their previous conversation, but his attention kept straying back to the Kryki of years before. Henley had always admired Kryki for his willingness to stand straight up for his beliefs, but Henley had to admit that he had never really understood Kryki or felt comfortable close to Kryki's fanatic obsession with intergalactic brotherhood. Now Henley felt as if they were talking about someone he had never really known at all.

"Excuse me, Lieutenant," Henley said, suddenly interrupting Conlaura's recitation, "but if your people think the Last Signalcrew is hiding Kinderman, why don't they just haul all those people into jail and find out from them where he is?"

Conlaura looked startled for a moment, then laughed. "I wish we could, and I'm sure my superiors wish they could, also, but I guess you haven't heard about the new legislation."

"I don't follow you. What new legislation?"

"The Tri-Cameral and the Combined Committees passed a new series of laws several standard months ago called the Evidentiary Statutes, or Evis Laws, as the public calls them. It is now illegal to arrest anyone without substantial claims of evidence verified by a judge."

"That's insane."

"It's worse than that. The heart of the Evis Laws reverses the concept of guilty until proven innocent. Now all arrestees must be treated as innocent until proven guilty."

Henley let out a low whistle. "And the Service is going along with this anarchy?"

"For the time being it is—mainly because the laws do not apply to the Service itself."

"I should hope not. It's frightening to imagine the trouble that will cause," Henley said, yet even as he spoke, he felt a certain attraction to this revolutionary idea. It might be good for Sondak, and it certainly would reduce the suffering of those who would otherwise spend years in jail before finally being declared innocent. Still, his fear of the idea was stronger than his radical attraction to it. He wondered if Ruffendamal had—

"Chief? Are you all right?"

"Yes, of course," Henley said quickly. "Did we talk about Ruffendamal last time?"

Conlaura leafed quickly through the transcript and held up a single page. "No. He's not on the list."

"It's not a person. Ruffendamal is a place, a private, secret retreat for artists and writers and actors and lots of other creative people—and it's on Nordeen."

"I never heard of it."

"That doesn't surprise me. It's built around an oasis in the middle of the Musgrave Desert. Tell your headquarters that if Kryki's not there, he's probably left Nordeen."

"How can you be so sure?"

"I don't know, but I am. He's secretly funneled money into Ruffendamal for years, and that's where he always went for what he called his rejuvenation periods."

"I'll certainly pass the information on, Chief. Now if we can resume the review of your—"

"Not now, Conlaura. I just told you the most important thing I know. You relay that information as fast as you can. Then if your people come up dry, you and I can talk again."

"Begging your pardon, Chief, but regulations say that—"

"Damn the regulations," Henley said, rising to his feet, "and pass on the information."

Conlaura rose hesitantly. "You're sure, Chief?"

"Do it," Henley said, giving her a quick salute as he opened the door.

As his junior in rank, she had no choice but to return it. "Very well, Chief, but I hope that doesn't put both of us in a sling of trouble."

"It won't. Just do it." He left without waiting for her reply. For some reason that wasn't clear to him yet he felt angry and agitated—and a little guilty—as he began climbing the ladders up toward his cabin.

Why had he been so eager to help the M.G.s find Kryki? Wasn't that a betrayal of friendship and trust? No, he decided. He and Kryki had never been friends. They had only been acquaintances who had admired each other's work. Kryki had violated whatever trust was involved when he had blown his way out of prison and killed innocent people in the process.

On sudden impulse Henley headed for the troop bays of the Three-Seventy-First Legion where he knew he would find Ingrivia and Denoro. He wanted his mind filled with honorable troopering, not politics and fanaticism.

Denoro greeted him at the door of Delta Company's bay. "You come to join us for the invasion of Yakusan?" she asked with a grim smile.

His mind was so cluttered it took Henley a moment to react. "I thought the fleet was going to soften them up for a while?"

"So did we, but the colonel just got new orders. The Ukes are breakin' up, and we're going in."

"How soon?"

"Eighty hours till mothership departure. You comin'?"

"Yes," Henley said without hesitation. "If you've got room for me, I'm wouldn't miss it for anything." A cold chill snaked along his spine, and he knew he was going to hate it again when the fighting started, but he couldn't imagine himself anyplace else.

*   *   *

Season after season Leri had asked the Confidante to explain what it knew about the Verfen, and to tell her why she should go into space and leave her beloved Cloise behind. Season after season her Confidante has answered her questions with questions of its own that only made her angry. When Weecs came again to ask for her response, she chased him away with unexpected fury.

She returned to the Confidante, but finally Leri's anger boiled away the last of her patience. "You said you had answers!" she screamed. "Why won't you tell me? Why?"

"Do you need answers for your well-being?" the Confidante asked.

"I need them for my sanity."

"Will you listen with an open heart to all I have to say
before you respond?"

"Yes, of course I will listen. I always listen to you. It's you
who doesn't listen to me."

"Will you open your heart, daughter of Cloise, to what I
have to say? Can you accept the truth when it will be strange
to you? Can you believe that soon all will be well when you
and I journey to greet those who are called the Verfen?"

"Yes—uh, us? Together? You and me?" Leri was as startled
as she was confused.

"Can you understand that those who come, who are called
the Verfen, are flesh of my flesh and shell of my shell?"

Leri opened her mouth, but nothing came out. The
Confidante a Verfen? Her Confidante? Is that how it knew—?
Is that what it meant by—? Even the questions wouldn't form
properly in her mind. What was happening to her?

"Do you doubt that I asked for you to accompany me, Leri
Gish Geril? Are you disturbed by this information? Would
you deny me? Would you deprive me of my need for you in
this joyous hour?"

Leri swallowed twice, three times, before she could force
the words out of her mouth. "I do not understand, and I am
afraid," she said slowly. "Are we to go together to join your
sister Verfen? Is that what you ask of me?"

"Did you not ask to live with me for the rest of your life?"

"I did."

"Would you deny my need for you?"

"I did not know—I do not understand your need."

"Do not you and your people need the Isthians as they
need you? Why, then, can you not understand my need?"

Leri sighed deeply. "There is much about you I do not
understand," she said, "but I accept your need."

"Then if you and I and two Isthians journey to join those
who have come for me, can we not be four in person but one
in contentment for the rest of our lives?"

It was all too overwhelming. "Yes," she said in a shaky
voice. Leri had no way of knowing what might happen to her,
but as she spoke she suddenly felt warm and secure.

Then the vision returned and filled her mind, the terrifying vision of yawning jaws waiting to swallow her whole. Her eyes saw nothing else. Her heart pounded in fear. She wanted to scream, to beg, to plead for release, but the vision overcame her, and she fell headlong into darkness.

*   *   *

Quarter-Admiral Hew Rochmon sat dejectedly outside the Joint Chiefs' meeting room. From a military point of view he should have been one of the happiest people in the Service. With the Ukes's Q-3 Code broken, his Cryptography staff was providing the Joint Chiefs and the tactical commanders in space with a steady stream of useful information. In addition he had implemented his plan for sending false information to confuse the Ukes, and it was working brilliantly, almost as though Charltos were gone and they were facing some lesser commander.

Now the Joint Chiefs were about to award him the Medal of Legions, an honor almost always reserved for combat commanders. But Hew Rochmon was anything but happy. He was tired in body and spirit and depressed by his personal life.

Why? he wondered. Why had Mica so unequivocally rejected his proposal? Was it because of Stanmorton? Or was it because she truly found him unworthy of her love?

That had to be the answer. She knew about him. She knew how limited he was, how reluctant to totally commit his emotions. She knew, but she didn't understand. How could she? Even he didn't understand what made him this way.

All he wanted was for her to love him. To love him so that he could recapture his own ability to love. Was that too much to ask of her? Was that so wrong? Did she think she would find something stronger than that, something more romantic?

He shrugged his shoulders. It didn't matter. Not now. He had already decided that he would leave the Service as soon as the war was over. He had some credits saved—enough to leave Nordeen and set up a new life somewhere else. There were other women out there who would welcome his attentions, who would give him the kind of—

Shouts and scuffling interrupted his thoughts. He looked up in time to see a strange bearded man wearing a purple-and-red striped long coat running down the hall toward him pursued by several M.G.s. Behind them there were many other people fighting in the hall.

Without thinking, Rochmon jumped out of his chair and ran toward the man. Something rang loudly in his ears and slammed against his chest.

"Stop!" he shouted as he spun and fell backward. "Stop," he gurgled again as the man leaped over him.

Rochmon rolled to his right and tried to stand. Dark waves of pain tore through his chest and his mind as he reached his knees. He looked up as the madman burst through the double doors into the Joint Chiefs' meeting room.

"For peace and brotherhood!" the man shouted.

Seconds later an explosion blew the doors back and threw Rochmon to the floor. Chunks of debris rained down upon him. Dust clogged his nose and throat. He fought to breathe, then to move. Screams and shouts filled the air.

Another explosion rumbled in the distance. The floor underneath him vibrated violently. His mind threatened to close down, but Rochmon fought for consciousness.

Close by he heard groans of pain. Again he tried to get himself up on his knees. His arms and legs trembled. His chest screamed out in pain. He ended up sitting dazedly on the floor, staring into the shattered remains of the meeting room.

He saw bodies and gore and a strange piece of purple-and-red striped material draped over a pair of unattached legs. For a moment he didn't understand what it meant. Then he remembered the madman and slumped into unconsciousness.

Rochmon awoke to the sight of a medic and a Guard Officer who immediately began questioning him about what had happened. He didn't stay awake long, but every time he awoke, someone was there to question him, forcing Rochmon to remember bits and pieces of the events.

That's how he got his information, in bits and pieces. Stonefield was dead. Avitor Hilldill was dead. They wouldn't tell him about Admiral Eresser for a few days until they finally said she was recovering. General McLaughlin and Admiral Lindshaw had been out of the room when the bomb went off, and both were uninjured.

The bomber had been some famous poet named Kickerman, or something like that. No one seemed to know why Kickerman did it, and Rochmon didn't care.

The doctors said it would take several months for Rochmon's wounds to heal, and that was just fine with him. Someone else could collect his medal and finish the war in his place. The only thing Hew Rochmon wanted was sleep without dreams and some peace within himself.

34

"Is that it?" Marsha asked. "Aren't they going to say anything else? Or are they gone?"

"That is very difficult to say, Partner Yednoshpfa," Delightful Childe said with a little shake of his proboscis. "The Verfen do not seem to observe courtesies of parting."

"It's impossible," Lucky said. "How can a bunch of aliens no one has seen for two hundred years just space in and announce that the war is over? That's the craziest thing I ever—"

"You heard them as well as we did," Delightful Childe said. "They said they could not put an end to this insane human conflict, but they could protect us from it. I believe them."

A brief thought of her father crossed Marsha's mind, and she knew she was still worried about him. No matter what had happened between them she would probably always worry about him. "But how? How are they going to protect you? Are they going to kill all us humans? Is that how they'll protect you?"

Lucky reached for her hand and squeezed it gently. "Don't jump to conclusions, Mars. If they could make Delightful Childe exit subspace just to talk to him, and just as suddenly start talking to us here on Oina, maybe they actually do have some power to protect all the neutrals."

"You're the one who just said that was impossible!"

"I don't know, Mars. I really don't. Maybe it's only impossible for us to imagine, but wouldn't it be wonderful if they really could protect us?" In spite of his better judgment

Lucky was hoping against logic that the Verfen could live up to their claims.

Marsha shook her head. Something deep inside of her was turning over, stirring up sediment from emotion that had lain undisturbed for a long time.

"Regardless of what happens, my partners, for us here on Oina it is no longer our problem," Delightful Childe said, knowing all too well that duty to Oina would probably deny him escape from the problems that faced the galaxy.

Marsha fought the tears that threatened to flood her eyes. She felt like she was teetering on the edge of an abyss, and that now only her much-neglected faith in God steadied her.

"Hold your faith, Marsha Lisa Cay Yednoshpfa," several melodic voices said from Delightful Childe's communications speaker. "We have come to stop what violence we can, not to commit new violence. Please accept our truth-saying."

The three of them looked at each other as though to confirm that they were all hearing the same thing.

The tears stayed in her eyes, and suddenly Marsha asked, "Are you connected with God?"

"Retain your faith," the Verfen voices answered. "All things are connected to all things."

"Of course," Delightful Childe said with a fluttering sigh. Deep in his heart he felt a warm flow of understanding as though he instinctively knew what the Verfen meant.

"That's no answer," Marsha protested, but already the turmoil inside her was settling down. "Give me a straight answer. Are you connected with God?"

The speaker remained silent.

Marsha looked at Lucky and knew he was puzzled by the whole exchange. Then, in a brief flash of insight, she recognized the answer the Verfen had given her. Like a great cleansing force, it swept through her mind and opened her way to peace. She saw it in a pictureless way and heard its silent music. There were no words to describe its effect, but Marsha was caught up in a bright wave of self-assurance. Delightful Childe bared his blunt yellow teeth on either side of his proboscis and gave her his Oinaise version of a smile.

Lucky turned from one of them to the other. "Why are you both smiling?" he asked.

"Because I believe Partner Yednoshpfa and I both understand the Verfen's answer," Delightful Childe said, seeing in her eyes a look that matched the feeling in his heart. "It seems the Verfen have left us with a bit of truth."

"Now I'm the one who's confused." Apprehension rippled down Lucky's spine. "Did I miss something here?"

"Take him to your rooms and show him," Delightful Childe said to Marsha with an expansive wave of his seven-fingered hand. "Then he will understand."

Feeling happier than she had been since before the war, Marsha took Lucky's arm and pulled him out of his chair. "Remember that old fiche of *skona* sayings I found on Patros that time?" she asked as she led him out of the communications room and down the hallway toward their suite. "Well, it's like that saying, the one I could never figure out but couldn't get rid of. Remember?"

Lucky remembered only too well, because she had recited it over and over until he had thought she would space him crazy. "The one you kept repeating about the old man's walking stick?"

She smiled. "That's the one. *If you have it, I will give it to you. If you don't have it, I will take it away.* It's true for faith, or love, or anything else, Lucky," she said, as sure of her words as she had ever been. She knew that somehow in the openness of sharing themselves with each other she could make him understand. "Now we have love, so let's give it to each other."

As he looked into her eyes his apprehension melted away. "I don't think I understand about the stick," he said, answering her smile with a mischievous grin, "but I suspect what we're about to do doesn't have anything to do with sticks and *skona* sayings."

"Everything's connected to everything else." She dropped her hand from his waist and squeezed his rear end.

It was enough for Lucky that she loved him and wanted him. If she needed some strange philosophy of faith, that was all right with him, just so long as they stayed together for the rest of their lives. From the look on her face and the feeling in his heart, somehow he suspected they would.

* * *

Pajandcan felt great empathy for Schopper's predicament, but the final decision had to be hers, and she wasn't quite ready to make it. "Are you sure this is the only way?"

"Depends on whether or not the crypto kids are right. If they are, if the Ukes do have our people imprisoned down there, how can we do anything else?"

"I don't know," Pajandcan said with a shiver. "I didn't think there was any way I could hate the Ukes more than I did after Matthews." She paused for the brief flash of memory that always accompanied that name. "But slaughtering prisoners? How could they?"

"They think they're better than we are just because they live a little longer and they're closer to their Terran roots. Killing our people doesn't mean anything to them."

Pajandcan leaned back in her chair and rubbed her temples, feeling the pressure of one of her recurring headaches. "My people thought they were better, once—*homo electus*, a separate race they said. It was nonsense, stupid nonsense."

"Doesn't matter what any of them think. We have to save those prisoners, Admiral, and we're going to need all the help you can give us."

"The Ukes are already scared and broken up here."

"But not down there. This will be our first planetary invasion against a Uke home planet. It's not going to be easy like it was back on Thayne-G. The best we can hope for is to control Syberal City and its starport and to rescue our people in the prisons we know about."

"That's what worries me. Your legions are battle weary, and mine are practically untested." Pajandcan rotated her shoulders, trying to relieve the routine stiffness in her once-broken back. "There's still the blockade alternative."

"Not if they're murdering our people."

"No, I suppose not." She closed her eyes and sighed before looking at him again. "All the troops are ready?"

"As ready as they're going to get anytime soon."

This invasion was going to cost thousands of young lives, but Pajandcan knew that her mind had already made the decision. It was her heart that was reluctant to accept it. "Very well. We land them as you have suggested, an hour before the dawn over Syberal City."

He stood up immediately and saluted her. "Thanks, Admiral."

She stood and held out her hands. He accepted them, and arms crossed, they shook. "Good luck, Schopper, and good hunting."

                    *   *   *

For the first time in her life Leri saw a Confidante outside
its grotto —her Confidante, a huge mass of wrinkled gray flesh
protruding from a pale blue shell. Despite her fears, and
despite her vision, Leri was comforted by the Confidante's
presence. Two Isthians clung to her back, one mute, one
not—both ones with whom she had previously shared exchange.

Even now Leri felt a sense of awe. Above them, descend-
ing slowly through the haze, was a Verfen ship. It hardly
looked large enough to carry the Confidante, much less her,
too, but she trusted that it could.

"Farewell, Honored Leri," cried voices from the cliff behind her. "May the Elett bless you always. Farewell, True
Confidante. May peace be your life's blessing."

Leri acknowledged their cries with a small fireball sent
straight over her head that burned out well below the de-
scending Verfen ship. As she watched its glow fade she
wondered if her people were close enough to see the Isthians
on her back, then wondered what they thought of the exposed Confidante. None of this was normal, but then nothing
seemed normal anymore, and nothing ever would be again. It
had all changed from the time the first humans arrived, when
she was but a gupling, to now when she was leaving to live
with a race of Confidantes.

Fear shivered through her again. The mute Isthian stroked
her nipple with soothing little purring sounds. Slowly Leri let
herself relax and watch the Verfen ship land quietly in the
middle of the canyon.

"Are you ready to leave now, daughter of Cloise?" her
Confidante asked.

"I am ready," she answered in a voice that trembled with
emotion. She wasn't ready. She would never be ready. But
her Confidante had convinced her that this was the choice
she was meant to accept, that it needed her as much as she
needed the Isthians.

Like a gigantic snail, the Confidante began moving toward
the waiting ship. Leri slithered along beside it, more afraid
with every passing spinelength, yet more determined not to
let her fear show. When they reached the ramp of the ship,
they paused.

"Will you follow me still?" the Confidante asked.

"Yes, I will follow you as best I can," Leri answered.

Slowly, the Confidante humped itself up the ramp and into the ship. Reluctantly, Leri followed into its dark interior. When her tail was completely inside, the ramp began lifting with a quiet whine. Leri panicked and spun herself around.

"Can you be still now, Leri Gish Geril, companion of my life?" the Confidante asked in a musical voice.

Instead of answering, Leri sought the Confidante's reassuring bulk and curled herself up against it.

"May we share the exchange now?" the speaking Isthian asked. "We are both in need."

It seemed an odd time, but Leri could not deny their needs any more than they could deny hers. "Yes," she said softly, "but since we are to share the remainder of our lives together, please tell me your names."

"We have no names in the sense that you mean them. I am but the brother of he who does not speak."

Leri thought about that for a long moment as the Verfen ship vibrated with a steady hum and the nonspeaking Isthian began suckling deeply on her nipple. "Then I shall call you Speaks and your brother Speaks Not. Is that acceptable?"

"That is acceptable."

The first exchange soothed her body and her mind, and Leri let herself relax to its rhythms. The second exchange put her to sleep only to be awakened soon after by the Confidante's voice.

"Will you wake, please, daughter of Cloise?"

"I am awake," she said.

"Will you see the journeycraft that carries us home?"

Leri looked over her head and for the first time saw a clear opening in the roof of the ship. Through that opening she saw stars and in the middle of the stars a huge and wonderful sight. The journeyship was ablaze with strange lights and the outline of—suddenly she laughed, her heart filled with joy and happiness.

"What pleases you so, daughter of Cloise?"

"Your ship," she said with great pleasure. "See the opening we approach—the opening like great jaws? Oh, Confidante, those are the jaws of my vision! But I'm not afraid! It was their strangeness that frightened my dreams."

"Can you rest easily now?"

"Forever," Leri said, letting her coil relax. She did not

know what the future held for her, but she was sure in her heart that whatever happened she would be contented. "Forever," she whispered again as she drifted back toward sleep.

"Yes, forever," a voice said.

She thought it was Speaks's voice, but it could have been the Confidante's. Whichever, she was happy.

*   *   *

It was the place Frye hated the most in the whole universe. It was the place of dreams—where he knew he was dreaming but couldn't break free from the darkness of the dream. He hated it most because he felt so helpless there—and Frye did not like feeling helpless.

In the dream he was surrounded by Sondak's fleets, thousands of ships that fired repeatedly at him.

No matter what he did, he couldn't fire back.

Nothing worked. Everything jammed. Vinita cried out for his help. When he reached for her, she disappeared through a black shadow. His ship rocked and rattled with explosions. Dark winds shook him. Soft claws cut into his flesh.

"More bad news," Melliman said as she shook his arm. "I think you need to hear this. Frye? Frye? Wake up, Frye."

He rolled on his back and rubbed his eyes as the dreams slipped like quicksilver through the crevices of his brain. Only the image of Vinita remained as he opened his eyes. He stared at her for a long moment before he realized with a twinge of sadness that it wasn't Vinita at all.

"I'm awake, Clarest. I'm awake. What's wrong?"

"We've exited subspace and entered the Alexvieux Five system, but you're not going to like what we've found."

Slowly, his mind cleared, but his heart still trembled in the cold, dark shadow of the dream. "Tell me."

"Marshall Zanazuza sent ships, but not the ones you told him to. We have one first-war launchship, fifteen troop carriers, ninety-one armed lightspeed freighters, and three hundred twenty-two unarmed ships of miscellaneous classifications."

"My ears must still be asleep," Frye said as he sat up and threw his legs over the side of the double bunk.

She sat beside him. For a moment she only looked at him, then tears ran from her eyes, and she buried her face into his shoulder. "Zanazuza betrayed us. There is no battle fleet here," she said through quiet sobs.

Now Frye was wide awake. "No fleet? But he confirmed my orders. How dare he disobey!"

"Oh, Frye, I'm sorry. I'm so sorry."

Even as her words tore at his heart, Frye was unangered, as though he were suddenly drenched by a great calm. He gently pushed Melliman away from him and raised her face to look at him. "There's more, isn't there?"

She nodded mutely, her damp cheeks shiny in the light.

"Tell me."

"Yakusan has been invaded. Chadiver has declared itself neutral. Gensha's defenses are crumbling, but they got those messages to us. It's over, Frye. It's over." She threw her arms around him and sobbed uncontrollably.

"It's all right," he said, stroking her hair. "It's going to be all right . . . because it's not over. Sondak may think it is, but I know better. Zanazuza must have known what he was doing when he sent those ships here." Frye's words sounded ridiculous, but he needed to believe them, and he did. "We'll talk to their captains, to the ranking officer. We'll count every weapon and prepare our counterattack. But it's not over. No, Clarest, it's not even close to being over."

"Don't you understand?" she asked through her sobs as she pulled back to look at him. "There is no fleet here—no real fleet. We've lost, Frye. We've lost."

"Alexvieux will make a good base," he heard himself saying. "We'll establish ourselves dirtside first, and then . . . and then . . ." His voice trailed off as he saw the strange expression on her face. "What am I saying? Why do I suddenly feel like we have to go dirtside?"

"Attention, Admiral Charltos," a voice said through the speaker in the bulkhead.

With an odd sense that he knew what to expect, Frye opened the command channel and said, "Charltos here."

"Sir, I think . . . I think you'd better come up here. We've just been contacted by some aliens—the Verfen they claim to be—and they're demanding to speak to you."

"Very well," Frye said. "I'll be right there." When he realized how pleased he felt just because the Verfen wanted to talk to him, something frightening twisted in his brain.

"Quickly, Clarest," he said, not wanting to believe what he was thinking, but at the same time feeling driven to communicate with the Verfen.

As soon as they reached the bridge plural musical voices addressed him in concert from the transceiver. "Admiral Frye ed'Laitin Charltos, you have reached your final destination."

Frye would have laughed if a feeling of total belief hadn't swept through him. Yet the core of his being resisted that overwhelming feeling. "Who are you?" he demanded. Glancing up at the tracking screens he saw nothing but U.C.S. ships. "And where are you?"

"Do not concern yourself with that, Frye Charltos. Truth be it to say that you should abandon your vessels of war and make your new home on this planet you call Alexvieux Five."

"Of course," Frye said, turning to Melliman. "Don't you see, Clarest? It's all so logical that I—" Again something inside of him resisted, but he didn't know what to say.

"—and calculating landing orbits of the *Deci*—"

"Preparing shuttles and assembling landing—"

"—previous scientific base as suitable—"

"No!" Frye screamed at the voices from his own fleet and the Verfen. "Stop that!" Part of his mind wondered what all the excitement was all about, but the military part of him continued to protest. "Stop that! . . . Leave us alone. . . . Please?"

There was no stopping the preparations for descent to the surface. Ships without landing capabilities began transferring their people and equipment to ships with those capabilities. Yet as those preparations increased, Frye's protests diminished.

Because of the Verfen.

Wasn't this what he wanted, the Verfen kept asking? Wasn't peace the thing he had sought? Wasn't peace the thing he needed most in the galaxy? Total and utter peace?

The more they spoke, the more Frye agreed with them and the more difficult it became for him to resist. It was almost as though the Verfen's first attack on his mind had pushed him off balance, and no matter how hard he struggled he could never right himself. Around him, everyone else, including Melliman, went about the business of preparing for landings.

Finally, after twenty hours of their inescapable questioning, Frye disapprovingly watched himself yield to their pressure and begin directing the preparations for setting up a permanent base on Alexvieux V.

Over the ships' transceivers the lilting Verfen voices praised
his actions. But part of Frye's soul seethed in defiance, and
he knew that as soon as he regained his mental balance, these
aliens would no longer be praising him.

35

Henley awoke with a start as the company slowly came to
its feet with a faint rattling of equipment. A quick check of his
chronometer showed he'd been asleep less than thirty minutes. At least we're still going downhill, he thought as he
stood up and fell in again behind Delta company's First
Platoon.

His relief was short-lived. The platoon turned uphill after
only a few hundred meters. For the next three hours it was
all Henley could do to put one foot in front of the other over
tree roots and rocks as he and the four thousand troops of
Ingrivia's task force snaked in long lines through the forest
toward their objective.

When the slow pale dawn spread through Yakusan's skies,
the task force settled into hundreds of small bivouacs well
inside the forest. Without thinking, Henley shook off his
equipment with the rest of First Platoon and sat down. After
ten local days—almost eighteen Standard days—of trudging
across Yakusan's hilly terrain, his body no longer ached. It
was numb with fatigue.

As carefully as he could in the pale light, he poured and
drank a small cupful of his precious water, wishing there
were some way he could bathe and sleep for a few quiet days
in a clean bunk. Then he lay back, thinking about a bath and
within seconds was asleep.

When he awoke, he quickly ate some battle rations, drank
a little water, and went looking in the dim forest for Ingrivia.
He found her in a lean-to eating a cold meal with Denoro and
the commanders of the ten Z-companies and six heavy weapons companies that made up her task force. "Did I get here
in time for the briefing?" he asked.

"That you did, Chief. The Colonel was just about to start," Denoro said. "Want something to eat?"

"No, but I'd take some water if you have any extra."

"Sorry. Everyone's short. We have some teams out looking, but they haven't found anything yet."

"Here's the update," Rasha'kean said, setting down her mess kit. "Brigadier Elgin and the rest of the legion reached Syberal City at dusk yesterday. He began evacuating' our people at first light. That means he wi'not be available to support us directly. However, he believes he will be able to supply limited air support by midnight."

"In other words," one of the commanders said, "don't plan on us gettin' any help."

"Correct, Bryant. But according to recon, we wi'not need it if we can catch the Ukes by surprise. As soon as it's fully dark, we move out in three columns. I'll take the first column along the top of the heights. Captain Virzi will lead the second column to the west of the summit. Colonel Davmichele will follow with the reserve in support." As she assigned units to each commander, Rasha'kean felt strong confidence in the plan she and Denoro had developed and a sense of satisfaction that she was gaining some measure of revenge for the death of her father in a Uke prison.

Henley watched her with great interest, marveling at how much stronger she had grown since he first met her. There was an air of assurance and authority about her that was hard to ignore. No wonder Elgin had put her in command of the task force.

"Now, if you have no questions about your commands, I'll let the X.O. give you the information Delta and Axle Recon obtained."

Denoro nodded. "Thank you, Colonel. Our two Recon platoons added a great deal of detail to our satscan maps, and as you can see from the additions we've made on your copies there are several important factors we didn't know about before. The first is that this town which we've given the code name Bilewood to is exposed to attack from the north, and that happens to be where the prison is located."

Rasha'kean listened with pleasure as Denoro laid out the attack plan. Virzi's column would move as quickly as possible to reach the north end of Bilewood while her column neutralized the Ukes on the west side of the valley. Davmichele was responsible for keeping their line of retreat open and supplying reinforcements if and when they were needed. It's a good plan, she thought as she looked up and caught Stanmorton staring at her.

Henley met her questioning gaze with a smile and a nod. Later he would tell her how impressed he was.

"Any questions?" Denoro asked.

There were always questions, and this time was no exception. Henley took advantage of the time to stand up and stretch his tired body by walking around. When the command meeting finally ended, he approached Ingrivia. "Colonel? I'd like to ask a favor of you. I want to be with you at the head of the column."

Rasha'kean gave him a quiet smile. "Already planned on it, Chief. Figured you'd want to. Did you stick with Delta First?" When he nodded, she continued, "Then you're already in the right place. Delta and Axle Recon platoons will lead the way, but Delta First will head the column. Be ready to move out as soon as it gets dark."

"Thanks, Colonel," he said with a nod. "See you later."

Later came much sooner than either of them expected.

A Uke patrol made contact with Echo company. The Ukes were quickly repulsed in a brief firefight, but Rasha'kean decided to begin the attack early. Since the Ukes already knew they were in the forest, there was no sense in waiting for a renewed attack.

Yakusan's sun had barely slipped over the horizon when the recon platoons led the way out of the forest. Close behind them in the bright twilight came the first column with Denoro, Henley, and Rasha'kean in the middle of First Platoon.

The route recon had chosen was just over the crest of the heights from the summit. Denoro had placed Haultcour's platoon on the high flank. The column had only moved a kilometer when the Ukes began sporadic firing up the slope from their emplacements. Haultcour was smart and refused to return fire and give his platoon's position away, but the Ukes kept sniping away at his troops whenever they moved.

Rasha'kean checked her map, then turned to Denoro. "Five full kilometers to Bilewood. We ca'not afford to let them hold us up here. One-C-Three," she said into her communicator, "this is One-C-One. We need two platoons of reinforcements to suppress fire at coordinates X-ray seven-seven-nine, Yo-yo three-two-eight, over."

"One-C-Three copies," Colonel Davmichele's voice said quietly in her earpiece. "Recommend one weapons platoon and one Z-platoon."

"Recommendation accepted. One-C-One, out." Rasha'kean switched channels. "Haultcour, two helpers on the way."

"Copy, One. Thanks."

To Henley the five kilometers to Bilewood seemed like fifty. Every couple of hundred meters the head of the column was stopped by heavy fire from the Ukes. Ingrivia had dispersed all but Delta Company and half of heavy weapons company H-Fifteen in concentrated pockets along the summit. They were pouring fire down on the Ukes, but receiving almost as good as they got. Davmichele was sending Spur Company and two more heavy weapons platoons from H-Nine, but they had not arrived yet.

Below Ingrivia's column on the west side of the summit Captain Virzi's column had moved slower than planned, but now Virzi reported his companies in position north of Bilewood.

Rasha'kean checked her red-lit chronometer. "Give us forty Virzi, then initiate Operation Freedom."

"Copy One-C-One. One-C-Two, out."

It seemed less than forty minutes when the firing started north of the city. As Henley peered from behind the rocky wall Denoro had designated for him, Delta First and the weapons platoons opened fire on Bilewood's southern defenses.

Within seconds the night was bright with firing. Yellow, red, and white tracers snaked like living snakes through the darkness. Flares lit the sky and ground with garish brightness. Explosions rocked both ends of the city and the summit of the heights.

Fragments of rock and metal rained down on top of Henley. Beside him a rifler screamed and fell across his legs with an ugly thud. He carefully rolled her over and knew immediately that she was dead. The smell told him.

In the shock of anger and fear he picked up her rifle and took her place between the rocks. Muzzle flashes made targets easy to find, and he was quickly returning Uke fire, caught up in the intensity of the battle.

Rasha'kean huddled in the narrow defile that had become her command post. Virzi reported light resistance from the Ukes, who were falling back into the city. Bullets whined over Rasha'kean's head. Stones rattled down on her helmet.

She huddled deeper, trying to make herself as small as possible as she listened to Captain Bryant's voice in her ear.

"This is Echo-One. We've just demolished the prison gates. The guards have several automatic weapons, but we can take them."

"Reinforcements!" Denoro shouted. "I'll place them." She left the defile to position them to reinforce Delta.

"One-C-Two, what's your status?" Rasha'kean said into her communicator.

"Flanks holding. Fire and Echo now inside."

"This is Echo One. We've found them, Colonel, but they don't look good—worse than the last ones. We'll need help getting them all out."

"Copy, Echo One," Rasha'kean said, but where was she going to get help? She had already spread the task force as thinly as she dared. "One-C-Two, can you assist?"

"Can do, C-One if you can cover our rear."

"Negative." A close explosion momentarily deafened her. "Hold one," Rasha'kean shouted as Denoro jumped back into the defile. "How are the Ukes holdin' out?"

"Not too well," Denoro shouted back.

"Think Virzi could bust through them from behind if we gave him enough covering fire?"

"If he takes that main road that leads up this way."

"Good." Rasha'kean made the only decision that made sense to her. Uke rounds still sang over her head, and she dared not stretch her column any thinner, but she could provide covering fire for Virzi and the freed prisoners.

"One-C-Two, mass your units around our people and fight toward us through to the southwest corner of the city. There's a road that leads from there to here. We'll pour in on them from the front. You attack them from behind. Got that?"

"Copy, C-One. Give'em hell."

Henley was looking for more ammunition when he found Ingrivia and Denoro in the defile.

"What the tensheiss are you doing here?" Denoro yelled over the racket of weapons.

"Looking for ammo. My platoon's running short."

"Your platoon?"

"Dinsmore is dead, Colonel. I just sort of took over. Gave our position to a platoon from Spur Company and came looking for ammunition."

"They've been relieved?"

"That's right, Denoro."

Rasha'kean handed her communicator to Denoro and turned to Stanmorton. "There's ammo up ahead, Chief. Get your platoon and come with me. Denoro, you're the C.P. I'm goin' to try to get closer to give Virzi more support."

"But Colonel, you shouldn't be doing that. What if—"

"D'not tell me what I should and shoul'not be doin'. Just hold down the Command Post. Tell Davmichele to keep callin' for air support, and get me that recon sergeant, Bledsoe."

"Aye, Colonel."

Henley followed Rasha'kean from the defile to where his weary platoon was waiting. When the troops saw that Ingrivia was going to lead them, their spirits brightened immediately. As they filled their pouches with ammunition, Sergeant Bledsoe joined them and led them to the forward elements of the company at the head of the road that cut down the slope into Bilewood.

"Everything from here down to that bridge is exposed, Colonel," Bledsoe said, pointing through the pale light of a small moon toward where the road crossed the dry riverbed.

"Then we'll be settin' up on the other side of the bridge. Look, you can see from the firin' where Virzi's troops are fightin' toward us. Let's go."

The Uke gunners didn't spot them until the platoon had almost reached the bridge. By then it was too late to stop them. Led by Ingrivia on one side of the bridge and Henley on the other, they ran down the near bank, across the dry, sandy bed and placed themselves just below the top of the bank on the other side.

Bledsoe fired an arching flare up over the outskirts of the city. When the flare reached its zenith, Delta First opened fire on the Uke positions less than one hundred meters in front of them. Henley was filled with an exhilarating fear as he carefully sent one shot after another into the enemy.

The Ukes returned fire for several minutes. Then a series of explosions ripped their positions apart.

Virzi was breaking through!

Rasha'kean immediately moved Delta First up over the bank. In low crouching runs they formed up with their backs at an angle to the road as they provided covering fire. She marveled at the sight of Virzi's column firing its way out of the city with the ex-prisoners hurrying as best they could down the road between the lines of soldiers who protected them. They moved like a sluggish, phosphorescent liquid, but they moved!

Faster than she thought possible, Virzi's rear guard left the last of the city buildings behind. "Prepare to withdraw," Rasha'kean shouted.

Henley waved in acknowledgment and passed the word through his half of the platoon. They fell back across the bridge with Virzi's rear guard, still firing at the Ukes and still taking casualties of their own.

Rasha'kean was halfway up the summit, moving backward with Delta First, when a flight of fightercraft roared up the valley. Their thundering cannons ripped the earth in front of them, filling the air with a deafening rain of rubble and bodies. She paused to admire them, feeling at once relieved and happy.

Something exploded directly in front of her. A brief, painful roar frightened her from the inside out. For an aching moment the scene before Rasha'kean froze in a bizarre, buzzing pattern of lights. Then darkness overwhelmed her as she fell to the ground.

For Henley the next thirty minutes were like moving through congealed time. Everything and everyone moved with agonizing slowness.

As soon as he reached Ingrivia, he knew she was badly hurt. Blood was coming from both her ears. The front of her uniform steamed with dark gurgling froth.

He screamed for a medic as he dropped his rifle and lifted her into his arms, surprised by how heavy she was. Others came to help. A stretcher appeared, then Denoro. They were running with her to cover, to safety. Tears ran down Henley's face.

Two medics huddled over her working frantically to seal her sucking chest wound as she rested in Denoro's lap. Finally, one of them looked up and shook his head.

As though on cue, Rasha'kean opened her eyes and found herself looking at Stanmorton. She felt surrounded by a quiet calm. "Tell me . . . my mother," she whispered.

"Your mother was the bravest person I've ever known," Henley said in a voice shaking with emotion. "You're just like her."

"Thanks . . . thanks, Chief. Denoro?"

"I'm here, Colonel."

"I ken this hill's too hard to bust." Rasha'kean did not have the energy to say anything else. She closed her eyes and drifted off into the peaceful warmth of sleep.

Henley was never sure about the sequence of events that followed. Sometime before dawn the fighting stopped. Colonel Davmichele passed on a message from Brigadier Elgin that the war was officially over. The Ukes had announced surrenders at Yakusan and Gensha. Then another message came, something meaningless about peace and the arrival of the alien Verfen.

None of it mattered much to Henley or Denoro. The two of them stayed with Ingrivia long after the medics had moved on to the wounded whose lives could be saved. Somewhere in the midst of all those events they said their silent good-byes and placed her body aboard a morgueship.

By then they knew that Colonel Rasha'kean Ingrivia had been killed by a rocket fired short of its target by one of Sondak's own fightercraft.

36

Henley went to the Troopers Club aboard the *Menard* well before he was supposed to meet Mica. He knew he needed some time to prepare himself for seeing her again.

It had been a long time since their brief hours on the *Walker*, a time when he had again seen too much pain and dying to be sure of his personal emotions. Her choice of the Troopers Club for a meeting place told him she was being cautious but told him nothing more. He didn't mind her caution. He felt his own sense of reserve about facing her—a reserve that made him afraid to hope for too much between them and told him he had already let his hopes get out of hand.

When he arrived, the place was half full. As he made his way through the tables along the perimeter, Sergeant Denoro waved to him in invitation to sit at her table. She was alone, but as he joined her, Henley noticed a certain resigned presence about her that he understood without trying to explain it. It was a presence that came from battle experience and nothing else—the experience they had shared with Rasha'kean Ingrivia.

Mica had seen Henley enter the club and was surprised when he sat at a table with a Planetary Sergeant. She rose and moved to join them, but suddenly hesitated, unsure that she would be welcomed. Yet she was drawn toward them and moved to a bulkhead support close to their table where she could hear what they were saying without being seen. Leaning against the support, she knew she had no excuse for such shameless eavesdropping, but she couldn't stop herself. She needed some inside line, some clue to Henley's emotional state, before she confronted him with her own feelings.

When Henley's drink came, he raised it to Denoro. "Here's to victory and a safer place than the last."

"Hell," she said with a tight smile cutting the weathered wrinkles of her face as she touched her glass to his, "there ain't no such thing as a safe place, Chief—despite the crap those new aliens are shoveling on. It's wherever you find your ass in a moment's peace that counts—nothing else—'cause no place is safe."

She took a sip of her drink and looked at him with bright gray eyes. "You still gonna keep writing about the war? Or you gonna go on to something else now—something neat and civilian?"

Her question touched a nerve Henley had been afraid to touch himself. "I don't know if I'll ever be able to stop writing about the war," he said finally. "It's too much a part of me—like it is a part of you." He wanted to turn away from this subject and the raw feeling it caused in his gut, but the very vulnerability he felt forced him to touch it, to probe the rawness for understanding that might help it heal. Somehow he felt that she might— "Tell me, Denoro, how has the war affected you?"

She snorted. "That's the stupidest question I ever heard you ask. You've been there. You know the answer—same as I do." She waited a moment, as though expecting him to respond, then the brightness in her eyes flared for a moment.

When Denoro continued, there was a quiet intensity in her voice. "This is my second war, same as you, and you know the worst thing about it? It's that part of your humanity," she said slowly, "a big part of it—your *kindu,* your soul, whatever the hell you want to call it—it's never gonna be there again."

Behind the support Mica felt suddenly guilty and paralyzed at the same time—afraid to move and afraid to keep listening. This was not what she had wanted to hear.

"It's gone, dammit," Denoro said. "It's gone . . . and you don't *know* it. You don't know it's gone until it's over. Then you start missing it. But it's too late."

When Denoro hesitated, Mica wanted to step from behind the pillar as though she had casually walked by, but now fascination mixed with her guilt as she focused on Denoro's every word.

"Makes the second war easier, I guess," Denoro said quietly, " 'cause you already lost whatever it was that kept your *kindu*—your soul—alive and well. It's easier to fight if you're half dead, you know that?"

She paused again, and Henley knew better than to interrupt her, even though everything she said rasped across the exposed nerves of his own damaged soul, saying things he had been unwilling to face in himself.

"Who the void doesn't want to be loved?" Denoro asked with renewed intensity as she leaned across the table toward him. "Everybody does. You got to want to be loved if you've got anything inside you at all—anything worth keeping, that is. But to be loved, you got to give it. . . . I can't give it to nobody no more. I can't. It's not in me. I just can't do it."

With a quick wave of her hand and a flashing scowl she sent an approaching trooper away from their table. "Like right now," she continued, "my father's back on Mungtinez, and he's sick, real sick. I can't even bring myself to cry about that. I didn't go see him when we were there, and I can't even bring myself to go home to him now. I *should* do it. I know I should."

Denoro took a long breath, and there was a look of angry amusement in her eyes. "The war's over. And if you want to believe what the Efcorps is saying about that bunch of stinkin' aliens nobody's ever seen, there's never going to be another war. How about that? Never going to be another war. Like all of a sudden the Ukes are going to quit starting them and we're going to quit stopping them." She paused again, the look of amusement fading as quickly as it had come.

"What does it matter, Chief? What the hell does it matter? We busted the Ukes, and now I've got time to do anything I want. What I should do is take some of this back leave I've been tacking on my R-and-L tab and ship my ass home right now, because my father might be dead tomorrow, and home's where I belong."

Suddenly she slapped her palm flat on the table. "But I can't go, Chief. You understand that? War or no war, the Service is all I've *got*. I can't give nothing to nobody anymore— even my father. It all got stripped away while I was busy duckin' frags and huggin' rags. Like some thief snatched it away before I even really knew what it was." Her voice shook with emotion. "Now it's like I'm standing naked all the time, and my duffel's empty. There's nothing left to give. Nothing."

Henley wanted to stop her now before her pain overwhelmed him. But part of him wanted her to continue, to spill the pain for both of them. He needed her to say what he knew he would never write.

"You know," she said with a bitter laugh, "I wanted a family once. Still think it would be nice, sometimes, to have a mate and some children I could watch grow up. But there's no spacin' way I could do it now. There's no spacin' way . . . It's not that I'm too old to have children . . . it's just that there's no way I could . . . give . . ." She leaned back, head down, with a soft, shuddering sigh and slowly covered her mouth with her hand.

Words were supposed to be Henley's specialty, but he could never put it more eloquently than she was doing. "I know," he said quietly as leaned toward her, forcing his burning gut muscles to relax. "I know what you feel."

The sadness Mica heard in Henley's voice made her heart

go out to him, and without thinking, she forced herself away from the pillar and into his line of vision. She wanted to shout "hello" and break the dark spell Denoro had cast over him, yet she hesitated once again.

"There's so much," Denoro said, moving her hand up to shade her eyes. "Oh, god, there's so much missing." There was no self-pity in her voice, only a tone of resignation. Her hand slowly fell away from her face in a helpless gesture of acceptance.

For the first time Henley understood that he only shared part of her loss, and he prayed he would never feel the same engulfing emptiness that Denoro had revealed to him. Yet he wished that both of them could cry together, here and now, if only for temporary relief from their anger and grief.

"Hello," a voice said softly as a hand touched his shoulder. Henley started violently as he looked up to see Mica standing beside him.

"I am sorry, Henley. I thought you saw me." She hoped the guilt she felt didn't show on her face.

Henley looked up at Mica and realized that while listening to Denoro he had completely forgotten she was coming. Now he suddenly wished that she could have heard Denoro's . . . what? There was no name for those kinds of things, no adequate label for confessions of the soul.

"It's all right," he finally managed to say as he stood up and took her hand. "This is Sergeant Denoro."

"My honor, Commander," Denoro said, her gray eyes now hazy and distant.

"Thank you," Mica said as she slipped her hand out of Henley's and sat in the empty chair between him and Denoro. "It's nice to meet you. And here in the Troopers Club, please feel free to call me Mica."

"Then how about a drink, Mica?" Denoro asked a little too eagerly. "We'll continue the victory celebration."

"Thank you." Mica sensed that she had broken the intimacy between Henley and Denoro.

Henley ordered her drink, another for himself and one for Denoro, whose glass was almost empty. Denoro declined, claiming that she had duty the next work watch. Henley knew it was a lie but let it pass. When the drinks came, the three of them toasted victory, then Denoro left. After watch-

ing her disappear through the growing crowd, Henley turned
to Mica and realized he was very unsure of what to say to
her.

*   *   *

Frye Charltos wept.

He wept for Vinita, and Marsha, and Clarest. But mostly he
wept for himself. The war was over. He had lost.

Whatever else would be recorded in the annals of the
United Central Systems, it would always be known that Admiral Frye ed'Laitin Charltos had led the U.C.S. to defeat.

Whatever else would be recorded, it would always be
known that he had failed in his ultimate duty.

He sucked in a deep, rasping breath and forced himself to
sit upright. He watched as his hands took the ceremonial
pistol from its plush lined case, listened as a tear fell loudly
on its stainless-steel barrel. It was a weapon from Earth, over
a thousand years old, handed down through the generations
of his family. Never before had it been required to salvage
the family's honor by taking the life of one of its own members. Now it was. Now there was no choice.

Slowly, his thumb pulled the pistol's hammer back until it
clicked twice and locked into place. Slowly, his hand raised
the cold muzzle to his head and steadied it against his tem-
ple. Slowly, his finger pulled the trigger.

Instantaneously, his scream mixed with the searing explosion from the pistol.

In the cave on Alexvieux Five there was darkness without
end as something warm pressed itself against Frye and wrapped
around his chest and held him steady. Heavy sobs echoed
from cold walls.

A familiar voice spoke soothingly in his ear, calming him,
reassuring him until gradually he realized that the sobs were
his own and the voice was Clarest's and the warmth was her
body pressed against his.

"The nightmare again," she said, kissing his forehead as he
stopped crying.

"Yes," he whispered. "But don't worry, Clarest. I am going
to beat it, just as one day we will beat every Sondak ship in
space back to the surface of their planets."

It would take time, he knew that—more than his lifetime.
But when he was gone, Clarest would continue the cause,

and after her there would be others to follow. There was a debt of revenge owed against Sondak, and always there would be those willing to fight to the death to repay that debt.

The dream, the nightmare of suicide, was a stupid thing, an archaic ghost that could never stop him from fighting back any more than the alien alliance could. The aliens had caught him off balance once, but it wouldn't happen again. He would prepare those who followed him to deal with any aliens foolish enough to stand against a rising tide of revenge. And he was positive the U.C.S. would rise up against Sondak again, and again, and again, until they achieved total revenge and victory.

Frye had no illusion that he would be alive to see that day, but from his final command here on Alexvieux Five he would rebuild that dream, starting with his child—the one growing now in Melliman's womb—and that child might live to see the day of triumph now lost to him.

That was enough hope for Frye Charltos. No invisible alien could dictate terms to him or stop him from moving toward his goal. No alien could quench his fires of revenge. In the seeds of the children and grandchildren and the great-grandchildren of the U.C.S. lay the seeds of final independence and victory over Sondak, and Frye had committed his life to making that victory possible.

* * *

"How's your father?" Henley asked lamely, breaking the silence between them.

"He's negotiating the final terms of surrender and peace with the Ukes at Gensha. Pajandcan's joining him with a delegation from the Verfen—if you can believe that. They claim the right to some voice in the peace terms, but no one's taking them very seriously."

"Except for your father, the new chairman of the Joint Chiefs, who believes in closer ties to all the aliens."

"Exactly—but Pajandcan seems to support the idea, as well." Mica's smile was awkward and brief. "But enough about that. This is the victory celebration, isn't it? How are you?"

She looked uncomfortable and Henley wanted to—to what? He didn't know. "I'm all right," he said finally, "but I've missed you a great deal."

"I've missed you, too, Henley, but I'm not sure—that is, I don't know if we missed each other in the same way."

The pain in his gut tightened, and Henley prepared himself for the worst. "Are you telling me good-bye before we've had a good chance to say hello?"

Mica was surprised by his question but not by the wealth of affection she felt for him. "Just the opposite," she said, reaching over and taking his hand. "I'm telling you that I *missed* you. And . . . oh, hell, I just want to know if you missed me the same way."

Henley understood now, and it frightened him more than any rejection she could have given him. "I still can't tell you that I love you," he said, staring at their clasped hands. "I'm not sure I know what that means anymore, much less whether I know how to love anyone."

"I know," she whispered. "I understand." She wanted to say much more, but suddenly there were no words. Mica knew she had enough love for both of them without words.

He leaned forward, folded her hands into his, and looked into her eyes. What he saw was her affection for him shining through her tears. Her radiant joy burned off part of the darkness he had shared with Denoro and gave him reassurance. Henley wished he and Mica were somewhere private so they could just hold each other.

"Mica, I can only offer you what I'm sure I have to give," he said slowly, "devotion and loyalty. That's it. I don't know if that's enough for you . . . and I don't know if that could ever grow into love."

"It can," she said. He had told her what she needed to hear, and now she knew that whatever darkness the future held, it also promised something bright and good and joyous that could blossom for them out of the emotionally ravaged fields of war.

"It can," she repeated, smiling now through her tears and stroking his hand. "We can grow anything we want."

His smile answered hers, and for reasons he did not fully understand, Henley believed her.

APPRECIATION

Sometimes after completing a work of fiction it seems both appropriate and necessary to give credit to those people who were involved in ways that cannot be handled in a normal dedication. This is one of those times. Consequently, there follows a brief list of some of the people who helped me along the way.

The Norwood Clan: Marie, Richard, Sandy, David, Dixie, Mary, Margaret, Margot, Ivy, Ivan, and Butch (the honorary Norwood).

The Soldiers: W01 Anderson, General Deane, Nicholson, Apfel, Buckbinder, Jamey Druid, Danny Boy, Michaels, and forever in memoriam, Major Watters and Bobby Brooks.

The Teachers: Frances Caveness, James York, Jake Kobler, Richard Owsley, Giles Mitchell, Pete Gunter, and Bob Hughes.

The Emergency Consultants: George and Lana Proctor, Raymond Flowers, and Bob Vardeman.

The Doctors: James B. Shackleford and David M. Beyer

The Assorted Book People: Karen V. Haas, Bob Silverberg, Poul Anderson, Norman Spinrad, Mike McQuay, Suzette Haden Elgin, Richard Curtis, and Lou Aronica.

The Very Special Friends: Ralph Mylius, Joy Spiegel, and Gigi Sherrell.

My Father: Warren Heller Norwood, who, at a time when very few people understood, gave me a safe and healthy outlet for the deep anger I felt about *my* war, and who thus helped keep me off the list of serious casualties.

Mel White

ABOUT THE AUTHOR

WARREN NORWOOD began writing when he was nine and got hooked on science fiction when he was eleven, reading Tom Swift and Tom Swift, Jr. books. At seventeen he made a serious commitment to become a writer. College, marriage, the Vietnam War, and eleven years in the selling end of the book business intervened before he saw the publication of *An Image of Voices*, the first book in his Windhover Tapes series. The other books in the series are *Flexing the Warp*, *Fize of the Gabriel Ratchets*, and *Planet of Flowers*. Warren was twice nominated for the John W. Campbell Award as one of the best new writers of 1982–83 and also cowrote *The Seren Cenacles* with his best friend, Ralph Mylius, author of the "M.A.C. Gate" stories.

In addition to writing, Warren currently teaches a course on "Writing Fiction for Profit" at Tarrant County Junior College in Ft. Worth, Texas. He is also an avid wildflower photographer and a self-proclaimed pseudobotanist.

After living in Missouri long enough to fall in love, Warren now has a small house out in the country a couple of miles outside of Weatherford, Texas, where he is currently working on a long science fiction novel set in west and north Texas seventy years from tomorrow.

On sale in February . . .
the science fiction publishing event of the year

HEART OF THE COMET

By Gregory Benford and David Brin

The Nebula Award-winning author of TIMESCAPE and the Hugo and Nebula Award-winning author of STARTIDE RISING join in the creation of a groundbreaking vision of the future—the saga of an astonishing mission to Halley's Comet in the 21st century.

Buy HEART OF THE COMET, on sale February 15, 1986 in hardcover wherever Bantam Spectra Books are sold, or use the handy coupon below for ordering:

Special Offer
Buy a Bantam Book
for only 50¢.

Now you can have an up-to-date listing of Bantam's hundreds of titles plus take advantage of our unique and exciting bonus book offer. A special offer which gives you the opportunity to purchase a Bantam book for only 50¢. Here's how!

By ordering any five books at the regular price per order, you can also choose any other single book listed (up to a $4.95 value) for just 50¢. Some restrictions do apply, but for further details why not send for Bantam's listing of titles today!

Just send us your name and address and we will send you a catalog!

ELIZABETH SCARBOROUGH

- ☐ 25103 Bronwyn's Bane $3.5(
- ☐ 24441 The Harem of Aman Akbar $2.9(
- ☐ 24554 Song Of Sorcery $2.9(
- ☐ 22939 The Unicorn Creed $3.5(

URSULA LE GUIN

- ☐ 23906 Beginning Place $2.7(
- ☐ 23512 Compass Rose $3.5(
- ☐ 24258 Eye of the Heron $2.9(
- ☐ 24791 Orsinian Tales $2.9(
- ☐ 25396 Very Far Away From Anywhere Else $2.5(

ANNE McCAFFREY

- ☐ 23815 Dragondrums $2.9(
- ☐ 23459 Dragonsinger $2.9(
- ☐ 23460 Dragonsong $2.9(